Apache Death Wind

A Novel By

Denis J. LaComb

Apache Death Wind

Published by BAMs² Publishing
A division of Sharden Productions, Inc.

Credits:
Book cover illustrations and design by Vida Raine

ISBN: 978-0988420333
ISBN-13: 978-0-9884203-3-5

To Sharon who believed in me at the beginning and still does after all these years.

To my children, Brian and Melanie, who continue to inspire me.

To Michelle for her help in the editing of this work.

To Vida for her help with book design, blogging, web design and other sundry crafts of writing and publishing.

CONTENTS

PROLOGUE

March, 1861, Glorieta Pass, Apache Canyon, New Mexico Territory

Seven men lay flat-bellied in a muddy rut that was once a road. Seven pairs of eyes were glued on the gray finger-thin outline of a sentinel slowly pacing back and forth along the Union picket line. The men remained motionless, like torn dolls cast astray. Their gray uniforms had been reduced to dirty rags that blended into the moonlit shadows blanketing them.

The silence was deafening, washed out only by the constant drone of insects gnawing away at the men's exposed skin. Cavalry horses snorted in the distance and voices from obscured tents filtered through the air. The smell of cooking pots, mixed with campfire smoke, wafted over the muddy cut in the field.

Escape was only a tall grassy ridgeline away. Freedom was so close the Confederate soldiers could practically taste it, yet far enough away that an open run across the scrub brush would mean risking everything.

After the battle at Glorieta Pass near Santa Fe, escape and survival were the only options left for the tattered Confederate forces. Reeling against the onslaught from Lieutenant Colonel J.M. Chivington's Third Regiment and its cavalry contingent, the Confederates under Colonel Scurry had been broken. Outnumbered and outgunned, they had fought the blue coats to a bloody standoff that allowed only a small fraction of the Southern forces to pull back and escape the Union cavalry's flanking movements. With their supplies and ammunition gone and their forces shattered, a nighttime retreat was the only option left for the remaining Confederates.

After all this, groups of hard-rock miners, the worst kind of mercenary fighters, were still combing the hills for Confederate survivors. Brought down from the Colorado Pikes Peak region, these miners wanted to fight and kill and be done with it, so they could return to their mines. The battle was long over, but the killing of gray coats continued.

The seven rebel survivors had escaped the initial slaughter and eventually gathered one by one until they were a unit again. Bloodied, hurt, and near-beaten - they were still Confederate sons of President Jefferson, every one proud of their Southern heritage. As the moonlight cast a dull pale over the darkened landscape, the rag tag column started to stir.

A shadow melted out from under the trunk of a sycamore tree. It paused for a long moment, and then signaled the others to follow. Each man arose slowly as if tied together by an invisible rope. The line moved in quick succession, scurrying toward a distant ridgeline like a disjointed caterpillar. No one made a sound. The men moved hastily through the thin waves of tall grass and scrub brush, each one of them bent over. Occasionally one or more of the men would throw a fleeting glance over their shoulder towards the dim outline of the sentinels on the picket line.

Limping behind the others and losing ground with almost every step, a man of medium build hobbled with the aid of his crudely fashioned juniper branch. His leg was wrapped in filthy bandages that reeked of an open draining wound. His face was dark - matted with dried blood and three days growth of beard. Like the others, this was his first taste of defeat and he meant to avoid capture, even if it meant his death.

Only a few hundred yards more, he thought to himself, as he pushed along trying hard to keep up with the others. If only they could reach the river and the mountains beyond. They would be safe. There was no food, few weapons, and no help nearby. Yet they still had their freedom for now and the chance to escape their blue coat victors.

The distance between the laggard and his comrades continued to grow. The man struggled to close the gap to no avail. The men up ahead were but a smudge just below the ridgeline.

The line paused and the stray soldier moved to cut the distance between them. As he exerted himself, sharp pain kept knifing into his crippled leg and he was forced to slow down. He slouched to the ground, resting his aching leg. Pain from the open wound and the forced march was excruciating. It was pulsating through his body and almost numbing his extremities. He clamped down his jaw to stifle the screams of anguish inside.

Waist-high brush now blocked most of the moonlight for the men lying prone at the base of the ridgeline. It cast shafts of light that sliced the straggler's haggard face. When the line began to move again, it took the wounded man longer to get up. He staggered to his feet, forcing back the fatigue gnawing at his bones. Once on his feet, he could see the moon, hung like a Chinese lantern, casting its eerie glow over the field ahead. The black shadows danced over the gray ridgeline. The enemy encampment was now but a shadowy frown on the horizon. Freedom was almost theirs to taste.

Up ahead, river sounds played music to his ears. He bore down until he was actually gaining on the last man. He could now just barely see the caterpillar's tail topping the ridgeline, then disappearing on the other side. The straggler knew that already his companions were gathering on the steep embankment. They would be debating the best place to slip into the swift current that would sweep them past the miners and Yankee soldiers and on to their freedom. Muted voices drifted back to the straggler, urging him onward. According to plan, no one would wait for him. If a man fell behind, he was on his own.

The straggler recklessly jabbed his makeshift crutch into the ground. He could not, he would not, be left behind. This rebel had fought too many battles for far too long to lose it all to a Yankee bullet. His awkward stance caught him off balance as his crutch sank into a pocket of soft soil. The earth gave way to the juniper branch, throwing him off his feet and pitching him backwards down the slope. Cursing beneath his breath and ignoring the blinding pain, the straggler resolved to get up. The voices up ahead were growing dimmer, moving down the embankment away from him.

Soon he thought he heard water being disturbed. The voices mixed with sounds of the river as it splashed against the escapees. The others were now wading into the river, seeking out the fastest current in its middle. The first ones were quickly engulfed as the river began to carry them away to freedom and their long journey home.

Fearful of being left behind, the straggler half-dragged himself to his feet. He pushed forward until he was moving back up the grassy rise. He persevered until he crested the peak from which he could see the riverbanks. Below, framed between a grove of pine and spruce, he could see the last of the others glance back before descending into the water.

It was old Peterson, an elder country gentleman. Peterson, the oldest among them was always the one to look out for everyone in his unit. The straggler wanted to shout out to the old man - to say he was almost there. But the numbing pain clamped his mouth tight. His rubbery legs started to give way again, tipping his balance. He caught himself before the fall and landed on his knees. Pain shot up his leg to his side and back. He would drag himself if he had to, to get to the river and his freedom.

Suddenly he heard a shout.

An explosion of gunfire shattered the night calm. Finger licks of flame poked out of the darkness from across the river. Men screamed and shouted and pitched forward into the water. Others cried in pain, splashing out of the river. They began retreating back up the crumbling embankment, only to be cut down before they reached high ground. Only three men made it back up the slope, scurrying on their hands and knees to the top of the ridgeline.

The straggler quickly moved backwards, half-crawling, half-stumbling his way back to the tall grass that quickly wrapped around his tattered body.

Peterson was the first to claw his way back over the ridgeline. He slid down the grassy slope and struggled to his feet. He ran toward the waving curtain of grass near where the straggler was now crouched. A bullet slammed into the old man's back, throwing him forward. He staggered back to his feet, fell to one knee, and struggled up again. He began stumbling toward the brown waves of grass that offered concealment. Another bullet ripped off his tattered cap and took half his brains with it. His dead body hit the ground, sending a shower of blood into the straggler's face. The straggler could see Peterson's open dead eyes and bloodied head. He turned and scrambled away as best he could.

Voices arose behind another survivor, followed by more gunshots. First off to the right. Then to his left. The man was surrounded. Yankee shouts and curses erupted all around him as the Union soldiers moved in for the kill and cleanup.

A wave of blackness enveloped his brain as the straggler laid his head to the ground.

The two remaining Confederate troopers stumbled into the grass, ignoring the body of Peterson and the straggler's body just a few feet away. Shots erupted again in their direction. The surviving soldiers raised their hands and shouted, "We surrender! We surrender!"

"We got 'em!" a voice shouted off to the left.

"The other one is on your right!" another Yank yelled in return.

"No mercy!" someone shouted.

Others laughed. More shots were fired. The gray coats screamed. Then silence.

More voices, getting louder, slapped the straggler back to consciousness. The sounds of boots, miner's boots, came crashing through his numbed brain. It jerked him back to his senses. He could hear the loud moaning of one of his companions. Another shot rang out. The man screamed. More shouts and a cheer.

"I got him. I got me the son-of-a-bitch!" someone shouted in the distance.

"Shut up, you old sogger. Show me the body," another voice barked back.

Despite his leg and the caked blood blinding his eyes, the straggler pulled himself to his knees and edged back through the tall grass that concealed him. His hunting instincts were still strong, as was his thirst for survival. Dragging his bum leg behind him, the wounded man half crawled, half walked along a grassy wash, trying desperately to put dirt between him and the voices. Hollers raised again in unison as they found the last Confederate body. He headed in a half circle toward the riverbank, aiming to enter it far from the massacre scene.

As he moved closer to the river, he could hear voices from across the river answering those voices behind him. The miners and troopers had been planted on both sides of the river. It was a perfect ambush. A trap that could only have been planned and implemented by Chivington or one of his officers. A trap meant to kill, not capture the rebels. It was Chivington's way to eliminate the opposition for good.

Whatever hatred the lone Confederate soldier might have felt, whatever all-consuming passion for revenge that might have pounded his brain, it was now lost to pure animal instinct. A gut level need for survival that drove him on. He could hear the river churning up ahead. He still had a chance to escape his Yankee hunters.

Already Yankee voices were readjusting their positions as they began a sweep of the grassy field behind him. Someone was counting bodies as they moved through the tall grasses. Then the straggler could hear the soldiers and miners fanning out, directly behind him and to his far right. They were widening their search area for stragglers.

The sound of the rushing river came like a soothing melody sending a feeling of relief sweeping through his brain. The sound of the river was growing louder. Behind him the voices in the field continued, but didn't rise in alarm. He still hadn't been spotted. He was close, so very close to freedom. Then he thought he heard new voices, much closer now, off to his right. He moved faster, mindful of the noise he was making but unwilling to slow for one moment.

Now he was out of the grasses and much closer to the river. He could just barely see the crumbling banks of the black river and darkness below. More voices arose, closer now. They broke his concentration. The Yankees were closing in, coming toward him along both sides of the riverbank. Soon they would be on top of him. Black forms materialized out of the woods across the river. The Yankee sharpshooters would see him in seconds.

He heard footsteps pounding up behind him. He struggled to turn around. Out of the darkness, he saw a Union officer brandishing a sword and rushing toward him. The blue coat swung his sword up for the kill. The straggler reacted with a savage thrust of his crutch into the officer's groin. The blue coat doubled over, collapsing to his knees. The straggler smashed his crutch across the officer's face, sending him sprawling backwards.

More Yankees appeared out of the darkness and began shooting. The straggler fell back over the embankment and rolled over and over as bullets cut the air above his head. Miners and soldiers were running through the grass across the river, closing in. The straggler threw his body off the edge of a small crest above the riverbank into the darkness below.

Even as he fell, tumbling over the loose dirt and rocks and vegetation, he could hear the miners shouting, the bullets whistling by his head, and the officer's voice above them all. The water hit him across the face, stinging his eyes and lips as he sank beneath the black water. His head popped up once, breaking the surface just long enough for him to suck in air before disappearing beneath the black surface again.

As the straggler sank back down, bouncing off bottom rocks, and struggling to hold his breath, the same persistent image captured his mind. He saw the bloodied face of that Union officer, the ambushing officer, and the frenzied look of hatred on his face. He saw the man's up swung sword meant to slice him in half. The anger and rage on his killer's face. The lust for blood in his eyes. And the lone rebel survivor knew that if he ever saw that officer again, he would kill him. He would make him pay for what he had done to his companions.

CHAPTER ONE

September 1867, Arizona Territory

The land was dead. A dried up, washed away expanse of nothing but sand and rock for a hundred miles in all directions. Nothing moved. Little was alive. Overhead, the sun poured its stifling brightness over everything. It was a vast wasteland of dust and dirt and death.

Or so it seemed. Beneath the blistering sun, cracked and baked rocks, arroyos and canyons, the hunters and the hunted continued their centuries-old pattern of life and death. Before the US Cavalry, it was the Mexican Federales and local militia. Before them, it was the Spanish who foolishly traversed the barren deserts in search of gold. Before all of them, it was the natives from the East, the Comanches and Kiowa who dared venture into Apache land. All met, all fought, and most never survived an encounter with the elusive Apaches.

To the unsuspecting eye there was no one, nor anything threatening, within the distant horizon. There was but sand and sun and sweltering, choking heat. No cloud in the sky to offer up a respite of shade. Neither tree nor rock outcroppings. A stranger to these parts would see only a dried up sameness. But a stranger to this land would not survive a day on his own.

Those unsuspecting eyes usually belonged to settlers or cowboys newly arrived from out East. These new arrivals were always the first to die from Apache arrows, lances, or knives. Caught in an ambush they hadn't seen coming, no time to react before feeling their life blood drain from their body. The fortunate ones died quickly. The unfortunate ones died slowly, knowing who their killers were and how they were about to die.

Two Indians, naked other than breechcloths and sleeveless cotton vests, worked their mustangs through the rocky entrance of a canyon's narrow mouth. Their red turbans, a clear indication of their status as army scouts, were the only strong color amidst the surrounding monochromatic landscape. The land laid quiet and still. Neither scout said a word, nor looked at the other as their agile ponies walked, undirected, along the rock walls and through the scant opening.

Towering above the scouts, a blue, cloudless sky capped twin rock outcroppings that bridged the canyon walls. Silence hung heavy between the crags and boulders, punctuated only by the soft footfall of their horses. Occasionally a bird would appear overhead, soaring on the heated air currents that rose up off of the rocky terrain below. Silently, it would float in slow lazy circles high above the scouts until disappearing behind some towering butte or ridgeline.

The scouts rode methodically with only a seldom glance exchanged. A tightening of thigh against their mounts signaled an occasional pause eventually followed by cautious movement again. Their black eyes swept the ground, looking for crushed grass or plant discoloration, sure signs they were close behind the war party they were pursuing.

They were Tonto Apaches, under loose contract with the United States Cavalry. To their leader, Delshay, chief of the Tonto tribe, they were traitors. Like the Chiricahuas, the Tontos were a small tribe constantly at war with the Mexicans and Americans.

Weeks earlier, Delshay had disappeared with the remnants of his tribe, but these two stayed behind. Both bachelors, they preferred scout duty to running and hiding in the mountains - again.

One scout wore a crumpled felt Hardee hat, gray with alkali dust, over his turban. His brown body was bare besides a faded crumpled vest and breechcloth. Across his saddle lay a Winchester Carbine, model 77- loaded and cocked. Around his waist was an Anson Mills woven cartridge belt favored by the Apaches.

The other scout wore a dirty gray bandana that stood out against his cracked skin and piercing black eyes. Over his barrel chest, he wore a faded blue shirt vest, regulation Army issue, and a loincloth. His weapon of choice was a .45/70 Trapdoor Carbine. His cartridges were in a Dwyer pouch favored by the white man.

Both Apaches were lithe and sinewy, with sharp features beneath their mop of black, course hair. Their hair hung to their brown shoulders. Both rifles had been blued by the Army to cut down on glare from the sun. The Apache scouts were the eyes and ears of the U.S. Cavalry patrol spread out behind them.

The Cavalry patrol that followed the two scouts was probably a quarter-mile to half-mile behind. They kept a fair distance to avoid ambush and yet stayed close enough to close in on an unsuspecting foe if the opportunity arose. Their baggage was minimal; down to the clothes on their back and 50 rounds of ammunition each. Trailing behind the column, four mules carried 150 rounds of extra ammunition and the standard rations of hard bread, coffee, and bacon. The patrol was packed for just one thing: to travel hard and fast.

Yet three weeks of trailing scarcely seen pony tracks had worn heavily on the troop and the scouts. The raiding party or parties were out there, somewhere, in the distance or too close for comfort. It was the scouts' job to find them before getting found themselves.

Two weeks into the pursuit, a prairie fire appeared, moving swiftly down a broad grassy valley the troop had just entered. Winds swirled and rolled down the alluvial fan, pushing the flames higher and faster than anticipated. The troop beat a hasty retreat and had to wait for the conflagration of smoke and ash and flames to subside. By then, the tracks in the grasses had been eliminated and only ash and charred scrub brush blanketed the valley floor. The Apaches had managed another delay for the troopers and added two days of traveling before their trail was found again.

The Captain had pushed his troops hard. He extended the normal one hour march interval to much longer lengths and cut the rest shorter. The normal 15 to 20 miles per day had grown to over 30 miles per day and they had nothing to show for it. The troopers and their mounts were feeling the stress and strain of the pursuit with no contact yet made.

The unshod pony tracks the Tontos were following lead straight into a tightening canyon confine - perhaps straight into a trap. If it was a trap, the pony tracks on rocks would begin fading fast. Army eyes would be distracted from the shadows and crags among the rocks. The troopers would push themselves deep enough into the rock stockade walls until there was no place to turn, no place to hide or seek shelter. A withering fire of carbine and arrow would then rain down on the column until the pursuers become the hunted and the dead.

The scouts spoke silently to one another without words. Quick glances and barely discernible nods conveyed their messages back and forth. Their eyes and posturing at the rising slopes and towering canyon walls communicated a deep concern for a possible trap ahead. The silence was maddening.

After cutting the renegades' trail three hours earlier, the scouts had hastened their pace. As the hours wore on, the pony tracks had become more and more pronounced. But more disturbing, the tracks had grown in number as more parties of two and three warriors joined the main band. No attempt had been made to cover their trail. Was it a raiding party? A war party looking for a fight? Perhaps young bucks on a killing sweep; the signs said it all and yet said nothing.

Now those same pony tracks headed deep into the winding canyon, disappearing around a wide curve in the sandy, rock-strewn bottoms. Unspoken, unmentioned, a bad feeling moved in as third partner to the scouts. The tracks were pronounced - too pronounced. They were enticing, an invitation to follow when none should have been intended. The signs were clear but uncertain and the scouts felt uneasiness for the first time in their pursuit.

One Tonto kicked his wiry mustang around and sent him into a gallop, riding back toward the Cavalry moving up quickly to close the distance between column and scouts. The first scout watched him leave, even as he scanned the rough outcropping along both sides of the canyon rim. Years in the canyons and mountains had made the Tonto cautious, wary, and suspicious. And it had saved his life on more than one occasion.

Weeks before, word started to trickle into the fort about a raiding party of Apaches hitting the ranches along the Arizona border with Mexico. Chiricahuas, Jicarillos, Mescaleros; the band didn't matter. They were raiding farmsteads and ranches and had to be stopped. The reports were sketchy. They came from Mexican freighters and the occasional drifter or cowboy who happened upon a burnt out ranch or bleached white bodies staked out in the sun.

The raiding party or parties were hitting isolated ranches and farmsteads. Rumors and wild tails of an Apache uprising made the job of selecting troop strength even harder. A small troop could move fast and handily track down the raiders. A large troop would be much slower but better equipped if the raiding parties combined to become a formidable foe.

When Delshay broke away with his band, the die was cast. Army command had to respond before those scattered bands of Apache tribes converged into an even more threatening force to reckon with.

Closing the distance from the Tonto scouts, the troop moved up swiftly despite the heat, heavy in the afternoon sun. It weighed upon the land and slowed the movement of everything, a yellow-white ball of fire burning down on the waiting soldiers, bowing the heads of their horses. The clear blue sky offered not one rag-tag cloud for protection. A solitary vulture could be seen wheeling high above, in search of prey. Even the lizards, normally placid statues on the sun-baked rocks, lay panting in slim slivers of shade.

The patrol consisted of the usual regulars: battle hardened non-coms and fresh recruits from out East. There were a couple of casuals; recruits out of the guardhouse or hospital. Few were clean-shaven. They wore mustaches, burnsides, imperials, and dun dreary whiskers. The more experienced soldiers whispered warnings to the fresh meat about watching their back and keeping their eyes peeled. In a firefight, the veterans would keep themselves alive first and worry about the virgins later. A soldier's life depended on his own skill at survival and honing his killing instinct. The Apache would show no mercy. The U.S. Cavalry would do the same.

The troopers wore regulation blue blouses and light blue trousers, now both a uniform shade of gray from the dust and dirt that hung in the air. The flanks and shoulders of their horses were darkly patched with sweat. In the oppressive heat, they could only move so fast without risking the lives of their mounts.

As the patrol picked up its pace through the dead land, the only sound was that of shifting saddles and the off-key clinking of metal gear rubbing together. Commands came in the form of raised hand signals.

Captain Miles Branan, ten years a veteran of the Army in the Southwest, watched the Tonto scout approaching him fast. The captain was a medium-build man, with a jutting chin that accented his high cheekbones and one narrow-slit eye. The other eye was covered with a black patch. His mouth was a gash tipped by a pencil-thin mustache. A cruel scar ran a deep crevice down his check. He was a United States Army Cavalry officer and looked every bit the part. He was all-military and it defined his essence.

But there was something about his appearance that belied his intent. He was military alright, but more than that he was a hunter; born out of the skirmishes and battles of the civil war. Honed by the bloody encounters at Chatsworth, Blue Mountain, and Gettysburg; Captain Branan had learned the art of war - to kill or be killed. To outsmart, out maneuver, and compel the enemy into a fight he knew he could win.

The Apaches were no different than the blue bellies he had defeated years before. They were the enemy now. It was his job; no, it was his responsibility and his honor, to hunt down and kill as many Apache as he could find. Men, women, even the children were fair targets to eradicate. They were a scourge he meant to eliminate from the earth once and for all.

There was nothing physically remarkable about the man to set him apart from the troopers he commanded. The difference became apparent only when he spoke. He spoke only in sharp, commanding tones, never offering or accepting an excuse. He prided himself on his calculating judgments and emotionless decisions. His reactions were precisely metered. He knew what he wanted and how he wanted it. He would accept nothing else. Second best was never good enough. The troopers knew it and he was determined to make certain the hostile Apaches realized it before this mission was complete.

Branan's uniform rarely showed a wrinkle, a near miracle in the heat and dust of their trip through the desert country. He wore leather gloves that he brushed constantly against the saddle horn and his legs. It was a habit of impatience, which he wore proudly.

Waiting behind the captain were two lines of troopers, 30 men in all. A film of fine alkaline powder faded the coats of both soldiers and horses. They wore the sifting dust as their own badge.

These men were the regular army of the Southwest. The Irish and Germans, young and old, veterans and ex-rebels: galvanized Yankees to the others. They were called 'soger-chaps' by complaining settlers. They could never do enough to satisfy the whims of migrating farmers, ranchers, traders, and townsfolk. They hired on at 13 dollars a month and didn't much give a damn what the world thought of them, just what they thought of themselves. They were the protectors of the settlers, the government's peacekeeping force, the Indian Bureau's thorn-in-the-side, and the Indian fighters: the dog faced pony soldiers who fought and died in such similar Apache pursuit missions. The troopers sat without comment scratching at the hair on their face, irritated in the hot sunlight.

Sitting at ease, next to the silent officer, waited Sergeant Davis. He had spent 25 years in the Army, the last 10 in Arizona. He had seen officers come and go, and he had lasted longer than most of them. He had led his own command in the war and won a medal for it. But he was not officer material. He was a non-com, born to be one of the troop. He was not an old man but his appearance betrayed him. His face had not fared well against the ravages of the country and its elements. His reddish checks hung loosely on his face, below eyes tired and haggard eyes. He kept his eyes glued on the rocks and clumps of prairie sage lying strung across the flat plain before the canyon. He'd kept his hair for 10 years in Apacheria by relying on himself and his troops. Apache scouts, even Tontos or San Carlos, weren't about to change that.

As the sergeant kneed his mount up to the captain, Branan was pulling a pair of binoculars out of his saddlebags.

He turned to the non-com, "Sergeant, take the first two squads in a skirmish line along the East side of the canyon entrance. The rest of the detail will follow me. Once you've reached the canyon mouth, I want those squads deployed on either side, just in case. Work the scouts farther into the canyon, flanking both sides. They can smell trouble faster there than we can spot it."

"Begging your pardon, Captain," The non-com began; "But the horses are exhausted. They need a rest."

"Sergeant, we'll stand to horse after we've explored that canyon. Not sooner!"

The command was brisk, without pause or a chance for comment. The captain had given an order and it was law; unquestionable, irrevocable. An act set into motion.

The skirmishers moved out quickly. Finally, there might be some action. An encounter, maybe even a fight, waited. After three weeks of sore butt slogging along, almost anything would be a relief to break the monotony of the patrol.

The captain lifted his glasses and probed the cracks and crevasses bordering the canyon's rim. His surveillance for hostile signs was self-satisfying. He knew that even if they were there, he would never see them. Not unless they wanted him to. The captain had fought Jicarillos and Mescaleros for two years and had never taken a prisoner. Twice he had trapped a party in a narrow canyon and fought them to the end. They never surrendered. They never left any whites alive that did.

Now the captain was deep in the desolate wilderness of the Arizona-Mexican border country, chasing an Apache known to the whites only as the Fox, with 30 or more fellow Cherry Cow Apaches: Chiricahuas. Three times the captain had sighted the renegades and three times the Apache band had simply disappeared. It was like fighting a legion of ghosts.

The Tonto reached the troop, reining in his desert pony in front of Branan. He spoke rapidly in broken Spanish and gestured toward the second scout left back inside the canyon. His words and gestures made a strong argument for caution entering the canyon ahead. But Branan was having none of it.

"Pony tracks don't lie!" Branan said.

The scout continued, speaking slower and more clearly. The Captain was unimpressed. He waved the scout to be quiet and snarled back: "Go back and resume your patrol. Follow the tracks as far as they take you. We will proceed behind you at a reasonable distance".

The scout began to protest.

Branan listened inattentively, dispassionately, and then dismissed the Indian with a wave of his hand. "You have your orders. Carry them out." The Indian wheeled his mount, and dashed back toward the canyon.

"With the Captain's permission," the sergeant began, "I think that Ta-nay is right about the canyon being unsafe, it's too close to being comfortable. It doesn't feel right."

Before his last words were out, the sergeant realized he'd done the wrong thing. Right or wrong, trap or not, if the canyon was the fastest way to catch the hostiles, then the captain was willing to risk his command to accomplish those ends, and that was that.

Captain Branan smiled. It was a forced contraction for his face. "The scout gets paid to tell me what he's found." he said, "I'll make the decisions after that." Branan paused to let the words sink in. He meant to make a point. "Is that understood, sergeant?"

"It is, sir," Sergeant Davis said in a controlled tone of voice. He knew he should have kept his thoughts to himself. But years in the military, especially fighting the Apache, had made him a very cautious man. Still alive after more firefights with the Apache than he could remember, Sergeant Davis wasn't used to the captain and his mechanical mind.

The sergeant called out the first two squads and moved them into a walk-trot toward the canyon entrance. He tried to push his disparaging thoughts of the captain out of his mind. But they persisted, scratching their way back in. Whether the Apache were within the canyon or not, the sergeant felt the hostiles were nearby and probably knew the troopers were there. No surprise here for either party. But not knowing just how large the raiding party or parties were left the sergeant with a tight knot in his stomach. And all the past battles didn't make him feel any better.

For three weeks the captain had tracked the renegades trail. First they traversed the mountains and lost some of their supply mules the second week. Then they crossed the desert during the day, despite the heat. And now the canyon, despite the Tonto's warning. The captain had pushed his men at a killing pace and they'd taken it. And they would continue to take it. They were professionals trained to do a job. After two weeks the men realized this officer wouldn't quit until the hostiles were stopped or out of reach over the border. He'd never give up on the chase.

Sergeant Davis admired and hated the old man for that. Already they'd lost two men and a third to courier their bodies back to the fort. The Apaches must have lost some warriors but they never left any bodies, only traces of blood and one dead pony with its throat slashed. Sensibility and logic were lost in this situation. The Apaches were growing bolder each day. Now the captain was matching wits with them. Branan intended to counter their movements step for step. He would go where they thought he wouldn't dare and he would find and kill those hostiles.

But the captain knew, logical or not, these Indians were different than before the war. The Apache had been spoiled by years of freedom from cavalry patrols and a decrease in settler traffic into their lands. They'd been emboldened by raids into Mexico and against settlers on both sides of the border. These renegades were three weeks into a killing spree and spoiling for a fight. If they tied up with the Comancheros and those bandits had rifles, grave trouble lay ahead for soldiers and settlers alike in the territory.

Wind stirred the tuft grass and a faint breeze touched the tired faces and lifted a few eyebrows. Yet it failed to lift the penetrating heat persistently taxing the column. Men and horses hung their heads, narrowing their eyes to cut out the harsh glare of bright sunlight. Dark patches of sweat grew larger on their worn heavy shirts and beads of perspiration ran freely down their faces.

Davis' column moved steadily down the gradual slope toward the canyon entrance. They rode through clumps of sagebrush and creosote, and worked their way gingerly through the tall saguaro cactus and thorny ocotillo shrubs. The Tonto was now but a tiny figure against a backdrop of shale.

Unlike his tired troopers, Captain Branan sat ramrod straight in the saddle, looking straight ahead. His back was dark patched and his eyes blinked out the tiny trickles of salty sweat running off his furrowed brow. Yet he gave the stifling air no mind. He had a mission to accomplish and a reputation to guard. Both were more important than the weather or mood of his sergeant. He'd been a captain three years and was determined to win his major's bars before most other men. The right results with the Apache might do it for him. Or at least put him on the right track.

Time was running out. The Apache had hit two ranches with the column's dust only hours behind them. Those ranches had given the Indians fresh mounts and more scalps. All the more reason he had to destroy them before they crossed the border into Mexico.

"Captain."

A voice broke him out of his thoughts and back into the blinding sunlight. Branan turned back to a corporal carrying the ensign. The trooper was pointing toward the distant ridgeline, his face taut with squinting eyes.

CHAPTER TWO

A half empty bottle lay cradled between the man's crooked leg and his rifle butt. The bottle's owner, in a right stupor from the heat and rye whiskey, leaned against the hogan of his friend, Navajo Joe. Neither man was in the mood for talking that morning. A drunken night of reminiscing and bemoaning their fate had worn both of them out. There was little more to say to each other.

Overhead, the midday heat was boiling up like gelatin waves off the hard-baked campgrounds. Only a razor thin line of shade deflected the midday sun from burning the two rye-soaked relicts as they lay slumped against the hogan. Flies buzzed about and bugs crawled over their blanket but neither man noticed or cared. Finally the old Navajo turned to his friend.

"Whiskey's good," Joe said to no one in particular. His companion said nothing but just nodded in agreement.

Joe was a half-breed, part Mescalero and part Mexican. He was born in the Sierra Madres of Mexico and ended up here after a lifetime of nothing jobs and failed attempts at farming. Even now his expert tracking skills only brought an occasional job from the Army.

"I've had better rot-gut but not from you," Joe's friend finally commented as he intently watched a fly circle around the lip of his bottle. "If you're going to buy hooch," he added: "Get something better than this slop that Indian agent is selling you."

"You're drinking it," Joe replied with a laugh as he grabbed the bottle. "And besides it's all I can get," he added. The rest of what he mumbled was lost as he pressed the bottle to his lips and turned it skyward, barely disturbing the fly still there.

Joe's companion smiled at their scattered verbal exchange. He and the old Indian had been friends for a long time. So long, in fact, that he'd forgotten when he and Joe had actually met for the first time. Probably some mountain trails high in the Sierras when Joe was still trapping there. Whenever it was or wherever it was didn't matter now. They met, formed a friendship, and now spent time together when they could and disappeared from each other's lives for months at a time. Joe once had a wife and then he didn't. He had kids and then they were gone. But Joe always had his hogan just outside the army fort, and occasionally his friend, to sit and drink and talk. They would revel in times past - both good and bad.

Joe's friend peeled off his faded, worn buckskin shirt and even in the false shade of the hogan, his skin shone a deep copper. He was a white man, burnt from many months traversing the desert and worn tough from trapping in the rarified air of the high Sierra Madres. His buckskin breeches were quilt-marked with strips of deer hide and black with dried blood from trapping and skinning. It was shiny in spots where he'd cleaned off his greasy knives and nearly all the fringes had been cut off for thongs. Dark hair hung abundant and dirty, curling over his ears. A thick mustache obscured his upper lip and from it a cigarrito curled smoke toward dark smoldering eyes; unfocused, unassuming, and vacant. Navajo Joe raised the bottle again and pronounced it good. His face cracked into a silly grin, which exposed three front missing teeth. He took a hefty swig and belched satisfaction. The whiskey was a fitting gift from his friend, the Indian agent, but as always, it never seemed to last long enough. It was root medicine. He liked it and it liked him. The whiskey brought back friends and they brought stories; rekindling memories of the old times when he was in the mountains, hunting, trapping, and fighting Apaches.

The white man stared at the bottle and felt its warmth curling around in his belly. The whiskey was like a mirror. It stirred up memories that his trapping and hunting and roaming could usually quell. But the whiskey also rained an avalanche of disturbing images on his mind and ushered back flashes of the war.

The War Between the States had steeled his hatred of the hard rock miners and the treachery of that Yankee officer who orchestrated the massacre of his men. He never stopped lamenting the failure of his Confederate army to stop the blue coats in those New Mexico Mountains. It was a part of the man's background that he couldn't let go… a history that was meant to be forgotten. If only he could forget.

Now it was just a small footnote in the history of the war, a minor skirmish among the more famous battles. But to the relic of that former soldier, it was his Waterloo.

It was the image of Colonel Chivington and his force of hard rock Pikes Peakers backed up by 300 regular infantry and two batteries of artillery that wouldn't fade away. They had lain in wait and with an ambush straight out of the textbooks, they had made mince meat of the unsuspecting Confederate columns along those New Mexico mountain trails. They brought an end to any effort by the South to capture New Mexico.

Capture New Mexico! Now it seemed almost ludicrous to think that the South could have done it. Especially after what Chivington had done to those rebel forces.

But it wasn't such a farfetched idea back when the man, still a boy, had joined up to fight the blue-bellies. It wasn't such a hard thing to imagine for a young kid straight off the farm and eager for a fight. Not with old buddies to join up with and a new uniform and plenty of ammunition and that spine-tingling Texas war cry to scream out his lungs. It wasn't hard to imagine those rebels running over anything in their path, all the way to those famed California gold fields.

Another swig. Another cigarette. Navajo Joe babbling on about something again. The white man glanced at his friend, the bottle, his own horse hobbled on a strip of course grass, then back at the campground. It wasn't hard to imagine back then. The wonder of youth and its blessed ignorance.

The boy and his gray-coated companions hadn't stormed all the way through New Mexico. Not even as far as the other end of Apache Canyon. Chivington, with his muskets rattling and those big guns booming, had ripped the rebel forces to pieces. And when those Johnny Rebs were staggering back, carrying their wounded with them, Chivington's cavalry came down on both flanks, crushing the rebels underfoot.

Damn it to hell! Navajo Joe was asking questions again, mumbling to himself and laughing at his own jokes. What was he doing here? The white man thought to himself. Again! Hadn't the last drinking spree been enough of a headache? Headache! What's a headache when you owe your life to a man? … red man or white.

He remembered escaping with several others in the dead of night. He remembered that wild grass field and Peterson. Long gone Peterson! Oh, the ambush and that officer with his sword. And making it back to the foothills behind Johnson's ranch just as Chivington came down off those canyon rims and sent the rear guard of the Confederates running for their lives. He remembered lying there and watching the wagons go up in smoke. All that ammunition, supplies, rations, even the surgical stores all destroyed. And then those miners yelling and whooping it up as they systematically knifed and bayoneted dozens of mules and horses. And the few prisoners they captured and what they did to them.

The rest was a blur. A blessed relief he couldn't remember. He hadn't gone back to his unit, or whatever replaced it, after that battle at Glorieta Pass. He'd gone into the high mountains, away from the fighting and senseless killing along the Texas border. He'd stayed in the mountains for years, long after the war had moved out of the Southwest and the only fighting was against the Apaches, Navajos, and Comanches. He had grown up emotionally, mentally, and physically hard in the high reaches of the Sierras. He found what satisfied him and made him his own man. He'd found his own kind of peace.

But the years had been hard on him and he carried that lifestyle on his back with scars and aching muscles from too much heavy lifting, and too long in the cold and misery of those long winter nights. It was time for a change, time to head toward something different.

The hunting had grown sparse. There were now too many ranchers, too many farmers. Apache ambush from young braves trying to prove their manhood or renegades just off the reservation was always a danger. Change was in the air. The army, fresh off the Civil War, had reinforced their garrisons and filled their ranks with fresh recruits, eager for a fight against any hostile forces. The West was changing, and not for the better.

The man had no grudge against the Apache. Some were his friends. He understood their unwillingness to give up the land they considered no one's, least of all the white man. Navajo Joe understood this but he also could do nothing about the passing of time and the slow elimination of the Apache from their own lands.

A crude passing of air from Joe turned his friend's eyes up off the ground. His friend was mumbling in broken Spanish again. Nothing had changed with Joe, not even after rheumatism had crippled one side of his body and tied him down to his hogan and as far as the saloon in town. Nothing else had changed much either. The young Indian girls, the virgins, still wore ornaments in their hair and gave him inquisitive, forbidden stares. The old wrinkled women still sat all day and gossiped. And the old men still sat in the shady entrances to their jackals and stared out at nothing … day after day.

Within an hour the heat had moved most of the Indians back to their own rancheros. Only the two old friends sat under the slip of shade and ignored the sunlight, the flies, and the gritty sand blowing about their faces. They chose instead to concentrate on their bottle and the lies it produced. Navajo Joe ventilated himself again and spoke.

"It's good that you've come, my friend," he began, "Now we can go back to the mountains. To the place where we first met during the heavy snows. There will be plenty of deer and mountain sheep. We can get plenty drunk, have a good time. No pindah lickoyee! No pony soldiers."

The smoldering eyes met Joe's. He understood what his friend was suggesting but he couldn't lie. Not even to Joe. "No, my friend, we can't go back to the mountains. You're too old. Your people won't come and get you this time. Those were good times. But they've passed. We've got to live with what we've got now."

"But what do we have now?" his friend protested in the middle of another swig. "No good horses, no women, no more pelts, not even a warm lodge for the winter. How can we be happy at having nothing?" He shook his head gravely and drained the rest of the bottle quickly.

The man's eyes gave Joe an understanding nod. Comfort him, the man thought. Don't lie, but damn it, don't forget what he did for you in those snows.

The man had encountered his friend Joe on a mountain trail the day after fighting three Apaches. You'd be one sorry son-of-a-bitch if it hadn't been for Joe and his skill at digging slugs out of pus-swollen legs, he thought. He saved your life. But even that wasn't enough to keep the man in the territory. It was time for a change and the man meant to make the most of it.

No more daydreaming with Joe. No more empty nights talking about women and forgetting what they were once like. The man had made up his mind what he was going to do. And he knew Joe would be disappointed.

Although the man's unshaven face's was lined from lack of sleep, his eyes were still alert. They scanned back and forth past the slouched shoulders of Joe, the distant outline of the fort, and the infinite desert rimmed on two sides by mountains.

This then would be his last ritual to perform. This would be his last gesture toward at old friend before heading west again, only this time all the way to California. No more mountains. No more trapping. No more hiding out from roving bands of bandits and Apaches and trigger-edgy miners looking for gold. Arizona was one life, the mountains another. Now California would be his last. He'd stay there until whenever, but he'd stay there.

"You keep looking out to the mountains. I think maybe you want to go back soon. Back to the good times." The Indian stared with vacant eyes, smiled his broken grin, and rubbed his Spencer rifle with affection. Joe hadn't heard a word his friend had muttered and if he had understood the words, he wouldn't recognize their meaning. Joe was lost in his own world. And it was slowly closing in on him.

In his younger days, Joe had been a good hunter and fighter. He'd counted coup against the Apache and fought Mexican bandits when they attacked his village. But he'd been too good, too sure of himself. An Apache gunshot had taken off his arm and with it his ability to fight. His manliness had been robbed.

Joe and the white man met high in the mountains in the middle of winter. Joe had his knife. The man had a muslin bag of whiskey bottles and a swollen leg that was draining the life out of him. It made for a fair exchange. They lodged in an old miner's cabin and stayed for a week. Joe dug out the Apache slugs and his friend fed him whiskey. After that the man made it a point to visit Joe in the spring or fall and bring him whiskey. It was all Joe wanted. That and the stories, exaggerations, and lies about the old times.

When the second bottle was empty and pitched into the bushes, the man reached inside his saddlebag and produced a third. He teethed out the cork and spilled the reddish liquid down his throat. As he upended the bottle, his eye caught sight of something moving off to his right, something fast approaching. It was a rider, traveling hard. As the rider got closer, the man could see it was a trooper, his lathered horse almost to the point of faltering. He was stepping short and almost tripping over the stubby bushes which dotted the desert flats.

The rider raced past the prone pair and his dust slowly settled over both men. The white man fished out the makings of a cigarette and rolled one. The tobacco tasted good to his whiskey-numb mouth. The Indian pulled out a corn-shuck cigarette and lit up.

"More trouble," he muttered under his breath.

"What kind of trouble, Joe? Apaches again?" the man inquired.

"Cheeracows! The one the pony soldiers call 'The Fox.' Good name for him. 'Pindah lickoyee' are stupid! They can never catch him. Not even the mad one called Branan is going to catch that damn Indian. The Army will never do it in a thousand moons. Pony soldiers don't think Indian. They think white and fight white." His voice had suddenly sobered up in his anger. "You were still in the mountains when that Apache left the reservation. He took 30 warriors with him. People say he's probably meeting up with bandits. Maybe Comancheros to get more guns."

The man's dark eyes suddenly jerked up. "Comancheros? This far West?" he asked. "Is there truth to that rumor?"

Joe shrugged his shoulders. "They think it is so." he answered. "I think I need another drink".

"Here, keep it," his friend said. "I'm going to get a little shuteye. Wake me when it's sundown. I want to go into town for some food and more whiskey. Tonight we'll celebrate some more before I leave."

Joe smiled his stupid grin and cuddled the bottle against his belly. "We'll get plenty drunk tonight. Raise a little hell again. Just like the old times."

Just like the old times, the good old times. Lying back upset his equilibrium and the man could feel the whiskey weighing down his head. His eyelids grew heavy and he felt himself being swept away down a foggy well that clouded out the sunlight. The quiet and the desert heat wrapped up tightly against his ears. He couldn't feel the heat slowly burn into his long legs as they stretched out into the brightness. All was peaceful. The man's snoring grew louder. Peace at last, for a while.

Joe tossed back the bottle and snorted out the drops which had run into his nose. He coughed and belched and smiled. Tonight would be a good night, but what of right now? His friend was sleeping, dreaming of the mountains. Joe didn't have any more whiskey. What now?

Irish Troubles

"There are evil men about, Charlotte, you must be careful.

The young woman nodded her understanding even though she wasn't sure what her father was saying or the reason for his heightened concern. The old man had grown increasingly edgy and cautious over the last couple of months. It was almost as if he knew that change in their lives was eminent and possibly dangerous. But he said no more. The warning was but a casual comment, not meant to alarm or frighten his daughter. But the effect was unsettling nevertheless for the young woman raised in a very comfortable household.

Times were changing in Philadelphia and not for the better among Irish immigrants. The Irish were still not welcomed among the populous and animosity was rising among the other businessmen at their success. There were growing rumors afloat about possible reprisals for the business deals of the micks and wops who often collaborated on deals amongst themselves. Their exclusion of the Protestants and inclusion of the occasional Jew did little to enhance their reputation among the business elite.

Yet for all the threats and an increasing undercurrent of ill will, Charles Butler Barrington was not about to let any rumors stop him from acquiring more property in the city and expanding his other holdings. But now sinister rumors pointed to maneuverings by his enemies that might endanger his only daughter.

Charlotte Rose Barrington was the only daughter of this successful and prosperous family in Philadelphia proper. She was raised with all the tradition and pride of a family used to hard work and even harder times. She carried her pride quietly and with reserve. Yet she understood the stock from which she was born. And her pride in her parents had no bounds. Her red hair and equally bright mind was a testament to her parents' strict upbringing and the unlimited opportunities offered her at every stage in her relatively young life. Her parents' wealth offered but one more avenue for her to explore all that the large city had to offer. Not bad for her father, once a simple Irish immigrant who only a generation ago had snuck aboard an English freighter bound for the new land and now was a major real estate holder of fine city property.

As an only child to her now elderly parents, Charlotte had learned the refinements of a fine lady. She had earned a fine education in private schools. She had done charity work to help the less fortunate, and she had traveled up and down the East Coast accompanying her father on business trips.

But while these experiences had strengthened her self-confidence and steeled her determination to make her parents proud, it had also widened Charlotte's connection with other women her own age. The beautiful young woman had become somewhat of an anomaly among her friends who thought only of marriage and babies.

Charlotte had found time to learn to ride a horse, shoot a gun, and learned as much as she could about the untamed land to the west. Her teachers were the furriers that cared for her father's horses. Then the family's old cook and her husband, the gardener, filled Charlotte's mind with tales of the new territories being established out west and the adventurous lives lived out there.

The new territories were being turned into farms and towns and growing cities. Opportunity was everywhere just for the taking. Charlotte was intrigued. Society life wasn't right for her despite her parent's desperate desire to make a lady out of her.

Charlotte's parents were on the fringe of Philadelphia society. Their money had bought them partial entrance but their Irish-English heritage barred real acceptance by the elite. Charles' ambitious business dealings had only heightened his estrangement from the power brokers in town.

Charlotte's own place in that gentile society hardly assured her of a future bound for marriage and children and a place on the social registry. Instead she had to bank on time and changing attitudes toward the Irish before she might be fully accepted. But that was something she was neither willing nor capable of doing. She was too impatient, too anxious to fill her life with adventure and meaning and fulfillment. In whatever form that might take.

There were only a few family relatives to the Barrington's on the East Coast. Those that were nearby did not get along with her parents. Most were poor Irish who envied her father's success. Only one other man came close to her father in terms of his own success. Uncle Badger. Her mother's brother; once a staple at most family gatherings, had long since disappeared into the West. Now he was seldom heard from. And within the Barrington household, he was never talked about. When Charlotte would ask about him, the subject was changed. It quickly became apparent to even a very young Charlotte that Uncle Badger was a closed subject in her family. And she was never told why.

When pressed by Charlotte, the household help whispered that Uncle Badger was somewhere out in the southwest territories. It was rumored that he had become a very successful rancher and horse breeder. The help claimed that at first he would often write to his sister asking for money and loans. He encouraged the Barringtons to come out to visit his ranch. He had even hinted at great wealth to be gained in purchasing the many acres the government had set aside for land development. Yet even if she wanted to honor her brother's request, Charlotte's mother would never agree to bring her family out West. Even when the train tracks finally got to the New Mexico territory and she was assured of safe passage from the Indian troubles, Charlotte's mother refused to let the family travel out west. Pretty soon, Charles had put his foot down and correspondence with her brother ceased. He was seldom heard from since.

Charlotte's idyllic world ended with the stock market crash of 1866. Her father's investments in stocks, bonds, and real estate took a nose dive and their standard of living with it. Compounding the radical change of lifestyle was the tragic death of both her parents in a suspicious fire not long afterwards.

Charlotte came home late one night after volunteering at the poor farm to find her house ablaze. Frantic firemen were running around the building, seeking a safe entrance to find its occupants, to no avail. Orange-red flames poured out of every window and heavy black smoke towered up above the deadly infernal.

Charlotte became hysterical, screaming for her parents. There was no answer above the crackling and hissing of the terrible fire in front of her. She tried to enter the front door but was tackled by a burly fireman who pulled her, kicking and screaming, away from the intense heat.

In the end, everything was lost; the Barrington's financial wealth, their home, and their standing in the business community. Most tragically, Charlotte's parents were now gone, their bodies found on the second floor landing.

Charlotte had gone from landed gentry to poor house candidate in less than an hour.

Rumors grew rampant that the fire had been intentionally set. Whispers in parlors and saloon backrooms said it was the work of business associates seeking a piece of the growing Barrington holdings. Police investigated the claims but found them unsubstantiated and quickly dismissed the talk as bar room banter and society envy.

It made no difference to Charlotte. The deed was done and the young woman suddenly found herself without parents or wealth. All the trappings of her once privileged life had ended in one tragic evening. The young woman had gone from a life of privilege to one of meager subsistence. She had but one thing in her favor now. A fierce determination to make something of her life, by her own devices.

Charlotte Rose Barrington would rise up from the ashes of her parents' tragic deaths, her loss of wealth, and stature in the community. She would become her own person, relying on the skills her parents taught her and her own innate ability to fend for herself.

As the weeks dragged by, there were fewer and fewer friends to come by her new home, a small rented apartment she shared with her parent's former cook and gardener. Once close friends had disappeared and only the help could be counted upon to be honest with the woman who had always treated them with respect and dignity.

A resilient and feisty young woman, Charlotte would take charity from no one and soon found herself near penniless and with little prospect for a future in Philadelphia. The old cook had taken her in and gave her a place to live until she could get back on her feet. Creditors were kept at bay by a frying pan and shotgun when they came banging at her door. But they persisted until every penny that her parents had saved was spirited away and divided up among the crooked politicians and questionable business associates.

"What are you going to do, Miss?" the old cook asked Charlotte one night after porridge and stale bread.

"Head out West, I think," Charlotte answered with a smile.

"Out West! Oh my, why would you do such a thing? It isn't safe. You might be killed." the cook offered.

"If I stay here, I might be killed as well," Charlotte replied, shaking her head in disbelief. "Father's enemies will stop at nothing until all the Barrington's are dead or gone. They now own most of Philadelphia. No Irish allowed."

In the spring of 1867, Charlotte left by train for the West and whatever that vast land might hold for her. She hoped that time spent on Uncle Badger's ranch would provide the funds to continue on to San Francisco or perhaps beyond. She would do housework, cooking, cleaning, whatever her uncle asked of her. Just for the opportunity to earn enough to continue her journey further West.

Charlotte's first real stop was the hamlet of Irving; hundreds of miles away from the hustle and excitement of the big city. It was also the first real sign of trouble for a woman traveling alone. Early that morning Charlotte got off her train to switch trains heading for Chicago. The small depot emptied quickly as the other passengers either boarded other trains or the waiting stagecoach. She was soon alone on the platform waiting for her train to arrive.

A smartly dressed man appeared out of nowhere. Two companions, not so well dressed, trailed behind him. They quickly assessed the situation and approached Charlotte. The three of them kept looking around as they moved toward her.

"Morning, Madam," the stranger said, "Might I be of assistance to you?"

"No thank you," Charlotte replied as she tried to move past the man. She had neither the time nor patience for honkytonkers, gamblers, thieves, pimps, and whoremongers. Their intention was clear and she would have none of it.

"This is not the place for a young attractive woman such as yourself traveling alone," the man offered as one of his companions stepped in her way. They had her surrounded.

Charlotte turned and smiled at the leader of the pack. "I'm quite capable of taking care of myself, Sir," she replied. "Now kindly step aside and let me proceed."

Smiling a curt, almost sneering grin, the stranger slipped his hand in a vest pocket and in doing so revealed a small derringer there. "I don't think so," he began. "A young girl like you needs a place to stay. Perhaps even work. I have work for you at my saloon. Doesn't pay worth nothin' but the fringe benefits feel real good." His companions laughed and punched each other on their shoulders. They moved in closer to Charlotte.

She stood her ground.

"Sir," Charlotte began, "I travel where and how I chose. It doesn't concern you. Now please step aside."

The stranger smiled and continued to block her way. "A woman such as yourself, traveling all alone, just might get lost or disappear and never be found. You best come with me and don't make a scene."

"Do what he says and you won't get hurt," one of the thugs laughed. His companion slugged him on his shoulder again.

"Your threats don't scare me. Now get out of my way!" Charlotte snarled, raising her voice as she lifted her chin.

No reply but for a smile and then a smirk from the man. Charlotte would have none of it. She was tired and dirty and in need for food and water. She pushed past the man.

He quickly swung around as she passed and grasped her arm in a tight lock. "I told you a woman alone is not safe, even in a busy place such as this," he said. "You're coming with me."

"Sir," Charlotte said in a calm, deceivingly quiet voice. "You have but a moment to release me and be on your way or I shall end this conversation with you once and for all. Which will it be?"

The man grinned and then turned to nod at his two companions. This feisty redhead was one solid cut of stone, he thought to himself. He liked that in a woman. It would be a challenge to break her down as he had done all the others. If she wouldn't come of her own accord he just might have to persuade her in other ways. He started to say something to his companions, his back half turned to his latest conquest.

Charlotte did the two-step, imitating a dance step she knew so well. Pivoting on her left heel, she shot her right hand into the man's vest pocket and grabbed the derringer. Then she shifted to her right heel and drove a clenched fist into his throat.

The blow hit him directly in the Adam's apple. He went down in a gurgling heap. Charlotte stepped over the gasping, heaving body and smiled at the other two men. The derringer was now inches from their faces. But it was not the small pistol that stopped them cold. Instead it was the look on this woman's face; cold, determined, ready to kill at a moment's notice. Charlotte's stance was rigid. The Irish woman was mad and looking crazy.

"Your friend will live," Charlotte said calmly as she moved the pistol barrel from one face to the other. "But he won't be talking for a very long time. Another inch to the right and he would have choked on his own vomit. Leave now or I will shoot the both of you where you stand."

They stared at her in disbelief. Never had they seen such a woman. Her face was a placid façade, void of any emotions. Her eyes were piercing and deadly. The anger there was palatable. The tiny derringer floated in their faces. The two men had no doubt she would kill them both without a hint of hesitation. The two thugs turned and quickly backed off the platform and retreated out of sight.

The stranger rolled on the ground, coughing up blood and vomit. Charlotte bent over him and whispered in his ear. "I won't kill you this time. But if I ever see you again, Sir, I will place a bullet between your eyes." The man looked up at the unflinching face of the young woman. "Now nod if you understand what I am saying," Charlotte said.

The stranger's terrified eyes looked up at the redhead and managed a feeble acknowledgement. Charlotte smiled again and moved down the platform as the loud shriek of her approaching train cut the silence.

Death in the Hills

The first Tonto, cresting a series of small ridgelines within the canyon, flicked his glass mirror back and forth. Almost immediately, a flash came back, acknowledging his signal for the column to proceed. In the distance he could see the column slowly begin to move, sending out flankers as it entered the narrow confines of the canyon entrance.

Slowly, the Tonto nudged his pony down off the ridgeline and worked his way deeper into the canyon. Silence followed his every movement, heightening the uneasiness that rode along with him. His dark eyes darted back and forth, taking in a dozen images at one time. Nothing seemed amiss or out of place. Nothing moved but for the dust always twirling in tiny spouts of brown in the open areas.

The Indian paused for a moment and took a pinch of hoddentin and threw it up toward the sun. Then he put another pinch on his tongue and yet another on the crown of his head. Medicine to make his journey safe: that and a cocked rifle.

Where the canyon opened up, cactus and scrub brush blanketed the canyon floor, providing dozens of perfect hiding places for an ambush. But years in the mountains and canyons had perfected the Tonto's instincts and he kept a wide berth of the undergrowth and accompanying arroyos. Siding up against the far canyon wall, he moved slowly and cautiously. His partner Ta-nay might question moving so far ahead of the column, but he was confident of his instincts. He might be younger than Ta-nay, he thought to himself, but he knew just as much and he would prove it. He rode easily in the hot sun, ever alert for any signs of danger.

Suddenly his pony stopped dead in its tracks. The horse's head lifted up and his nostrils flared. The Tonto swung his carbine up, cocking the lever as he did so. He looked around, quickly trying to access his situation.

The black-feathered arrow flew straight and true, hitting its intended target dead center. The Tonto's body flinched, stiffened, and started to sag. He looked down at the arrowhead protruding from his chest and raised his arms to ride away. A second arrow found its mark higher up near the base of his neck, and the Tonto fell foreword, collapsing off his horse.

They appeared from among the rocks. Swiftly and silently, the Apaches scooped up the body and carried it away, leading the pony behind them. As quickly as it had happened, the Tonto was gone and no trace of his body remained.

The war party spread out, filtering among the boulders and moving higher up the side of the canyon wall. Carbines and bows at ready, they waited for the column to appear.

The column entered the canyon with a cautious but steady trot. Up ahead, the first two squads had passed through the narrow mountain gap and spread out, flanking both sides of the entrance.

As he passed by the skirmishers, the second Tonto studied the canyon's baseline and accompanying ridgelines for his partner with no luck. The first Tonto must have moved over the series of rolling crests beyond and deeper into the canyon, he thought. Too far out for his liking but his partner was never one to heed another's warning.

"Sergeant, move your skirmishers out quickly. We don't want an exposed flank. Carbines at ready." The sergeant kicked his mount and motioned the two squads out.

Branan drew out his binoculars and studied the canyon baseline up ahead. A million places to hide. A million shadows. Or were they? One Tonto distracted by his partner's absence, the second Tonto nowhere in sight. He kicked his mount and moved the column straight ahead giving them ample distance from the canyon walls, and a possible ambush.

Jail Time

Joe and his companion were fast asleep in the hot noonday sun. Far off in the distance the sound of something resembling voices arose. They pricked at the snoring man's ears but were unclear and he couldn't see a thing for the darkness. A dream, yeah, it was only a dream.

But then the sounds grew louder. The man tried to ignore them by rolling over and covering his head with an arm. That didn't work. The sounds persisted, growing louder until they tugged at the man's consciousness and finally broke through.

He came awake with a cold sweat start. Both shirt and pants were soaked. His vision ran in blurry waves, which gradually began to slow down then fade into something recognizable.

"Alright, get up!" A voice came through the fog. "Colonel wants to see you," the voice continued jabbering, shouting on until its noise began hurting the man's ears. The sound echoed in the man's head and scrambled his brain. His watery eyes tried to focus on something bluish towering over him. But the more he looked up, the more it hurt his head.

"Could you talk a little softer?" the man countered in a barely audible voice. The blue form moved closer, raising its own voice by several decibels. "Get off your sorry ass! You're under arrest." Behind the thundering voice, two other blue shadows clicked their rifles to port-arms.

"What the hell are you talking about?" The man muttered as he tried to slide his back up against the side of the hogan. His vision was beginning to clear and he could make out gray, dust-lined boots. There were three pairs of boots, faded trousers, and the stocks of army carbines. Army rifles! Now what the hell did they want with him?

The blue form bent over and materialized into the red-splotched face of a sergeant; bad breath and teeth missing. "One more time, pilgrim. You're under arrest for selling liquor to an Indian. Now get off your backside or I'll drag you to the stockade by your heels. Colonel wants to see you in the morning once you've sobered up. Now move!"

Movement was a painful effort the man couldn't force. The sergeant did it for him. The tight-faced non-com motioned his men, and with a jerk, they lifted the man off the ground and pushed him toward his horse. The man started to protest but his words fell on deaf ears.

The ride back to the fort joggled his body and knocked his brain back and forth inside his head. Even in the pain of his hangover, the man had time to think about what had happened to Joe and how the army had found out about their drinking spree.

They put him and the Navajo in a small cell at the end of a row of six others. Joe lay curled up on a cot next to his, happy in his dreams and stupor. The white man lay back on his cot and stared up at the adobe ceiling whitewashed gray. He'd seen that color before in much the same kind of cell, but it didn't stop him from coming down to drink with Joe. Twice before the same thing had happened; Joe had left, gotten into a fight at the fort, and bragged about his whiskey-laden friend back at his hogan. It was usually the sheriff who hauled him off to the jail, not the Army. And why would a Colonel want to see him? It didn't make sense.

The darkness closed in again. The man's eyes grew heavy. His pounding head subsided in its pain. Sleep came gradually to him again.

CHAPTER THREE

The man's second awakening matched his first in both pain and intensity. His morning came on quicker and without the customary cold sweat. But that was about all. His pounding head fared little better this time although his vision had become steadier. He recognized the familiar gray ceiling of his jail cell, the smell of dank adobe bricks and the snoring of Navajo Joe. The half-breed was still sound asleep curled up like a baby on his cot.

Rolling his head to one side, he saw he was in a small cell. The rank bunk he was laying on smelled as foul as his own tired body. It was a flea-ridden, foul-smelling mattress over a wooden frame, which squeaked loudly as he shifted his weight. In one corner stood a washstand with a clay pitcher on it and a galvanized tin basin next to that. It was all standard equipment for a transient jail cell. He barely had enough room to stand, which he wasn't about to attempt in his condition.

Later that morning, they would haul his sorry ass in front of the colonel or some magistrate. He'd pay his fine and be on his way. This would be the third or fourth time around again with Joe … hell of an average for a wandering scout and his drunken companion.

Sunlight streamed through a small three-barred window above his head and he had to shield his eyes from the light's intensity. The slant of the rays told him it was early morning. A little too much brightness for sore eyes that early in the day.

He must have slept all night!

Sounds of the Post's early morning activity came through the window and reminded him of his long-planned journey now postponed for another day. Thanks to Joe's drinking and no common sense on his own part, but he didn't mind. The fine was worth spending time with an old friend. A friend he would probably never see again once he left the fort for the California coast.

Easing himself out of the cot, the scout gingerly stood up. The clay floor spun around and he fell back, crashing down onto the cot. His head felt as if it had split open and he muffled a moan of pain. Then he carefully slid off the cot and crawled on hands and knees to the washstand and poured some water from the olla over his head. The warm liquid did little to help the pain but did wash one layer of dirt off his face. Resting back on his haunches, the room again began to spin around and he had to quickly sit back on the mud floor until the momentum slowed.

Got to slow down and go easy, he swore at himself, *I'll waste the whole day in bed. Christ, I can't do that. The mountains are waiting!*

As the man sat motionless, the room slowed its spinning. A breeze, filled with fine parade ground dust, began to filter through the cell window. It touched the man's sweaty neck and felt good. Sounds of marching drill squads picked up.

Morning duty. Police patrol and marchin' time. *What memories,* he thought. Cold beans and sowbelly. Saturday nights in town. Rebel gray everywhere. "Goes with the pretty girls and the pinching," the old veterans told the young pup after that first night out on the town.

Civilian voices mixed with soldiers' commands and tin cups clanged against coffee pots. He was back in his cell again. One stupid civilian prisoner dumped in an Army cell on charges of drunkenness.

The sounds outside had aroused something long forgotten. He was curious about the fort. Moving slowly so as to be sure he had gained some semblance of a conscious state, the scout climbed carefully to his feet and went to the sun blasted opening on the wall. He rested his chin on the narrow wooden ledge and looked out into the center of the fort.

The fort had been built of adobe, wood, and stone, whichever was in more abundant supply at each stage of its construction. He'd seen several like this one before. They were spread far and wide across the Arizona and New Mexico Territories. Forts had grown from small frontier bivouacs to much larger trading and routing establishments. Each one was a stopping off point for many of the settlers and migrants heading out West. The scout's cell was part of the older section of the fort which stood conveniently close to the guardroom along a broad avenue fronting the troop barracks.

From his vantage point, the man could see a storehouse, quartermaster's headquarters, and most likely the commanding officer's headquarters with its long ramada. Outside the quadrangle, though he couldn't see the rough board houses, he knew those women he heard chattering would be the married men's wives. Their voices rolled across the parade ground, despite the low murmuring civilians and nickering of horses in a corral nearby.

He spotted his horse easily among the better-fed, stronger army grays and bays. It stood out like a scarecrow. The old swayback rough-coated beast had survived two deadly winters on meanness alone. It was a companion and a pain in the backside. But he was the only horse the man had. A good horse cost more pelts than last winter's total catch. He'd have to tolerate that animal until he reached his beloved mountains.

Unless!

Unless he could get his hands on the fine looking blue appaloosa in the corner of the corral. An appaloosa was as fine a horse as a man could ever want, especially for long distance travel. He'd have to wheel and deal for that one. And with what? He had little money, no worthy horse to trade and only a Spencer repeater for protection. He couldn't bargain his rifle away or it might be his scalp someday. A man needs capital to invest and he only had a couple of coins to his name. So that took care of the Appaloosa for now.

Close to the corral, the early morning campfires of the civilian contractors and their crews glowed. It was a motley collection of muleskinners and teamsters resting between long pulls back and forth along the trails across the territory. The man knew them to be a mean bunch. Men toughened by the elements and as ornery as their mules. He had seen those bull-whackers on the trail and admired their skill with the whip. One drunken skinner had taken three bits off him by flicking a fly off his mule's ear with a long black snake whip.

Beyond the corral and stacked freight wagons, the man could see several teams from an immigrant wagon train, all lined up for a pull-out soon.

Draggled-skirted women and rag-tag children scurried about the canvas covered wagons in seemingly total confusion while the men folk harnessed their horses and mules or grouped together for early morning coffee.

The only troopers he saw were casuals, new recruits and men out of the guardhouse or hospital. All second rate troopers. There wasn't a seasoned veteran to be seen. But it was still all too familiar. Faded blue tunics. Dusty parade fields. "Boots and saddles" followed in 15 minutes by "to horse" and another patrol was off. Rough board houses and barracks. *No thanks*, he thought to himself. *No thanks again!*

Traffic passing by his cell window scarcely gave the prisoner a second look. A few urchins would stop and stare, and be quickly smacked into motion by their sober-faced parents. Women looked down at the ground in passing and the men folk didn't bother to look at all. Only an occasional soldier would give him a second look, be glad he wasn't there himself, and go about his business.

No one cared about the prisoner. The scout was a surplus piece of humanity in a sea of busy activity. He was a casual observer of work and sweat, of hot coffee and bacon, and freedom beyond the awakening horizon. He was not a part of anything and wouldn't be until he was free. Life was sweeping by him and the man felt funny inside, out of place. He felt frustrated for not staying in the mountains and his warm winter cabin. Mad because he had to see Joe, though the man wasn't really that kind of friend. More of an obligation, and the scout kept his word. So there he was paying the consequences. *California, I'm comin'. Sooner or later, I'll be on my way.*

The man slipped back onto the cot, fished through his shirt pocket, took out a rumpled piece of paper, and rolled a cigarette. It tasted a little better than yesterdays; not much of a breakfast though. Joe still snored and sputtered his liquor away and ventilated. He'd be back squatting in front of his hogan and drinking before nightfall.

As for the scout, he gave it a couple of hours, two or three at the most, before he'd be taken before the commanding officer, dressed down military fashion, given a fine, and sent on his way. Sheriff or Colonel, drinking was drinking, and it wasn't murder. *So what the hell,* he thought. *I'll be patient, and it'll get over and I'll be free of this stinking place.*

A fly lighted on his hand and he watched it intently, gradually losing focus as he did. A voice caught his attention.

"You Burns? The trapper and scout they call Jeb Burns?"

The man looked up at a kid sprawled out on his cot in a cell across from him.

"I am."

"What they got you in for?" asked the kid, probably no older than 17 or 18. His head was shaved. A deserter most likely.

"Drinkin', I guess," Jeb Burns replied. "How'd you know my name?"

No response. The kid just stared at him and looked back down at the ground. "Hear things around, that's all," the kid answered and then rolled over, his back to Burns.

Somewhere outside a horse stamped and nickered. There was a clang of iron on iron. The voices continued but were farther and farther away.

He sat very still and hardly noticed the sounds drifting into his cell. The fly buzzed around his head and left. He felt very much alone.

Voices again broke through the quiet. This time they were very close and at a whisper. They were close enough, in fact, to be in the same cell as Jeb's. Only Joe's snoring filled the long dank hallway. No. They came from behind him, just outside his cell window.

Burn's instinct to peek out the window was stifled by natural caution born in the war and tempered in the mountains. The whispering grew a little louder. He sat still, dragging on his cigarette, listening.

"No, Edward, I know I heard it right! That trooper said the Colonel's got to get supplies out to a patrol in the field. And soon! Most likely its ammunition and rations. But it doesn't matter. Quartermaster can't hire Injuns 'cept for scoutin' and no contractor is going to risk his men resupplyin' the Army. Not when there's plenty a money to be made haulin' freight or takin' passage with them settlers. The Colonel's stuck and he'll be more than willin' to hire us on as scouts until the job's done. He ain't got no choice!"

A more controlled voice greeted the first one with disdain and skepticism. Jeb sat up on his knees, inching closer to the window to catch all the words flying back and forth. The first man wasn't about to be put aside that easily. He grumbled at his companion's cautiousness and continued.

"It'll be a week's easy work and a way to get outta here. Christ, if it's gone south, what more could you ask for? Escortin' Army stuff is the best protection we got. What the hell have we got to lose?"

Way out of here? Jeb cocked his head. *It didn't make sense. How could taking Army supplies through hostile territory be considered a safe thing to do? For anyone!* The men were talking nonsense and Jeb was intrigued.

The second voice broke louder this time, more adamant. "What have you got to lose, you ask? Your hair, that's what!" He spat out the words with earnest. "Do you think those contractors are refusin' the Colonel cause there's no real money to be had running supp-lies to some damn fool officer caught in a patch of trouble? Hell no!"

The first voice started a protest but the second man cut it off, more vehemently this time.

"They aren't going out because there's Cherry Cows raidin' south of here. That's why! It's one thing to haul freight armed to the teeth with a parcel of heavy guns or haul ass with a bunch of settlers coverin' your back. It's something else to risk your neck on a supply march."

He paused, still angry. "Why hell, you don't even know where that patrol is at or what kind of trouble it's gotten into. And for what? Nine dollars a month, regular quarter-masters pay. Bullshit! I ain't riskin' my hair for that."

There was a pause long enough for the anger to settle in on both sides of the conversation, and then it began again.

"Then what the hell are we gonna do to get outta here smart guy? There's no work out here. Them teamsters can't stand the sight of no one but their damnable smelly mules. And the ranches aren't hiring this late in the season. Leaves robbin' a bank as the only answer and there ain't one of them for hundreds of miles. We gotta get outta here, don't we?"

No answer from the other side.

"So how do you propose we do it?"

There was still no response forthcoming.

"We coulda stayed in Yuma," the second voice countered, "If you hadn't been so damn stupid and bushwhacked that settler."

"Deserved it for calling me a boy," came the response.

"Still stupid of you!"

After another long pause the two men continued to argue, taking up where they had left off, but now in softer tones, dropping their conversation as other voices drifted by.

Burns finished his cigarette and closed his eyes, half-listening, half-dreaming of the mountains. Whoever these two men were; saddle bums, bandits, con men, or two stray farmers looking for work, he was sure of two things. They were stupid! And they just might be very dangerous if they went on such a patrol. But what the hell did he care? He wasn't going. He hadn't a concern in the world until the Colonel called for him. And he got the fine paid and was on his way.

"Alright, we'll talk to him. But just talk, that's all. If it sounds too risky, we'll forget the whole thing." the other man agreed and they left, their voices trailing off the porch.

Curiosity topped caution and Jeb knelt on his cot, watching the two men cross the parade field. They both wore blue denim pants, woolen shirts, and matching leather vests. One wore a kerchief around his neck. The other had a small forge cap, cocked at an angle, on his head. The second man, the shorter of the pair, wore a new colt, hung low-gunfighter style, on his hip. He tough-walked and rode his thumbs in his pants belt. The other walked with a more noticeable, tired gait.

Jeb's dark eyes trailed the pair as they passed through the varied collection of humanity criss-crossing the parade field. They disappeared into a row of migrant wagons. Their clothes labeled them as cowpunchers or bronco-peelers but the conversation he had overheard suggested something else. Like perhaps holster men-gunfighters or bandits.

His curiosity was aroused all right. *I'm probably imagining things again. Too long in the mountains this time. Almost forgot the way a lot of these kind talk when they're by themselves. Talk is cheap. It doesn't label a man unless he's heard or overheard. And they didn't expect to be overheard by anyone. Much less someone stuck in a jail cell. Whatever they're talking about doesn't concern the likes of me,* Jeb told himself. *Forget the whole incident.*

The sound of an iron door squeaking open turned Jeb's attention back into the dim cellblock light. Someone was entering the row, perhaps coming to get him. A young soldier, pimples still blotching his face, carried in a tray of mess hall slop. He slid it under the cell door and turned to leave when Jeb called out to him.

"Hey, Trooper, when are they gonna take me out of here and let me go. I got time to make up and places to go."

The youngster spun around. "What are you caterwaulin' about?" he spat back. "You got your sorry ass in here. Don't yell at me to get you out. That's for the Colonel to decide. And I expect he ain't about to do it until he's ready."

"What are you talking about?" Burns gave back. "I'm in here for drinking, not killing. How much of an offense is that anyway?"

The trooper approached his cell, a bit cautiously, and wary of the stranger. He stood his ground and looked tough. At least he tried to. Then he said, "The way the Colonel feels today, he ain't gonna concern his self with no drunk. He's got rations and supplies to get outta here and not enough men to do it. Old Captain Branan's done it again. Strung his self so tight, he'll need help from us to get his self out of trouble again. So don't go crying to me about your gettin' outta there. Until this thing is settled, the Colonel's not about to worry about you or your Injun friend." Then he added with a sneer, "Eat hardy, squaw man."

Ambush

Ta-nay was looking for his partner and feeling increasingly uneasy. Both knew the danger in this kind of terrain. It was a maze of blackness and shadows and eerily ominous light shadows that twisted and curved over and under jumbled piles of rock. Boulders cast deep shadows among the rocks. Arroyos hid shallow recesses where an Indian could lay prone until someone was practically on top of him. Chaparral was the perfect cover to hide behind before launching arrow or lance into the back of an unsuspecting prey.

The Apache scout was growing increasingly worried about his partner. He should have been on the ridgeline or cresting one of the rolling slopes that blanketed the canyon bottoms.

Yet the other Tonto was nowhere in sight. Nor his pony, a jittery young colt, never prone to a quiet trot. If there had been a problem, Ta-nay never heard a thing. If the other scout was far ahead, out of sight, he was very foolish indeed. Silence enveloped the canyon but for the two squads of skirmishers spreading out and their muffled footfalls.

Then, up ahead, near a jumble of boulders and rock at the base of the canyon laid his friend. He was settled in against a large boulder, carbine at ready, waiting for Ta-nay. Strangely his pony was nowhere in sight. Perhaps gone lame and in the shade. Or run off for some reason.

Ta-nay nudged his pony into a trot and moved quickly toward his partner. There would be words between himself and the younger scout. Captain Branan would never tolerate a breach in security from either scout. It would be trouble no matter what happened here.

Closing in on his prone partner, Ta-nay saw no movement from the other scout or acknowledgement of his closing presence. As he drew even closer, he noticed the legs were splayed out and the head tilted back against a rock. Was he asleep, hurt, or worse? Something was not right!

Suddenly Ta-nay set his pony back on his hocks. The lithe animal sprayed sand and pebbles as it slid to a halt. Sliding off the mount, the Tonto fired rapidly into the shadows up ahead. Two Apaches sprang out from behind a large boulder, firing wildly with their Winchester rifles. Slugs whistled by Ta-nay's head as he steadied his carbine and got off three shots before feeling a bullet rip through his tunic and shoulder blade. He staggered back and caught another slug in the stomach. Falling backwards, he rolled to one side and got off another shot before a third bullet ripped through his neck.

"Column halt, arms at ready," shouted the captain, instinctively bringing up his carbine and aiming at the boulders nearby. In rapid order, rifles and carbine flew out of their scabbards and focused on the bordering ridgeline.

For the most part, these were seasoned troopers, and like any well-oiled combat machine, they knew instinctively what to do. Veterans shouted directions at recruits and in doing so calmed their already jittery nerves. Horses bellowed and blew out of their noses. The column stood at ready.

The air was still and quiet. Men silently scanned the horizon and nearby protrusions for any sign of the enemy. Nothing. Dirt-crusted fingers gripped the rifles and carbines and the men waited, but not for long.

Suddenly a blanket of arrows arched up over a ridgeline, sailed high up into the sky in an ever-widening fan, and then rained down on the column. The onslaught was swift, silent, and deadly. Shot from an angle behind and to the left of the column, no one saw or heard the assault until the first troop lurched forward, an arrow protruding from his back. Others quickly followed, tumbling off their mounts.

"Break right," shouted the captain and echoed by his sergeant at almost the same moment. The column broke right and dashed toward an arroyo in the distance, trying desperately to distance themselves from the cascade of arrows. As the column raced toward the nearest arroyo, Apache marksmen suddenly materialized from among the scrub brush and chaparral, firing at the column of troopers as they dashed by.

The column spilled into the arroyo, losing several troopers and their mounts in their mad dash for cover. "Dismount and fire at will, pick your targets," came the next order. Tight discipline among the older men held the younger ones together like glue. Shouts and screams intermingled with the steady staccato of Apache Winchesters, which was answered, in turn, by the hollow crackling of Spencer carbines. This chorus of rifle and carbine fire bounced back and forth among the rocks and boulders.

All too quickly, Captain Branan realized he had been funneled into a trap. The hostiles were surrounding his arroyo and cutting off any chance to escape. Apache archers were already gauging the distance to the arroyo with strategically placed arrow markers that were, even at that moment, marching across the parched ground toward his meager concealment. The apache attack had been perfectly timed to pin the column between two lines of hostile fire and catch them in the crossfire. Dismounting had been a costly mistake. Three troopers already lay dead on the ground.

"Sergeant, mount the column and get to the next arroyo, hold steady there. Move out!"

"Captain," responded the Sergeant as he turned and shouted to mount up and charge the next arroyo. Seasoned veterans grabbed young recruits and together they mounted up and dashed away from the swiftly approaching Apaches.

Branan rallied his own squad from among the skirmishers who had dashed back as soon as the attack had begun. Together they held a rear guard stand as the other troopers dashed toward the arroyo. Moving back and forth in the now empty arroyo, they fired off quick shots before ducking down for cover. Rifle slugs and arrows cut the air about their heads.

"Steady men. Aim at the shadows. Pick your shots," the captain shouted as he moved among the standing and kneeling soldiers. With a calmness born out of numerous fire-fights with the hostiles, the veterans methodically sought to find their marks among the unseen enemy. Having moved out of range of the unseen archers, the column now focused on finding their targets. Frustrated archers grew brave and topped the ridgeline, quick enough to fire an arrow, and then drop down again.

The troopers began to find their marks as one Apache after another jumped up to fire only to be cut down by multiple carbine slugs. Captain Branan looked over to where the Tonto had first spotted the hostiles. A glance told him all he had to know. Both the Tonto and his mount had been cut down by a fusillade of arrow and bullet. They lay crumpled on the ground, in a growing puddle of blood red sand. The other Tonto wasn't far away, slumped up against a boulder.

In the meantime, the Sergeant and his men had reached the arroyo, cutting down several hostiles as they charged up and over the arroyo embankment. One troop gathered the horses in a ramada while others provided covering fire for Branan. Seasoned veterans calmly sided up to the cactus and rock and began to pick their targets.

Branan rallied his troops and followed the Sergeant until he too was in the safety of the arroyo. He spread his troopers out in a skirmish line and held steady fire at the quickly fading hostiles. Gradually the firing grew sparse, then stopped all together.

In time, silence came back to the canyon. Except for the buzzing of insects on dead bodies and muffled talk among the troopers, no sound could be heard. Branan sent a squad to flank the scene of battle. Minutes later, as the captain had expected, the troopers appeared across the canyon floor where the archers had launched their attack.

"As expected, Sergeant, they're gone," the captain said, almost matter-of-factly. There was no hiding the distain and frustration lathering his voice. "Collect the dead. We'll have to bury them here and come back for them later." Count out the ammunition that's left and give me an accounting. We still have plenty of miles to go until we get to the ranch."

CHAPTER FOUR

They came for him an hour later; three stone-faced troopers and a sallow-skinned, elderly sergeant. The enlisted men were armed with Civil War Henrys carried at port arms. The sergeant wore a sidepiece and a depression where his mouth began and ended.

"Christ, you guys look like an execution squad. You're after the wrong hombre," Burns joked. They returned his joke with cold stares. The scout rose, still chuckling at the seriousness of it all.

"Button up, Mister," snapped the non-com, unlocking the iron door and letting it swing back, clanging against the side. "The Colonel wants to see you." He stood firmly in the doorway, one hand on the bars, the other on his sidepiece. The men behind him mumbled "Probably a God-damn galvanized Yankee."

"At ease, troopers," snapped the sergeant. Jeb ignored their comment.

The noise woke Navajo Joe who peeked from under his arm. He muttered something indiscernible and buried his head back under his sleeve. Burns laughed and followed the sergeant down the hallway.

He had guessed right about the headquarters building. It stood almost directly across from the guardhouse. It was a crudely built affair of adobe and rough planks. The floorboards squeaked as the party stepped onto the brush-covered porch and marched through the open door. Seated inside, along the wall, were two young enlisted men. Their haggard faces and head cradling made the him smile. They were probably there for the same offense as his. Poor bastards, the Army would show no leniency for them.

Another sergeant, with a horse face of granite, sat behind a crudely fashioned desk sorting paperwork. His eyes shot up behind a wire-rimmed pair of glasses as the party entered.

"Sit down," The non-com snapped to the prisoner and nodded the others back out the door. Jeb hesitated, looking down on the non-com, eyeing his faded blue tunic and parchment-like skinny face. His first reaction to a command was to freeze. He was his own man. He listened to no one, especially not someone in the Union Army.

"You deaf? I said sit down."

Jeb cracked a smile back at the sternness and sat down. Instinctively he reached into his pocket for tobacco.

"No smoking," growled the sergeant, casting the prisoner a piercing look. Jeb cupped the tobacco pouch in his hand, sorely tempted, then put it back and looked over the room.

It was large but nondescript. Regular Army sameness. All by regulations even to the construction of their buildings. The room was little different from the one he had joined up in years before. It was small, cramped, hot, and stuffy. It smelled of sweat and gun grease and leather. To him, all non-coms seemed much the same. Little time for civilians and lots of enlisted ass to chew. A necessary hinge to keep the military fighting tough.

A door behind the sergeant opened. Burns looked up as an officer came out. He was a tall man, wire-taut and strong, but his face was lined and showed signs of fatigue. He approached the prisoner - hand extended.

"Mr. Burns, I'm Colonel Kincaid. I understand you've been our guest since last night. Come into my office. I want to discuss something with you."

Jeb Burns took the officer's handshake apprehensively then followed, still a little surprised, into his office. He caught the sergeant's hard look as he passed by.

Now what the hell was this all about? he thought. *All he wanted was a small fine and an open door to get outta there. What did the Colonel want with someone like him?*

The Colonel's room was a small cubicle with a desk in one corner and a large territorial map pegged to the wall behind it. Dotting the canvas map were colored markings, indicating the regular stage routes, relay stations, ranches, and small establishing settlements. A window, wooden shutters drawn back, looked out across the parade field. Through it a yellow hazy shaft beamed through to the floor. A fireplace had been built in the corner using the walls for supports. Except for one chair, there was no extra furniture in the room. It was sparse. Clean and efficient. Just like the officer presiding there.

"Sit down, please," offered Kincaid, seating himself in a cane-bottomed whirligig chair behind the desk. "Smoke 'em if you got 'em," he added as he drew out a tobacco pouch from his breast pocket. Jeb obliged and slumped back into a rickety chair, and crossed his legs. "Don't mind if I do," he said, pulling his own pouch out.

Friendly kind of soul, he thought. *So what's wrong here? Something is amiss. This isn't the usual treatment for a drinking offense. Not when it concerns feeding liquor to half-breeds or Injuns. The Colonel has something else in mind. Something more serious.*

Kincaid offered him a light but he waved it off.

Digging into his back pocket, Jeb found his last match and cupped the cigarette; he lit it and drew in heavily. Then the officer began reading off a paper on his desk.

"Your name is Jacob Burns. You answer to Jeb Burns. You've done trapping and hunting in the Sierra Madres, the Chiricahua Mountains, the Guadalupe's, and most everywhere you could go for pelts. What interests me though, especially now, are those mountains directly south of this post. You know them well. Probably as well as any miner could. My report shows that you've been here three times before trading your furs in town. Each time you and a half-breed by the name of Navajo Joe have gotten drunk and thrown in jail."

Wait a minute, Jeb thought. *This smells like trouble, sure enough.*

"Well, Colonel, I may have had a little too much to drink, but I didn't cause any trouble. Joe just has a habit of spreading the word around about me being his friend. I know you got a law about giving liquor to Indians but it won't happen again. I'm on my way to California. Leavin' this part of the country for good."

Burns smiled. There, it was all out. Damned if he hadn't even apologized for that half-breed and all. What he'd do to get the hell out of there.

Colonel Kincaid wasn't impressed. "Your drinking doesn't concern me. That isn't why you were thrown in jail. I knew you had a reputation for knowing those mountains better than any man. That's why I wanted to see you after you had sobered up."

"Well, Colonel, I've been there before if that's what you mean. But no man really knows those mountains that well. Only the Apaches do. I was just lucky enough to stay clear of them and still get some hunting done. I don't favor the thought of going back there. Not if it's true what I hear about that pack of cherry cows on the loose."

"But you've been there. You've crossed them. That's the important thing."

Christ, Jeb thought, *he isn't even listening to me. He's got one thing on his mind and that's all.*

"I'll come directly to the point." The Colonel began, stubbing out his just lit cigarette. He leaned forward, eyes piercing the scout's gaze, almost challenging him, daring him to not look away as the officer spoke.

"You've been around these parts long enough to know when trouble is brewing. The Apaches have a long history of raiding Mexican villages and towns up and down the border. Been doing it for years. After Colonel Gonzalez…."

"In the Presidios," Jeb stated.

"Exactly!" The Colonel shot back. "He cleaned them out of Sonora and most of the Chiricahuas moved to Northern Mexico and some spilled over the border. It was quiet for a while with the exception of a raid here or there by some young bucks wanting to make a name for themselves. Then we got word of more possible trouble. With a new twist…."

"Like Ramos?" Jeb asked, referring to a Mexican town wiped out by the Apaches after their band was tricked into coming to the town for a feast and then massacred by the locals.

"Not another Ramos, this happened on this side of the border," the Colonel replied, "But it still spells potential trouble, a lot of it, for the ranchers and wagon trains to the southwest of here."

"Three weeks ago my third in command, Captain Miles Branan, left with a detail of 33 troopers for a sweep of the district's southern boundary. His plans were to get as far as the town of Wilcox, to replenish his stores from the Southern Pacific Railroad supply yards there and coordinate a sweep with a group of Tombstone Rangers. They were going to pick up the new heliograph to communicate their positions and trap any renegades in between their two forces.

"Using those vigilantes, now that's inviting trouble," Burns interjected.

The Colonel ignored him. "Two days out on patrol, he got word that a band of renegades had started raiding just south of here."

"I heard the same," Jeb volunteered to a stern face.

"Let me finish, Mr. Burns," Kincaid snapped as he absentmindedly lit another cigarette.

"Supposedly they were also to meet up with a group of bandits, Comancheros probably, to trade their goods for rifles. Apaches don't usually trade with bandits, Mexican or whites. But riders from both Fort Apache and Fort Thomas reported a band of Comancheros had attacked one of the new supply trains from Fort Union and taken several boxes of rifles. They were last seen heading due south. If that report is true and those Apaches are going to meet up with the bandits, Captain Branan may be in grave danger."

The Colonel paused long enough for effect, and then continued. "There are other bands, Chihenne, Bedonkohe, and Chokonen who might join the fight if these renegades are successful."

"Two weeks after Branan left, three of his troopers came back: two across their saddles dead, one half-dead. Now a dispatch rider came in last night with word that the captain has fought four skirmishes with those hostiles but still hasn't stopped them. He's low on ammunition and rations and he needs fresh supplies right away. If those Apaches are going to get new rifles, they may be baiting the captain on, leading him close enough to the border so that those Indians could fight him and still make it across the border if the going gets rough."

The Colonel paused a second time, his jaw locked in place, the furrows on his forehead waving up toward his hairline. "The captain will not stop his pursuit. With proper supplies and enough ammunition, the captain can hold his own against those hostiles even if they are armed with rifles. And he may be able to nab the Comancheros at the same time, but he needs those supplies. That's where you come in."

Jeb Burns sat up in his chair. "Wait a minute here!" he protested. "I'm here because I got a little drunk and my friend has a big mouth. I didn't volunteer to be here. You got the *wrong* man."

Colonel Kincaid waved Jeb back into his chair, took a long deep pull on his extinguished cigarette, not noticing it was out. "I'm well aware of the circumstances which brought you here, and what the offense means in terms of time spent in jail."

Then he leaned forward, his face suddenly void of the slight curl of lips. He was serious, deadly serious. "I also know that as commanding officer of this post, I can let you sit in that cell for as long as I deem it necessary. And that, Mister, might be a long time." He paused for effect. "A very long time."

Jeb's face went slack. The colonel wasn't kidding. The son of a bitch meant every word of it. Flagrant violations of a man's rights were accepted and understood in wartime. But what the hell was the Colonel pulling now?

A weak smile came back to the colonel's face. "But listen. For someone who knows those mountains, this trip would be nothing more than another hunting expedition for you. Going over the mountains would bring you only a couple of days away from a ranch near the border. That's where the captain has arranged a rendezvous. No one knows those mountains like you do. I think you're the man to take those mules over the hump."

"You do. Do you!"

"Yes, Sir, I do."

"Good-bye, Colonel," Jeb said, starting to rise.

"Sit down!" Kincaid snapped at the prisoner.

Burns collapsed back in his chair.

Any trace of friendliness had vanished completely. Hard red lines erased the forced composure. The colonel was mad. Not yelling mad … calm, serious mad. Calculating, yet weighing his words for the reaction he knew he had to get.

"Now, I'm going to tell you something whether you're interested or not." He paused. The effect took hold. He had Jeb's attention.

"The Army has been facing a tough time of it since the War. Congress is making decisions every day that affect every life out here on the frontier. President Johnson is doing the best he can. But with all due respect, he isn't Army. He doesn't understand what it's like out here. And the general public, the ones that count back East, don't want a large Army. The War Department has got the Army divided up into nineteen territorial departments and five geographic divisions. Most of the garrisons are small, one or two companies each. Do you have any idea what that means?"

A shrug of shoulders greeted the question. Jeb knew enough of the Army to know when to let the wind blow and when to ignore it. This was one of those times he'd better lend an ear.

"Just as I thought," the Colonel said. He jammed his cigarette back into his mouth, lit it for a second time and drew deeply on it. He continued. "Two years ago, the Army de-mobilized more than 800,000 men. General Grant had proposed a standing Army of 80,000 be maintained, but the Secretary of War whittled that request down to 50,000 soldiers. Right now that force has dwindled to little more than 40,000 troopers spread across the whole of these United States. We have less than 50 posts established throughout Indian country. "

The Colonel stabbed a pencil down on a stack of papers and continued, "The troopers I'm getting now from Jefferson Barracks in St. Louis are young and inexperienced. Tough to train before I have to send them out on patrol and likely as not to be killed or wounded if there's a fight with the Apache."

The Colonel couldn't tell if the prisoner was getting the point or not. He continued: "And if that isn't enough I've got citizens coming in here every day complaining about Indian harassment while the Jack Tars are feeding them hymn books instead of the proper rations they're supposed to get. I closed down the Indian ring that was operating before I arrived but new faces just keep popping up and causing problems with the Indians."

Burns started to speak but the Colonel cut him off. "It just feeds the anger of the malcontents who are looking for a reason to leave the reservation.

The government, or I should say Crook, pursued a policy of pacification while the populous wanted extermination. Where does that leave me?" the colonel asked no one in particular.

A raised hand.

"Yes."

"Colonel, with all due respect, I don't see what this has to do…."

Fiery eyes met the scout's. It was the wrong thing to say. Old Jeb Burns still wasn't a part of the system. Prisoner or not. He should have kept his mouth shut.

"Don't you see? We have a responsibility here. If Captain Branan can stop and destroy that pack of raiding Apaches, the others might stay on the reservation or at least remain at peace. But to catch those hostiles, the captain needs supplies. And I need someone to deliver them."

"I hear say that Crook is on the trail of Geronimo and his Chiricahuas down in the Sierra Madres. Can't he take care of the problem?" asked Jeb.

"You heard right," confirmed the Colonel. "But for precisely that reason, he can be of no assistance. He has his hands tied trying to find those renegades. He's too far south to be of any help to me."

Jeb shrugged his shoulders and said "What about your own men here? Its looks like a post full of casuals but surely you've got enough to take those supplies to the captain. If not, then some of those Mexican mercenaries I saw back in town. They can track the Apache as well as any Apache can."

Kincaid let out a sigh of emotion. He was tired. He didn't want to continue talking, persuading. But he had to.

"Mister Burns. I can't spare one jack man. And the Mexicans won't take the work, don't ask me why - probably scared of a band this large. There are still a lot of Apache women and children held as slaves by the Mexicans. We've talked to the authorities but they won't budge. That just feeds the Apache rage against every Mexican around. And the other garrisons nearby; Lewis and La Paz, are too undermanned to be of any help".

He paused for a moment and continued, "My second-in-command, Major Hellerman, has a full company of cavalry establishing another garrison west of here. He's been gone for a month and isn't due back for another three weeks. He can't spare a squad in that territory. There are too many Apaches close by. It'd be too much of a temptation. That means that this post, for its size, is critically undermanned. And I can't spare a soul. I've got to depend on civilian labor. But more than that I need experienced men. Mountain men. Men who know those mountains South of here. You seem to be that man!"

The Colonel's voice dropped suddenly. He was talking in a whisper as he leaned forward over the desk. "I'm not begging you, Burns. I'll pay good money and drop the charges against you. But if you turn me down, I won't say how long you'll be in jail. That's it then. Take it or leave it. What's your choice?"

"You're a persuasive man. But you minimize the danger. Who's to say those mountains aren't crawling with Apaches? One man alone. I'd have a hell of a time handling four mules, much less watch out for redskins."

Kincaid allowed himself a smile. He knew then he had his man. "You won't be alone, I've hired on three other men to accompany you. They should be useful with the mules and provide adequate escort. One can soldier, I know that. But the other two you'll have to chance. They're all that's around and willing."

There it was then! All laid out neatly, and Jeb had taken the bait. Once bitten, he would have a hard time backing out. He remembered the two men arguing outside his cell window earlier. The whole picture was beginning to take shape. Those men had come in that morning and made their offer. The Colonel, wary of their lack of skills, put them off until he heard about Burns being locked up and remembered him from the sheriff in town. He put two and two together and had his solution in hand. The promise of a long term in jail if Jeb didn't take the job was just the icing on the cake. Colonel Kincaid had his solution and not a Yankee to risk in the process!

"Those two men you mentioned. Are they cowboys, just drifters? A tall guy and one shorter, a kid. They came in this morning, offering to take those supplies out. Am I right?"

Kincaid crushed his cigarette butt against a metal ashtray and let a smile crack. He had his team. The supplies would go out. The smile grew across his face.

"That's right, and they're willing to take whatever risk might be involved. Trouble is that they don't know those mountains like you do. You and the fourth man for this trip. He's a trapper and scout. Rumor has it he was friends with Old Gabe, Jim Bridger, back in the days. He knows his mules. Probably done some prospecting, too. He's from over by Santa Fe. A bit grizzly for my taste but I think you can depend on him."

The Colonel stood up into the blue haze, which hung low over his desk. He looked satisfied. He began talking about the Captain and the hostiles he was chasing, but Jeb Burn's mind was a million miles away. The scout leaned back in his chair, balancing himself on its two back legs.

What the hell was this Texas-born wanderer getting himself into? he questioned. First he got thrown in jail because of Joe, again! Now he was joining a couple of strangers, probably dirt farm cowboys, to deliver supplies … and ammunition! *A week's worth of work to reach some damn captain hell bent on destroying the Apaches and making a name for himself. How did I get into this mess?* Jeb pondered his situation for a while longer, and then decided to make his move. *If I'm going to do it, I might as well try to get as much as I can in the bargain.*

"Alright, Colonel, you got yourself one reluctant scout for one, two weeks at the most. Regular scout pay plus a new horse from quartermaster. That Appaloosa will do just fine."

"Whoa, who's making the offers around here?" asked the colonel.

"Colonel, I'm not risking my neck on that flea-bitten old nag of mine. He isn't worth one shell in my rifle. Now if you want me, then I want a chance to make it through this job with my hair intact." Jeb's voice came on strong, cloaked in a matter-of-fact tone of voice, but strong nevertheless. Now it was his turn to smile.

"The horse is yours, Mister Burns. Anything else?"

"No, the horse will do."

A knock sounded at the door. The Colonel called the sergeant in.

"Those two men are back, Sir. Shall I let them in?" he asked.

The Colonel nodded.

Two cowboys passed the sergeant and entered the room. They were the same two cowpokes that Burns had overheard in his jail cell. The first to enter was the younger one. He strutted into the room with a gamely step. But his youngish pockmarked face betrayed his age. His companion, a close look-alike, had a face to match his walk: tired, lined, and haggard.

"Gentlemen," the Colonel began, "This is Mister Burns. He'll be taking this detail through the mountains. Mister Burns will be in charge." He turned to Jeb. "Mister Holden and Mister Ransis."

The taller man nodded at Burns but the younger one stood his ground, eyeing the scout up and down, noncommittal. He wore a single-action, 45 caliber, six shot U.S. Army-issue Colt. That was an officer's sidearm, Jeb thought, now where in the hell did this kid get such a weapon?

The kid glanced at Jeb's old six-shooter and his faded, rough-worn trousers. A slight smile curled his lips. Well, more a sneer than a smile.

The scout had been sized up, classified, and laughed aside. All by a kid not more than 18 and a face full of pimples.

"You sure about the way to get through them mountains?" the youngster asked, with a cocked eye.

Jeb held his tongue. This one might be dangerous. Not because he might be fast on the draw. More likely he would be ruthless. A shot in the back would be more his style. And these were the two men talking about having to get away. They didn't know it, but Burns was already very familiar with their style and their true motive. Better he should keep that secret to himself. At least for the time being.

"I'm sure," he replied blandly.

The door opened suddenly and a huge man stood in the doorway, the sergeant protesting vainly behind him.

"Colonel, I told him..."

Colonel Kincaid waved the sergeant back and nodded for the man to come in. The man's bulky frame practically filled the entire doorway. His leather hat, squashed down, tilted down on a face of bushy hair.

The man wore leather breeches and a buckskin shirt. It was open half way to the chest and revealed a broad front of thick black matted hair. Dirty black fringes, many missing, laced his pants and shirt. He wore a looped cartridge belt called 'fair weather Christian belts' by the troopers. Every loop held a shell.

Resting against his leg stood one of 'Beecher's Bibles,' a Sharp's single-shot, breech-loading rifle. It was partially wrapped in an Indian sheath, beaded and fringed.

A pair of coal-black eyes stared out above a shaggy brown beard, which hung in strands down to a red bandana around his neck. Nestled in his belt was a hunting knife, encased in a leather sheath, which stuck out from his protruding belly.

The trappings were clearly that of a mountain man, a trapper more at home in the wilderness than in civilization. He carried an animal smell about him and his cheek was puffed up with a wad of chewing tobacco, which he worked back and forth.

He said nothing, standing in the doorway. His cat-like eyes covered the room in a sweep, sizing up everyone, judging them by his own standards.

Now there is one hell of an Indian-fighter, Jeb thought. He had met others like that one when he was in the mountains. Men left to themselves not for a winter, but for several winters. Alone for years on end except during the trading season. They knew how to fend for themselves. He knew of their calculating instincts and animal reaction, all of which would serve this patrol well in the mountains. This one would be a good man to have on his side.

"Pony, come in."

The man leaned his rifle against the doorsill and approached without sound, despite his girth, on silent moccasins.

Kincaid pointed toward the two men. "This is William Ransis and Edward Holden." He turned to Jeb.

"Pony?" a voice exclaimed next to Burns. Billy turned toward the mountain man, sizing up the old man. He locked his legs apart, rigid like a statue. He'd make himself known right away. Billy was someone to reckon with.

The mountain man turned in mid-step and stood before the youngster. His bearded face revealed no emotion, no reaction to the sarcastic-edged remark. He looked down on the pockmarked face, the hands nervously twisting the gun belt. He knew the type; he knew how to handle them.

Pony smiled, a wide grin revealing a mouth full of yellow and missing teeth. The quick reaction startled Billy. It disarmed him completely. He'd expected either a cowering admittance or a confrontation … either one of which he knew how to handle. But the smile was something else.

The room fell silent. Outside sounds came in and fell on deaf ears. Three pairs of eyes stayed glued on the two men confronting one another. One smiling, the other nervous, liable to react without thought or reason.

"Yeah, Pony! That's my name. Not my real one, but it'll do." The smile was frozen in place, like a mask. The mountain man pulled a piece of reddish tobacco bar from his belt and tore off another chunk with his yellow teeth. He chewed it slowly, and then offered it to the young man.

Billy, confused and taken off guard, nodded dumbly.

Pony wouldn't let it go at that. He grabbed the boy by a shoulder and laughed out loud. Billy stared at the man laughing at nothing. He wasn't sure how to react.

"You want to know how I got that name, I'll bet," Pony asked, shaking the boy back and forth, laughing louder. "Got it when I was about your age. Just as young and dumb. Didn't know much but didn't think anyone else did either. I was up in the Bitterroot Mountains, sidetracking Shoshones, and trying to get enough plews to make a little money. Me and three other coons was caught in the open and attacked by them Injuns. I got away with one horse. A skinny nag. A pony. Hid out for a week and then without a thing to eat, I ate my horse. Tasted right good after a week. So that's how I got my name."

Billy tried to stand his ground, even as the mountain man's huge paw was clamped down tightly on his shoulder, forcibly shaking him back and forth with his own laughter. The boy wanted to break away, to distance himself from the leather-covered giant towering over him. But the mountain man's actions had thrown him off guard. He could hear the others laughing at him. The old man had told a story and ridiculed him at the same time. He felt anger climbing up inside himself but he was too confused to know what to do. Then, with a flick of his wrist, the mountain man released the boy and pushed him back against the wall.

Still laughing, Pony turned to the Colonel and said, "Right inquisitive young man you got there Colonel. I hope he's as good with his scouting instinct as he is with his curiosity. He'll need it out there. Anything could happen." The last statement brought a lifting of the eyebrows and another grin aimed at Billy.

Colonel Kincaid grabbed the pause to make himself known again. He moved his pointer off his desk and up against the canvas map.

"Gentlemen, I think it's time we get down to business now that you're all here." He motioned the men closer.

Billy and Edward stepped up while Jeb and the mountain man stood their ground. Each was sizing up the other out of the corner of his eye. They had both immediately disregarded the two cowboys as irritants and of little value on the patrol, but each regarded the other with a great deal of caution. Wariness of strangers was born quickly in the mountains and tempered by scraps with danger almost every day. They weren't about to open up easily with one of their own ilk.

Kincaid was speaking. "You'll leave as soon as ordinance has issued you the necessary rations and ammunition. Quartermaster has the mules ready to go. Each man will be issued blanket, saddle and bridle, haversack, tin plate and cup, canteen, and eight days cooking rations. The mules will carry the ammunition, some rations, and salt."

The colonel had found his men; his part of the job was completed. Now he had only to depend on them. "Mister Burns will lead this detail. He's been hired on as scout. Pony will handle the mules. Mister Holden and Ransis will ride escort. You'll be paid at the end of the month. You'll have to fill out a form with the sergeant out front in order to get paid."

The two cowboys eyed him apprehensively. "Why do we have to wait that long?' I thought we was gonna get paid right away," Billy whined.

"Civilians get paid like everyone else. At the end of the month. This is no exception," Colonel Kincaid remarked. He kept his formal composure. He turned back to the map.

He ran his pointer down from a dot which identified the location of the fort to a brown squiggly line running perpendicular across its path.

"That's the hump," the Colonel began, "The fastest way to reach the border. A man named Badger owns a rather large spread down near the border. That's where Captain Branan intends to meet you. Mister Burns and Pony, I won't pretend I can tell either one of you very much about that area. I'm sure you've been there enough to draw me a map of the area."

Jeb Burns and the mountain man listened intently. The two cowboys looked around the room, distracted by the activity outside the Colonel's window.

The colonel continued, "I'll fill in the details with Mister Burns. Pony, I want you to get the mules ready. You two fellows can get the supplies together. You'll leave within the hour."

The three men filed out of the room and Kincaid turned to the scout. "Well, what do you think Mister Burns? Will they be of any help?"

Burns pursed his lips, thinking, wondering why in the hell the Colonel even bothered to ask him. "The one called Pony will be alright. I know that kind. They can work like demons. The other two I'm still not so sure of. But why do you bother to ask me? I took the job. I'm committed. What do you care what I think of the others?"

Kincaid returned the question with a knowing smile. Burns needed no more. For better or worse, he was in for eight days of hard riding and more than enough danger. The Colonel got what he wanted and Jeb was it.

Burns turned to leave.

"Good luck."

Jeb glanced back. "I wish you meant that, Colonel, for my sake instead of just your own."

Then he was gone tramping down the rough board planks toward the blue Appaloosa, and the only good deal he had wrangled out of that morning.

CHAPTER FIVE

The column of troopers pulled out of the draw with their horses at a walk. It had been two days since the ambush and tensions still ran high. After the attack, the troopers had buried their dead and rested the horses. Scouts went out looking for dead Indians and found none. Blood stained rocks and gravel pinpointed the accuracy of carbine and pistol shot but the scouts found no bodies.

The Apache had vanished as quickly as they had appeared. Back into the crags and crevasses that hid their escape from the fusillade of army bullets. Gone to fight again when the advantages suited their style of attack. Back to kill when they chose to do so.

Walking two abreast, rifles at ready, the troopers crawled up the draw and automatically scanned the surrounding sage and sage. The mid morning air was hot and growing hotter. The terrain was still. A feeling of uneasiness had settled over the troopers since leaving the canyon bottoms and traversing distant plateaus.

Another ambush could come at any time and from any direction. Branan had quickly surmised that the canyon was an ideal place for an ambush. The Apache knew these mountains like the back of their hand. A shallow arroyo or draw could hide a large enough force to wipe out half the troop before they could see their attackers. It was a game of cat and mouse that the captain meant to win.

Lunch was hard tack and sour water. Shade was almost non-existent, so the troopers settled near sentinel cactus and chaparral trying to stay cool. Outriders had moved into a screen of high burnt grasses to cover their flanks. The less movement, the less sweat trickling down their necks and foreheads. Most of the men were silent, saving their breath for something important to share. None was forthcoming.

With squinting eyes against the sun's harsh glare, Sergeant Davis tried to penetrate the shimmering land stretched out before him. Beyond the heat waves lay a basin and from the liquid movement before it arose the sentinel spires of saguaro cactus. Tuft grass, intermingled with sagebrush and greasewood, lay like a blanket before the column.

"No sign of them, sir," he commented to the Captain.

"One Apache is enough for a war party," came the response, without emotion, from Branan. Silence fell between the two again.

Captain Branan noticed the smoke before Davis did. Just beyond the brown blanket, behind a series of low-lying hills, a dark smudge hung smoldering. Two, maybe three miles away. It was a hazy shaft of gray-white smoke curling upward, like some sweep of an artist's brush against an empty blue sky.

The Apaches had found their prey, whatever it was. An immigrant wagon train, Mexican freighters crossing the border, supplies for the next town … someone had crossed paths with a raiding party. Caught in the open, their prey wouldn't have had a chance.

"Sergeant, assemble the men, we're moving out," Branan barked out the order.

"Sir. Skirmishers first?"

"Right! Send out a squad. Not too far ahead. My guess is that the Apache are gone already. But," he added, "we can't take any chances."

The Sergeant quickly moved back to the squads, spreading the men out as they saddled up for the ride toward the smoke.

Branan moved up to the head of the column. The troopers eyed the drifting smoke and knew what it meant. Best guess, there would be only enough time to dig the shallow graves and then move on, hoping the next time they might be ahead of the marauders.

The captain tightened his lips. His slit-eyes swung over the valley basin and foothills beyond. He probed the ground and sky for some sign; dust, smoke, trampled grass - any indication the Apache might be still around, but he found none. The Apaches had done their killing and looting and left, probably for more game on their way to the border. Unless he could stop them!

Branan waved the outriders forward then signaled Davis. The Sergeant halted his squad until the Captain caught up with him. Skirmishers flanked the column and worked the scrub brush.

"Sergeant, as we move in, I want a perimeter defense. Detail a burial party. Then take a squad and sweep the area beyond." The Captain paused to collect his thoughts. "I doubt there'll be survivors but we've got to look, just in case. Tighten security. I don't want to get hit while we're burying what's left of those poor devils."

The column moved out at a hard gallop into the basin toward the dark smudge, trailing behind the outriders who moved out at an angle in a fanning motion.

The first thing they came across were two oxen shot full of arrows. Both animals were lying by the curled up body of a boy. Branan drew up and reined back his mount, scanning the ground. Two more bodies lay nearby also cut down by arrows and lance. They were probably herdsmen, hurrying strays back to the wagon train. The Indians had caught them in the open. Moving ahead, the captain counted two more boys and a child. There was blood on the ground where they had fallen.

Cresting a low running hill, the captain reined in. He saw all that remained of an immigrant wagon train. The sight tightened up his throat and drew a hushed silence from the men.

The Apaches had done their job well. There wasn't a wagon left that hadn't been torn apart or torched by their whirlwind attack and savage destruction. Everywhere the troopers gazed, the scattered bodies of oxen lay beside those of settlers … men, women, and children. Several looked like pin cushions, stuck full of arrows. The smoldering ruins of four Conestoga and Murphy wagons still crackled and sputtered, sending up thin whiffs of gray smoke. The smoke trailed off across the motionless column, stinging eyes. The little equipment that hadn't been torched was scattered about the ground. Even the water barrels had been smashed to splinters.

Branan looked over the destruction and felt anger welling up inside. He had seen the Apaches' savage work before. He had buried men caught alone or in groups by roving bands of Apaches. A month before he had buried an entire family out on the river flats, and each time it chipped away at his soul, just as the war had done. It numbed him and steeled his resolve to rid the country of this scourge to the white man.

It wasn't that way at the beginning of his military career. Not when he was with Chivington in New Mexico but later at Brandywine, Gettysburg, and Antietam. All the killing and destruction had done a job on him. It left him a calculating, emotionless thing feeling nothing for the Apache but contempt. The war had driven out whatever warmth that might have existed within him.

He was an officer and he was alive. He meant to keep it that way. Anything that stood in his way had to be driven aside, in whatever manner available. Compassion, feelings, sympathy for the plight of the red man meant nothing to him.

Sergeant Davis came back with his squad. He slid out of the saddle slowly, careful to hide a pained, teeth-clenching grimace. His rheumatism was acting up again, shooting lightning jabs of pain through his lower back and legs. Despite the pain, Davis walked erectly to the captain. He slapped his pants of the alkali powder and reported.

"The hills are clear, Captain," he said. "We found where a bunch of them had been waiting. Looks like they stayed there for some time like vultures, waiting for their prey. Best I can figure those poor devils must have walked right up on top of them Injuns before they got hit. There's four dead up there. Three women and a boy."

Branan gave the sergeant a cursory glance and at-eased him with a nod. He turned to his mount and fished a leather map out of the saddlebag. Laying it across his saddle, he fingered the route they had taken from the fort. The captain knew there was still a long hard ride to the border. His supplies were to be delivered to Badger's place. Since it was the only large settlement between the Apaches and the Mexican border, the hostiles were likely to be heading there right now. There would be trouble. The kind of trouble Branan relished; his own Indian-fighting kind of trouble.

"Sergeant," he motioned the non-com over. "Give the men a 20 minute rest. Feed and water the horses. This will be our last stop until we reach the Badger spread. If we're not too late already!"

"You think they'll hit Badger's place before they cross into Mexico?" the sergeant asked.

Branan didn't bother to look up from his map. He slowly folded the leather into tight squares. His voice steady - determined. "They'll hit it alright. To replenish their stock and get supplies and kill a few Anglos and Mexicans in the process." The captain slipped his map back into its pouch. The business of soldiering was a dirty business.

"Badger's likely to have a full crew this time of year. But even so, he isn't strong enough to stand off those devils if they hit him without warning. If he's caught in the open, working his ramada or fixing fences, he won't be able to hold them off for long."

A long pause punctuated the air. The sergeant stood his ground, waiting. Branan stared off into the distance, his eyes unfocused and glassy. Finally he spoke, "I want them, Sergeant, so badly I can taste it in my mouth. And I mean to have them."

He turned to the sergeant; his eyes suddenly clear as crystal, full of hatred. "If I have to push this troop to the limits of their endurance or even beyond," he continued," I intend to do it. Nothing is going to stop this company from catching and destroying those savages. Nothing!"

"Understood, Sir," the sergeant replied and turned to go back to his troops.

"Thank you, Sergeant," the captain said. *I hope that sentiment goes with the troop also.*

The sergeant turned back to face the captain. "It's been a rough three weeks," The captain said, "I know that and it's not going to be any picnic from here on. We'll ride straight through to the border. I intend to catch those hostiles before or after they reach Badger's place. Inform the troop, sergeant."

The sergeant, having heard it all before, simply replied "Understood, Sir," and then continued on his way. Seasoned veterans didn't need formal speeches to know the kind of trouble they were in or the danger facing them as they got closer to the border. The troop already knew what the captain intended to do. It was the only thing he could do. They all knew this was just the beginning. There would probably be lives lost on both sides before the company returned to the fort.

Cool Reception

Charlotte Rose Barrington was all alone in another indistinguishable frontier town. A hard scrabble town no different from the dozens she'd passed through on her way out west. She was thousands of miles away from anything familiar and had nowhere else to go. She couldn't turn back now. There was nothing for her back in Philadelphia. She was just one of hundreds of travelers heading to someplace unknown - a young woman in a world of men and whores and suspicious womenfolk looking out for their own.

After leaving Chicago, Charlotte had traveled to Barrel Rock, Missouri, following a sliver of information once passed on by a distant cousin on the whereabouts of an uncle's ranch. In Barrel Rock, she'd picked up more cursory information on his cattle trading. Bills of sale indicated he was still in the Arizona Territory.

Uncle Badger, estranged brother of her mother and hated by her father, was supposed to be in the territory, somewhere near the Mexico border. She heard talk from her parents that he ran a very successful ranching and cattle operation.

Over the years, her parents had made comments about him but their muted mutterings were unclear. They were gone now and the reported cousin in Barrel rock had no more information to give her. There was no one else in town that had more information to add. Just press on, Charlotte thought, until she found his ranch.

Thus far, the trip had been a tiring series of one-night stops at questionable lodgings. But a ready smile, enough hints of ample breasts, and a quick wit had served her well so far. She found companionship where she could - a lodging house one night, a stagecoach station the next. There was usually some lonely cowboy or farmhand who would take up with her for a meal and conversation. Just talking, she offered nothing else. It was a safe pleasant arrangement that satisfied both parties.

Four weeks later, Charlotte finally arrived at the Badger Ranch by hitching a ride with the overland stagecoach that detoured to the ranch just for her. A pretty smile can work wonders, especially among old stagehands lonely for female companionship.

They grumbled on about Apache troubles but Charlotte saw nothing and let their musings pass. There were always wild tails of Indian and cavalry battles back East but no one she knew ever came back to verify the tall tales. The redhead smiled to herself. The stories were probably nothing more than stirring adventures dreamt up to keep the young boys and old men occupied at the corner grocery store or local saloon.

The final miles to her uncle's ranch found Charlotte sequestered on top of the overland stage, nestled in between an overweight driver and his rail thin shotgun partner. Talk was held to a minimum even though Charlotte tried her best to engage the both of them in even the simplest of conversations. As the stage rode through the fenced-in ramada, Charlotte braced herself for a quick exit. As the stage rolled to a stop, Charlotte made her move.

"Gentlemen, it's been a pleasure," Charlotte said as she suddenly slid over the lap of the startled shotgun man and down the side of the stage. Most of the ranch hands were out riding herd on the stock and horses. Only a skeleton crew manned the premises. The few men who were left at the ranch could only stare in wide-eyed disbelief as the redhead dropped off the stage. It made quite a stir among the startled crew. Even after her arduous journey, Charlotte felt alive with a renewed confidence now that she had finally found her new home.

But a warm welcoming reception was not what she got. Startled looks and suspicious eyes greeted her behind a wall of silence. Charlotte paid the onlookers no mind. She had arrived after weeks of hard traveling and she meant to make herself a home at her uncle's place.

Uncle Badger stood on the veranda, hands on his hips. There was another man standing next to him, watching Charlotte intently as she approached. Badger stared at the strange woman, trying to figure out where she had come from and what the hell she was doing so far away from civilization. Her auburn hair and fair skin made Charlotte stand out from the dark skinned Mexican vaqueros and sun drenched ranch help. She had a beauty about her and a softness that set her apart from the other women Badger had been with on the frontier. As Badger stepped off the veranda, all he could mutter under his breath was "Who the hell is that?" Badger's partner, a refined gentleman, stepped off the veranda with him.

The ranch boss could smell trouble and it was strolling toward him in a long dress with high firm breasts that moved as the young woman approached. Suddenly, she was standing right in front of him, smiling and extending her hand. She was young, full bodied, and very attractive. Badger's mind went blank.

The woman had arrived unannounced and caused an immediate stir among his men. She was not a welcome addition to his ranch. Not when it was full of young boys and haggard old men unaccustomed to a woman like her. There was no place for women on Badger's ranch and he meant to keep it that way.

Charlotte was out of place there. She realized it almost immediately when she looked into the cold vacuum that was her uncle's eyes. And it was reinforced by his limp handshake and reserved demeanor. *No one,* Badger thought, *let alone this young woman, is going to get in the way of my ranching operations.*

The other gentleman spoke first. "Ma'am, what brings you to the territory?" he asked.

Charlotte just gave him a quick smile and turned her full attention to her uncle.

"Uncle Badger," Charlotte began, "I'm Charlotte Rose Barrington, your niece from out East. Your sister's daughter. I've come to stay with you for a while, if you don't mind."

Ranch hands began to gather around, anxious to find out more about this beautiful woman suddenly on their ranch. Several sharp words from Badger sent them scurrying back to their chores. Still, a few lingered behind.

The gentleman smiled even more but said nothing. He seemed to be delighting in the quandary that Badger suddenly found himself in. Charlotte glanced at him a second time, held her gaze for just a moment, then went back to focusing on Badger.

Uncle Badger's response was curt and to the point. "You sure as hell can't stay here," he replied. "I don't know what my sister was thinking. I 'ant seen her for years. Lost touch long time ago."

Charlotte started to speak but Badger was hearing none of it. Badger cut her off with a wave of his hand toward his straggling crew. "The rest of you get back to work. Now!" The remaining ranch hands immediately started to move away. Badger turned back to Charlotte, his disapproval still etched on his worn granite face.

"You shouldn't have come. My sister had no right to send you out into the territories. It's not safe for a woman here, especially with the cherry cows taking scalps and cutting throats of any white or greaser they come across."

"She didn't send me," Charlotte shot back. "I came on my own. Both mom and dad passed away about three months ago. There was nothing left for me back in Philadelphia. You're the only relative I have now."

"Don't make no difference," Badger repeated, "No matter to me. You can't stay here."

"Badger, have a heart," the gentleman began. "The girl … this woman, needs a place to stay. At least for a while. You must have a spare room on this ranch of yours?"

"I said to stay out of this." Badger replied. "Our business is horses and cattle, not my niece. This doesn't concern you."

The man laughed. "If you won't take her, then I'll have to extend my own offer of shelter and hospitality."

"Like hell you will!" Badger shot back, giving the man a stern look.

Charlotte smiled at the man. Their eyes connected for just a brief moment then Charlotte turned her attention back to her uncle. "My Mother often spoke of you. You're the only kin I have."

"I'm right sorry about that," Badger answered, "your mom and dad and all. But it doesn't change anything. This is no place for a woman." He paused to correct himself then continued, "A girl. No place at all."

Charlotte started to protest but he cut her off. "It's not safe with Apaches around and these men. They've never had a woman out here. Too much commotion. You'd be a real distraction. And I don't need any more distractions with all the other troubles I got to deal with."

"I can cook," Charlotte argued.

"Got a cook," came a quick retort.

"I can do laundry," she said.

"Cook does that too!"

"I can help her," Charlotte continued.

"Him," Badger corrected the girl, "and the China man doesn't need any help."

"Won't you let me stay for a little while?" Charlotte began to plead with her uncle. "Just let me work for you and earn some money. Then I'll be on my way."

"Where do you think you're going to?" Badger asked.

"Maybe San Francisco. If I can't stay here. I've heard wonderful things about that city."

"Fools talk!" Badger shot back with growing distain in his elevated voice. "There's nothing but death and destruction between here and the Coast."

"Maybe that's true," Charlotte replied, "But please let me stay and work some. I'll leave soon enough. I have no place else to go. Let me earn a little money and I'll be on my way." Charlotte wasn't ashamed to change her tone to a pleading instead of an arguing if it would help her cause.

Badger was in a bind. He couldn't just send her off, not without a horse or escort. And he sure as hell wasn't going to dispatch one of his own men to get her back to the nearest town or settlement. Damn bad timing on her part.

He needed every man jack he had. Besides, Badger reasoned, any escort with a woman like that would have a hard time keeping his hands off of her. Badger looked down at Charlotte's chest. The opened necked blouse and heaving breasts didn't help her cause either, he thought. He caught himself before she noticed his stare. Damned fool didn't understand what a woman could do to a man, alone for months at a time, dressed the way she was … and looking the way she did.

"Again, Badger, if you won't …"

"Enough, already!" Badger shot back at the man. "She's my niece. She stays with me." He took a deep breath and lowered his tone of voice at Charlotte. "For just for a little while. But you'll work to earn your keep. No slackers on this ranch. And you'll stay the hell away from my men. Is that understood?"

Charlotte nodded her understanding.

"You can bunk in back of the cook's cabin. There's a small room there with a cot. Not much but it'll work for you."

Charlotte forced out a cheerful smile and extended her hand. "Thank you, Uncle Badger. I won't be a problem, I promise. Just give me some time to earn my keep and save enough money for a good horse and supplies. Then I'll be on my way."

"Fool's talk, girl," Badger shot back. "You're just full of fool's talk. Your parents should have raised someone with more common sense than you obviously have. Remember what I said about staying away from my crew."

Charlotte dropped her hand to her side and continued her forced smile. "There won't be a problem, I promise," she said.

"Make damn sure there isn't," was all Badger replied as he turned and fast walked away.

Charlotte was left standing on the veranda with the refined gentleman.

The man extended a hand as he tipped his hat. "Name's Matthew Tailor," he said. "I'm sorry you weren't able to take me up on my invitation. I expect it would have been more a hospitable arrangement than what you'll find around here."

Charlotte smiled at the handsome stranger, but said nothing at first.

"At least you'll be safe while you stay here, Miss Barrington."

"Thank you, Mr. Tailor. I hope my stay here will be pleasant but I can assure you, it will be brief. I don't intend to stay where I'm not welcome. I will do whatever is necessary. I will earn my keep then be on my way."

"Well, before that happens," Tailor replied, "I do hope we get to know one another."

"We shall have to see," Charlotte answered, in a noncommittal tone.

Uneasy Ride

Four men rode out of the fort as a yellow burn of sunlight began to crest the hills around them and grow in intensity by the minute. Jeb Burns could feel the penetrating heat warm his shoulders and knew it would be another scorcher. Behind the four followed a string of three California pack mules, a cross between the burro and the pony. They were strung out with aparejos and pack diamond-hitched on their backs. There were enough supplies for several more weeks if the four men could reach the troopers in time.

The party swung off the main post road and headed into a southeasterly wind just picking up. It sprinkled their faces with stinging sand and dust, promising another miserable day. They rode past straw-thatched buildings of adobe bunched together. Homes of the hangers-on; the vajeros and peons looking for work and a handout. Children ran among the mules and wrinkled old men under wide sombreros watched them from the shadows of their jackals. Women stopped their gossiping long enough to watch them pass and dogs barked in the distance. Behind the adobe houses, scattered among the folds of the land, they could see enclaves of wicciups, peaceful Indians too old to fight or hunt.

The village gradually fell behind and the land spread out before them. The wind died down until it hardly rippled the grass and the heat came back, more intense this time. After two hours of steady riding they came up on a little creek, almost dried up in the sun baked land.

Pony's eyes scanned the ground looking for dead insects along the shallow banks. There were none. The water was safe to drink. He nodded to the others.

As his horse dropped its muzzle into the straggle of water, Burns looked across the sweep of desert before him and wiped his neck. His eyes gazed out but couldn't identify much for the shimmering waves of heat rising up, wrinkling the air. The cowboys were talking but he didn't hear their words. He leaned on the mare's neck, easing the pressure on his spine and back muscles. The horse stood still, ears twitching occasionally, head immobile. His eyes rolled back toward Jeb once then back again. They waited a long time in silence, casting little shadow in the hot sunlight.

A low, faint sound emanated from the horses throat and the scout moved out of his daydream. Jeb sat up straight, the leather saddle creaking at his movement. That was the only sound. He looked around. Pony and the others were sitting apart. The hirsute trapper gnawed on his plug of tobacco as he worked the mules. The other two were arguing again. The mules contented themselves grazing on clumps of course grass.

Pony threw a blind over the eyes of each bronco mule. Then heaving and tossing the encircling ropes, he tightened the diamond hitch securely on each back. He checked for any straps with signs of wear, then mounted up and corralled the mules behind Burns.

No one had said a word since leaving the post. Billy and Edward spoke only to one another and quietly. Pony worked the mules and contented himself with chewing and spitting tobacco. But now as he moved the mules, he sided up next to the scout. His bearded face was devoid of expression. His voice matched that with monotone.

"You know this here trip reminds me of a little scrap I had down on the Brozos, riding with five other coons, crossing a plain. No cover for miles around. We came up on some Comanches. They started yelling and hollering. So we cut the throats of our mules and dropped down behind them. It was a stand-off, but we had to leave all them fine pelts right there. That hurt. Wagh!"

"You think that might happen here?"

Pony tipped his head sideways in puzzlement. "Well, sir, it just might. Won't be on no plain. Ain't none around here. But they might catch our scent. Hunt us down if they're around. If that happens, them mules is gonna have to go. Supplies or not. I ain't about to give my scalp away to no Apache to save some broncos."

Burns gave him a silent glance; his face blank, revealing no reaction. The mountain man had warned him. But he didn't have to be told what to expect in case of trouble. That was one thought he had tried to push as far back in his mind as he could. Pony's reason for joining up was as mysterious as those of the two cowboys. His enthusiasm for the captain and his company didn't need questioning. Now Jeb could only hope they didn't run into Indians before making it to Badger's spread.

"Well?" Pony asked inquisitively, expecting an answer from Jeb.

He got none.

Burns kicked his mare's flank. "Let's move out." A chuckle burnt his ears from behind.

Yellow dust rose about their horses' hooves and settled again over the dry grass and mesquite brush. Stretching away miles ahead was the purple line of a mountain chain, growing bluer and hazier until lost in the hot brilliant atmosphere of the desert horizon. Overhead stretched the deep blue of another cloudless sky. The ground stayed flat, unbroken for many miles, and then gradually grew pockmarked with wandering arroyos and yawning gaps where the earth had split open and heaved up, many centuries before. Sage clumps gathered around the open scars and near the towering saguaro.

The party moved up the long slope of a mesa toward the mountains. They entered a break in the foothills and gradually the grade became rougher, more broken. The mountain mass in front of them grew higher. The land began to buckle up, steeper this time. Finally they reached a short plateau and stopped.

"We'll walk them from here on up," said Burns, tossing the bridle reins over his horse's head. He noticed Billy check his own saddlebag discreetly when the boy thought attention was not on him. The two had some secret between them. Besides their real reason for going on this mission. Jeb's curiosity was aroused again, but he dismissed it. There was more than enough to concern himself with. He didn't need the strange actions of those two tinhorns to confuse him even more.

Pony strapped his Sharps across the pommel of his saddle. Then he carefully tied down a carpetbag he had produced out of his saddlebag. The other two were curious, watching his actions.

Billy asked, "What's that for? Never seen no one with a bag like that 'ceptin those damnable carpetbaggers back home." Edward nodded agreement.

"It's my medicine bag. Given to me by an Apache … after I took his scalp and cut out his heart." He burst into laughter, slapping the saddle again and again.

"Let's go," Jeb said, moving out.

Burns lead the party followed by the two drifters and the mules behind them. Pony took up the rear keeping a distance between the broncos and the two men. The mules seemed to know instinctively they were his charge. An occasional stop resulted in a sharp whack across the rump and soon a common understanding was reached between mountain man and mule.

The afternoon heat made the party's ascent even more difficult. Though they were free of the haze and choking dust of the desert floor, the sun beat down more unmercifully and baked the rocks they leaned against. The party wound its way among trees and brush, scrambled up precipitous slopes, then picked its way across fields of scattered rock. The horses had to be lead carefully over the smooth surfaces of large flat boulders and nudged over large humps of rocks sprinkled with brush.

The slopes grew steeper and the men had to stop to catch their breath in the overheated rarified air. "We'll stop here for a rest," Jeb announced.

Edward and Billy fell to the ground, trying to steady their runaway breathing. Burns settled down between two rocks, wiggled his butt between them, and dared a cigarette. Pony gathered the mules together and checked their cinches again. The double diamond hitch was holding well. Satisfied with their tightness, he tore off another wad of tobacco and moved next to Burns.

The mountain man settled against a huge boulder then looked out across the vast emptiness below him. The base of the mountain chain looked small and far away. Brilliant sunlight made a harsh glare of the land, distorting everything on it. He chewed his tobacco slowly, methodically, and spit out a long yellowish stream. It splattered against the rocks leaving a brownish squiggle to the ground.

Pony spilled the contents of his medicine bag on the ground. A jumbled collection of quartz crystal, petrified wood, concentrated sandstone and galena lay in a heap. The mountain man's gnarled fingers spooned the contents around and around in a swirling motion.

"They tell you anything?" asked Jeb.

"Not yet," replied Pony, "but they will. In due time. Message isn't always clear at first."

Jeb just smiled. He knew enough not to disregard the medicine of the Apache totally. Nor their superstitions. But as a white man, he didn't know how much to believe either.

"You never did answer my question back there," Pony began. "But I don't suppose you're the kind of critter that would."

"It didn't need answering."

Pony laughed. "You fought Apaches before?"

"Couple of times. In the Sierra Madres. I was lucky. I got away."

The mountain man sent another stream of brown juice capping some rocks. He puckered his lips. "I fought 'em. But I'll tell you that Apache ain't half as bad as them damn Blackfeet. I've been fighting Blackfeet almost all of my life. If it weren't for that sickness that wiped them out, I guess I'd still be fighting them. 'Rees is just as bad. They used to do anything to get you close enough to kill. Offer friendship, pelts, wives, anything. Then they'd come after you like Old Ephraim screaming for your blood."

"I take it you've been in the mountains all your life?" Burns asked.

"Yep, As far back as I can remember. Had me a Hawkins then. There weren't no finer rifle made. None as true as a good Hawkins. These newer ones may be faster loading, easier to handle but they don't take a shine to a good .50 caliber Hawkins and a horn of Dupont." Pony's eyes had a glaze about them.

"Then why the Sharps?"

Pony laughed. "I'm gettin' old. Don't have the steady aim for a Hawkins. This here Sharps makes up for that. I just gotta come close to do the job."

"Do you think we'll cross the Apache before we get to Badger's place?" Jeb asked.

Pony paused then chuckled. "The problem with fighting or evading Apaches is predicting what they'll do next. Once you've figured that out, you've got a fighting chance."

"Your prediction then?"

Pony shrugged his shoulders. "I got no idea what they'll do next. Keep killing, I guess. Take the cut-arms, the Cheyenne. Them I can predict. Sioux, the same. But Apaches, little chance of knowing what they'll do. There's only one thing I'm sure of."

"And that is?" Jed asked.

"They'll hit us when we least expect it. That's a guarantee!"

The scout rolled another cigarette and let the silence fall again between them.

What a strange crew, Jeb thought. *Two drifters, who ask - no, practically beg for an assignment with no idea of what they're getting into. Then this mysterious mountain man who talks a lot but says only what he wants you to hear.*

Pony hadn't said a thing of his past or why he had taken the assignment. The bickering of the two men was beginning to wear on his nerves and the mountain man made him feel uneasy. Jeb wondered why Colonel Kincaid had been so sure of Pony and his ability on this mission. Perhaps he knew something Burns didn't. But then again, perhaps he didn't … and didn't care. With the colonel it was hard to tell.

The horses, which had grunted their way up the slope with long and labored breathing, now stood, head hung, almost asleep. Burns watched them and smiled. *Tough cavalry horses,* he thought, *as smart as any trooper in the field.* They'd grab a chance to sleep at every opportunity. He thought about his mare back at the fort and wished he'd shot her before leaving. It would have been a fitting end to their relationship.

Finishing the cigarette, the scout rose. Pony climbed to his feet and saying nothing, moved toward his horse. Billy and Edward sat still, looking up at Burns, their eyes riveted on him.

"Come on, we've got to make the summit by tonight," Jeb said. "Can't chance a climb in the darkness." He turned and walked to his horse.

"We aren't going, not right now, we need more time to catch our breath!" Billy whined.

Jeb stopped in his tracks. He turned and looked down on the two. Billy spoke again.

"You can't expect us to burn our ass in that desert, then climb this mountain to the top all in one day. We volunteered to get those supplies out but we aren't going to kill ourselves doing it."

Burns regarded him with a cautious eye. "Look, we don't have time to stand here and argue the matter. Fact is we don't have much time until sundown. It's a hell of a lot safer up there than it would be down here." He paused to let the words sink in. "Now let's move out!"

Without waiting for a reply, Jeb turned and walked to the appaloosa.

Pony stood behind his horse, leaning across the saddle, staring at the two men. His paw rested on the Sharps, its black barrel aimed directly at the two. They noticed the rifle and the mountain man's placid expression. A slight curl of his lips was all that greeted them.

Billy started to say something but Edward told him to shut up. He pushed the youngster up and toward his horse. Pony walked past them, without looking in their direction. Behind him the two muttered to each other and the mountain man heard the word 'crazy' drift back to him.

The climb to the mountain's spine was strung with loose shale, which made footing hazardous and tricky. The broncos picked their way more easily than the heavier, clumsier cavalry mounts. Burns and the mountain man worked their horses gingerly over the gravel, taking each step one at a time. They climbed in silence, concentrating on the treacherous footing. One slip might send them, animal and man, crashing to the bottom.

Edward and Billy, unaccustomed to the thin air and forced climb, worried more about themselves than the animals. Edward kept stopping to catch his breath and lean against the flank of his jaded mount. Billy kept up a stream of curse words flying at his horse and the mountain. He yanked at the bridle rein and jerked the horse's head.

Pony looked back at the stragglers. He cast a grin at the scout and turned back. Jeb knew what he was thinking. He thought the same thing. Those two might become a real burden, perhaps a danger before they reached the Badger spread.

CHAPTER SIX

After Badger and his crew had gone back to their ranching chores, Charlotte and the gentleman walked to her new quarters behind the cook's cabin. He was quick to grab her traveling bag and walk alongside her as they crossed the dusty grounds.

"You've shown a lot of spunk by coming this far west all by yourself," he began, "more so than any other woman I've ever met."

"You should get out more often," Charlotte replied with a smile.

The gentleman laughed and beamed at the comment.

"Well spoken, Miss … Charlotte … may I call you by your first name?" he asked.

"I think for now, since we really don't know one another … I think we should be a bit more formal. Don't you agree, Mr. Tailor?" Charlotte replied.

"Absolutely." The man was quick to answer. "Please don't mistake my comment for boldness. I take pride in my gentleman's stance in this harsh and dangerous environment I find myself in out here. I would never try to take advantage of a woman, especially one of your class and style."

They entered the cabin and Mr. Tailor set Charlotte's bag on the small cot in one corner.

The room was sparsely furnished with a cot, water basin, and ceramic pot in another corner. A rough cut piece of glass was hung on the wall. The only light came from an open window facing the back fence line.

After Charlotte had quickly perused the room, she smiled at Tailor and stepped back outside. He quickly followed her.

"I'm sure you're tired after your long journey. Let me take you to the main ranch house for some fresh water and bread. Badger and I were just doing business when you arrived. The jam is still fresh as is the bread. We can get to know one another a little better. Is that agreeable with you?"

"It is," Charlotte answered. "Fresh water and a light snack would be wonderful, as would your company."

Mr. Tailor beamed and grasping Charlotte's elbow he led her back to the main ranch house. They settled on the wide veranda and Tailor summoned the cook to prepare their light meal. As they waited for the bread and water, he edged his chair closer to Charlotte's and began talking.

"I've been in the territory for more than a year now, although it seems much longer. Like you, I am also of Irish descent and lost my parents at a relatively young age. I took my inheritance and used it to buy several ranches which I blended together into one rather large spread. Almost as large as Badger's here, but not quite." He glanced over at Charlotte who was staring out at the mountains that surrounded them.

After a brief pause, Charlotte looked over at him with a smile. "Forgive me, I am listening to you but can't help but wonder what is over those mountains yonder."

Tailor smiled at Charlotte. "More sand and Apaches. More hardship and hard work. That's what it takes to be successful out here. Your uncle knows that and is a harder worker than any man I know."

"Why did he have to be so rude to me?" Charlotte asked.

Tailor laughed. "By our standards, he was just speaking his mind. I'll grant you your uncle can be an ornery cuss but he is a good businessman. He does well trading with the locals and has a large contract with the army to supply them with horses. You'll have to get used to his behavior because he sure as shootin' isn't going to be changing for anyone … or anything." Tailor leaned in close to Charlotte's chair. He lowered his voice as he spoke into her ear. "You'll do just fine. And if it's agreeable with you, I'd like to come back soon and get to know you better."

Charlotte smiled. "If you wish, that would be agreeable with me as well."

Tailor returned several times over the next couple of weeks. He always found Charlotte busily engaged in some ranching chore but managed to pry her away from her duties for a talk on the veranda or behind the cook's cabin. He was always the gentleman and quick to respond to her every need.

He talked about his ranching operations and the future of the territory. A good woman beside a man would make all the difference, he told her. Of course, children to work the land and continue his name for future generations, was very important. Matthew told Charlotte he intended to become rich and would like nothing better than a strong woman at his side. Charlotte smiled at his rambling and said nothing. She admired the man's ambitions but wasn't about to show her appreciation so early in their relationship.

Work on the ranch was hard but Charlotte was quickly learning the intricate maneuverings of Badger's ranching operation. The ramada had grown appreciably since she first arrived. Strong horses were being culled from the rest of the herd and sequestered back in the large barn. The other less able horses were corralled with the rest of the stock for sale to the army. When Charlotte asked one ranch hand about the culling, he quickly turned and walked away. When she mentioned it to Badger, he exploded in expletives and told her to mind her own business. He told her she didn't understand the business and to keep to her chores. She quickly demurred to his wishes and never asked about it again.

Although the ranch hands were still curious and some a bit lecherous toward her, Charlotte still felt she could handle herself. One day, Matthew announced that he had to return to the east coast for business and wouldn't be around for at least a month or so.

Charlotte was disappointed. She'd grown accustomed to his frequent visits and their light but interesting conversations. Now she felt quite alone and vulnerable on the ranch, but Tailor assured her she would be all right and despite Badger's apathy toward her, she would be in no danger from the men or the Apaches.

Matthew Tailor had misjudged the situation and Charlotte felt increasingly uneasy among the men who said nothing … just stared at her body whenever she passed by. After Badger's latest outburst, Charlotte wasn't about to mention it to him. She was on her own and would have to deal with her situation as best she could.

But things worsened and finally Charlotte felt threatened enough that she decided to leave even if Matthew wasn't coming back any time soon. She would write to him once she'd settled down somewhere. She missed his company already.

Uncle Badger was right about the men staring at her. Back East she had encountered the same kind of staring. It was more of a leering, men undressing her with their eyes, and snide remarks made out of ear shot, but their meaning understood.

Yet here the ranch hands' behavior was even worse. Charlotte knew that most of these men had been with women, but no one like her. They were used to the whores in town with their gaudy cribs or the other kind who traveled about using any flat surface to ply their trade. At Badgers ranch, the men would either laugh directly at Charlotte or just stare at her breasts, her body, and what was underneath the pinafores and skirt.

Charlotte always ate alone. Badger was never around and when he was; he was too busy with the livestock, the ramada, or his men to bother with her. He acted as if she had never arrived in the first place. He was distant and distracted and obviously anxious for her to leave. Living conditions on the ranch were deplorable but it hardly mattered to her uncle. Badger liked to point out the ranch was no place for a woman and the hired help wasn't significant anyway.

By the end of the first month, Charlotte smelled worse than the horses she had to groom. Despite her misgivings of bathing in the rusty old metal tub behind the cooks shed, she knew she had to get the dirt off her body. With the help of two reluctant wranglers, Charlotte managed to drag the old relic into an abandoned tool shed nearby. The two men left laughing and Charlotte quickly gathered up some rags for bathing. She thought if she was quick enough the other men wouldn't be alerted to her activity. She was wrong.

Charlotte's first bath made her feel more than uneasy. She was standing in a dark room with a pitcher of rancid water and dirty rags. As quickly as she threw off her clothes and began to pour the warm water over her head, she could feel prying eyes watching her through the cracks in the wall. She could hear their whispers and chuckles. *Catch a sight of my breasts if you want,* she thought. She was tired of feeling filthy and willing to endure the embarrassment of leering men just to clean herself off. *You won't see anything more than my chest. I'll turn my back on you for that.* Charlotte knew she would either be dead or a whore if she stayed too long. She needed a way out of there. And soon!

Charlotte caught the young cowboy eyeing her by the second month. True to form and after a lifetime of learning, she didn't let on. She could be a coquette and a charmer at the same time. She could do it without sacrificing her principles of engagement. Her glances back at the boy were meant to seen accidental, held only for a moment. Charlotte would give him enough visual feedback to hold his attention and yet not give him any more encouragement than that. No one suspected anything and she wanted it to remain that way, for the time being at least. There were soon enough glances between them that both understood a conversation would occur very soon. This just might be the ticket Charlotte was looking for. A means to escape the ranch and an escort out of Indian danger.

The end of the second month came and went. Neither one of them made a move. Charlotte was growing impatient. The harassment had only increased. Charlotte worried that one of the crew might take it to the next step. She feared for her safety and her virginity. So anxious to make verbal contact with the boy, Charlotte made her move that weekend.

Badger had ridden out early that morning to skirt the boundaries of the ranch and check for livestock that had wandered away. A group of heavily armed men rode with him. The young boy was left behind to mind the stock and feed the smaller animals.

Once her uncle was out of sight, Charlotte purposely ambled toward the old stone barn, kicking stones as she walked. Once behind the barn, she began grooming one of the stallions. Charlotte knew the boy would soon be by to check the stock. Then she would have her chance. The boy arrived ten minutes later.

He came up behind her while the remaining ranch hands were splitting up the ramada and shoeing the stock. They were the only ones near the barn. Charlotte could feel his presence behind her but she never let on. She continued grooming the horse's back and rubbing her hand alongside his neck. Finally the boy coughed once and Charlotte turn around, pretending to be startled by him standing there.

She smiled and stopped her grooming. The boy visibly relaxed at her smile and awkwardly removed his wide brimmed sombrero.

"You're not safe here," the boy began almost apologetically.

Charlotte looked at the boy but didn't say anything

He continued in a soft voice, "Mr. Badger's right about this not being a place for a woman. Only kind of women that ever come here are … you know … they don't stay long. Just enough to … you know.

Charlotte slowly smiled at the boy and crossed her arms. *Words of wisdom,* she thought, *from a young boy maybe in his early teens, pimples and all.* But he seemed sincere.

"Yes, I got the point not long after I arrived," Charlotte said. "You came here to tell me that?"

"No Ma'am, I just don't want you to get hurt … or worse!"

"Like by his men?" she asked.

The boy was almost embarrassed to answer. "Something like that," he paused, then quickly added, "You know what I mean."

Charlotte had been in tough situations before. She knew herself and what she could do if she were attacked. She answered confidently, "I can handle myself, but thanks anyway."

The boy wasn't to be discouraged so quickly. He argued "Not if several of them want to have their way with you, you won't!"

Charlotte was undeterred. "Uncle Badger wouldn't let that happen."

"Badger is not what you think he is. He may be your kin but all he cares about is this ranch and making money. No one and nothing is going to get in his way. If those men want to get to you, they'll grab you and take you away. Then they'll say you ran off. Badger may care but there won't be much he can do about it."

The boy paused and continued. "Besides, I heard say he has been making deals with some of the locals and cutting out the Army horses. Keeping the best ones and replacing them with local stock that isn't as good. That would be big trouble if he gets caught."

"You mean cheating the Army?" Charlotte asked.

"Exactly," said the boy. "They'd throw him in the stockade and close down the ranch if they find out. Now I just heard say about it but I'm betting it's true and that's probably another reason why he doesn't want you around. So's you won't find out for yourself." The boy looked around and continued speaking in a soft voice. "My mother raised me a Christian and I know things are not right here. You best be gone right soon if you know what's good for you." The boy paused then added, "No disrespect meant, Ma'am."

"I'm beginning to think you might be right," Charlotte confided in the boy. "My uncle is a strange man, not like I expected. I wanted to wait until I'd earned enough money but if you could get me a good horse and enough supplies to last until the next town, I would be deeply in debt to you. Is that something you think you could do for me?" Charlotte asked.

The boy smiled.

She had him!

The boy's chest swelled and his ego enlarged. "Better do it soon," he cautioned her. "Don't let those men see you much. They're pretty randy about now. Haven't been with a woman for months 'cuz Badger's driving them so hard."

"I know what you mean," Charlotte nodded in agreement. "You can help me then?"

"Yeah, I can help you," he said without hesitation.

There it was done! She had her ticket off the ranch and out West. An escort and companion until such time she had a better offer or was in a better situation. A boy who could help and didn't want anything in return. Could it get any better than this? Charlotte had her luck back and her virginity intact.

Confrontation

When the party of four finally breached the sharp ridgeline, the sun was beginning to sink beneath the horizon. Behind them stretched the valley's arid desert looking like a great sea bed with the water gone. It was a barren land even from that height. Nothing seemed to move or even live there. It looked as if it had been forgotten by God himself. Now at dusk, an eerie reddish-orange glow from the sun spread like a giant paintbrush across the land, casting it for a moment, into almost a pretty picture.

The scout slid his Spencer out of the boot and untied his bedroll from behind the cantle. He laid them by a pile of rocks where he intended to build a fire. Then he took off the McClellan saddle and laid it down for a backrest and pillow. As he took out a brush to rub down his horse, he noticed Pony had already begun to unload the mules.

The two cowboys had been quick to roll the saddles off their horses. They flopped them onto the ground and lay down beside them. Neither one moved, each taking turns with a canteen. The flanks and shoulders of their jaded horses were darkly patched with sweat.

Burns grew angry. "Better rub those horses down now, and then you can rest. Can't chance them getting chilled or sick."

Neither man moved. Jeb continued rubbing down his horse. Pony watched the three of them from his position off in the corner of the camp site. A slight curl appeared on his lips again.

"I said you'd better …"

"Oh, Christ, give us a break," Billy broke in, slapping his kepi to the ground. "We busted our ass getting up this damn mountain. You want them rubbed down, do it yourself." Then he laid back, his breathing still heavy. Edward's face was flush with uncertainty. He looked up at the scout, then quickly away into space.

The anger was slow in coming. But the fuse had just about run out. All day the scout had listened to the boy's bitching and cursing. All day he had held back from saying anything. There was too far to go and too great a chance of trouble to risk a confrontation with one or both of the men. Despite their pettiness, when the bullets were flying, their extra guns might make the difference between life and death. But they had pushed Jeb too far; he couldn't risk losing those horses just because of a couple of tinhorns masquerading as horsemen.

Jeb moved toward the two prone men. As he moved, he became aware of eyes watching him from behind the mules. It was Pony, rubbing his beard, chewing tobacco, and watching him, silently. The mountain man had been watching Burns since they'd left the fort. He was judging the man and trying to file him into some kind of category. This was the confrontation he had been waiting for.

"I'm not going to tell you again," Burns said, standing between the two men, "I want those horses rubbed down. Right now."

Billy looked up, gave him a cold eye, and then lay back down again. Edward sat up on one elbow, watching the younger man, not sure how to react.

As Jeb got to within a foot of the two men, he reacted suddenly, without warning. He reached down, locked his hands into the boys leather vest, and jerked him to his feet. The move startled Billy. The scout held him off the ground, his feet dangling. Billy tried to speak but sputtered his words instead. Jeb's fists held the vest tightly, straining against the boy's armpits. Burns face was only inches from Billy's face.

"Now rub those horses down and cut all that bullshit talk of yours!"

Jeb opened his fists and Billy fell back a foot, stumbling to catch his balance. The boy was livid and fighting mad. His hand instinctively fell to his side, brushing against the holster. A cough spun him around. Pony stood leaning against his saddle, hairy paw resting on the Sharps.

"Come on, Billy," Edward said, pushing the boy toward their horses. He turned back toward the scout. "We didn't mean to make no trouble. We're just a little tired, that's all." Billy gave him a glaring look.

A wind began to pick up, whistling across the mountaintop. The two men finished their horses in silence and then joined the scout and mountain man by a small campfire. Edward joined in the small talk but Billy refused to look up. Instead he continued staring down at the small coffee pot and the crackling twigs underneath it.

The mountain man took out a muslin bag of beans from one saddlebag and mashed them in his hand. Then he rolled the reddish pulp into a ball and laid it on a flat rock by the fire. When it was finished, he lopped the ball into his mouth and chewed it, the steam rising between his lips. "Wagh!" he exclaimed, "That is good."

Edward looked at him in puzzlement. "Do you always eat that stuff?" he asked.

Pony laughed, "Hell, no! There was a time we'd have feasts that'd last for weeks. Drinking and eating and making love. Right shinin' times."

Trickles of saliva caught on his beard and got lost among the matted strands. Pony looked away, his mind suddenly back in the mountains, among his friends. "Yes, Sir, we'd have some times. Roasts, hump ribs, boudins. My squaw would make me some of them cornballs and dip them into all that meat and gravy. Fine shinin' times!"

Jeb finished his meal and sleeved his lips clean. He rolled a cigarette and stuck it in the corner of his mouth. Billy mumbled something incoherent and left for his bedroll. Jeb wanted to question Edward about the saddlebag he and Billy were watching so closely but he decided to let it ride for the time being. Pony was rattling on about his mountain friends and his skirmishes with the Blackfeet and Rees. Edward sat listening intently. Jeb laid back and looked up at the inky darkness growing above him. The stars were barely visible pinpricks.

Jeb thought about the words Pony had mouthed with a grin as they sat down by the campfire that night. "You got yourself two problems there," the mountain man had offered.

Jeb's first reaction was not that he had two problems, rather three. The mountain man increasingly began to weigh on his mind. Pony didn't need to take this kind of job. With his trailing skills and knowledge of the ways west, he could have easily hired on with any number of wagon trains and made a decent wage to California. If not that, he could have hired on hunting for the Army. It wasn't good pay but it was steady.

Instead he chose to go on a patrol through hostile country to deliver supplies to a column hot after Apaches. It didn't make sense, and neither did the care with which he guarded his medicine bag. It was the first thing he set by the fire and the first thing he tucked next to his saddle. He guarded it with more than normal concern. That puzzled Burns. Perhaps the medicine bag held some clue as to Pony's actions.

They broke camp before daybreak to start down the other side of the mountain. The climb down appeared as treacherous as the way up. The slope, which dropped off at a sharp angle, was sprinkled with loose dirt and boulders. Far below, they could see a mask of brush concealing the bottom and whatever might lie beneath it.

Jeb hesitated a moment then moved out. The appaloosa cautiously put its head down, one leg forward, and edged over the side. The loose earth crumbled and slid away with each step. Man and animal moved cautiously, fighting gravity's pull. The mules, urged on by Pony's throaty grumble, dropped their hindquarters and half-slid, half-walked down the slope.

Man and animal came down in a weaving, jerking line, bringing a wave of dirt and small stones with them. They plunged through a wall of brush at the bottom. The cool morning summit air was replaced by the heat of the bottomland. Sweat trickled down their faces. Billy and Edward reached for canteens to slack their thirst.

"Easy on that stuff," Jeb cautioned them, "We've still got a long ways to go and no guarantee we'll find water before we get there. You've got to make it last."

Billy jerked the canteen from his lips. His face was cut with anger. His eyes narrowed into slits and he spat out. "Listen, I've had it with your goddamned orders; first those horses, now the water. Get off my back, old man."

Edward started to talk and Billy cursed him quiet. The boy's anger had taken control of his senses. He had pushed himself into the confrontation and wouldn't be satisfied until he had proven to himself and Edward that he was a bigger man than that drunk Colonel Kincaid had hired for this job.

The metallic click cracked loudly in the still morning air. It came from the right of the scout. He turned slowly, still keeping his attention on the fuming boy. Pony was behind him, mounted and leaning forward with an elbow resting on the pommel of his saddle.

Billy eyed the man and looked straight into the barrel of his Sharps. It only seemed to heighten his anger.

"Stay out of this, Pony," warned Burns.

But the mountain man ignored him. He sat straight up, his paw still on the trigger guard of the rifle. "No, I got me something to say to this kid still on his mama's tit."

Billy's face flushed redder than before. His hand slid to the butt of his colt. His legs stiffened. He braced himself for the draw.

"Come on, Billy, forget it, let's just go," Edward said, his voice almost pleading with the boy.

"Shut up," snapped Billy, his eyes still pinned on Pony.

Pony's throaty voice scratched. "Boy, you've shot off your mouth for two days now and I'm getting tired of it. Now you either button up and finish the job you signed up for or you're gonna be leaving right now."

Jeb nudged his horse between the two. "Nobody's leaving this party until those supplies have been delivered," he said. His eyes darted to Pony than back to the boy.

He noticed Billy's face had begun to perspire. Sweat ran lines down his checks. His hands twitched on the holster. It was apparent the boy's insides were caving in the face of certain death at Pony's hands.

One of the horses snorted. A bird chirped nearby. Everyone stood very still.

"Let's move out," Jeb finally said, breaking the deathly silence.

Without a word, Billy turned and stumped to his horse. Edward followed, trying to talk to him, but Billy wouldn't hear a word. He jerked himself up into the saddle and sat, beet-red face, fuming with hatred. He was like a wounded animal, only more unpredictable and dangerous than before.

Burns moved to his horse. Swinging up, he looked at Pony. The mountain man threw him a cross stare and said "Man steps between two people like that is courting trouble. Next time you might get killed." He sneered again, as he had done to Billy. Then he ushered out the mules.

Jeb watched the leathery mountain veteran move by and felt a cold chill in the morning heat. Pony had told him something be hadn't better forget. The mountain man obviously wasn't averse to killing when it suited him, be it an animal or another human being. He would surely kill Jeb if the scout got in his way. To Pony, people were as dumb as animals. He had conquered the mules … perhaps the men were next.

Jeb kicked his horse into a walk-trot. He moved down the slope into a series of breaks surrounding the mountain's base. The sky was clear except for a few white puffs off in the distance. The heat promised more dust and short tempers. Equipment rattled against the horses' movements to cut the stillness. The miles began to fall behind and the sun grew hotter with the day's length.

Billy set his forage cap well over his somber eyes and settled into a grumbling conversation with himself. Pony had humiliated and shamed him in front of his partner. He had been faced down, laughed at, again. Jeb had seen others like Billy; short-tempered, keen for a fight, too sure of themselves to control their runaway tempers. They were a dangerous lot to have on any trip, but especially one as dangerous as this.

The hours went by slowly. Sand flies buzzed the horses and sent the broncos kicking ribbons of the air. Pony tried to calm them down. Ripping off the branch of a juniper tree, he swatted the flies until they were left behind. Dust rose behind the party and followed them in a gray transparent haze.

Burns kept the party going all day. They ate in the saddle, chewing on hard tack and jerked beef. They rode steadily; climbing low ridges, skirting higher ones, and galloping across open stretches. Around mid-afternoon they crossed a trail of unshod pony tracks. A small group of eight Indians heading south. The trail was days old, but the identifications read clearly. Apaches riding south, working their horses hard. Probably a war party … possibly meeting up with the main band of renegades the cavalry had in pursuit.

Burns and Pony looked at one another, then the surrounding hills. Nothing moved. Not a thing stirred in the stillness. Their eyes met and they understood one another. If the Apache were still around they would find out soon enough, when the hostiles wanted them too.

Near dusk they came across more pony tracks, different from the first ones they had run into. They followed the trail for a while, then left it and cut across country, alternating between a walk and run until darkness had crept over the land.

The scout called a halt by a patch of cedar breaks. A little stream, scantly a foot deep, flowed by the trees before disappearing behind the folds of a high ridgeline. The stream based a grassy hillside, which provided some protection in case of attack.

Saddles and packs were laid on the ground and aparejos unhitched from the mules. The animals were herded against the hillside and tied off in a makeshift rope corral. Each man rubbed down his horse and then Pony perched himself on a rock above the camp and elected himself first shift guard. He took out a corncob pipe from the medicine bag he carried everywhere with him and lit up. He scanned the canyon perimeter, the animals grazing, and the other three men. His lip curled and his jowls tightened. A strange sinister mask appeared on his face, then disappeared as he slipped his hand into his medicine bag and pulled out a handful of human hair.

The scout gathered twigs and dried grass and laid branches of curl leaf over them. The flame was hot but smokeless. The coffee tasted better than Santa Fe rye, washing away the thirst and tension of the day's ride. He took some biscuits and beans out of a muslin sack and laid them over the jerked beef to warm. He topped off his meal with two cigarettes, smoked slowly. He felt settled, though still numb from the day's long ride.

Neither cowboy bothered him with conversation. An uneasy truce lay between them. Jeb felt Edward wanted to say something, but Billy's insolence dominated them both.

The moonlight cast an even glow over the campsite as Burns climbed up the hillside to relieve the mountain man. They said nothing in exchanging positions, not even a nod. Jeb settled in at the base of the rock, using it for a backrest. The horses and mules grazed contentedly.

The scout looked up and caught sight of a great horned owl, wings spread wide, floating above the canyon floor, searching for prey. He heard the sounds of the nocturnal animals, sleeping during the day, now out hunting and foraging for food. Crickets chirped and insects buzzed. Time passed slowly.

Voices rose from the camp. Burns looked toward the flickering fire. Billy and Edward were standing across from Pony, hurling words at him. The mountain man's medicine bag was between them, half-opened.

Jeb ran down the slope, moving carefully through the animals least they get spooked by the sudden movement. As he dropped down under the rope, something happened by the campfire.

One moment the two drifters were straddling the pile of embers, edging closer to Pony, their hands hanging from their gun belts. The next moment Pony had leapt up, hurling himself bodily into the pair. It happened in a split second, without warning.

By the time Jeb reached the fire, Billy and Edward were sprawled on the ground. Billy lay curled up, clutching his groin. Edward was flat on his back, arms outspread, knocked unconscious.

"What happened?" the scout demanded.

Pony shot him a glance then went back to a strip of meat roasting. As he squatted down, he rifled fingers through his unruly shock of hair. "I caught that young coon going through my medicine bag. Should have killed him!"

Burns exploded. "Don't we have enough to worry about without you getting into a brawl with those two fools? If you hanker so much for a fight, wait until we reach the ranch. You can do all the fighting you want with the cavalry's blessing."

"Next time," Pony interrupted him. "Next time I won't fight them. I'll kill them. Kill them both."

The curl appeared on his lips again and Jeb knew he meant every word of it. Killing seemed to be an easy answer for him. Whatever conscience he had was buried deep under that course hide of weathered skin. He was closer to an animal than any man Jeb had run into. And it made him uneasy.

A faint moan turned his attention. Billy still lay curled up, catching his breath, hands clutching himself. Edward had sat up, shaking his head slowly. Neither said a word.

The scout squatted beside them. "If you two pull something like that again, anything, I'll have you both humped across the back end of your horse all the way to Badger's place. With no pay on the other end."

"Christ," Edward muttered, "that man's crazy. We didn't touch his bag. Billy just picked it up to look at it when he was gone. We didn't mean no harm."

Jeb ignored his pleading. "Billy has the watch after me, in two hours. Then Edward, you'll take it until morning. If either one of you fall asleep or move from that spot, you won't ride to the ranch right side up. Next time, I won't try to stop Pony. Next time, you won't have another chance, now get up!"

Billy stumbled up the hillside at the appointed hour. He walked gingerly and eased himself down carefully. He didn't look the scout in the face or say a word. He was obviously still in great pain.

Jeb went down to his campfire. Pony was still squatting by the coals, putting them out piece by piece with streams of tobacco shot from his mouth. His black eyes followed the scout down.

"You done it again! You got in the way."

Jeb's eyes shot back. "And I will until we get to the ranch. Then the hell with all of you."

The statement brought a chuckle from Pony. Yellow teeth shone in the moonlight. "I like you. You're a coon all right, but not too smart. That boy comes near my bag again, I'll have his scalp!"

Jeb hid any reaction. He laid a cup of coffee on the few remaining red coals. Pony sent another stream off into the darkness. "Don't try to be a hero. His won't be the first white scalp I ever took!"

Jeb caught himself, but too late. Pony had noticed his eyes dart up, surprised.

"Yes, sir. In fact my first scalp was a white mans. A no-good Iowa man named Marshall. When I was with a brigade back in the '30s. Old Marshall had been fired from one brigade and taken on by another as a retainer. He ran off one night with the captain's rifle and favorite buffler horse. The old man swore he'd pay a bounty of $100 for that varmint's scalp. I took it. And the captain paid me." He paused for effect. "I was 19 then," he laughed.

The scout cupped the lukewarm java between his hands. There was nothing he felt like saying to the trapper. He rolled a cigarette after the coffee and studied the outline of Billy silhouetted against the hillside. If they didn't reach the ranch by the next day, there was bound to be a confrontation. The mission might fail. The Colonel would be after his ass again. That of course, all presupposed that they could even reach the ranch without running into Apaches first.

Dark Shadow

He came in the middle of night, slipping quietly into Charlotte's room and up to the end of her bed. He stood looking down on her sleeping body, his eyes roaming over the soft skin that moved under the thin cotton slip she wore.

The dark shadow was more than a little randy and he meant to have her. A strong smell of whiskey permeated his clothes and his breath. In his gnarly hands, he held a burlap pouch which he intended to slip over her face and hold her down as he spread her legs and penetrated her with his pent up need.

The shadow moved silently to the head of the bed. He leaned over and dropped the bag on the girl's sleeping face. Instinctively Charlotte awoke and tried to rise up. The man pushed her back against the pillow.

"Lie still," he whispered "or I'll kill you. This won't hurt much. Better than dying for nothing".

Charlotte struggled to catch her breath and pushed against the weight heavy on her chest and shoulders. The pressure intensified; holding rigid against her. She thought she recognized the voice, muffled even as it was, but she couldn't believe it. Not Badger, not her uncle trying to rape her.

Charlotte struggled and he hit her hard against her face with an open paw. She collapsed back against the pillow and tried to scream as he ripped her bodice open and struggled to get between her legs.

For just a moment then as he bore down on her, she threw her whole body against him. He pushed back, working a knee between her legs. He pressed down harder against her stomach. Charlotte beat against his back. He hit her again and she fell silent.

Then it was over as soon as it began. Warm liquid hit her stomach. The man grunted and swore then lifted himself off of the girl. Charlotte struggled to get the bag off her face. When she finally did, she was alone in the room.

There had been no penetration, just warm liquid on her belly that ran down her side.

Charlotte sat up, rubbing her cheek where he had hit her. She listened intently as footfalls moved away from the door and then were gone. It was utterly silent in the room except for the pounding of her heart against her exposed breasts. She tried to get up but fell to her knees and began sobbing.

It was her uncle. Charlotte was sure of it. Her uncle had tried to rape her. At that moment, she made up her mind. She would be gone by morning. She would go straight to the sheriff to report him for rape and cheating the Army. No dirty scoundrel was going to have her in that way and get away with it.

CHAPTER SEVEN

Branan's column cut the hostiles' trail early the next morning. Unshod pony tracks led straight along the almost perpendicular side of a rock-strewn bluff then cut down into a series of breaks, which formed a maze of trails.

Fresh hoof prints had joined the main body at several points until they numbered close to thirty, maybe forty warriors. The killing party was moving at a fast pace, making no attempt to hide their trail or conceal the direction they were heading. It was obvious to Branan's keen eyes that they were heading toward a specific objective, and in a hurry. They knew the cavalry was only a half-day behind but they were taking that chance. The Apaches were emboldened by the hour. Their direction would cross some part of the Badger spread for certain.

Branan hated feeling helpless, yet that was exactly how he felt at that very moment. It burnt his stomach and robbed any taste from his mouth. After the first two weeks and three bloody battles, he hadn't been able to stop the Apaches. It seemed all he could do was clean up the destruction they left behind. While attacking ranches, their sorties had freshened their own mounts, while the cavalry rode the same jaded horses mile after mile. Now the bastards were riding hard toward what was probably their last major raid before crossing into Mexico; and all Branan could do was doggedly pursue their tracks and hope beyond hope he might be able to catch them before the border.

Sergeant Davis took a long swig from his canteen and wiped his lips with a dust-laden sleeve. The air was still crisp and fresh with no indication of the coming heat. Davis had spent many years pursuing Indians; but this was the first party that had been so bold, so ruthless in its attacks. Even with the close proximity of the border and assured refuge from the cavalry, the Apaches seemed intent on reaching the Badger spread for one last raid.

Davis vaguely remembered old man Badger from the time he had to oversee the selection of new stock for the Army in his territory. He assumed Badger was probably gathering horses around this time of year to sell to the Army. The old man made it a point to hire top broncobusters, vaqueros from ranches across the border, and skilled cowboys on the drift. They broke his stock and provided ample protection at the same time. Badger used to brag that the ranch had never been raided, not once.

If the Apaches were going to attack his ranch, it would be planned, with the odds almost even and the risks higher than an Apache normally wanted; yet all indications were that the hostiles were willing to take that chance.

"They must be spoiling for a fight if they're going to try Badger's place this time of year," Davis said out loud. Branan didn't respond. He was still lost in thought.

The column rode through a series of winding canyons and moved toward a gradual slope rising up ahead to a plateau. Far up the slope, the outriders were moving into a screen of high brown grass that billowed like wild wheat under the wind. Their silhouettes were like jabs of blue-gray toward the clear sky overhead.

A rising sun clawed its way into the sky just above the troopers as they wound their way out of the last canyon. It sent a mellow glow among the canyon's spiny cactus forest of organ pipes, saguaros, and chollas. Leaving the confines of the canyon, the troopers blinked as the first rays of sunlight dipped down the chasm's rock sides and painted a cluster of palo verde trees a golden hue. Within the recess of the canyon bottom, the air was still cool and clear but as they moved into the sunlight, the heat began its assault.

A shout brought up all eyes. Branan saw his outrider, a half-breed by the name of Saulis, atop a plateau. He was silhouetted against the sky, waving his rifle in the air. The captain spurred his horse into a gallop while Sergeant Davis brought up the column. The Indian was pointing toward a spot over the plateau.

It was several finger licks of black smoke, thick and fat, trailing off across the close horizon of a low rolling ridgeline. Judging from its size and angle of direction, Branan knew immediately its cause.

"That's it," he shouted. "They've hit the Badger place!" He shot up his gloved hand.

"Column, move out!"

Sergeant Davis spurred his mount beside the captain's. He noticed the look on Branan's once tired face. The officer was coming alive again. Something was stirring behind his eyes. The fighting spirit had returned. The old Captain Branan was there; loose, daring, hurting for a fight.

As his hands urged the bay faster, the captain shouted over to Davis. "Send out three more sets of flankers. We aren't stopping in those hills."

Davis reined back. He heard the words "chance an ambush" but the sentence was lost in the wind and pounding of horses' hooves.

At last, thought the captain, I've got my chance to catch them and cut them to ribbons. His prey now seemed within easy reach, especially if they were being held up by the heavily armed ranch hands. If his troopers could sweep down behind the Indians, he'd have them trapped in a vice between the ranch and his men. He could crush them between two cross walls of gunfire … if they were still there.

Sergeant Davis shouted back the orders. Six men split off from the twin files. The non-com knew in the back of his mind that the Apaches might still be hiding in ambush, waiting for the column to come streaming into the folds ahead. That was a calculated risk that had to be taken.

Along the twin files of faded blue, carbines came out of boots, reins were tightened, and hats jammed down tightly. Grim faces reflected knotted stomachs. They rode in silence. This was it. After all their chasing, all the dust they had eaten, the daily punishing sun, it all came down to this final chance for a fight.

Moments before Branan's column crested the ridgeline overlooking Badger's place, the two remaining walls of the fire-gutted main house collapsed in an explosion of sparks and flying embers. Only a blackened chimney remained standing like a sentinel above the twisted, smoldering ruins. Behind the house, another pile of smoking debris lay heaped where the bunkhouse once stood. Two Murphy wagons, feathered with arrows and splintered by slugs, lay on their sides in the yard smoldering wisps of gray smoke. Two horses lay dead beside them. Only the old stone barn had escaped destruction in the whirlwind attack. Several ranch hands probed the smoking roof for smoldering ashes while others poked through the oil paper windows.

Around an empty corral, a group of haggard, bloodied cowboys watched the column charge down the grassy slopes toward them. Some were sitting exhausted; others lay in their own bloody clothes. No one said a word except an old timer who cursed the army approaching.

"All right, enough of that," snapped a large, heavy-set man with two folds of chin and a protruding stomach. For all his great weight and bulk, the man moved easily and with an air or authority about him. As he stepped into stride to meet the column, a group of men fell in behind him.

The column reined to a halt amid a swirl of dust. Davis cut out two squads, which circled the group to sweep the woods behind the ranch yard. The half-breed loped off to search the mesquite and sagebrush for pony tracks. Captain Branan and the rest of the troop quickly dismounted amid an air of heightened frustration. Badger's voice exploded before Branan's foot hit the ground.

"I wish to hell you'd come in here that fast 20 minutes ago, captain. We sure could have used you then!"

Branan ignored the outburst. He turned quickly to his ensign, "Corporal Reynolds, take a squad and attend to the wounded. Russell, take three men and help out with that barn."

The officer turned back to Badger and his men. Glancing over their shoulders, he saw the blackened ruins of the house and bunkhouse, then the empty corral. He had missed the Apaches again by only minutes. With fresh stock and more warriors, the hostiles would be across the border by now. They'd have a lot to celebrate in Mexico. The old ulcerous irritation came back hard, burning inside Branan's gut.

The Captain dropped his eyes to the rancher. "Mister Badger, I'm Captain Branan, Third Cavalry. What are your losses?"

"Losses, hell I don't know … four or five men. But listen, I think they got my girl." Sweat streamed freely down the old man's puffed checks. His voice was controlled but cracking with frustration. "I need some of your horses or your men. They run off all my stock. I've got to catch them savages."

Branan's voice rose firm against the frenzied rush of the old man. "Wait a minute," he said, "You don't have a ghost of a chance of catching up with those savages. No one is leaving this ranch without my permission. Now try to calm down. You say they took your daughter?"

"Well," Badger stammered, "not exactly. That is, I didn't see them take her but …" The old man paused, looking down at the ground.

"I don't understand," Branan began, "they did or they didn't take her?"

"I'm told she left and hasn't come back yet. I think they took her."

Branan peeled off his gloves, slapping them against his pants. "Mister Badger, let's step over here," he said, motioning toward the charred ruins of the house. Badger followed, shaking his head disgustedly.

"I lost some good men and most of my stock; damn near enough to put me out of business."

Branan interrupted him. "Corporal Reynolds, move the horses into the corral. Set up a defense perimeter. Once Sergeant Davis gets back, he'll assign positions." He turned back to the old man. "You say your daughter hasn't come back. Where did she go? And when?"

The rancher glanced back at his men, most of whom were watching the pair. "Listen," he said, "I don't want them to hear what I've got to say." He moved farther away until they were standing within the heat of the ruined house.

"Alright, now what is it that's so secret about your girl being gone?" Branan asked.

Badger hesitated, searching for the right words to use. Branan grew irritated. Another new problem! He needed all the information he could gather on the raiders, right then. Now a missing girl compounded it!

"Well, Mr. Badger, I'm waiting. What can you tell me about this raid and your girl being gone?" The officer's voice was controlled, but tense with frustration and pent-up anger.

The old man rubbed his hands and began. "Look captain, I got a good ranch here. I sell you Army boys the best stock in this territory. I got good hands, no grub-liners or sun-grinners; just top riders - best bronco-peelers this side of Tucson. But it's no place for a woman, much less a girl like Lottie."

"Get to the point, Mr. Badger!"

Badger looked into the Captain's eyes and felt a chill go through his body. He caught his breath, "Lottie is not my daughter but she is kin. She showed up here, unannounced, couple of months ago. I told her this was no place for a woman. Hell, she's just a girl. Anyway, I think she got mad and just run off with one of my hands … stupid boy himself. Some of the men know about it but I don't like to talk about it in front of them."

"How long did she leave before you were hit?"

"Don't know for certain. I was out checking for lost stock when we sensed trouble and came back here fast; maybe an hour or so before we were attacked. I didn't see her go myself," he said, still gazing off into the distance. "When I got back we shored up our defenses and they hit us. In the confusion, I didn't pay attention to where she might be at. Then afterwards, one of the men said that Bradford was gone and the girl with him."

"Is it like her to do something like that?" Branan asked.

"Maybe I should explain something," the old man said. "You see Charlotte isn't my own. She's my niece. Comes from back East - Pennsylvania. She came out here when her parents died." He stomped his boots on the ground and continued. "I didn't like the idea of having a woman around here, so I made it plain and simple to her. But I didn't expect her to run off like that. I need to know what happened to her."

Branan glanced over at the ruins of the ranch and felt something for the old man. *Woman trouble on top of all this,* he thought. *Glad I'm not married or involved myself.*

Badger continued mumbling out loud to himself. "There's been some trouble around here on account of her."

The captain cocked an eye. "What kind of trouble?" he asked.

"Well, I had to hold rein on a couple of my boys. They were constantly at each other's throat because of her. Anyway, my cook tells me that he saw the girl leave shortly after our line rider left for the camp to bring them supplies. That was before those red devils hit us. I'm afraid they might have been watching the ranch the whole time and saw her leave."

"They may well have," Branan agreed.

"And if that isn't bad enough, I got reports there's bandits prowling around here. One of my line riders was bushwhacked two days ago. I think he stumbled into them on his run. Captain, you've got to help me. I've got to get her back."

One of the outriders returned. It was the half-breed, Saulis. Branan waved him over and talked rapidly in Spanish. They squatted down on their haunches and drew lines in the sand. The lines formed a fork, which gradually widened then split apart. It pointed in the direction of the border then swung east. Fingers flashed, once, twice. Branan nodded understanding, then rose and motioned the scout back to his horse.

Turning to Badger, he said, "We found your girl's tracks. She walked her horse out of here, then caught up with another rider about a mile west of here."

"That would be Bradford, then!" A ray of hope kindled in the old man's eyes. "Did he find any sign of her? Is she all right?"

"He also found a small group of tracks that broke off from the main party and followed the girls' after your line rider."

Badger's face turned ashen.

"My man didn't follow the tracks any farther. I've sent him back out. He'll find out what happened to the girl. If she's all right, he'll bring her back. If the Apaches have her, he'll follow them to the border, but not across it."

"Why not across it? I've got to know what happened to her."

"You know we have no jurisdiction in Mexico. We're under strict orders not to go across the border."

"So that's it," Badger said icily. "Those murdering devils wait on the other side until you leave then they come back and hit us again." His face strained anger. "No, Sir, not on your life. I'm not sitting here and waiting for them to come back. I'll go to them first."

"What you do after the Army leaves is your own business, Mr. Badger. I can only advise you, but while I'm still here no one is to cross my defense perimeter … no one! My men will have strict orders to stop *anyone* attempting to break out … by any means."

"So we wait?" The old man said with strained control.

"We wait!" replied the Captain.

"Patron!"

A vaquero was pointing toward Sergeant Davis and two troopers approaching. They had an old Indian whom they prodded along with their carbines. The Indian stumbled and almost fell. They pushed him on. The ranch hands moved en masse toward the Indian, their voices rising in vengeance.

"Hold it!" Branan barked out.

The men slowed, startled by the officer who quickly stepped in front of them. Branan unlatched his holster cover and rested palm on the butt of his revolver. Two troopers moved up quickly beside him, carbines at ready.

"What are you doing?" demanded one of them, angrily. "Let us have at him, we'll teach him a lesson he'll not forget." Tense voices rose up in support. Hard faces lay on the officer, waiting for a reaction.

Branan planted his feet apart, indicating no intention of moving away from the angry crowd. He said, "This prisoner is under my jurisdiction. Now go back and let us take care of it." His eyes shined with determination. His tight set jaw remained firm. He was not about to be pushed aside by a group of vigilantes.

Badger stepped up beside the officer, his tired face stern with control. "You heard what he said boys; we'll have to let the Army take care of this one. Don't you worry, we'll get our chance soon enough."

The captain moved Davis and his prisoner away from the ranch hands.

"Where did you find him, sergeant?" he asked, eyeing the bent figure before him.

Davis pointed toward a grassy slope running out of the woods at a gradual rise until it knolled and dipped down into a series of low foothills. The grassy slope was cut with depressions and shallow gullies, like slashes through a green blanket.

"We found this one back there lying by one of Badger's men. Injun must have chased him into the gully and then fought it out hand to hand. Injun won but he took a licking. The herder is still back there, cut up something horrible. Guess the Apaches must have missed this one in the confusion of the raid and left him behind. He's an old thing but he might know something."

"They usually do!"

The captain called out a short, stocky trooper from the corral. "Private Sanchez, I want you to interrogate the prisoner."

As Sanchez started to question the prisoner in Spanish-Apache, Branan studied the face for some clue, some indication of what might make him talk. He had tried questioning Apaches before and had yet to meet with any success. Most Apaches had a steel-trap mouth. It never opened unless they wanted it to.

The Apache was elderly, his face a sea of wrinkles and old age blotches. His once jet black hair bore many strands of silver. Despite his age and the beating he had taken he stood rigid, frozen in place. He continued staring off into space as the trooper talked and shouted and cursed in his face. No expression escaped the facade.

They worked on the spindly old man for two solid hours; never letting up, never stopping. They went back and forth between threats and abuse to calm gentle talking … nothing worked. Indifference was chiseled on his face.

The pain was returning for the hundredth time that day to Branan's gut. He felt tiny rivets of sweat sting his eyes with salt. Frustration mounted its ugly head again, forcing him into a corner and robbing him of a chance to find the Apache; if by some slim chance they hadn't crossed the border yet. The answer was standing in front of him with its mouth clamped shut. He couldn't be rash. He must be calm, careful, and deliberate in his actions. But damn it, he had to get that information.

The officer stepped up to the Indian, his face inches away. His hand drew out and up his cap and ball Colt. The long black barrel passed the weathered face and leaned against the Indian's temple. The metallic trigger click cracked loudly. Branan's eyes sought out Private Sanchez.

"Now you tell this miserable son-of-a-bitch I'll blow his brains out if he doesn't tell us where his people are heading to now!"

Sergeant Davis was surprised, shocked almost. He hadn't expected the captain to go to that. He had no doubts the captain just might execute the prisoner if he thought it practical. A study of Branan's intense face matched up against the serenity painted on the Apache's face brought home the realization to Davis that the Indian would not break. Not even under the threat of death.

Branan was also aware of the Indian's fierce resistance, but his patience was wearing thin. Time was running out. His supplies were due in a day or so. If they came in, he had to be ready for the pursuit again. The missing girl presented another problem he didn't want to think about, but predominant among the irritations was the aged man resisting his might and authority.

"Sergeant, get the whip from that Murphy in the yard and bring it here."

"Sir?"

"The whip, sergeant! Bring it here," Branan's eyes flared over to the non-coms and held on to them. A savage curl replaced the taught strain on his face. He had a plan and, regulations be damned, he was going to try it. An officer had a responsibility toward his men and the settlers in his district. One man talking might save hundreds of lives. That alone was justification enough. No hearing board could deny that. And if he found and destroyed the hostiles, they might even give him a medal for it.

Badger, who had been standing behind the captain for a long time, finally broke into the conversation. His voice carried a strain of urgency. "Look, Captain, I know you figure that Injun is important. But won't you reconsider going after my girl? One scout ain't going to find anything. You need a posse for that. I mean, what if she is a prisoner or something, she'll need help. And now!"

The captain turned to repeat his stand. His face was flush with pent up anger. Before he could reply, voices rose from the defense perimeter. A rider was approaching. It was the breed riding past the soldiers. Hung across its saddle was a limp body. Even at a distance, everyone could see the shaft sticking out its back.

"That's Bradford," said Badger, rushing the rider. He helped slide the slack body off the saddle and laid it on the ground. The sight of what had been the boy's face knotted up his stomach. He quickly placed his hat over the bloody pulp. The cowboys milled angrily around the body. Badger tried to calm them down.

Branan motioned the scout aside. Sergeant Davis joined them. They spoke in soft voices. Saulis jabbed his finger toward the south. Sergeant Davis shook his head in quiet resignation. Badger looked on anxiously. When they finally parted, he rushed the Captain.

"Well, what did he say? What about my girl? Did he find her?"

"Easy," Branan cautioned him. "He found the spot where the Apaches jumped your man. There was no sign of the girl with him. Tracks indicate she separated from him before the apaches caught up with them." He turned his face from the piercing stare of the rancher. "If the Apaches wanted to catch up with her, they probably did. If not, she turned back to your ranch. My man didn't follow the tracks any further."

"That proves it as far as I'm concerned. She's not back yet and they're still out there. We've got to do something to find her."

"It's not as cut and dried as that."

The rancher flung his arms in the air. "Now what the hell's the matter? They've got my girl, damn it. You got a responsibility to get her back, or at least *try* to!"

Branan stiffened his back. His voice dropped down to almost a whisper. "Your girl may or may not have been taken by that party. If she was captured, she's either dead or across the border by now."

"How do you know that?"

'There's a chain of mountains Southeast of here."

"Yeah, I know them."

Branan began again. "The breed's been there before. He's certain the hostiles have left their women and children encamped there, waiting for us to leave. I'm going to bank on the assumption that if your girl is still alive they probably left her with their own. Once my supplies arrive, I intend to attack that stronghold."

"And my girl? What about her? Do we just leave her be and let her die?"

"If the girl is there, we'll try to rescue her. If not, we can capture some squaws and attempt to trade them back for her. Apaches are a proud people. They'll give up the girl to get back their own. That's our only real chance of getting her back safely. If we go after the party that caught her, they'll kill her before we get close to them."

"You sure there's women and children in those hills?"

"My man thinks so, and that's good enough for me." Branan turned back to the prisoner. "And if we can get this one to talk, he might be able to verify that."

Badger reached for the whip Sergeant Davis gripped in his hand. "Then let me do the honors," he said. The whip was a black cowhide, with frayed ends. It stretched six feet long and deadly.

The Apache's eyes suddenly twitched, focusing on the black coil, inches away. As quickly, the old man resumed staring into space.

Sergeant Davis caught the Indian's eyes. "He knows what you plan to do, Sir."

Branan told Sanchez to repeat the question one more time. The officer knew that a whipping was the most humiliating punishment an Apache could suffer. Perhaps the old Indian wouldn't think it worth concealing his information for that.

Branan was wrong. It didn't work. The Indian remained a statue. Sanchez grew visibly impatient, shaking his fist at the Indian, spitting out the words.

"Tie him to the corral gate," Branan finally said, "perhaps the whip will loosen his tongue."

Sanchez grabbed the Indian under one arm and jerked him into movement. The Indian hesitated, standing his ground. The private glanced at the captain then shoved the man into a stumble walk toward the corral.

Jim Badger stepped up behind the Indian and dropped the whip coil around his neck. He tightened the noose until it bit into skin. He then pushed the prisoner, like a slave, toward the corral.

The cowboys gathered inside the corral, eager for vengeance.

Davis and Sanchez lashed him, stretched out across the gate. His cotton shirt was ripped off and back laid bare. No sound was uttered. The Indian's eyes dropped down from the hate-filled ranch hands to the hard packed ground.

"One more time, ask the prisoner how many in the war party and if they are in those mountains," instructed Captain Branan.

No reply.

"Two sets of three, sergeant."

Davis nodded at the rancher. Badger smiled for the first time. His arm rippled muscles as he swung back with the whip and sent it ear-splitting across the Indian's back. It sounded like a pistol shot. A loud crack as the frayed fringes ripped across the tough Apache flesh. Streams of blood welled up out of the cuts where the fringes had passed. His body jerked with each biting snap. His eyes tightened. Still, he remained silent.

Laughter rose from the smiling faces inside the corral. One spat at the feet of the Indian. By the time the second round of lashings passed, the old man's body sagged against the gate. His legs had buckled and he hung, straining at the rawhide bounds. His stone face still hung down, emotionless, but the tenseness had been drained of its energy.

The whipping had taken all the anger and hatred out of Badger. His arm hung limply to one side. He was tired. But he was still in charge. His voice boomed out and the men looked up, shaken out of their numb attention to the flogging.

"Alright, we got work to do," he said. "This is no time to stand around with your hands in your pants. Parish, take three men and start searching the barn for anything worth saving. Flood, you do the same with the shed.

The rest of you horseless cowpokes start clearing timber behind the barn. We got a building to put up." He flung the whip aside and moved through the men; pointing, pushing, and prodding them on.

Captain Branan moved past the men filing out of the corral. He expected to see some sight of pain on the Indian's face, but instead he confronted the same granite mask. Branan cut the rawhide straps. The Indian sagged to the ground, semi-conscious.

Branan called Saulis and had him take the prisoner away. The Apache was bound to a cottonwood tree and a guard placed over him.

A small fire was set separate from the main trooper camp. The officer dropped some coffee beans into his tin of water and waited. Sergeant Davis came over and sat down next to the officer.

Davis studied the captain's face and eyes, deprived of sleep for days. The crust was taking shape, settling in firmly. The captain was becoming the same kind of animal he himself was fighting. The mad dash into the ranch was one indication, the flogging another. He would chase those Apaches straight up the side of a mountain if need be, consequences be damned.

But more than the captain's daring actions; the sergeant was concerned about the girl. Captain Branan had given no indication he really meant to go after squaws in the raid. It wasn't his style. He was not a lenient man. It bothered the sergeant, rubbing him the wrong way.

Finally he had to ask. "What about the girl, Sir, do you really think they'll trade for her?"

Captain Branan looked up from his steaming cup then back down. He unconsciously loosened his lapel button and felt the air cool his hot neck. His mind drifted off; away from the ranch, the territory, the girl, Badger, and all the rest. He was back in that pass in New Mexico. He was leading his men down on the rebel gray. They were falling beneath his cavalry, running in all directions. Many were the men he slashed down that day with his saber. That night, he had caught those men by the river, all but that one … the youngster who kneed him, took out one of his eyes, and got away.

He was honored back then. Chivington personally gave him his captain's bars that same night. They thought him a hero back home. He was someone, not just another forgotten lieutenant in this man's army. Damn, he loved that feeling. He wanted that kind of recognition again. He wanted it now, on this damn patrol.

"Sir!"

The dream was shattered. He was hot and cramped and desperately afraid of failure. "What is it?" he snapped.

"About the girl, Sir."

"Damn it, sergeant, surely you don't think I was serious about trading for that girl! Apaches don't keep female prisoners. Badger should be smart enough to know that. Even if we did take some females captive, we have no guarantee the Apaches would trade. I'm not going to risk one trooper's life for some fool girl that can't stay out of trouble."

"And what about Mr. Badger?"

Branan's eyes caught the sergeant's and for the second time that day, looked into them. "Sergeant, I'll make the decisions around here. Badger is a frustrated old man. He's not even thinking right. I don't want to hear another word about that girl from now on. We're waiting for our supplies, and then we are going to hit that stronghold. Any more questions?"

Davis rose slowly, biting back the pain in his leg. He said nothing as he turned and walked off.

CHAPTER EIGHT

The pack train had entered a wide-mouthed canyon laced with cactus, twisted rock formations, and a dried out creek bed that meandered across the mouth and disappeared into the surrounding foothills. Jeb thought he vaguely remembered the area from his old trapping days. Nothing there was certain but a few rock formations were familiar enough to let him relax a bit and nudge his mare to a faster pace. If there were Apaches lurking about, it would be further up ahead and not here.

The canyon eventually spilled out into an expansive valley beyond. Jeb felt confident that valley would gradually become more plateaus, more canyons and finally a series of valleys, which bordered the Badger spread. The scout sent Pony out ahead to search for signs of trouble. He put the two cowboys in charge of the mules. They returned cold stares but obeyed him without any argument.

Pony rode point easily, keeping himself a quarter mile ahead of the party. At times, he leaned far over in the saddle, studying the ground for twigs broken, rocks or pebbles knocked about the dirt or faint hoof prints barely visible in the light dust. From his stopping and fingering of the ground, Jeb guessed the old mountain veteran was picking up plenty of signs. He studied the ground himself but could see no signs of Indians who might have previously passed through. *The old man is good, no doubt about that. He may be a little strange, but he's one good man to have in the middle of hostile country,* Jeb reassured himself,

For most of the morning, the party wound its way through the valley bottomlands. Pony kept disappearing among the mesquite and sagebrush then reappearing farther off to one side or the other. He was taking no chances on getting caught off guard. Billy and Edward kept up a constant hum of jabbering back and forth. Burns noticed Billy more than once jab his finger at his saddlebags to emphasize a point.

It tickled Jeb's curiosity. The young boy was talking about those saddlebags again. He had done it several times during their march and each time it visibly bothered Edward to see him do it. The scout reined in until the two came abreast.

"You do a lot of talking about those saddlebags," Jeb said. "What have you got in them that's so interesting?"

Billy's brow furrowed. "Nothin'," he snapped, looking over at Edward for back-up. "That's right," his partner agreed quickly, "nothing that's of interest to you."

"Just curious," Burns said, making his point. Then he added for spite, "Just so it doesn't slow you down." He reined over and moved away. The mumbling behind him lifted a smile to his face.

But the scout wasn't deceived by the two slacker cowboys. There was something in those saddlebags that the cowboys were dead set on keeping a secret. It might be their reason for wanting to go on that mission so much. It might also be their reason for not wanting to take any chances climbing that mountain or crossing the desert without a lot of water. They were being overly cautious on a mission where hesitation might mean instant death. If their little secret was stolen contraband or currency, there was nothing Jeb could do about it. He wasn't the law. Nor did he particularly want that responsibility. His job was to get those mules and supplies to the Army column at Badger's place. Of course if he did get there, the Army might be interested in those boys - especially if there were a bounty on them. Now that was something Jeb could use more of, all the way to California. Until then the two grumblers would have to fend for themselves. Jeb had more important things on his mind; like getting safely to the Badger spread, for one thing.

By mid-afternoon the heat had become direct and merciless. The sun drove down from a cloudless vault; its penetrating rays slowed the broncos to a walk. The men hung their heads, eyes squinting on the ground, away from the sharp reflections and refractions in front. Only Pony kept up his pace, stopping occasionally until the others made up the distance.

Jeb felt the sweat run down his back, soaking his shirt to a vinegar-sweet odor. The stickiness settled in around his gun belt and pants. Even his tattered bandana kept out little of the sun's rays. He could feel his neck burn. Edward and Billy grumbled about the heat and kept taking nips from their canteens. A gruff warning from Burns brought only a curse and reluctant acceptance.

Once free of the valley bottomland, the party worked its way toward the plateau ahead. Upon summiting the plateau, the country stretched out before them, falling into nature's disordered arrangement. Arroyos slashed the land and where they did not run; rough outcroppings and uplifted lava beds tossed and heaved the surface into a jumbled mass of rising and falling ridgelines and neighboring depressions. It would be a very difficult land to traverse and a good place to stage an ambush.

Burns followed Pony into a shallow arroyo then up the other side. He reined in and looked back. In the heat waves, nothing was distinct except the mesas and hills. He sat for a moment drawing in burning heat as he caught his breath. The two young men looked up at him and continued past, cursing the countryside, the heat, the mules, and the colonel who had hired them for this mission.

Another hour of steady traveling brought the party close to another plateau. They rode up an incline with the horses' hooves clinking on the shale. They came onto a broad butte which, five miles distant, eventually fell into a series of rolling hills. Lacing the hills were valleys and one of those would lead to Badger's place.

Pony hadn't slowed his pace once he reached the butte. Already he was far ahead of the others. His horse sent up plumes as it kicked through the dust of a hundred sun-baked seasons on the face of the butte. The mountainous structure was a half-mile wide at its broadest point and the sides dropped off abruptly in places, straight down to the rocks below.

When Burns and the rest of the party reached the other side of the butte, Pony arose from the shade of a large boulder, threw away his cigarette and quickly put himself out ahead again. He led them down the rough cutaway trails, carefully skirting the large patches of loose shale. One wrong movement, one hesitating jerk on the reins, one push too fast on that slippery surface and a man or mount would end up spread all over the slopes bottom - gone to the four winds.

Once they reached bottom, Pony again galloped ahead and maintained the old distance he kept for himself. On the way down, the scout had scanned the terrain carefully. He noticed the sliver of a creek which ran parallel to their trail. Running almost the length of the valley floor, the creek moved between two thin rows of low-spreading cottonwoods, willows, and stubby reeds, As the willows and reeds gave way to more scrub brush and mesquite, the stream grew thinner and gradually faded away from the valley bottom and moved back into one of the many depressions which trailed into the main valley.

A faint gray wisp of smoke against the clear blue sky caught Jeb's attention. Pony must have seen it. He was riding back, flailing his legs in the rush. His Sharps was out in one hand high above his head.

"Well, coon, we got trouble!" Pony shouted as he ground his horse to a stop. "Whatever that was is burnt out by now." The mountain man's eyes flashed something strange, something primal. His keen instinct for fighting was aroused and he felt it surge throughout his body. The others could see it too.

"H-how," stammered Billy, "How can you be so sure? I mean maybe it's just a field being cleared."

"Aw, shit, boy," growled the old man, "it ain't no field being cleared. It's Apaches sure as hell!"

"How long ago do you think they hit the place?" asked Jeb.

"By the looks of that smoke, I'd say they probably hit it this morning."

Jeb's brow buckled. *The cavalry column should have already been there,* he thought. *Either there are soldiers at the ranch right now or we are in grave danger. We might be heading straight for a trap. This could be suicide.*

Billy's Colt was out of his holster, circling with his nervous arm. "Well, what are we going to do? Do we still go in?" He looked around nervously. Edward locked his eyes on Jeb.

Pony split open with a grin. Yellow teeth showed again. Jeb drew in deeply the stale hot air. He looked up into the waiting faces.

"If we push it hard from here, we stand a fair chance of making it before the horses play out. Let's go!"

He kicked his horse into a gallop. The others spurred their mounts, keeping tightly behind him. Pony moved back to the mules and cursed them on.

They moved rapidly down the valley bottom, keeping the creek and its concealing foliage at a distance. The dust rose thick and heavy, choking them. The hooves pounded out a steady rhythmic beat. Dark patches grew larger on their shoulders and flanks. The men pushed on. The mules began to slow. Pony kicked out at them. It did no good. The heat was getting too intense for a hard ride to anywhere.

"We can't keep up this pace," Pony shouted at the scout. Jeb nodded his understanding. He tightened back on the reins and slowed his mare. Behind him, the others almost caught him then backed off themselves. Another dried-out creek bed appeared to one side, disappeared, and then reappeared again like a dusty, dirty line in the crusted earth.

Everything was still going by in a blur. The thickets which bordered the creek had crept in closer. Trees thick with summer green moved in, narrowing the trail. Jeb angled his Appaloosa away from the creek. But the horse could smell water ahead. It fought Jeb's pull on the reins, trying to angle back toward the creek.

The gunshots came without warning. Dull cracks breached the background of pounding hooves. Bullets whistled past the men, kicking up tiny purrs of dust ahead of them. Burns threw a glance over his shoulder, catching the tag end of motion in a clump of cottonwoods off his right shoulder. Apaches were breaking through the willow thickets, their faces and ponies painted for war.

"Pony," Jeb shouted, pointing his rifle at Billy and Edward, "Let them take the mules, we'll cover you." Billy and Edward looked back and grew alarmed. The young boy almost lost grip on the bronco's lead rein as Pony crashed his horse into Billy's and passed over the reins.

"Whadda we gonna do?" Billy shouted.

"What do you think?" shouted Jeb, angry and alarmed. "Grab the train and lead those mules. Don't let them run off. We can't lose those supplies."

Billy went stammering. Edward was visibly scared.

Jeb shouted again, "This is what you two signed up for. Now, damn it, earn your pay!"

A shrill piercing cry baffled Jeb's ears; a white man's yell. He jerked around in the saddle. It was Pony reining in his mount, swinging his Sharps down on the approaching horde. He meant to face them alone.

Edward pulled out his carbine and snap-fired three rounds. Billy locked down on the ropes bunched in his hand. Jeb slowed, shouting at Edward. "Find a target, steady your aim." His shouts fell on deaf ears.

Behind him, Jeb could hear Pony firing his single-shot. Its crack sounded loud amid the clamor of battle. He swung his mare back around.

Pony was keeping pace to the party, but angling away from it. He was twisted in the saddle, directing the horse with his knees - Indian style. With each crack of his rifle, another Indian tumbled out of the pack and disappeared into a cloud of dust behind it.

Jeb reined in long enough to fire four rounds into the mass of hostiles then spurred his weary mount back into a gallop. As he threw another glance back, he could see the swarm of Indians veer off in a flanking sweep toward the creek.

Before the first wave of attackers could swing back once more, Pony had whipped his tired mount into a burst of energy. It kicked up great clods of earth as it tried to catch up to the rest of the party.

The Indian wave came back, flanking out yet farther apart. Dust rolled thicker; blocking out the Indians for a moment and making targets harder to come by. Then they were back, through the filtering dust and dirt, almost parallel with the party. They were gaining quickly on the faltering mules. Bullets cut the air among the party of four.

"Put them in the draw," shouted the mountain man. Billy didn't hear a sound from Pony. Only his own heart beating and the hideous war cries right behind him. The mountain man edged in closer to the boy. Burns swung in closer, intercepting him.

"No," Jeb shouted back, "we keep them here or they will bolt." The rest of his words were lost in the pounding hoof beats and shrill war cries. Both Edward and Billy had stopped firing and instead hung low over their horses' manes, urging them faster.

Pony cursed the scout with silent lips then swung his big rifle back at the Apaches. He fired at the closest painted face and brought the Apache down in a cloud of red dust. Jeb was firing off to his right but his concentration was on the Apaches closest to him.

One buck had swung over to one side of his mustang, firing from beneath his horse's neck. Pony fought his balance, as he jammed another cartridge in the breech. A bullet fried the air, inches from his face. The burst blinked his eyes.

Jeb swung around to look for the others. Just in time to see Pony and his horse collapsing into a large clump of sagebrush.

Pony's mare stumbled, caught itself, then crashed foreward. Pony rode him down, hitting the brush at an angle, spilling over to one side. He landed in a heap then rolled again as his horse crashed down next to him. His Sharps was still locked in one hand. A cloud of dust swirled up from the point of impact.

In a moment, Pony had snapped himself up off the ground and sprinted through the brush, ducking bullets which flew past his head. Several warriors split off from the flanking wave and rode down through the low-lying brush, straight at him. Their painted faces echoed shrieking yelps. Quartz-shod lances flailed the air at him.

Like a statue, Pony knelt on the ground. He was locked in place. His hands worked mechanically: firing, dropping another round into the breach, firing, and then repeating the motion. The first warrior caught a .50 caliber slug center in his face. He was dead before he tumbled backwards off his pony. The second buckled over and slid off his mount with a keening yell. The last Indian caught a slug in his horse's chest. The mare took a couple more steps and pitched forward, spilling the Indian head over heels.

Pony was almost on top of the Indian before he hit the ground. The shock hadn't slowed any of the Apache's instincts. He rolled over once and met the mountain man with a savage slashing motion of his knife. Pony ducked the killing arch and smashed his rifle butt across the Indian's face. Blood burst from the red man's nose and mouth but he remained on his feet, staggering, trying to catch his balance. Pony leveled his rifle and fired point-blank into the man's chest, opening a hole to his spine.

Neither man in the party had noticed the blue curve, which appeared at the far end of the valley bottom. Dust rose up from the blue line. Then a pennant appeared at the head of the line. A column of blue troopers, twin files, with carbines flashing in the hot sun, swung into the valley floor.

Jeb rode up, reining back in a plume of exploding dust. "Get on," he shouted to Pony as he extended his arm to the mountain man.

"Not likely," came the reply. "Get off your mount and hold your ground, cavalry's a comin'."

Jeb spun around in time to see the first of the column breaking through the willows and thickets behind him. Bill and Edward had stopped close by in a shallow draw, circling the mules around them for their protection.

The din of battle had swept all around Pony as he had fought. Now it encircled the four men as the Indians swept by, heading for the charging blue line.

Burns knelt close by, firing into the mass of warriors that were pressing in on both sides. The mules and two cowboys had disappeared in the dust cloud swirling around them. Blue-clad figures were smashing into the lead Indians. Riderless horses dashed through the dust and disappeared. Out of the whirling dust cloud, figures darted in toward the troopers, firing into their midst then dashing away.

The Apaches were making head-on runs at the entering cavalry column, charging them so close their horses almost scraped against one another. Soldiers and Apaches were firing point-blank into each other's faces. Hand to hand fighting erupted along the line of troopers.

The dust and dirt was everywhere – choking and stifling. A dark, thick cloud hid much of the battle and killing. Through the enveloping blanket, Jeb could see Pony running among the sagebrush firing, reloading, and firing again. He was almost as fast as Jeb with his repeater. Lances glittered in the pale air and arrows flew thick in all directions. Another riderless horse dashed by and three troopers chased after two warriors who hung low on their mustangs.

Suddenly a shrill ear-piercing whistle sounded. The Apaches began to break off their attack. From all sides, the Indians began to quickly draw back, firing slivers of arrows and bullets to cover their retreat. The dust effectively blocked out their movement. A bugle sounded and a line of blue charged past Jeb to pursue the fleeing Indians.

Suddenly out of the dust cloud settling over the swarm of milling horsemen, an Apache burst through, bearing down on the mountain man. The Indian carried a lance, which he drew in tightly against his side. Jeb wild fired his last round. It went high. He leapt on his mount; probably too late. Pony was on his own.

The mountain man tried to jack another cartridge into his breech but it jammed up, rendering the buffalo rifle worthless. The Apache was almost on him, his heels flailing the pony's side. Pony stood his ground, bringing the rifle back in an awkward stance.

A second before impact, the mountain man leap out of the way, swinging on his heels to put him to one side of the horseman. He heaved his rifle out and across the rider with all his might. It caught the warrior's side as he charged by. The force of the blow pitched the Apache off his horse.

The Apache landed head first into a pile of rocks. He staggered to his feet with a burst of energy then began to reel from the impact. His lance hung broken in one hand. He saw Pony running toward him. His hand groped for his knife. He found it and lashed out at the mountain man, trying to scream as blood bubbled on his lips.

Pony let out a loud guttural roar and crashed his Sharps into the Apache's face. The Indian fell backwards and Pony leap on him, driving his rifle butt down against the Indians skull. It cracked open with a sickening sound. Dropping the rifle, Pony whipped out his hunting knife. He grabbed the Indian's hair and with a quick circular motion, he cut along the hairline, ripping the hair off his head. A yellow teeth grin came to his face. He held up the scalp, blood still dripping from it.

Burns rode up just as the hair came off with a ripping sound. He reined back in disgust. He had seen it before in the mountains after the war, by white man and red alike. But it still brought a knot to his stomach. Pony hadn't noticed the scout come up behind him. He went up to the other three Apaches and began to lift their scalps. Jeb turned away. He felt suddenly exhausted and sick.

The gunfire had died down now with only a few scattered shots off in the distance. Troopers milled around, trying to settle their spooked horses, and find wounded companions. The scout drew in by a heap of boulders. All four mules were down but the ammunition was secured. His job was done.

Jeb sat slumped in the saddle, too tired to even climb down. His shoulders ached and he felt stabs of tension in his knotted stomach. Off in the distance a bugle sounded recall and order began to come back to the milling horsemen. A sergeant pulled together a squad and began helping with the wounded.

The scout wiped salty, crusted moisture from his face and neck. He eased himself out of the saddle, settling slowly to the ground. The Appaloosa turned its head back. Jeb patted its mane. The scout leaned up against one of the large gray chunks of rock and fished out the makings of a cigarette.

As he flashed a match up against the cigarette, an officer rode by still brandishing his revolver. A streak of dark blood dyed his faded blue tunic with spots of red. The company was quickly divided into squads and specific duties were called out. The cloud of dust and dirt had settled enough for Jeb to see Billy and Edward walking back toward the soldiers.

Jeb fought back an initial impulse to shout out his anger. The two tin horns had let the mules go down, affording protection for themselves. If it hadn't been for the cavalry, they would have walked to the ranch without their charges. Now they were shouting greetings to the troopers, acting like conquering heroes. Jeb felt weak and empty inside.

The sound of the creek crept back into his head. His blue Appaloosa was pulling at its reins, turning his head toward the water. Jeb pushed himself off the rock and in the momentum he began stumbling toward it. As he got closer, he could see Pony down by the water. He had stripped off his buckskin shirt and was washing himself. A blue-red welt ran the length of his back, splitting open in parts. Dried blood matted his hair down by the temple. Yellow teeth greeted the scout.

"Well, coon, that was some fight. Got me five good scalps. Apaches. Best kind." He splashed the water into his face and chuckled to himself.

Jeb turned a cold shoulder and knelt in the water. Even the warm liquid felt refreshing and cool after the heat of the valley bottom. But Pony wasn't going to let him go that easily.

The mountain man waded back to shore and pulled his buckskin shirt back on. He piled up his gear and the medicine bag and started to leave. He turned back to the scout, who by then had fallen back with exhaustion, his legs still dangling in the water. Pony said, "You know I thought for a minute there I was gonna go under. That old mare just dumped me and died. Ha. And three varmints right on my tail, planning to count coup with my hair."

Jeb wasn't listening, but Pony's words kept scratching at his ears. "You ever decide on another one of these trips, Coon, let me know. It was right profitable, if you know what I mean. Ha." With that Pony turned, gathered up his gear, and walked off. His self-satisfying laughter drifted off slowly.

As the scout had slumped back onto the shore, he felt his energy slowly draining away. His head dropped and the feeling of relief settled in. His job was done. Jeb had no more obligations but to himself. All he had to do was get back to the fort, collect his pay, and be on his way.

The voice awakened him with a cold start. His head swung up before his eyes had a chance to focus. Someone was approaching. A sergeant slapped off a tiny cloud of dust from his hat and stepped up next to the scout.

I'm Sergeant Davis," the non-com said. "The Captain would like to talk to you." Then he added, "We sure are glad to see you and those supplies. After the fight we just had, there's not one trooper with more than a half dozen shots left at best."

Jeb mumbled something under his breath and crawled to his feet. He threw the reins of his blue around a dead tree stump and followed the sergeant toward the other soldiers. The officer moved out from among the men and toward the sergeant and himself. Jeb's eyes suddenly narrowed, focusing, blinking away the deception he thought he was seeing.

Even in his exhaustive state, Jeb couldn't believe his eyes. His memory had gone haywire; putting an illusion right in front of him. Now more than ever, he sure could have used a strong drink. He thought he was seeing the man he had vowed to kill the first chance he had.

But it was no mistake. It was the same pointy chin. The same high cheek bones and a cruel slash for a mouth. The eye patch confirmed his gut reaction. Jeb's pace slowed down. He knew the man he was approaching was the same officer who had tried to kill him that black night years ago at Glorieta Pass.

The initial shock brought a new wave of perspiration popping out along his dirty forehead and down his back. Even in the heavy somber heat of the desert afternoon, the scout could feel his stomach tense and tightening. He sieved off the salty sting from his eyes. He felt his revolver; hung heavy at his side.

The captain was standing there in front of him, inches higher than him, his hand outstretched. He kept his eyes down, shaded by the brim of his soiled dirty hat.

"Mister, I want to shake your hand," the Captain began. "You've done a fine job getting those supplies here. Now we can finish the job we came to do." Jeb nodded in acknowledgement and said nothing. Perhaps his dust-laden clothes and bearded face was enough to disguise his true appearance.

The captain was still talking, but the words made no sense. Jeb was looking at him but his mind was focused someplace else. He was back in that wheat field, staring at Peterson's bleeding face and dead eyes. He could hear the shouting and feel the miner's heavy boots tramping through the corn stalks, hunting him down. And he could see the officer, younger then, waving his union sword, trying to cut a much younger Jeb to pieces. The rest was a blur, lost in time.

The voice was coming back. The captain was still talking. "Come on into Badger's place. We've got some food there. We leave first thing in the morning for the Apaches' hideout. The force that hit Badger was only half the main body. The rest are holed up not too far from here. You're welcome to come with us if you want."

The scout nodded absentmindedly but said nothing. The officer and non-com were turning now, moving back to the troops. Jeb turned and started walking back to his blue, suddenly very confused and not sure what to do next. He swung into the saddle and sat in place for a moment, trying to sort out in his jumbled mind the curious events that had just unfolded before him. It was the same officer that tried to kill him during the war. No doubt about it. But he hadn't recognized Jeb. And even if he did, the war was over. The blue and the gray were at peace. Galvanized Yankees were a part of many companies. The past had been forgotten. Or had it? *What of Peterson?* Jeb thought. *What about the others? All those men cut down on the banks of that river without warning or a chance to surrender. Whose idea was it to stage an ambush there? Whose idea if not the officer in charge?* But it was too confusing. What could Jeb do about it? He was only one man. The war was over. Yes, the war was over for him.

Jeb leg-slapped his mount and it started off at a canter. He'd get something to eat and drink. Some rest. He'd think about it in the morning … if at all. There was suddenly much too much on Jeb's mind and he needed time to sort it all out.

Evening came none too soon for Jeb. The ammunition, Spencer carbine cartridges and .44 caliber Army revolver shells, was distributed to the troopers with the evening meal. Cold beans and sowbelly for everyone! Jeb wanted to pass it by, but his growling stomach couldn't let him. He found a spot away from the troopers and cowboys and settled in by himself.

When he first arrived in camp, Jim Badger approached him with questions concerning any Apaches he might have seen. Jeb just shook his head and said, "Sorry." He had nothing else to offer. The old man wandered off unsatisfied and grumbling.

Billy and Edward had quickly mingled in with the ranch hands, bragging about their dash down the valley and the Apaches they took down. Jeb listened for just a moment then dismissed their bantering just as quickly. They were exchanging tall tales by the main campfire. The scout could see their profile and gesturing arms casting wild shadows on the ground. He looked around for Pony but the mountain man was nowhere to be seen. He's probably in the brush, Jeb thought, counting his scalps again.

The spot Jeb had chosen to bed down was near the ruins of the main house. Wafts of black soot rose up as a breeze caught it and curled it high into the darkening sky. The heat had subsided but the wood still crackled and broke as cool night air washed over the ruins.

Behind the scout, a line of drab tents and some sheds made of boughs beside an acequia made up most of the Army camp. The ranch campfire and lean-tos occupied an area bordering one side of the corral. Ringing the camp at staggered distances were the guards, constantly prowling its perimeter - waiting, listening, watching.

The ground was mostly sand; easy to hollow out a place for Jeb's hips. He had laid his saddle down for a pillow and picketed his Appaloosa a few feet away. The sergeant had wanted him to place his mount in the corral like everyone else. Jeb refused. Politely, but he refused. Cupping a coffee tin in one hand, Jeb laid back and flipped the blanket and ground sheet over his legs. The sky was a ceiling of gray pearl changing hues to black. Tiny pinpricks of light spotted the ceiling. A breeze had gradually picked up, cooling away the day's heat.

Tomorrow Jeb was going back to the fort with some of the foreman's crews. They were going back to town for supplies and ammunition. En route, they'd take back the Army dead and wounded. Branan still intended to find the Apache stronghold that next day. Jeb wanted no part of it. As for Pony and the other two, the scout could have cared less. His job was over. He didn't want to see them again.

Voices rose up from one of the Army tents. Jeb rolled over on his side to see who was making the fuss. He recognized two men standing outside a tent, silhouetted by a flickering lantern. It was the captain and the old man, Badger. They were arguing and letting their voices run out of control. Badger was waving a fistful of shells in the officer's face. The scout could barely hear his words, "…find my niece myself if you won't."

Jeb didn't want to hear any more.

"I can't wait for you to find some squaws to trade."

The scout laid back. He had heard enough.

A girl was missing from the ranch. More problems he didn't want any part of it. He was going to California and that was all there was to it. A missing girl was no concern of his. The voices rose higher, breaking into the soft talk around both Army and cowboy campfires. Heads turned to see what was happening.

"You will not leave this camp tonight," the captain shouted at the rancher, his hands planted firmly on his hips. "If you attempt it, I'll have you placed under military arrest. You have my word; a negotiation will be made for your niece once we have taken the hostile stronghold. Not before. Now that's final!"

Even in the darkness, the scout could still see the intense fury pent up on the old rancher's face. He could almost feel the explosive power ready to burst wide open between the two men. A trooper appeared out of the tent shadows, carbine at port-arms. A murmur arose from the cowboys. Several stood up. Before they could move, Badger spun around and stormed away, gritting his teeth in anger.

Jeb studied the captain. He wondered what, if anything, had crossed his mind when he first laid eyes on Jeb. Every indication made was that he hadn't recognized the scout. Even if he had remembered that night Jeb wasn't sure what he could do about it. The war was over, right?

But what kind of man kills so many others in cold blood and then tries to cut up a wounded man as a topper. What kind of mind does that take? Would fighting Apaches in the territory change a man for the better? A smile came to the scout's lips. No, that was unlikely. More realistic, a man would probably get worse out here in this Godforsaken land. *It was a good thing he didn't recognize me, because I'd probably have to kill him if he did. Kill him before he tried to kill me again.*

After several hours, the camp had grown quiet. An occasional nicker from the corral broke into the cowboys' murmurings, but that was all. The campfires were faint red coals glowing in the darkness.

The man appeared from behind the blackened stone chimney. He moved cautiously, in a glide - Indian fashion, making no sound as he passed the silhouettes of soldiers talking around their tents. His boots seemed to float on the ground as he skirted the corral, soft-talking the horses inside, and approached the sleeping scout. The blue twitched its ears, lifting its head. The dark figure sidled up to it and gently rubbed its mane, calming it down. Then it turned to the prone figure wrapped in a blanket.

Squatting three feet away, the man looked straight down into the black barrel of a Colt staring back at him. The hat tilted back and revealed two eyes, tired but still keen, looking up at him.

"It's foolish to walk that quietly around camp unless you've got a good reason. You could get your head blown off!" Burns looked at the surprised face and smiled. Badger returned the smile weakly and said, "My name is Badger. I asked you about seeing Apaches earlier today."

"I remember. I told you we didn't see a thing until they hit us. Only tracks we saw were miles north of here. They couldn't have been the same ones you're looking for."

"Yes, yes, I know," Badger said impatiently. "But I'm looking for more than just tracks. The Apaches got my niece this morning. They grabbed her after she left here to follow my line rider. They killed Bradford. I'm sure they've got her and someone has to bring her back, or at least tell me what happened to her.

"Why are you telling me all this?" questioned Burns.

The rancher eased off his haunches to the ground. He curled his legs up under him Indian style. "Mister Burns, I'll be honest with you. I like your style. I remember hearing about you after you brought some furs into town years back. I was just getting started then. I was looking for good men. I was going to offer you a job but you got dog-ass drunk with some injun and the sheriff threw you in jail. You were gone by the time I came back looking for you."

"You make it a point to hire drunks?"

"If they're good," he said. "Your reputation says something else about you. I've heard that you're an excellent shot, a good horseman, and you can handle yourself well in a tight spot." The old man let the words of praise hang. He burrowed a cheroot out of his vest pocket and offered it to the scout.

Jeb took the cigar and lit it with a red glowing stick. He studied the face across from him. Even in the moon-washed light of the ranch yard, he could see the furrows and tension lines on the man's face. Badger was nervous, high strung and hiding it poorly.

The scout took a long drag on the cheroot and blew out the blue smoke slowly. "Mister Badger, people will say a lot of nice things about a man that buys them all drinks on the house time and again. I wasn't careful with my mouth or money when I was drunk. Thanks for the smoke but you got yourself the wrong man."

Badger wasn't in the mood to take a quick rejection. He leaned forward, lowering his voice even more, "Look, someone has to go after Lottie. Despite what the captain says, those red devils aren't going to keep her for long. I can't wait for him to catch up with that bunch and then hope he captures some Indian women or children. I need someone to go after her right now."

"What's wrong with your own men?"

Tension tightened up the rancher's face. His eyes narrowed to slits, filled with anger. He said, "It's not as simple as that. The captain has put a guard over the corral and my men. He won't allow anyone to leave camp until after he's taken those hostiles. The only men leaving will be heading north, back to town for supplies. We lost a lot of our horses in the raid. Until we can get more mounts from town or our boys bring them in from the range, we're stuck here."

"So how am I supposed to leave?"

"The mountain man knows a way out of here," Badger replied.

"Pony! What the hell's he got to do with this?"

The rancher ran his long fingers through the rumpled toss of white hair poking out from under his hat. "I hired Pony to do this job because I think he is one of the best trackers around. And he hates Apaches."

"Who doesn't?"

"I mean he hates them enough to get this job done. There's good money in it for the both of you. I can pay you well."

So there it was - temptation again. California was a long ways off. It would take several jobs along the way to get there. This could be one answer. He might make enough to ride straight through or, better yet, take a train all the way. 'Riding the rails to Frisco.' It had a ring to it.

"You bring Lottie back and I'll pay you $100. Gold!"

One hundred dollars! Is that the worth of a man's life? Here I am again, tempting fate by even thinking about a mission straight into some Apache rancheria, for what? ...Yeah, for what?

For a moment, a face came back to Jeb. So long ago he had almost forgotten it ... if a man can forget someone he once loved. A lovely young face lost in the desolate wilderness of central Texas ages ago. A girl probably as young as the one the old man had lost to the Apaches. Jeb tried to push the thought away but it persisted. It wasn't the old man he was turning down, it was that girl. That Lottie who had meant so much to the old man. That young girl at the hands of the terrible Apache.

Badger was still talking. He was saying things about the girl; her strong will. Burns didn't hear a thing. His mind was back in Texas long before the war, when he was barely a man-child. Just man enough to have a wife and a child coming, he was old enough for that. A sting burnt Jeb's fingers. He looked down and realized the cigar butt was burning his fingertips. His mind focused back on the rancher who was still talking.

"I want $50 now Mister Badger, the rest if and when I get back," the scout stated as he rose to his feet.

"You got it," Badger said, feeling relief drain through his body. "Pony is waiting for you over by the clump of chollas behind the barn. My men don't know a thing about this. They'll be asleep by now. No one is over there. That's my area to pull guard. The supplies and extra shells I stole for you are on the horse for the girl. It was Bradford's. It's a good gelding." He extended his hand, his voice almost pleading, "Bring her back to me, Mister Burns. Bring her back!"

Jeb took the extended hand and shook it limply. He didn't know whether to curse himself for taking the mission or be satisfied it might be the right thing to do. He wasn't sure of anything right then, except that he was going off with the mountain man after a girl he knew nothing about.

…if that really mattered.

CHAPTER NINE

It was well past midnight when Jeb and Pony slipped away from Badger's ranch. The encampment was quiet and still except for the sound of smoldering ashes where the ranch house once stood. Turquoise embers still crackled and split the wood as the pair passed in the distant shadows that bordered the inky darkness.

They crept out slowly and tried to blend in, keeping well within the black drapery of trees and tall scrub brush. For a good half hour, they walked their muzzled horses and lead a third one away from Badger's encampment. By then only a few scattered clouds offered scant protective cover from the full moon's pale wash.

Following Badger's prearranged instructions, Jeb and Pony filed through a narrow, sage-choked break in the obsidian rim of rough outcroppings and arroyos far behind the barn. The winding corridor was well camouflaged under a corrugation of long bluffs.

Neither man had exchanged a word that evening. They tied the canvassed supplies to their saddles, loaded their weapons and moved out, all in silence. The mountain man gave a yellow-toothed glance back at the camp and left. He wore an air of excitement about him that made Jeb uneasy. He seemed more anxious than before their journey started. A sinister look had returned to his eyes. He glided on padded feet, quickly and quietly, like an animal on the prowl.

Beyond the arena of broken bluffs rimmed by desert, the land heaved up again into sharper more defined ridges and deep arroyos. The pair moved toward the scaled narrow ridgelines, always keeping below the crest so that only their heads occasionally appeared over the edge. Nothing stirred the air except an occasional animal foraging for food in the darkness. The wind picked up, blowing a refreshing breeze across their faces. The stars twinkled overhead and their dark forms snaked along the hillside.

Jeb knew the danger they faced was two-fold; either making noise and alerting the perimeter guards or running into some Apaches positioned to watch the ranch. Neither alternative was pleasant to face, one meant jail, the other probable death. They stopped every few yards, ears keen, and tried to sort out all the nocturnal sounds.

The moonlight that earlier had shrouded their escape now faded as clouds gathered overhead. The blackness, though providing cover, cut their visibility range down to a few dangerous feet.

An hour crept by, then another. The two men were well within a jungle of brush-riddled arroyos and larger foothills. They had seen nothing nor heard any strange sounds. Pony loose-tied the Sharps to his saddle pommel. He swung to saddle. Jeb followed. The scout peered through the spindly foliage in front of them. He could see another stretch of desert, soft and beckoning, in the distance.

The mountain man tore off a plug of tobacco and spoke, "Beyond this here stretch of desert and such are the foothills to the Sierra Madre mountains. We've got to catch up to them Injuns before they get too far into those hills. If they're taking that woman to their camp, we need to get to her first. Once they get back to camp with her, we can hang up our hats. We'll never get her back."

Jeb savored a cigarette and scratched his unkempt beard. "So why'd you decide to go on this jaunt?" he asked.

Pony grinned. "No reason in particular," he answered. "Needed the money I guess. Anyway that camp was too crowded, made me feel all uneasy. I need room to breathe and move along."

"Bullshit!" came a quiet but firm retort.

The mountain man lifted an eye, shifting wads from one cheek to the other. He spat out a long stream which splattered against a rock. The grin broke into a smile. "Aw, coon, come on. Why don't you believe me? Man my age don't lie 'ceptin by accident."

"Man as old as you doesn't know the difference between the truth and a lie. Not when the lies roll off a tongue like they do yours."

"Now what do you mean by that?" asked Pony in a mocking tone of voice.

Jeb wasn't in the mood for Pony's bullshit. He said firmly, "Meaning just this. I came for the girl. Not Apache scalps. I want her. Not trouble. Don't bullshit me why you came along. We both know why. I'm not risking my neck so you can fill your medicine bag with coup."

There, it was said. Jeb had called Pony's bluff. "Either we have that understanding right here and now or we split. You can go after your scalps. I'll go for the girl."

The mountain man shrugged his shoulders. "Coon, you disappoint me!"

Jeb cut in, "Forget that. Can I trust you?"

"Sure, sure," Pony assured him, "if'n you just want to get her out and not a little game along the way, that's alright. I still need the money. I can get my scalps later."

The scout flicked his glowing butt into the darkness. "Let's go then," he said, kneeing the blue into a canter up and over the last saddle on the ridgeline. Behind him, the mountain man scowled. His brooding eyes cut his leather face with hatred. The eyes narrowed in on the nape of the scout's neck. *One shot there would almost take off his head. Or my Green River across his throat would be just as swift and quieter.* Pony felt tempted. *Not now,* he thought. *Later on, maybe.*

Pony's hunch was right. After an hour heading due south, they cut the Apache trail. The tracks headed parallel to their own with ten or twelve Indian ponies, one shod horse, and a mule - probably from Badger's place. They were heavy; still being ridden. The men kicked their horses into a gallop and rode on.

The border between the Arizona territory and Mexico is flat, expansive, and indistinguishable for a thousand miles in any direction. Stretched out before the two riders lay a flat gray blanket of sagebrush and mesquite dotted by tall fingers of saguaro and pipe organ cactus. The cacti looked like tiny protruding fingers across the wide vista as far as their eyes could see.

The miles fell slowly behind. They rode in silence again, with only the occasional clank of a horse's hoof striking bare rock to break the rhythm. The air was cool and dry. Their horses loped along, more alive in the night air than the stifling heat of the day. The Apache trail ran straight and true. No attempts had been made to cover it over. The Indians were feeling confident. Too confident, Jeb could only hope.

An hour later, the first false light of day began in the East. A reddening glow hazed the rim of distant horizon. The two men had traveled all night, alternating between a gallop and walk-trot. They were well into the desert expanse.

By midmorning the sun had curved up high into the cloudless sky. The heat had already grown intense. Burns and the mountain man wound their way among a grove of desert willows and stopped by a tiny circle of rocks among scattered pinon nuts. They were in a wide, shallow bowl; a rocky, wooded oasis in the desert.

There, carefully concealed, lay a few signs that the cherry cow Apaches had been camped in that spot early that same morning. The ash mounds were still warm and smelled of dripped meat juices.

The mountain man could identify it before he was out of the saddle. "Damn, that's mule meat," he exclaimed. "They must be feeling pretty safe. They're butchering some of that ranch stock even before they get back to their people in the mountains." He rubbed his fingers against one of the blackened rocks and licked it. "Rock's still warm," he said. "They're a couple of hours ahead of us. The wounded must be holding them back; they should be farther ahead than this."

The scout grounded his Appaloosa and searched the camp. He soon found where the raiders had their remuda bunched among some mesquite and then where the mule had been butchered. The remains were buried under a thin veil of dirt, enough to keep the buzzards away and keep the meat for other parties in that area. His somber eyes, squinting under the brim of his weather-beaten hat, probed the ground, the bushes, and the willows for some sign of the girl. He could find nothing. The Cherry Cows may have left her tied to her mount while they camped. Jeb looked up as Pony disappeared among the willows, following pony tracks leaving camp.

"Does her horse leave this place?" he asked the mountain man.

Pony looked back from behind a clump of trees several yards away. He ignored the question and kept scouring the ground for more signs. Finally he looked back and said, "They still got her … for now. Meaning they'll either sell her soon or kill her and go back to raidin' along the border. Suppose there's always a chance they'll try to sell her in Mexico to the Comancheros later on."

"Or keep her," offered Burns.

"Not likely," countered Pony, "unless some chief has an eye for her, but that still isn't likely. Only one I ever heard done that was old Red Sleeves up in Magnas, Colorado. Apaches don't hanker for white women. Not one that age. Besides their own women would kill her for certain if she was in camp for any length of time. They're crazier than the men folk when it comes to keeping white or Mexican prisoners."

Pony came back and settled down by the small fire the scout had made. He gnawed on his tobacco stick and picked at his teeth with a knife. A small tin pot of coffee warmed on the fire. The two men ate their jerked beef and hard tack in silence.

Jeb had been studying the mountain man since they left the fort almost a week before. His own mountain experience told him that trappers fell into several categories, none of which seemed to fit Pony. They were an individualistic lot, distrustful of strangers, skilled at any kind of hunting, and Indian-fighters par excellence. Pony fit that mold. He was like one of them, but only to a degree. There was something about him, something the scout could only sense at a gut level. Most mountain men were content to trap for pelts and hunt. They left the scalp hunting to the town folk and bounty hunters.

More often than not, trappers had to live amidst the Indians, trade with them and swap food stores and ammunition. Scalp hunting wasn't a way to solidify that connection with the Indians. It wasn't their kind of work. That wasn't why they were in the mountains. Scalp hunting was nothing new to the scout. He had encountered it before and even during the war, but seldom among mountain trappers. Pony set himself apart in that respect.

But there was something else that bothered the scout. Something he couldn't quite define even to himself. He didn't feel right about Pony's volunteering to go after the girl. It wasn't his style. He could make more than a hundred dollars working for the mines around Tucson as their supplier of fresh meat. That and bounty hunting for the territory and the two counties in Mexico: Sonora and Chihuahua would bring him more than a hundred dollars and not the risk he was taking right now. It didn't fit. There had to be some other reason he was going after the rancher's niece; something that the scout couldn't place his finger on.

"How long you been in the mountains?" Pony asked suddenly.

Jeb broke out of his thoughts and looked up. The mountain man was opened mouth, his knife still probing between his tarnished teeth. He was staring at the scout.

"Too long," Jeb stated plainly. "Some years before the war and then after it. I've hunted and trapped off and on most of my life, I guess. Tried scouting for the Army, but dealing with Union brass became a real burr under my saddle, so I gave that up. You?"

Pony was waiting for the question. He seemed to have a whole delivery all set to go. "Sonny, I've been working one bunch of mountains here and there ever since I begun with old Jim Bridger and Sublette back in '31."

"That makes you older than old and then some!"

Pony laughed heartily. "Hell, I was old before I got started. Back then them mountains belonged to us. Nobody was there 'ceptin that other fur company, the American Fur Company, that was trying to run us outta money. It was money back East that was trying to clean out those mountains."

"You weren't a free trapper then?"

A glint of recognition lifted the mountain man's eyes. "Ay, you know. No, weren't no free trapper. Not then. I was too young. There was a lot I had to learn first. Spent my first winter at old Gabe's camp on the Salmon River. We fought them Gros Ventres and Blackfeet the whole winter. Damn irritation it was!"

Jeb poured out two tins of coffee. Pony grabbed his mug and took a long deep swallow and sleeved off his beard. "Coon, I'll tell ya. I've been trapping in just about every mountain from the Missouri's headwaters to the starving Gila. But it's all changed now. None for the better."

He leaned back against a rock and let his gaze drift off. "Weren't bad until I guess the time of the migration. I guess around '34, '35. It got so bad, you couldn't travel in any direction without crossing their trails, settlers and the likes. Mormons came in '47. They were worse." His voice dropped, he wasn't concentrating on what he was saying. The thoughts were coming out, jumbled, and confused, telltale hints of his mind's workings. "I can still remember topping South Pass and seeing those damn Conestoga wagons lined up for as far as the eye could see. Sad. Families, women, children, oxen, taking it all away. Then the Oregon Trail all rutted and barren of grass. They ran over it until it was hard as granite. All of them; pork-eaters, Greenhorns, settlers, foreigners, injuns hanging on, too many of them."

"What did you do then?" asked the scout.

The mountain man looked up, still lost in his thoughts. "Nothin', just worked when I felt like it, but it isn't like it used to be."

As the mountain man had begun his oration, the scout's mind was also begun drifting back to his first days as a free trapper.

His first winter. What a baptism it had been. He and a party of five others had crossed the Great Divide just above Killman's Pass in the dead of winter. Deep snowdrifts bogged down their horses' legs, making the trek twice as long as normal. Shrieking winds howled through the pass, whipping icy blasts through even their thickest layered jackets and frosting the horse's nostrils. The cold numbed their arms and legs, robbing them of any feeling. Frostbite set in and three of the party simply slumped over in the saddle and never woke up again. Another lost his pace and was never seen again.

The scout hadn't forgotten that first winter. He had grown up very quickly back then. His reliance upon himself and not others had been kindled and nourished as the party staggered out of the mountains and every man went his own way. He was 16 and afraid, but he was alive, and somehow he made it to a town and a warm room.

"…round here for a couple of years. What about you?'

Jeb looked up. "What?" he asked, jerked out of his trance.

"I asked how long you was planning on staying in these parts?"

"Not long after we get the girl. I'm heading out to California."

Pony stuck his long Green River knife back in its beaded sheath and spat out a little blood with his tobacco. "What do you think she is like, this girl we going after?" he asked.

"Like a hundred dollars' worth of trouble," Burns replied, not bothering to look up.

"No, that's not what I mean. I heard some of that old man's boys talking about her. They say she's a wild one. Don't listen to no one. She sounds like one of those good old honkytonkers back in Santa Fe. I wonder if she's a looker."

Jeb let the question hang in the air. The girl was his ticket to California. That's all he cared about. That and getting her safely back to her uncle. She could outshine a coonhound or a fat sow for all he cared. He only cared about one female to grab from the Apaches and deliver home. It was less complicated that way.

Finishing his coffee, the scout left Pony to scratch in the sand with his knife. Moving through the brush, he noticed that the rocks outlined a shallow depression where a stream had worn the ground down centuries before. He selected a large boulder and curled under it to escape the direct sunlight. He sipped from his canteen and rested his head on his arm. Soon he fell into a fitful sleep, aware of the penetrating heat and trickling sweat down his face, and caring about neither.

Back at the campfire, the mountain man continued his idle sand-drawings. A crack on Pony's normally placid face marked the beginning of a sneer-smile-coming from inside his head. Unconsciously it grew wider as he thought about the rancheria he'd find somewhere up ahead. The Apaches would have to make at least one more night camp among the tangle of foothills and canyons before they entered the high country of the Sierra Madres. Normally Apaches never let their wounded slow down their pace. These did. The tiny droplets of blood Pony had wiped off the warm rocks told him what he had suspected. The wounded were still bleeding. That meant they'd call on a shaman; a medicine man to heal the wound. It was obvious the party felt they were relatively safe inside Mexico. There hadn't been a sign of vaqueros or Mexican army federales, and the U.S. Cavalry couldn't follow them across the border. The Apaches were safe, or as safe as they could expect to be anyplace else.

The mountain man had trapped in the Sierras on occasion. He knew of a place that few other whites knew about - Hidden Springs. Most likely that was where the raiders would camp before entering the Sierras. That was where he could find his scalps and the little white girl he found himself so curious about.

Methodically the mountain man went about his work; rubbing down his mount, polishing and oiling his Sharps, and checking his supply of shells again. Never can be too careful, he told himself. After a short meal of corn bread, jerked beef, and more muddy coffee, he lay back in the sun, and tipped his hat over his face. Soon a guttural, growling snore came from his fluttering lips. He dreamt of black shiny scalps and that little white girl.

The next day seemed like one continuous headache. The sun rose early and died late. The heat kept their riding down to a slow, safe pace. Luckily the Apaches were not doing much better. The Apache wounded still slowed their pace. For two solid days the Indians had moved south and the pair followed, at a distance. The Indians never stopped once. In the middle of the second day, Pony spotted the party moving out of a canyon. Jeb tried to spot the girl but the figures were too small, against gray-green hills and canyons and stretches of desert.

By late afternoon, they found a narrow, rock-strewn path, which worked its way up along a series of bluffs. Pony studied the ground closely. He threw a grin at the scout. "That's it," he said. "They're not more than an hour from here."

"How do you know?"

Yellow teeth flashed. The glint in his eyes was back. "I know," was all Pony said.

They walked their horses up the steep hillside until they found a spot gutted out by the trail, where they could leave their mounts. It was a little pocket of mountain mahogany, cat's claw, and blanketed grass tufts. There was a rock seep of water from someplace above. It would do just fine, thought Jeb. Even if their horses nickered, the sound most likely would not carry up very far; certainly not all the way to the top of the canyon or beyond. That relieved Jeb. But, he thought, if they were spotted it meant a hard fight back down to the horses before they could escape. That didn't set well with him.

They followed the trail until it took the form of a wild burro track; twisting and turning, back and forth, all the way up to the rim of the canyon above. The mountain man told Jeb that the track was the only safe approach to the Apache rancheria. There were two other main trail approaches but both were heavily guarded. Those trails dropped down into the encampment from the valley below.

The track they were following led above the camp and then circled down into a corner of the canyon. Pony doubted the Indians knew of its existence and even if they did they would probably feel safe and ignore it.

Once Jeb and Pony reached the top, both men crawled along a rock shelf and through a rim of dun rock to the edge of the canyon. Jeb elbowed his slim body through a narrow passageway of boulders and slid like a snake up to the very edge of the canyon's rim. Pony was too large to follow. He circled the huge rocks and dropped down beside the scout.

Through the haze of dying sunlight, Burns studied the rancheria below. Small figures of men and women moved about.

Men and women!

He looked again to be sure his eyes weren't playing desert tricks on him. No. There were children and women down there. Some were by the cooking fires, others washing in a small stream that circled the encampment.

"What the hell!"

"Figured as much," was all Pony muttered before rolling over on his back and pulling out a plug of tobacco.

"What do you mean?" Jeb asked. "Did you know they were meeting another party here?"

"I figured that's why they were going slow and caring for their wounded. They knew this other party would be waiting for them here. That's why they kept the little girl. They won't be raiding for a while at least."

"So she's safe for the time being," Jeb whispered under breath.

Pony sucked in his gut and spat out a stream of juice. He grinned. "Unless their womenfolk get to her. If some squaw down there lost herself a husband in their three weeks of raiding that someone ain't gonna feel like being kind to no white woman. If we don't get her out tonight, she's as good as dead."

The scout snaked up to the rim again. He poked an eye over the edge. The canyon wall below him dropped straight down, smooth and clean. An alluvial fan spread out on the bottom, where the rain had washed the cliff wall to a sheen. He looked along the wall. It was the same smooth, clean, sheer, pathless rock wall for as far as he could see. The darkness was quickly shadowing out the rocky outcroppings and cracks and fissures. Nowhere could he see a pathway leading down to the bottom of the canyon.

Before he could turn, Pony wiggled up next to him. As if reading his mind, the mountain man pointed toward a section of dun rock piled high far off to the left. Jeb looked and saw the trail leading down. It made him swallow hard and wish he were seeing wrong.

The trail, if it could be called that, was a twisting, barely visible ledge which wound along the rim for several hundred yards before dropping at a sharp angle down the far curving side of the canyon wall into the pool of gathering darkness below. Even from a distance, the scout could see that it was narrow, very narrow. It was less than four feet wide in most spots. It tapered off into black empty space on one side and up against a jagged dangerous wall of rock on the other. The mountain goat trail angled in spots sharply downwards. Loose rocks on the ledge would make footing little more than a step-by-step venture. It would be a chancy risk in the daylight and near suicide at night, but it was the only way down.

The pair moved back to a boulder pile where they could still look down and remain concealed. Jeb noticed a mule in a spit and small groups playing monte. Several Indians were drinking from small jugs. Tiswin! The fermented liqueur made from sprouted corn was as strong as any white whiskey made. If the Indians drank enough, it might make entering the camp a little safer. He mentioned it to Pony.

"Coon, you still got a lot to learn. You don't see their squaws drinking or their kids. They'll be sober tonight whether them Injuns is drunk or not. And some of them youngsters can spot a white faster than a lot of them bucks, drunk or sober." The mountain man pulled out a small pipe carved of bone. He lit up.

Jeb studied the encampment more closely. There was one wicciup which stood apart from the others. It was bordered in back by a clump of cottonwoods. An old couple sat in front, cooking over a fire. Pony moved next to Jeb, his pipe jutting from his mouth. Jeb nodded toward the lone hut. Pony shook his head.

"Most likely that's it. We'll find out once it gets dark."

Jeb sucked in his breath and slowly exhaled. "In a couple of hours," he said. The two men moved back into the rocks and settled in to wait for late night. Jeb fished out the makings of a cigarette and rolled the filled paper. He cupped a match against the paper. The aroma and taste softened the tension in his body. It made him relax.

Fat cumulus clouds promising at least some chance of rain began to gather overhead. Perhaps it would provide enough rain to cover their tracks into the desert if they ever got that far.

Two black forms; lumped together and out of place beneath the spreading cholla cactus arms, melted out from the web of darkness and cautiously snaked along a soft sandy wash. The two shadows crawled single file, skirting the open moon-washed river bottom and settled instead on its bank using the juniper trees and sage clumps as a cover. They followed the dry riverbank as it circled the Indian camp. Beyond the juniper and sage, the stream turned back toward the encampment and settled into a pool. A few dark figures still moved back and forth between camp and the water.

Over their shoulders, voices arose behind the two men. Most of the Apaches had stumbled back to their wicciups to sleep off the tiswin. But several groups remained, huddled around their glowing campfires, drinking and talking. Through the thick foliage, Jeb could see their dark faces reflected in the light. Only a stray dog's bark broke the low muttering and talking.

The two men paced themselves with the gathering clouds. As the thick dark shapes moved across the sky, the moonlight was blocked every couple of minutes, Jeb and Pony waited for the darkness and moved quickly but quietly to their next point of concealment. The air had grown noticeably cooler even in the canyon bottom. It dried their sour shirts and eased the soreness of necks burnt in the daylong sun.

The sky promised rain soon if Jeb could believe it. He wasn't sure. The scout had been in the mountains plenty of times when thick, dark clouds bunched up and then slowly drifted apart, without one raindrop. *Nothing,* he thought, *is certain in the desert until it happens.*

As they reached the thicket of cottonwood trees, moonlight laid a pattern of light over the two men. The shadows dissolved into faces; burnt wood faces, and white reflections for eyes. Their bodies slunk deep into the thick grass there and each laid his knife and revolver in front of themselves. The air was thick with the smell of tiswin and mule meat blowing in their direction. If it changed and a camp dog caught a whiff of white men, they were in trouble. And certainly dead!

Job thought about their slow procession down the rocky ledge and feared passing sentence on their chances of surviving, either in the camp or on their return back up the ledge. Especially if it began to rain. Twice he almost lost his balance when the ledge sloped dangerously outward, at almost a 45 degree angle. Loose rocks and soft tufts of course grass made the footing treacherous at best. With time bearing down on them, and the possibility of a hurt or injured girl on their hands, the climb back up might prove the final impossible obstacle.

Their avenue of escape was made even harder by the layout of the apache rancheria. The assortment of wicciups and several lean-tos were centered next to the small stream, which ran out and around the camp, on the opposite side of where Jeb and Pony were hiding. The camp was elongated, stretched out from the shallow pool down to the remuda. The rocky ledge leading back up to the canyon's rim was close to the remuda, sheltered only by a small switchback, which hide the trail from the ground.

If the rains came, and the downpour was thick enough, they might risk a direct run along the riverbank, straight back to the trail. If it didn't rain, their only option was to crawl back the same way they came. Slowly, cautiously and very time-consuming a retreat at best.

After a few minutes rest, Pony moved through the cottonwoods into a neighboring cholla's long dangling tentacles and eased up next to the spiny trunk. Burns moved in under one of the over-hanging limbs. Both men stared at the drawn, drunk faces reflected in the dim light. The girl was nowhere in sight. Only a couple of Indians remained huddled together, the dull humps of their wicciups like overturned bowls behind them.

Beside the scout, meshed in a web of patterned shadows, Pony's leathered face broke once more into a hunter's stare. A feeling; instinctive, natural, and savage, was reborn deep inside his consciousness. Pony's hunting prowess was on keen edge.

Jeb glanced over at the trapper and recognized the glazed look. The eyes were set, darting back and forth, taking in everything, and missing nothing. The breathing slowed down. Muscles bunched up beneath the worn buckskin. The mountain man's huge paw tightened up around his green river as one of the Apaches stumbled toward the pool to relieve himself. Pony felt the strong urge to try himself, to slip up to the man and count coup. He fought down the urge. His time was coming, he thought, there would be plenty of scalps before the night was over.

The two men waited with a patience born in the mountains. Time drifted slowly by. The night grew longer and their time for escape grew shorter. Overhead the black clouds had bunched up to block out the moonlight completely. Distant approaching thunder followed by flashes of lightning silhouetted the rim of the canyon. Rain could not be too far behind.

The old Indian in front of the lone wicciup hadn't changed position since they first spotted the hut. The woman had long since gone. The elder remained. His head continued to bob back and forth, as he drifted in and out of a shallow sleep. Jeb felt uneasy not knowing where the woman was. But there was nothing he could do about it, unless she was inside. He'd find out soon enough.

When the last of the Apaches had finally wandered off into the other dark huts, the pair left the cholla's sheltering darkness and snaked their way, belly-flat, over soft sand toward the hut.

The first drop landed on Jeb's shoulder devoid of any sound. The second landed on his hatband. He stopped and looked up. A third drop crashed into the bridge of his nose, splattering minute particles in both eyes. He blinked them away. Then the rain began in earnest.

Heavy wet drops began falling in a blinding sheet over the canyon bottom. As it increased in intensity, the raindrops became thicker and heavier until they were drumming on back and legs. Visibility grew shorter as the rain came down in volumes of thunder, rolling over both prone figures. A crescendo of thunder, lightning, and howling wind beat the rain against the ground.

The old Indian awoke with the first blast of thunder and lightning in the canyon. He moved slowly back into the hut. His hand pushed back the flap covering the entrance and he started to crawl in.

Pony hit him before he got his head in the door.

Leaping to his feet before Jeb could react; Pony dashed up to the old Indian and slammed his Green River knife into the elder's soft belly flesh. The old man gasped out a soft sound and slumped to the ground. Like a conquering animal, Pony straddled the body. He jerked back the head, grasping the hair, thick in his hand, and ran his knife along the baseline. With one sickening rip, the scalp came off. His first scalp for the night.

Burns rushed the mountain man, throwing his weight against him. They both tumbled into the wicciup. The mountain man rolled off the dead body. His hand jerked the knife up into Jeb's face.

"Whaddya doing, boy?" Pony snapped, his hand arched up, the knife inches away.

"You stupid bastard, I told you no scalp-hunting. We want the girl, that's all." Jeb spat out, furious at the mountain man. Even in the heavy downpour he could tell the mountain man was not himself. His eyes were strange - glazed, unfocused, and dangerous. He said nothing, letting the rain run off his lips. The hair matted down on his forehead and the mustache. Jeb turned around in the hut. He growled out a 'stay here' and rolled the dead Indian into a corner.

Jeb's eyes, though accustomed to the darkness outside, were not prepared for the blackness inside the wicciup. He could see next to nothing, just faint outlines and forms. There was no one else inside. At least none that he could focus on. The wicciup was customarily small and cluttered. Several bowls and a pile of small furs cluttered the ground floor. A blanket in the far corner covered a shape of something. But no girl! She wasn't there. Jeb felt his throat tightening. No sound outside but for the heavy constant pounding of the rain. He hoped the mountain man had regained his composure and be on guard. But he wasn't counting on it.

Before turning to leave, Jeb slid over to see what was under the blanket. He flipped back the cover.
His mouth dropped in surprise.

There, hidden under the old horse blanket, lay a girl staring back up at him. A beautiful young woman like none he had ever seen before. But before he could react, a leg shot out from underneath the blanket and hit him square in the groin.

Unconsciously he sucked in his breath in surprise and tumbled over in pain. The girl let out a gasp through her tied mouth and stared at the prone man on the ground. "Sorry," came a muffled sound from her lips. Jeb caught his breath and ignoring the pain between his legs, staggered back up to his knees.

The girl was as surprised as he was. He hadn't given any thought to her looks or age. It was simply some woman or some girl, this Badger's niece that he was after. But lying before him was one of the most beautiful young woman he had ever laid eyes on.

Her eyes caught his attention first. They were dark, black or brown he couldn't tell. And the hair, auburn, that seemed to shine even in the dull light of the wicciup. It fell in curls about her face, framing her strong cheekbones, tiny nose and smooth curve of her chin. She had the face of a catalog model Jeb seen back in the merchants store in Tucson. He hadn't seen such a woman as this on the frontier in all his years of wandering.

The girl's murmuring broke his stunned gaze. Only then did he realize her hands and legs were bound by rawhide strips. Her mouth was tightly bound with a cloth strip, affording only enough room to breathe through her nose. Her riding breeches had been torn by either cactus needles or Indian hands. Her calico blouse had been ripped open, exposing milk-white flesh down to her waist. He tried not to look at her firm breasts beneath the torn cloth.

A sigh of relief escaped her lips as Jeb untied the mouthpiece. Even in the hut's dim, hazy light, Jeb could see that the girl was in her early to mid-20s, a ripe age when most women had settled down and had a brood of children. Somehow she was much younger than he had imagined her to be. Her face was scratched and dirty. Only her eyes - dark like Jeb's and just as somber - peered intently, searchingly at the scout.

"Don't worry," Jeb whispered, trying to assure her. "You'll be alright. Your uncle, Mister Badger, sent us after you. Keep quiet and we'll get you out of here."

The girl nodded understanding. She hiked up her legs and tried to hide her exposed body, as she rubbed circulation back into her stiff joints. As she did this, her shoulders pressed together covering her exposed breasts. Her dark hair tumbled over her front.

Quickly the scout peeled off the old Indian's buckskin shirt, despite the blood hole in its side, and handed it to the girl. Without a word he turned his back to her. He could hear the calico being hastily torn off and the sound of leather on skin. Then he heard the girl reach past him and grab an old calico skirt in the corner.

Suddenly a gasp came from the girl behind the scout. The wicciup flap had flown back and an old Indian squaw stuck her head inside. A second gasp escaped the girl's lips as something grabbed and propelled the old woman through the doorway. Like an animal closing in on the kill, Pony rolled on top of the squaw, knife in hand.

Jeb was stunned momentarily, enough time for the squaw to squirm out from under Pony and leap back toward the entrance to shout her warning. Blindly following the flash of buckskin, the scout threw himself at the woman. His powerful hands clamped down on her ankles, trying to force her back. The rain was starting to ease up and her shout would carry far across the camp. Jeb could feel the woman kicking, fighting to break free. He pulled with all his might on the legs, desperately trying to get her back inside before she could scream. She kicked him square in the face, breaking his grasp on her ankles. She started to crawl to her feet to leap out the doorway.

Just as suddenly, the legs stopped kicking. The body went slack. The jagged tip of the Green River was protruding from her back. Jeb hadn't seen Pony pile on top of her and plunge his knife into her back. Jeb pulled the woman back from the entrance. A gaping hole in her chest was leaking out blood. Now the entrance to the wicciup was filled with Pony's bulky frame. He looked around and slipped back inside the tent.

The mountain man held his knife still dripping blood in one hand, and two black scalps in the other. He sheathed the knife and tucked the scalps in his belt. He shoved the woman's body off to the side. As his eyes fell on the girl they opened wide in amazement. A sneer curled his lips.

"Did you have to kill her? I told you to stay out front!" Jeb exploded.

Pony looked beyond the scout back at the girl. "Coon, I told you I had me some things to do. You ain't giving orders to me. Not now. Not ever."

Jeb quelled the impulse to drive his revolver across the mountain man's face. Pony continued to stare at the girl, saying no more.

Jeb purposely moved in front of Pony, blocking his view of the girl. Jeb gritted his teeth in fuming anger and spat out the words. "Listen, you ornery son-of-a-bitch, either you stick with us or I swear to God, I'll kill you right here and now."

Only then did the mountain veteran bother to focus in on Jeb. He looked back into the hate-filled eyes flanked by taut facial muscles and smiled. "Sure, coon," he said, "whatever you say."

Jeb clamped his mouth shut and bit his tongue. "We'll move out first. You cover us. We'll meet in the trees, and then leave together."

Pony turned abruptly and crawled toward the squaw's bunched up body. Jeb grabbed the girl's hand and quickly led her out before she could see Pony perform any more of his ritual scalp-letting.

Outside the heavy downpour was beginning to loosen up. Only the continuous rolling thunder claps broke the monotonous rhythm of the rain. Visibility was beginning to increase. The air was heavy with the smell of cactus and brimstone. As far as Jeb could see, nothing was moving outside. Even the camp dogs had sought shelter in the heavy rain.

Jeb and the girl ran, bent double, through the packed sand to the brush and cactus; then around the spiny tentacles to the grove of cottonwoods. Their rain-soaked clothes stuck to their skin and hair lay plastered to their foreheads. The girl pushed the tangled hair out of her eyes and watched the scout, not saying a word.

The pair knelt hidden behind the trees. They peered through the rain and watched for the mountain man who was supposed to be right behind them. But they couldn't see a thing. Pony was nowhere in sight. The girl huddled against the tree trunk, trying to escape the chilling rain. Her clothes pressed against her figure, accenting its fullness and shape.

Jeb tried to take her mind off the rain and the wait. "We've got horses just over this canyon. It's a treacherous climb up but you can make it," he said.

The girl looked up at Jeb with a forced smile. Then she dropped her head and pressed her arms tightly around her waist.

The rainfall was growing lighter. Already Jeb could see the wicciups hazy outlines. He could hear the swollen creek overflowing with the sudden accumulation of water off the canyon walls and base.

Jeb felt the sudden powerful craving for a cigarette to settle his taut stomach. He felt for his tobacco pouch but came up empty handed. It was missing. Perhaps in his fight with the old woman or his run from the wicciup to the trees. No matter. It was lost and the Apaches would find it for sure.

Jeb climbed to his feet. He would wait no longer. Pony would have to fend for himself. He motioned the girl to rise and turned to leave. She got to her feet then gasped out in surprise.

Jeb wheeled around, his revolver out and cocked. Ten feet away, in the dim light of the dying rain, stood the mountain man. Hanging from his bloody hand were four scalps. He raised up his hand and turned it. The scalps danced in the air, throwing off more blood. The girl let out a gasp and turned her face from the scene.

Jeb leaped forward in uncontrolled anger. He slammed against the mountain man and pushed him up against a tree. He spat out the words - his face inches from Pony's. "You dumb bastard, I told you no more scalping. I warned you!"

Pony tried to lunge forward, but the scout held him firm. His paw reached for the Green River but stopped in mid-air as Jeb's cold blue pistol knocked against his face.

"Aw, coon, come on now," he started to argue. "Whaddya care if she gets outta here alive?" He stuck his beard in Jeb's face. "Let me have a little fun. We got the girl don't we, what more do you want?"

Jeb slowly cocked the gun, pressing its barrel harder against the leathery face. "One more time, old man, and I'll leave you behind, without a horse or gun. One more time."

Pony pushed back the gun as Jeb eased off. He avoided looking Jeb in the eyes. His checks were tight with seething anger but he held it back. He tucked the scalps in his cartridge belt. Then with-out looking back at the girl who had turned back on the two of them, the mountain man left the trees at a run. The other two followed him at a distance.

Jeb took the girl's arm but she tried to move it away. He closed his fingers down hard. He wasn't in the mood to argue with the girl on top of Pony. They moved together, at a half run, down along the stream.

The climb back up the goat's trail was made even more dangerous by the rain that had washed down upon it. The trio moved cautiously, hugging the sides of the canyon wall as much as possible. Below them, each could see the round bowls of the wicciups growing more distinguishable in the growing light. They could hear the barking of dogs thrown out into the wetness. And the remuda shaking off the wetness of the night.

Halfway up the cliff climb, the girl stopped dead in her tracks. She pressed her back against the rock wall and refused to look up or down. The ledge had narrowed to just a couple of feet. Shale and loose gravel crunched beneath their feet.

"Come on," Jeb encouraged her; "You can't stop now".

The girl was adamant. She wouldn't budge.

Jeb hadn't the time to argue the situation. He wrapped one arm around her waist and practically lifted her off the spot and into motion again. She let out a gasp and seemed to come to her senses. Pressed against his body, Jeb could smell something sweet in the girl's hair. Her face was inches from his. A feeling, vaguely familiar crept into his mind. He was holding a beautiful young girl in his arms for the first time in nearly a lifetime. No, more than a lifetime … since before the war, long before. Then a loose rock snapped his attention back to the ledge and the dark hulk of Pony waiting up ahead.

CHAPTER TEN

A brown-backed scorpion moved across the alkali flats carving minute lines behind itself in the soft sand. Burning above, a whitish sun beat down unmercifully on the cracked land. It was the dead season when most animals were scarce on the desert flats. The arachnid was alone, moving effortlessly untouched by the crippling heat. After crossing a wide expanse of desert, the scorpion began climbing a sandy shale slope. Moving slowly but steadily, the scorpion's front nipper claws explored every item in its path; pebble, leaf, and plant, touching whatever it came across.

Suddenly it stopped dead in its tracks. Only its antennae twitched in nervous jerks. It moved cautiously, then stopped. It moved again, and then froze. The arachnid instinctively sensed a dangerous presence. Something flashed overhead, blocking out the light for a split second. The object careened out of nowhere and smashed against its back, slamming it to the ground.

The scorpion lashed out defensively, its slender jointed tail futilely jabbed at the ironwood shaft, glancing off it. The insect was caught, rooted in place by the shaft of wood. On the other end of the stick were two ruthless eyes, lacking all compassion.

Billy was at play.

It wasn't a smile on the young man's face but rather a slight change of stony expression as the eyes peered contently down on the helpless insect caught by a superior mind. The eyes, sunk deep in his sunburnt bronze face, lit up with cruel satisfaction. He imagined the deadly creature to be all those he hated so much, all those he'd like to crush with his bare hands.

Pinned down, its back being pressured to the breaking point, the scorpion fought for its life. It kicked out its legs frantically, clawing at the dirt. It fought until there was a trench on either side of its body. But even as he channeled down, the shaft pressed harder on his back. The curved tail repeatedly lashed out at the wood, leaving not a mark.

Crack! The back broke open. Green liquid oozed out, staining the light brown sand. The scorpion's legs jerked in spasmodic motion, its antennae waved limply back and forth like a flag hung on a still, windless day. Then it lay still. Billy had won again.

Satisfied with his kill, the teenager rose off his haunches. Wiping his wet, dirty brow, Billy turned back to continue his climb up to the top of the canyon rim. He used the ironwood shaft as a walking stick. Pausing for a moment, he looked up and saw a whisper thin shaft of smoke rise up from the canyon rim.

The young gunfighter broke into a labored run. He yelled at his partner as soon as he could see his head above the rim.

"For Christ's sake, Edward," the bellicose cowboy scolded his partner, "Don't you know enough not to burn wood that smokes? Do you want a pack of 'paches swarming down our throats?"

Billy was puffing hard, sucking in hot air by the time he got to the campsite. The small fire was in the shade of some mesquite trees. The horses were hobbled on a patch of galleta grass nearby.

Edward was not rattled by the youngster's excitement. "Oh, settle down," he said calmly. "For Christ sake, it isn't going to smoke that much, and besides, with the breeze up here and these trees, it'll be gone as soon as it rises." He cupped his tin and took a long swig of coffee. Billy stood impatiently by, looking down with a tense face.

"That's a fool risk to take when…"

"Relax!" Edward broke in. "We're home free. We got the money. We got good rifles, good stock. What more do you want?" He went over to the fire and, as if to push home his point, he dropped a few more pieces of wood chips into the fire. White smoke curled up and was quickly swept away as it cleared the trees.

"I still don't like it," Billy grumbled. He squatted down across from Edward and poured himself a cup of java. Edward took out the bacon and began cutting it for lunch.

"What were you doing down there?" Edward asked.

"Nothin' - just playing with a scorpion. Like I'm gonna do to that mountain man if I ever lay eyes on him." Billy was full of himself once again. He continued bragging. "That sonofabitch won't last a minute if I have at him. I should have plugged him back on that mountain when I had the chance."

His partner glanced up at the wandering eyes, the exaggerated gestures of Billy's arms, then smiled to himself and went back to cutting the bacon strips and laid them across the stick to sizzle.

He let Billy ramble on. It was better that way. The boy recounted their first robbery weeks before and the guard he blasted off the stage coach. And the other shootings after that, all of which culminated in that shipment of gold dust they almost polished off. It would have been theirs if it hadn't been for that cavalry patrol that came across the stage just as they were cleaning out the last passenger.

Their escape had been a frantic, toll-taking dash across half the territory. They escaped the cavalry patrol, but lost their third partner along the way. He was left behind, for the coyotes and Apaches to have at.

Billy recounted, with his customary embellishment, how they had talked their way into the mission at the fort just to get closer to the border; and how the scout and Pony had almost found them out. There wasn't much money left, but it would get them to Mexico.

"Listen, Billy," Edward finally interrupted his young partner. "Forget about them two. All you got to think about now is how to spend that money we got left once we're over the border."

Billy dropped his mumbled cursing long enough to smile at the thought. Edward continued, "God, I can't wait to get there. I'm gonna get me the biggest senorita I can lay my hands on and spend a week just wearing her out." He chuckled to himself and licked his greasy fingers. He pulled at one of the saddlebags and scooped out a handful of gold coins.

Billy picked some of them away, examining them. "You think Badger'll try to follow us?"

"Why should he?" asked Edward, as he shoved a bacon strip into his mouth.

"Cause we stole two of his best horses and killed one of his men, that's why!" Billy stated.

"He's got that girl on the mind. He won't come after us until he's got her back. By then we'll be too far into Mexico for him to follow."

"Fool shouldn't have gotten in our way," Billy stated.

"Shit, you'd have killed him even if he hadn't. Just 'cuz he laughed at you?"

"God-damned right."

"Right," Edward mocked him. "You let that temper of yours get out of control in Mexico and they're liable to hang you by the short and curlies. We need to keep a low profile. Let this whole thing blow over before we come back to the territories."

The young boy frowned and looked irritated. "I just don't like no one getting in my way," he snarled. Then sensing an impending argument with his partner, he tried to change the topic. "You think old man Badger hired those two to find his girl?"

Edward nodded. "Of course he did."

"Wonder what he paid them?"

The older man dropped the last greasy piece of bacon into his mouth. "What do you care?" he asked.

"Just wondering. You heard them wranglers say the girl is a real looker. Do you think…?"

"Here," Edward interrupted, handing him the skillet. "Wash this out and let's go."

"Damn it, Edward," Billy protested, "don't you listen to anything I got to say?"

The man stood up, irritated by the youngster's bickering. He snapped back, "Shit, you spend most of your daylight hours complaining about other people or bragging how you're gonna whoop their ass. Who cares what that girl looks like? We aren't gonna ever see her. I've had me a belly full of them slave-driving sonofabitches. I'm thinking about Mexico and that's all. You got other thoughts, keep them to yourself."

"Come on, Edward," whined Billy.

"Finish your coffee and let's go. That's the last you'll be eating until we reach Sonora."

The boy downed the last piece of bacon on his tin plate and chugged down his lukewarm coffee. "You're sure about that caravan that goes back to Mexico City every month?" he asked.

Edward nodded affirmatively. "That's right, every month - with a large escort of soldiers and civilians, at least 20 or more freighters each time. A few coins in the right man's hands and we've got us safe passage all the way down to Mexico way." He smiled to himself. He could see the brown skinned senoritas already. *It won't be long now,* he thought.

They broke camp quickly and rode down off the canyon rim and across the baked alkali flats. Billy rode in the lead; gun-ready and ever cautious, but more show than fact. He stared at the hills growing hazier in the distance.

"How far to them mountains?" he asked.

"We should be in them tonight. Take us a day to cross 'em. Then it's Sonora on the other side." Edward didn't like the idea of crossing those mountains or winding through the canyons and valleys surrounding its huge mass, but that was the fastest way to get over to Sonora. Chihuahua was closer but it didn't have the steady run of freighters going south. Sonora was their answer for safe passage out of the territories.

They rode in silence for a couple of hours. The day had begun fresh and cool but that quickly tore away as the sun climbed higher into the sky. By mid-afternoon, Edward heard birds chirping and went toward the sound. A shallow basin hidden among the stacked layers of boulders held a seep of water. They drank their fill and smoked a cigarette among the rocks. There was no movement around them - nothing in the air, and nothing on the ground.

"Hell of a place, ain't it, Edward?"

The man shielded his eyes, looking out across the wide sweep of land. "The Apaches can have it, he replied. Crushing his cigarette into the ground, the man rose. "Come on, we've got to move on if we're gonna reach those mountains by nightfall."

An hour later, beginning the ascent out of the desert flats and onto rising layers of dirt and rock, Edward reined in abruptly. He quickly dismounted and fingered the soil. It was the tracks of unshod ponies. Apaches!

The tracks were fresh indentations still untouched by time or the elements. Edward studied the terrain around him. There would be little protection if he and Billy came across the same Apaches in the open. And the tracks were heading in the same direction as they were!

"I don't like it," Billy protested in his best adult tone of voice. He cocked his new rifle. His eyes scanned the landscape probing for something, even if he wasn't certain what he was looking for. It still left a cold feeling in his gut.

"We're changing directions," Edward suddenly announced as he swung his mount around and headed up the slope at an angle away from the Indian tracks. "We'll go around those hills this way and hope like hell them Apaches aren't thinking of doubling back."

They had passed through a narrow valley and moved up into the folds of a second series of hills. The mountain spread out; more a series of high mountain buttes rather than a continuous link of mountains running in a chain. Between the rolling hills was a maze of trails to follow. Once out of the second series of hills, the two riders angled along a low-lying ridgeline and crossed it near the sweep of a plateau.

They rode up slowly, cautiously to the edge of the plateau. Then they sat on their horses, silently, patiently, listening to the wind for anything unusual. Edward twisted in his saddle, looking around. His body froze. He leaned forward toward the empty space beyond the plateau.

"Billy!" Edward whispered in a quick commanding tone. He slipped out of his saddle and motioned to his partner to do the same. Billy dropped out of his saddle, following his partners lead. A finger to the lips silenced any questions he might have had. Edward threw him the reins and motioned him back. Billy moved the horses into a chaparral grove. Then he crawled back to his partner, by the edge of the plateau.

For several minutes, they lay perfectly still. Edward refused to look up at Billy or answer his questioning eyes. Then they both heard movement.

It was the sound of hooves striking shale. Riders slowly came into view. It was several Apaches riding in a loose bunch. Several carried lances with feathered tips. Others had bows or carbines at ready. They were heading roughly parallel to the two men.

Edward touched Billy and motioned him to look away for fear of attracting the Indian's attention. Both men held their breath. The red-turbaned warriors were only a dozen or so yards away, right below them. If the Apache ponies sensed another presence close by, Billy and Edward were as good as dead.

Pressing their faces to the ground, both men listened to the movement below them. The Apaches made no sound except for the occasional click of hoof meeting stone. The Indians were studying the ground. Their markings indicated they were Mescalero Apaches, a long ways from their regular hunting grounds. Edward knew something had brought those Indians out on a search, but he didn't know what. The Apaches were past as quickly as they had appeared. Then they were gone.

"Christ," Edward exclaimed softly ten full minutes later, when he was certain the danger had passed. "They're more damn Apaches out here than the pack that captain was chasing. We gotta be careful. We'll camp in those hills tonight. Then move on about midnight. That should get us outta here by mid-morning tomorrow and in Sonora by tomorrow afternoon."

A Ruse

The race to find the Indians had been lost. There was no encampment of Apache women and children. The scattered remnants of a camp told the soldiers little beyond the fact that some Apaches had camped there briefly and then fled further south. No indication of how many, if any, warriors were in that group. A dead end chase for the cavalry once again.

Now Captain Branan stood on high ground, Badger at his side, scanning the distance with his one good eye, looking for any indication of Apache movement. There was none, and Badger was continuing his complaining about the two cowboys who had stole his horses and killed one of his ranch hands.

"Gonna hang those sons-a-bitches on the closest scrap of a tree I can find," he muttered and spat tobacco juice out of his puckered mouth.

"They'll be tried in a court if we ever find them," Branan interjected. "But chances of that happening are slim to none. They're probably down in Sonora or beyond by now. There's heavy traffic down there and an easy place to hide from the authorities."

"Still, if I catch them..." Badger began again, but the captain cut him off.

"I have more pressing issues right now and it doesn't include those two horse thieves. The Apache are either over the border now or close to it. A sweep to the North will catch any that have broken off for more raids up there. The others are long gone by now. You can do what you want Badger, I have my orders."

Badger kicked the dirt and spat out his tobacco again. He squinted his eyes against the harsh sunlight and spoke to no one in particular. "Still got to find out what happened to the girl. Dead or not, I got to know."

The captain let the old man go on. His rant was becoming painfully familiar. He kept muttering about 'finding out if she's alive or not.' It almost seemed as if Badger was more concerned about the girl's existence than whether she had been rescued. The captain thought it was a bit odd for an uncle talking that way about his only niece, but relationships were one thing the Captain didn't bother to worry much about. He had none, so why should he care?

"They said she was talking crazy the last week or so," Badger lied. "Don't know what that was all about." He seemed pensive for a moment, lost in thought. "She was strange all right. She had to be to come all the way out here and expect to stay at my place - just like that."

The captain began to move off, back to the column. He was lost in his own thoughts about the drifter that had brought in the supplies. Something about that man was strangely familiar, perhaps from past experiences or an old event in his army life.

The scout's eyes told the captain something. It wasn't just an unwillingness to look back straight at the captain, but also the way he handled himself - and a very slight limp the captain detected in the man's walk.

Hours in the saddle would cripple up anyone's ass for a good long time, but the eyes and the limp together made the captain feel inexplicably uneasy. As if something from his past was coming back to haunt him. Something he had left in the recesses of ancient battles and hard won victories; something he wanted to keep forgotten.

What it was the captain couldn't grab on to, so he let it go … for now. Both the scout and the mountain man had disappeared that first night, even before the two cowboys murdered the ranch hand and stole the horses the next night.

If, by chance, he came across either party, he would deal with them at that time. Badger could have his satisfaction of catching the two cowboys, but the other two, he'd just as well not see again. Something about the scout perplexed him, and he didn't know what the hell that was all about. It managed to afflict him nevertheless.

Crazy Eyes

Jeb Burns and the other two rode steadily through the still afternoon, thudding and clanking toward the ghostly hills. Heat wrinkled the air and weighed down heavily on all of them. The horses moved with heads hung in a drowsy trance. Their steps grew shorter as the mountains grew larger. They brushed carelessly against sage and thorns. Their riders seemed too tired to move out of the way.

A pale warning of dusk tinted the sky, penciling jagged outlines of peaks looming ever larger. It was the quiet, expectant hush of a dying day which hung over the land, peaceful and serene. But to the scout, it was a very deceiving scene. Dusk was a favorite time for Apache ambush, when most riders were exhausted from the heat and long hours in the saddle. The spring would be a lifesaver if it weren't occupied already. All they could do was get there and find out.

They entered the mountainous folds through a narrow, winding corridor squeezed between two rolling hills. They continued up onto a rock shelf bridging the gap. Crossing the short, wind-swept plateau, the trio descended into another series of breaks. They would wind in and out of them until they approached a thicket of mountain mahogany and cactus forms cradled in a depression. Centered in the green oasis, the trio could make out a spring. There was no sign of life around.

The horses smelled the water first, their heads suddenly up, muscles bunched as they strained to run. Sounds emanated from deep down their throats. Their hooves kicked up the sand.

"Careful," whispered the mountain man, cocking his Sharps. "Hold them still! If someone's there, we got trouble." He slipped to the ground, tossing his reins back to Burns. The scout handed both sets back to the girl. Then he and Pony cat-padded, bent double toward the thicket. Lottie waited, apprehensive. Seconds later, the scout reappeared and waved the girl in.

The spring was barely a foot deep, ruddy-bottomed and bordered with weeds, but it stretched for several yards, narrow in the middle and wide on both ends. By the time, Charlotte brought in the horses, sounds of splashing greeted her. She let the mounts eagerly join the two men splashing in the spring. She went to the other end. Both men had plunged into the spring, clothes and all. They were laughing and kicking at the brown swirling liquid. The mud ran down their faces as they rolled on their sides.

Charlotte, for a moment, forgot her company. She grabbed her calico skirt and lifting it above her knees; she jumped in, seat landing with a loud smack. Her clothes pressed tightly against her firm body as she climbed out. She didn't seem to notice it as she lay back on the sandy soil, feeling new energy surge through her whole body. Nor did she notice Pony's narrow eye-slits parading over her rising and falling breasts or the evil look he gave Burns after looking at the girl. Charlotte was too thirsty and too tired to notice. She kicked her legs, still in the water, and threw swirls of water into the air, laughing as she did it.

Jeb heard the laughter and felt good. He hadn't heard a laugh for a long time. It sounded almost refreshing. The two men flopped back on the ground and caught their breath. The horses stood, feet first in the water, and continued lapping up the water at a relaxed pace.

Pony saw it first, a small inconspicuous piece of clay. He looked around, alert and cautious, and then picked it up. "Scratch stick," he announced. "A raiding party's been through here. Can't tell when."

"A what?" Charlotte asked.

Jeb nodded in agreement. "It's a scratch stick," he explained. "Some buck left it after his fourth raiding party. Apache are very superstitious. The first four times a buck goes on the warpath, he can't scratch his head with his fingers or let water touch his lips. So he uses a scratching stick."

Jeb leaned over and picked up a small reed. "And he uses this," he said. "A drinking reed to get his water."

"So the Apache have been here too?" Charlotte asked, alert and very much afraid.

"Have been. Past tense." Jeb answered. "If they were still here, we wouldn't be alive right now."

Pony laughed at the two of them and shook his head in contempt. "Fools, I wouldn't have come here if I sensed there were Apache about," he snarled and turned away.

Dinner that night was a cold piece of jerked beef, frijoles, and morning biscuits. Although heat still rippled off the ground, Jeb heated a pot of coffee. Force of habit, he told himself. The bitter coffee felt good all the way down. Always did. Coffee and a cigarette if he had one. Simple pleasures for a simple man. If only it were true. He sleeved sweat off his forehead and leaned back against his saddle.

"Here," said the girl, holding out a dried, bent cigar.

Jeb took it and smiled.

"I got it out of my saddle bags. Must be one of my Uncle's."

He rolled the cigar in his lips. It was flaky, dried out. But he could smoke it. As he lit up, he caught the girl watching him but she looked away quickly when he glanced up.

The mountain man trudged away as soon as they'd finished eating. He took his medicine bag into the brush, moving along the waist high sage until the ground dropped him out of sight. Burns watched him go with intent eyes. He didn't like it. Twice before Pony had taken his scalps out and admired them until Jeb cursed and badgered him to put the grizzly trophies away. Pony's morbid fascination didn't particularly bother Jeb, but he knew it might upset the girl.

Soon they were alone in the dusk of a dying day. Jeb stared out into the inky blackness but couldn't see anything discernible more than ten feet away.

The girl moved back from the seep of water. Jeb turned around. Charlotte had moved across from him. She was wiping her hands on her skirt and pushing the hair out of her face. The water seemed to have brought her back to life. Her face looked fresh and clean. She seemed more at ease than Burns had seen her up to this point.

"Sir, it may seem a little silly to say, but we have not been formally introduced. I still do not know your name." The question came direct and with sincerity.

"Name's Jeb Burns, ma'am."

"Don't call me ma'am, please! Just call me Charlotte."

The scout raised an eyebrow, then smiled a slight curl of the lips and lowered it. He stared at the girl's beautiful eyes and handsome face. When he realized he was staring, he looked away, pretending to be listening to the darkness around them.

"Are you always so polite around women?" Charlotte asked in jest.

"Force of habit, I guess," Jeb replied, meeting Charlotte's smile with the wisp of a grin. He drew in deeply on the cigar and blew out a perfect blue ring which slowly spun through the dry air. They both watched it in silence as it slowly dissipated into the night air.

"What is your line of work?" Charlotte offered, trying to keep the words flowing between them. "When you're not rescuing damsels in distress, that is."

Jeb returned her stare and then seemed to break out of his mold. He raised himself up against the saddle pillow and took the cigar out of his mouth. He replied in a matter of fact tone of voice, "Sometimes I scout. Sometimes I trap. Sometimes I do what they call renegade riding; checking fence lines for ranchers. Some of the time, usually deep winter, I don't do much of anything."

"Then you're a drifter," Charlotte said.

"Sometimes," Jeb replied. "The back of a horse has been my home for many a year. That and a lot of mountain caves or miners cabins. Nothing permanent since before the war." He let it go at that.

They smiled together. The tension was slipping away between them. They could both sense it in their words and reactions to one another. Charlotte tried to carry the conversation forward.

"I read in the Tombstone Epitaph about those Tombstone Raiders and how they are fighting the Apache. Are you one of them?"

"Hardly," Jeb replied, shaking his head. "Most of them are riff-raff. Vigilantes or cheap tin horns looking for a thrill. They're no better than scalp hunters or bounty men. The troubles with the Apache won't stop as long as the whites kill the Apache and the Apache retaliates. Like a vicious circle of dogs."

"I cannot say I share your sympathy for the Apache," Charlotte said, "considering what fate has just befallen me. I was certain they were going to kill me."

"If not those warriors, then their women would have," Jeb answered frankly. "I wouldn't say what I feel is sympathy - just being realistic. There's killing on both sides and few people calling for an end to it without the extermination of the Apache and the other tribes for that matter. The Apache are a proud people and with chiefs like Hieronymo and Chato and Maugas, they have leaders who won't let their people die off without a fight. Like I said, it's a vicious circle." Jeb's voice began to trail off, his mind fixated again on some long forgotten skirmish with his Indian adversaries.

Charlotte looked up from the glowing embers and stared at this atypical man who seemed lost in his own thoughts. He wasn't what he seemed on the surface. Instead of the rough demeanor that she expected from a weathered old trail rider, Charlotte found in Jeb a cautious and reserved man who held back more than he was giving up. He was a far more intelligent and learned man than she had encountered during her brief time in the West. He was sympathetic toward the Apache but ready to kill them at a moment's notice.

Growing up, she'd watched her father bargain with other business associates. She learned to study their body language and the words they chose to use in negotiating. Jeb was among the best she'd heard. He was telling her the truth but not more than he thought she should hear. Yet for all the straight talk he was capable of, Charlotte could also sense that he had a darker side. She'd seen him face off with Pony and instinctively move to protect her. There was something beneath the man's façade he wasn't revealing to her. And even with her little time in the West, she knew no white man lasted in the mountains unless he was quick and cunning and willing to kill an adversary without hesitation.

"General Crook had the right idea. "He said to reason with the Apache and be honest. Show strength to backup your position and don't compromise on your own principles. The Apache respect that in an enemy, which is why they hate the Mexicans so much."

"Why the Mexicans?" Charlotte asked.

Jeb smiled. "Because Mexicans call themselves 'gente de razon' or 'people of reason.' The Apaches, all of them, are called 'barbaros.' With reasoning like that, it's not surprising that both parties just keep killing one another."

Jeb looked over at the girl and smiled. "Al Sieber, Crook's chief of scouts, once told me the Apache problems were just one stinking mess and the easiest way out seemed to have escaped most people. That was simply to treat the Apache right. See that they had enough food and clothes to keep them warm and let them live in the mountains around Fort Apache where they had been for years and years … centuries, really. And stop pushing them around. It was really as simple as that."

"And did they?" asked Charlotte.

"Of course not," Jeb replied with a sad smile.

Charlotte idly brushed the edges of unburnt wood into the remaining coals. The silence fell between them again and they let it linger there for a long time. Then one of them, Jeb couldn't remember who, began with an innocuous question. Just to say something. They spoke of the heat and the distance yet to travel … all of the safe things, but they were talking.

Charlotte poked at the fire's coals with a stick. A few remaining embers sparkled and leap up into the air. She looked over at the scout who was staring down at the fire, lost in his thoughts.

"Are we safe from the Apache now?" she asked.

Jeb glanced up at the half moon climbing in the sky. "You're never safe from the Apache, but they don't like the night. They prefer a full moon if they have to travel so they can see well in the darkness. They call it an Apache Moon and they won't travel far without it. Snakes spook them too, so do a lot of other superstitions that they've got."

"So we should be safe for the time being?"

Jeb smiled. "As you say, for the time being."

"Are there snakes around here?" Charlotte asked. "I hate snakes. I just hate them." She twisted her body and looked around the campfire.

"If you're worried I can lay out my rope. Rattlers won't crawl over a horsehair rope," Jeb replied, wondering how many questions the girl might have for him. The girl seemed satisfied with his answer. She sat back down and continued staring at the tiny flickering flames that curled up into the night sky.

Charlotte shook her head, which made her hair dance across her shoulders. "I feel incredibly grimy. Is there any place a lady might go to wash up? …I mean a private place."

Jeb pointed to a small knoll at the thicket's end. It was marked by a tall cactus void of any other vegetation. "There should be another small pool up there by the looks of it. Won't be much more than a seep but you can wash yourself and," he paused awkwardly, "you can do whatever you need to do."

"Are you sure it'll be all right?" she asked, looking around in the direction Pony had left.

"It's alright. He's gone to fashion his scalps. He won't bother you."

Charlotte wasn't sure. She wanted to clean up but shuddered at the thought of the mountain man prowling around outside camp. She looked to the scout for reassurance. His eyes held hers and spoke reassurance with a casual nod. She gave in to the scout.

"I shan't be long," she assured him.

"Take your time, ma'am … Charlotte," Jeb said as he slid down against the saddle. Charlotte smiled. She dug a towel out of her saddlebags and picked her way toward the cactus. She skirted the prickly pear and teddy-bear chollas whose thorns leaped out at her skirt and sleeves.

It was more a puddle than a spring. Its size had shrunk considerably that late in the season. Around the seep were shelves of bare rock where Lottie laid out her towel and nestled up to the muddy brown water. Looking around cautiously, the girl could see nothing above the sage except the crooked cactus directly behind her. It stood out against the fading skyline like a tall green scare-crow void of any clothes.

Peeling her buckskin shirt off, the girl cupped water and poured it slowly down her face and front. The brown liquid felt cool streaming down her dirty front and under her calico skirt. She rubbed the water over arms, face, and stomach. Muscles tightened at first contact, then relaxed as she rubbed the moisture in and grime away. Then she stretched her legs out the pool's width. Hiking up her calico to her pale white thighs, she dipped them in the water again and again, causing little ripples of waves back and forth. The tight-knotted muscles gradually loosened up a bit and she felt her whole body relax.

Amazing how a little water, even this brown mud, can mean so much, she thought. She smiled when she realized how she had taken something as simple as water so for granted. Now it meant the difference between life and death. *A bath like this means more than a dozen trips to the ocean back East.*

Something moved behind her. A boot crunched down on a dry leaf, then silence. Lottie spun around, rising off the ground, her skirt still bunched up around her thighs. Something was there. Someone was by the cactus - watching her.

Pony stepped out from behind the prickly trunk with a cruel smile and crazy eyes. He carried no weapon, nor did he have his medicine bag. He made no sound as he moved toward the girl, his eyes locked on her exposed cleavage. There was no mistaking his intent.

Charlotte screamed. She covered her breasts with her arms.

"I ain't gonna hurt you. Don't scream," he said through his beard. He flashed an even more gruesome smile and moved toward the girl. His eyes were like bug eyes - open but vacant. He almost seemed to be in a trance.

The sound of pounding feet came up from camp. The mountain man didn't seem to hear a thing. His attention was fixed on the girl and her heaving breasts. He pushed through the prickly pear and stomped over low-lying chollas. Both hands were dangling loosely by his side. Charlotte scrambled to her feet, dropping her skirt and scooping up her blouse.

"Pony!"

Jeb Burns broke through the brush, moving at a run. He carried his Spencer hip-high, and cocked. He moved in front of the girl, blocking Pony's advance. The Spencer was leveled at the mountain man.

"What the hell do you think you're doing?" Jeb said angrily. "Haven't we got enough to worry about without you getting fool ideas into your head? Go back to camp." He stood firm, bracing his legs. His hand rested on the rifle's trigger. Pony would have to get past him to get to the girl.

Like a charging grizzly confronted by a superior force, Pony stood his ground, pursing his lips. A look of puzzlement accompanied furrowed brows. Should he kill the scout right then or wait until later? His mind worked at the answer. His instinct wasn't working as quickly as before. Should or shouldn't he? He wanted the girl - badly!

The beard opened, revealing his barbaric yellow teeth. Pony snarled at the scout. "Alright, it's time we found out just how tough you really are. Either get outta my way or I'm gonna break your neck!"

Before Jeb could say a word, Pony moved forward. His huge arm shot up, slamming the rifle back against the scout's chest, shoving him aside. "Get outta my way," he growled. He moved toward Charlotte who backed up, one foot into the pool.

Jeb moved quickly. He took a step back, then thrusted forward and drove his rifle stock into Pony's kidney. The blow knocked the mountain man off stride. He stumbled sideways and caught his balance. His expression hadn't changed. He registered no reaction to the stunning blow. Charlotte's eyes were opened wide in fearful amazement. Pony sucked in his gut, his chest rising like a balloon. He turned to the scout.

"Put the gun away," he said with gritted teeth. "I'm gonna see what kind of scrambler you really are." He moved forward again. He snarled. "You want the girl? She's yours … if you best me. If you don't, I'm gonna kill you, nice and slow. After I've…"

The blow caught Pony just aside the chin. It snapped his head backwards and buckled his legs. He fell in a heap at the scout's feet. Jeb lowered his rifle and turned to the girl.

"You all right?" he asked.

The girl nodded weakly, still shaken by the entire incident. She turned her back to Jeb and slipped the shirt over her head, then turned back to face him.

Jeb reached out for her arm.

"Look out!" she screamed.

The solid blow hit the scout just below the nape of his neck. It pitched him forward, arms out flung, against the girl and sent them both crashing into the pool. The Spencer spun in the air and landed in a thorn bush. Jeb brought himself up, sitting in the muddy seep. Charlotte was saying something but he couldn't register the words. His head rang with pain. He fought to catch his breath.

"Are you okay?" she asked. He nodded dumbly.

Pony moved to the pond's edge, his paws stuck in his waistband. He was laughing, taunting the scout, and urging him out of the pool to fight.

Jeb climbed slowly to his feet, then out of the pool. Pony backed off, preparing for the final, fatal blow. Then he moved in, grunting. It was almost a growl, deep throated and animalistic. He rushed the man who stood wavering before him. He'd kill him once and for all.

Jeb waited until the last possible second then he jerked to one side of the mountain man's wild lunge. He chopped a taut, solid fist down hard on the thick-corded neck. It hurt Pony, drawing a deep gulping sigh from the hirsute attacker as he lumbered sideways, crashing into a teddy-bear cholla. Spitting out his tobacco plug, the man angrily backhanded the spiny needles off his arms and legs. He rubbed his neck. His breathing was deeper, heavier. He had been tricked. The scout had been faking his pain. Uncontrolled anger welled up inside. *Now,* Pony thought, *now I'll kill him for sure.*

Pony's next rush was a well-executed fake. He lunged, arms outspread, at the scout then sensing his opponent's movement, he quickly sidestepped

his stride and sent a balled up fist smashing into the man's chest. Jeb reeled back, shooting up his arm to knock away another blow, but missing a third which sent him spinning into a clump of sage. He flew over the brush, his legs in the air, and then rolled over in the dirt.
Charlotte gasped and Jeb fought to hold on to his consciousness. The ground was blurry and tilted. A haze of pain-laden scarlet floated like a trapped sunburst behind his eyelids. Jeb felt sick inside, his guts heaving up and down, in and out. He tried to steady himself as he arose, doubled over in pain.

Pony stood his ground, throwing glances over at the girl. She took a step toward the gun. "Do it, missy, and I'll kill him right now! You just stay where you are," he said. Lottie clenched teeth and stood her ground.

The mountain man bent over and took a piece of plug tobacco out of his leggings. He tore off a piece and chewed on it, open-mouthed. "Come on, Coon," he said mockingly, "Come and get me." He broke into a guttural laugh.

Then he grunted something and moved in. His huge paws spread out, ready. His beard jerked as he chewed. Red saliva formed on his lips. Jeb was still bent over in pain. He wasn't even looking at the mountain man. Pony could see the quivering legs almost buckle then steady just a bit. It's gonna be easy, he thought to himself. The scout is done for.

The realization he had been tricked again struck home with the split second show of Jeb Burn's boot. Pony's eyes widened. His mouth dropped open. His hands grabbed for his groin just as Burn's boot smashed into it.

Pony staggered back in pain. His legs started to buckle inwards. He looked with pain-filled eyes just as the scout chopped his fist across the man's throat. A choking gargling sound came from the man's lips as he fell sideways to his knees.

Jeb stood wavering, trying to catch his balance. Pony started to get up, slowly. Jeb danced one step, then two, and kicked up his leg straight into the mountain man's face. Pony's head snapped back with a sickening crack. His arms wildly flailed in the air, churning in circles. He stumbled backwards, trying to catch his balance. Blood flowed freely out his mouth and nostrils.

Even as he was stumbling backwards in awkward motion, Jeb was up against him, pounding his lightning fast jabs into the swaying buckskin form. Pony brought up an arm to ward off the blows. It did little good. Jeb stepped inside a looping left with a cutting blow to the chin. Pony's bloodied face had gone pale white. He moved his lips but nothing came out. His granite stature was beginning to crumble. A lucky blow caught the scout by the ear but he turned with it, glancing off of it. The blow was ineffective.

The mountain trapper swayed back and forth. His arms moved mechanically, disjointed. They were of no use whatsoever. A knee buckled and the man was down on one leg. He tried to raise himself up. Jeb locked fists and swung back. Pony looked up with glazed eyes in time to see the balled up hands smash into his face. That was the last thing he saw. Like a giant pine, the mountain veteran simply toppled over, face first, into the dirt. He landed with a heavy thud and a small puff of dust.

Pony's body twitched once … twice … then laid still. Faint moaning sounds came from his scarlet-streaked, swollen face. Jeb felt the steel-spring tension go out of him. He felt empty inside, exhausted, drained of all conceivable energy. His legs were turning to rubber and he had to swing his arms out to regain his balance. Then the girl was next to him, supporting his swaying body. He felt her arm around his waist and leaned against her for support. A faint scent of something fresh greeted his senses. Her hair felt good, curled over his scarred knuckles.

Jeb looked down on the battered form lying before him with scarcely any emotion - only pity and a tempered anger came through. Jeb moved away from Charlotte and toward the pool. He cupped water in his hand and felt its stinging effect on his lips. Watered down blood ran down to his chin as he splashed on the liquid. Charlotte handed him her towel. He pushed it away and used his sleeve. Then he cupped more water and went back to the still form on the ground. He let the water run in trickles down the swollen eyes and puffed up checks. Some ran in and then out of the redlined teeth. No reaction from Pony. The water sank into the sand. Pony lay curled up, almost embryo fashion, in the dirt.

Finally Jeb squatted down by the prone figure. He bent over so his lips were close to the man's ears. "Your word, Pony. No more trouble! Do I have it?" he asked softly.

Pony nodded weakly, not looking up.

"I'm holding you to it. Until she's safely back at the ranch. Otherwise, I swear to the almighty, I will kill you."

The mountain veteran nodded again weakly then vomited up the rest of his dinner. Jeb left him lying in the dirt. He picked his Spencer out of the brush and taking Lottie by an elbow he led her back toward camp. His only chance now was that the mountain man would keep his word. A man's word was sacred among the mountain men and Jeb hoped that would hold true until they returned to safety.

The girl's face was still pale and grave. She kept glancing over her shoulder at the still figure left behind. A look of fear and concern wore heavily on her face. Burn's face revealed nothing. He still sucked in air heavily, trying to adjust his walk to the pain shooting throughout his body. He lifted his hand and licked a bleeding knuckle. The movements brought him to awareness of a score of joints crying in pain, of an immense weariness that tugged at every fiber of his body. But he knew the real pain and aching wouldn't be felt bone-deep until the next day.

Charlotte looked up at Jeb as they moved through the brush. "Aren't you worried about him?" she asked," I mean, that he'll come back and kill us in the middle of the night."

Jeb tried a weak smile. It failed. "I've got his word. You heard him. For a mountain man that's usually enough. If Pony's like the other mountain men, he won't be any trouble; at least not until we get back to the ranch. By then you'll safe and I'll be on my way."

"But…"

"Look!" Jeb said, stopping to look down into the girl's worried face. His voice lowered. "Look. We don't have any choice. I can't kill the man. To disarm him would do no good whatsoever. So I've got to rely on his word. It's that, or leave him hog-tied to a cactus and hope he doesn't catch up to us." The voice dropped even more, edged with concern. "It's our only choice. Don't worry about it. Trust me. It is the only way."

"That's not what I meant," Charlotte let out. Jeb gave her a puzzled look. "Forget it," she said and moved on.

As they crowned the sage and entered the camp clearing, Charlotte studied Jeb's face. His words had come out as a simply stated fact of life. As if it were almost taken for granted. Like tomorrow would come as today had. He seemed neither concerned nor particularly worried about it. As they settled in by the remnants of the fire, Burns rubbed his shirt against the spots where the blows had battered him.

"Does it hurt much?" Charlotte asked.

"Not as much as it's going to tomorrow," he answered with a weak grin. Charlotte dropped down across from him, staring up at the twinkling stars, which dotted the clear dark sky.

Jeb studied the girl's face. She had a strong chin, probably from her European ancestry. Her cheekbones were smooth and curved just right, not stark and jutting like so many of the hardened frontier women Jeb had known in Tucson and Santa Fe. She was nothing like the soiled doves and painted pigeons who worked the back rooms of most saloons.

She was a stunning woman, yet nowhere as soft and fragile looking as those fancy ladies he had seen in the picture magazines long ago. There was toughness about her, a fiber that ran from her speech to her horsemanship. It was a characteristic he admired without being able to pin down exactly what it was.

Charlotte had survived her capture by the Apaches. The forced march and imprisonment hadn't dampened her spirit or her will to live. There was much more substance to the woman than her good looks and ready smile would allow to be shown. The scout was puzzled. He'd never meet such a woman in the tough and unforgiving world in which he lived.

The girl looked down and returned his stare with a smile. It disarmed him totally.

"What did you start to say back there?" Jeb asked. Charlotte ignored his question. He let it go. It was a baffling turn of events for both of them.

"Where are you from?" he asked without thinking. "I mean, your uncle said back East someplace."

"Philadelphia," she said, and then realized who she was talking to. The girl seemed to be searching for words. "A big city called Philadelphia."

Jeb smiled. He wasn't that foreign to this country. "I've heard of it," he replied. "Much too big for me. Atlanta was too big for me before the blue coats burnt it down." He let it pass. Enough said about that.

Charlotte continued, "That seems like such a long time ago. It isn't really, but it feels that way. I plan to travel to the West coast and another city called San Francisco, seeing as it didn't work out at Uncle Badger's." The words came out straight and true and totally devoid of any feeling.

"So your folks are gone?"

Charlotte looked straight into Jeb's eyes. They held firm, rigid, unflinching. He felt very ill at ease. He hated that he had started the conversation in the first place. He wanted out but didn't know how to change the subject.

Charlotte replied with a total lack of emotion. "They're dead and gone now… as is my life back East."

Change of subject, quick! Jeb thought. This was far too awkward to continue. He stammered, "If you don't mind my asking; why'd you come out to this Godforsaken place? I'm sure it wasn't the fresh air and sunshine that brought you."

Charlotte gave Jeb a funny look and a quick smile that released a lot of the trepidation in the air. "No," she said with a weak smile. "It wasn't fresh air and sunshine that brought me."

The embers luminesced her eyes, wide and soft blue. She paused before continuing and dug a comb out of her saddlebag. She started raking the comb through her thick copper hair, sending static electricity crackling on the ends.

Jeb watched her silently, wishing he had a cigar or cigarette - anything for his coffee nerves. He chewed unconsciously on his mustache and bit his lips.

Charlotte began her story in a voice soft and low.

"My parents were poor Irish when they first came to this country. They were Irish-English, actually, which is worse. They made it in a tough town with a lot of folks working against them. My father was a very hard worker and he knew how to buy and sell properties. He knew which way the trade was moving and where the next bunch of immigrants would be settling in. After some time, he held a number of properties and a lot of new immigrants beholden to him. That didn't sit well with certain types."

Charlotte smiled thinking about her parents and their hard work. "They didn't think the Irish should get ahead like that. They made it known that we should remember our station. It was the custom, they said. There was propriety to follow and it didn't allow for my people to accumulate a lot of property or money. They even called me a free thinker. I believe it scared them a lot."

Jeb smiled at Charlotte. He'd never met such a spirited woman as her. She was focused and sure of herself. Certainly nothing like the other women he'd come across in his travels. She noticed his smile and returned it.

"But last year's crash hurt my father badly and some of the other businessmen used that as leverage against him. Then there was a fire and my parents were gone."

"I'm sorry," Jeb said. It fell on deaf ears.

"I didn't feel safe there anymore. Those men wanted all traces of my family gone, myself included. I couldn't stay even if I had wanted to. So the West beckoned me and I had to answer."

"So Badger's place seemed like the answer?"

"Exactly," Charlotte replied, adding, "or it did at the time"

"And?"

"It didn't work out," was all she said.

Now Jeb was confused and intrigued at the same time. Something happened back at the ranch. But what? "So why did you leave so suddenly?" he asked. "Your uncle said you just up and disappeared. Left with some line rider."

Charlotte glanced sideways at the scout as her brush raked the curls for the last time. "Let's just say I had to leave, and I needed a way to get out of there. I found a friend, a boy, who agreed to help me get away. He knew the layout of the land well enough to guide me away from the ranch and directly west. He and I started talking and I convinced him to help me leave without anyone else seeing us go." She paused to collect her thoughts. "He agreed to help me get away. That's all. He didn't want any favors in return." She looked at Jeb again, straight and direct. "He was a nice young man. He was good to me. I liked him."

That was it. It was all out in the open and now he knew the girl's unsettling story. It left the scout having no idea what was to come next.

"So I left, and once we're out of this trouble I'm heading straight West to the coast."

"We've got to get you back to the ranch first," Jeb commented. "Your uncle is counting on us."

"Jeb," Charlotte began, her voice down an octave. "there's not a chance on earth that's going to happen!"

"What?" Jeb said, startled by the explosive statement from Charlotte.

"I'm not going back. Not ever. And don't ask me why. Once we're away from the Apaches, I will be heading out on my own. And don't try to stop me." Her Irish temper flared and Jeb saw the cold steel in her eyes.

"Ma'am…Charlotte, your uncle paid us to do a job. When I have a job to…"

"Mr. Burns, I don't want any trouble between us, please … but I can't … I won't go back there."

Jeb stared into the piercing eyes and held firm. Finally a smile cracked his rigid façade. The smile widened until it disarmed the woman staring him down.

Let it go, he thought to himself. She was tired and confused and scared. Once they were out of danger, she would come back to her senses and he could get her back to the ranch. Whatever happened back there couldn't have been that bad. Not enough to warrant her never going back. He'd be there with her just in case. He would do what he set out to do and that was that.

"It's late" Jeb began. "We can deal with it once we're out of danger from the Apache. No need to get yourself all worked up about it. We need to get plenty of rest because tomorrow we're going to have to push it hard to put distance between us and the hostiles."

"Just so you know…"

"When the time comes, Charlotte. You're going to have to trust me here."

Their eyes meet again, locked in place. A smile slowly began to curl up the girl's lips. The tension was gone between them then.

"Let's go to sleep…now."

Charlotte put her brush away and reached for her saddlebag. She drew out a worn tattered slip of a blanket. Then she flipped the blanket out and over her as she lay back down. She looked at Jeb as she curled up on her side.

"I'm trusting you," she announced softly and then added. Will you be close by?"

"Yep," Jeb said, "I'm not going anywhere." He stared at her still form until he could hear her steady breathing as she fell into a deep sleep.

He watched her for the longest time. The feeling of helplessness and confusion was almost overwhelming. He couldn't understand the feelings that were screwing up his head. He felt protective. Like a guardian suddenly assigned the job of helping and protecting and caring for a girl. No, a young lady who wasn't asking for help at all. But at the same time, a woman who had opened herself up completely to him; sharing and revealing intimate secrets about her past.

What the hell kind of a fix was he in now? Apaches hot on his trail, a crazy mountain man for a companion, and a fine young woman who was stirring up feelings he hadn't felt for a very long time.

A sound pricked Jeb's ear. He slipped out his colt and turned around in one quick, fluid motion. The blue barrel lined up on a dark figure standing in the clearing behind him. It cocked. Then the figure moved into the glow of moon-washed sand. Pony stood groggy and unbalanced from the fight. He stood for a time, like a drunk without a post to lean on, staring with vacant eyes at the glowing embers. The scout held up a tin of reheated java. Pony came forward.

"Here," Burns said, handing over the tin. The trapper grasped it with both bruised hands and slowly sipped on the black thickness. His face was badly swollen. Through the mangy beard, Jeb could see the lips were split and caked with dried blood. But the real hurt still came throbbing up from between his legs. The trapper dropped from his squat to a sitting position. He moved awkwardly and with visible pain.

"Tomorrow we go past the ruins, then Badger's spread another day from there," Jeb said.

Pony shook his head and continued to sip the java. When he finished, he cocked one eye up under a bushy eyebrow. He lowered the tin and said, "They're close. Real close."

Anxiety drained Jeb's face of emotion. "How do you know?" he asked.

"I found where they'd been waiting here for a long time. Waitin' to ambush us or someone else. Then another bunch joined them and they all left together. Maybe 12 hours ago. They was headin' in about the same direction we will be tomorrow."

"How many were there?"

"Dozen or so all together, but I figure there'll be more up ahead. If it's us they're lookin' for, we got trouble sure as hell."

"How can you be so sure?" Charlotte asked, awakened by their conversation.

"Apache viento de la muerte." Pony muttered. "Apache death wind. All the conditions are right for them to find us. No doubt about it."

"I don't understand," Charlotte said.

"Cutting signs for the Apache depends on weather and terrain. Both are right for them to find us soon. Wind is blowing out of the East now. It'll shift by morning and take our scent or anything else we kick up right back to the Apaches. They're in no hurry to find and kill us. Once they've got our scent they'll find us, sure as hell they will. Then they wait for the right moment and…"

CHAPTER ELEVEN

The Army column worked its way down off a series of rolling plateaus and into an expanse of flat lands. There was still no sign of the Apaches or the two missing cowboys from Badger's ranch. The hot air smelled of dust from the dry land everywhere. A slight breeze was blowing off the ridgeline, hardly disturbing the overwhelming quiet of the bottomlands. Captain Branan and Badger were lost in their own thoughts, oblivious to one another.

For Branan, the unfocused image of the scout was still lurking in the back of his mind. Even as he accessed and mulled his past actions, the captain couldn't figure out where he might have come across this man. *Nothing recent, that's for sure,* he told himself. Since the captain's move out West from one series of barracks to another; he had come across a lot of different folks, military and civilian, but none like the scout.

He wasn't union, that's for sure. He didn't have the military bearing or the familiarity with U.S. Army matters to be a veteran of the Army of the North. Probably a Galvanized Yankee, a Johnny Reb out of the service, and working the West like hundreds of others just like him.

But it was his face that Branan couldn't forget and yet still couldn't place. The black eyes, the piercing stare, the simmering of some kind of recognition underneath a facade of emptiness. The captain was uneasy. He looked forward to the time when he might cross paths with the man again. He'd have him arrested on charges of leaving the ranch against military orders. Then, when he was in custody, the captain would determine who he was and if he posed any danger to the captain.

Badger, for his part, was trying hard to hide his true feelings of anxiety about his niece. If she were still alive, he'd have to deal with her before she could talk. He was certain she knew far too much to stay alive. Bradford, that dumb kid, had probably told her about the army horses and the switching of stock. He was dead and the girl was the only liability left.

Even if she didn't know about Badger cheating the army, then his own attempt at 'having the girl' would bring him a prison term or even a hanging. A young girl like that, looking like she did, could turn the head of any jury of sympathetic cowboys.

Now Badger's only chance at avoiding the consequences of his actions was to make certain the Apaches had killed the girl. If she was still alive, he had to make sure she didn't stay that way.

Badger motioned toward a series of foothills in the distance. Even from their distance away, Badger could see the slopes were heavy with shale and loose rock, impossible for Army mounts to crest.

"Only two kinds of animals can climb that slope," he said, "mountain goats and Apaches; no difference between the two of them."

Branan smiled and said nothing. Badger rambled on, "Damn Mescalero is one of the smallest tribes among the Apache but one of the most troublesome. Wish you Army boys could take care of that problem before it gets any worse."

"We're doing everything we can, Mr. Badger," Captain Branan replied apathetically. "As a supplier of Army mounts, you should know better than most the situation that Washington has put us all in. I swear politics have killed more good troopers than any amount of Apache arrows could. Damn shame, the politicians just can't stay out of our way and let us get on about the business of cleaning up the West, the way we were meant to do. Damn shame!"

Captain Branan swung around to the first sergeant. "Sergeant" he said. "Take a squad and cover that ridgeline. Stay off its slopes, footing is bad. Keep the men alert for signs of the Apaches passing. Understood?"

"Yes, Sir!" The sergeant replied as he swung his mount around and waved for a squad of men to follow him.

The captain turned to Badger. "You do understand, Mr. Badger, that the chances of our finding your niece alive are getting slimmer by the hour?"

"Yeah, I understand, but I have to do something. She is my only niece."

"I understand your concern," the captain said with as much sympathy as he could muster. "The Army will do all it can. That's all I can promise."

"I may stay with you boys for a couple more days, just in case you find any signs of her - that she's alive, I mean." Badger kept looking ahead at the line of blue trotting along the bottoms of the ridgeline in the distance.

"You're welcome to stay with the column for as long as you like. My orders remain the same. Pursue the hostiles until contact is made."

The two men fell back into a quiet complacency; adjusting their saddle positions to relieve the constant pain in their backsides. The air remained hot and still. Only the sound of iron clad hoofs stepping and falling in the hard packed ground rose up to disturb their own world of silence.

Ribbon of Smoke

"It'll be light soon. If trouble's coming, that'll be the time it happens."

Pony's grim assessment captured the mood of the moment perfectly. Dawn was the preferred time for an Apache attack. Jeb and the mountain man knew it and could only wait to see if it would happen.

"You think they're close?" Jeb asked, scanning the ridgeline along with Pony.

The mountain man eyed the hills which were still dark and somber. Then he replied with a nod. "Oh, they're out there alright. If they don't see us or hear us or smell us, then we got a chance. Not much, but some." The mountain man gnawed off a piece of plug tobacco and chewed it slowly, his sore mouth giving him a stab of pain with every chomp. "We've got ourselves a couple of hours before we reach those canyons leading out of here. If they hit us before then, we'll pay hell getting away."

The horses clip-clopped along, their saddles creaking in the still gray hour of pre-dawn. The morning hinted of breaking clear and blue-skied, which meant it would be a very hot day.

As the haze gave way, Burns could see buttes and mesas lined solid against the pale gray horizon. He distanced the rock and clay sentinels at two or three miles away, with a foreground of broken, tortured land stretched out before them.

Charlotte was feeling better. The rest had eased her nerves. She woke with a start but without complaint. There was no breakfast that morning. They had ridden two hours before sunup, keeping to the jumbled hills instead of the quicker moon-washed canyon bottoms.

Rest had been a ten minute stop by a ragged seep, holed in a shallow cut of rocks known only to the nomadic Apaches and mountain men like Pony. The mountain man grunted familiar complaints and sharpened his knife. Charlotte soft-talked her spent horse, rubbing down its shoulders and flank. Burns kept to himself, scanning the dark curtain of hills for signs of trouble. Aside from the sounds of night creatures big and small, nothing unusual stirred.

As darkness slipped away, gathering in its shadows, the girl moved close to the scout. Her young face showed wrinkles of concern. She was worried about her mount. The mare was steadily growing weaker. It had worn itself badly during their frantic dash from the Apache rancheria.

Even the slower pace had done little to relieve its suffering. When Badger had given the horse to Pony and Burns, he cautioned them it was a fuzzy old bronco that had seen better days. However, under the circumstances, it was the only horse not taken that he could spare.

Jeb nodded good morning to the approaching girl and resumed searching the horizon.

"I'm worried about my horse. He's in bad shape. I don't think he's going to make it. What will we do?"

The scout threw her a quick look and motioned back toward the grounded horses. "Don't let it weigh on you," he lied. "If he goes, we'll have to double up. That's all there is to it. We didn't come all this way to be stopped by a lame horse."

"Oh," the girl said, resting her hand unexpectedly on Jeb's arm. He stopped to face her. "About last night, I gather some things were said that probably did not make much sense to you; about things back at my Uncle's place.

Jeb tried to look reassuring though he wasn't quite certain how to do it. "I think I understood," he said and then paused, searching for the right words. "It wasn't any of my business. I'm sorry if I took liberties with my inquiry."

"Oh no!" the girl said quickly. "It wasn't that ... but … you see … well, there are simply some things I do not wish to ever discuss."

Gently, without trying to draw notice to it, Jeb removed the girl's hand still planted on his arm and moved her toward the horses. He walked close beside her. She moved without complaint, her head bowed in silent thought.

She's all woman, Jeb thought. *Young, pretty … no, beautiful. Plenty of spirit; or spunk, depending on one's mood and tolerance level. She'd make a good wife if someone could tame her down a bit. That would be a man-sized task.*

Dawn's hush drew his attention away from the girl. He signaled the group to mount their horses. "We need to keep moving," Jeb said. "The Apaches are sure to be on us soon. Stay alert." A soft bird whistle, a sound, a pebble or anything that distracted them from their keen watch meant danger. If the trio stopped even for a second, a bullet or quartz arrow could be launched straight for their backs.

Pony cocked his buffalo rifle and laid it across his pommel. Canteens slouched against the saddles and Charlotte's horse paused to blow out his lungs. Fluid ran out his mouth. The animal wouldn't last much longer.

The growing sunlight first lit up towering peaks among the buttes then moved down among rocky outcroppings. It sent a mellow hue among the spiny forest of tall saguaros, organ pipes, and clumps of chollas. The only sound was an occasional crack of shod hoof meeting rock or shale laid open by time.

Jeb Burns' slit eyes scanned the rough outstretch of hills dotted with wisps of Palo Verde trees. He saw nothing unusual. Yet even as he absorbed the topography of the bottoms and surrounding hills, his eyes probed every rise, every dip for a sign of hostiles, Jeb's mind raced over the last evening, trying to isolate Charlotte's words, to remember exactly what the girl had said.

Charlotte's face, crystal clear and radiant, came back. Like a cloud, it floated inside his mind, hazy just beyond his consciousness. He remembered and then he didn't. She was telling him something with her eyes and gestures. There were those pauses and secretive glances. He could see her again and then he couldn't. She was there and then gone. The girl beside him wasn't the same as before. He wasn't the same person since last night. Maybe they were both different now and he didn't recognize it. His years in the mountains had numbed, almost buried his reflections of most things past. He wasn't ready for a girl like Charlotte to come into his life, not so quickly, not so strongly.

Suddenly his eyes, floating in a vacant stare, focused sharply. He thought he saw movement up ahead, but fastening his eyes on the spot, he could see nothing. Anxiety coursed through him. He imagined a set of eyes trailing his every movement. Cold metal locked on his profile as if his chin was resting in a barrel notch and someone's finger was on the trigger. The night air was quickly fading into morning warmth. Quiet stillness bothered him. Though natural and ordinary, he didn't like the perfect hush. He could feel that something was amiss.

The party moved into a shallow basin; a sandy-bottomed washout from the surrounding hills. Sand muffled the sound of their horses' hooves. The air released more whisperings of heat reflecting off rocks and boulders. There were few clouds to provide shade. Burns tilted his soiled narrow-brimmed hat lower in front and trailed a hand down his rifle boot.

They were fast approaching the spot where Burns first thought he'd seen movement. There was little room for cover. If anyone was out there, they'd be in a good position to fire down on the trio, and the three would pay hell seeking cover. Up ahead, the wash narrowed into a single corridor running between two large boulders then curving out of sight.

When they reached the boulders, Burns walk-trotted through. The rock sides were still cool and shade brought back a moment of evening coolness. Once out of the protective boulders, the wash dropped down into a large empty basin. Burns glanced at the girl but she returned his look with a blank stare. Her mind was on other things. Beads of perspiration had already formed across her forehead and darkened under her arms. Unwashed, tangled hair lay matted against her forehead, a shade darker with sweat. She fretted concern for her horse, patting its mane and stroking its neck. The gelding didn't respond as it plodded along weakly.

The basin was shaped like a huge kettle, rough-cut on the bottom. In the distance, they could see a series of breaks leading out of the basin. One of those canyons, Pony assured them, would lead them out of the mountainous range and back toward Badger's spread.

Loose reined, the horses picked their way down the tricky gravel slope into the basin. There was no room for hiding or to launch an ambush in the basin. There were no arroyos for Apaches to hide in or rolling hills to hide behind. Burns was beginning to feel a little better already.

Then it happened.

Gunfire cracked the still air. Charlotte screamed. Her gelding dropped, pitching the girl head over heels down the slope. A bullet split the air past Burns' head. He swung around, half out of the saddle, his Spencer cocked and ready. Pony was already out of his saddle and crouched on the ground, searching for a target.

"Freeze, or the girl gets it!" The voice was shrill and nervous. It came from the bare ridgeline directly behind them.

Pony started to ease back toward the scout.

"That goes for you too, fat man!"

The mountain man, his face taut, squinting against the sun, searched for the ambushers. He saw nothing; neither gunpowder nor smoke - not a soul. His big Sharps still rested ready in his hand, but he dare not use it.

Jeb looked back at the girl. She was slowly getting up, shaking dirt out of her hair and clothes. Her face was scratched and covered in a mask of dirt. Luckily she had pitched into a spit of sandy soil, which had broken the fall and not her back. Her skirt was torn to her knee and her shirt hung out all around her waist. The mare laid still, its legs frozen in motion and its long graceful head splattered with blood.

Pony kept scanning the jagged ridgeline. His body relaxed but was rigid, just waiting for a break. He whispered through his broken lips, "It's one of them two varmints that went with us. I recognize the bastard's voice."

Jeb felt intense anger and frustration boiling up. They were trapped, helpless under a grueling sun and the gun sights of hidden ambushers they couldn't see or hope to hide from. The girl was visibly shaken up, maybe even in shock, and her mount dead. Two people on a horse in rough desert country would wear an animal down quickly; and that was not to speak of the Apaches still roaming the hills, perhaps close by.

"There's one of them now!" said Pony, nodding off to their right.

Burns risked a glance over his shoulder. He saw Billy dropping off a large boulder and strutting down at an angle toward them. He carried a yellow boy: a new Winchester model 1866, hip-level, aimed in the girl's direction. He was grinning and chuckling to himself.

"Throw down your guns. Easy like," commanded the boy-man.

Jeb turned toward the ridgeline.

Edward's head appeared along the crest of the ridge. He crested the rim and stood straddling the rock, pointing another yellow boy down at the group. Missing teeth showed clearly in his smile. He wore two revolvers, low-slung, and smoked a thin cigar. His checks were dark with a scruffy beard. His eyes squinted in the brightness reflected off the rock.

Burns and the mountain man let their gun belts slip down their hips. The girl still stood by her dead mount, too numb and scared to move. She didn't acknowledge Billy's presence. Jeb knew they were trapped for sure. The basin behind them offered no protection. Billy had already sided up next to Charlotte, placing her between himself and the two men he still regarded with caution. Jeb could tell immediately the youngster was his cocky self again. His walk was like a tough strut. He had the upper hand.

"Back away from them horses," Billy ordered. They complied. The young boy ran his eyes over the girl's figure, concentrating on her buckskin blouse hanging out and the tear in her calico skirt. He liked what he saw.

"Now throw over the canteens," Edward called down from his perch above them.

"What the hell for?" Pony growled.

"Shut up and do it!" Billy spat out, training his piece on the mountain man's protruding stomach.

Edward disappeared for a moment then reappeared at a jog around the boulder. They collected the canteens and took turns drinking down the liquid greedily. The precious liquid dribbled down their chins and checks. Even as they lapped down the water, both held their rifles on their hostages. Neither Pony nor the scout doubted their ambushers would open up if either one of them made a move.

Burns grew irritated at the terrible waste of water. “Christ, take it easy on that water. It’s all we got,” he said with a snarl.

Billy dropped the canteen and jerked the Winchester’s long blue barrel straight into Burns’ face. “You keep your mouth shut. You hear? You ain't in charge no more. We’re giving the orders around here.” Then another thought came to him. “Anyway you got no use for this water, not anymore. Not when we’re done with you.” He broke into laughter.

“Shut up, Billy!” His partner warned him.

“Well, what are we gonna do with them?” Billy demanded to know, dropping the rifle out of Jeb’s face to his belly.

Edward regarded the youngster with a cold eye and then turned to the others. His face was caked with dirt and the water had run thin lines darkening the layer on his chin. A crude lip curl broke out. He said nothing, eyeing his prisoners and their female companion.

Charlotte felt uneasy with his stare. She pulled her calico together with her fingers and tucked the buckskin back in around her waist. A look of anger began to grow on her face.

“What do you want from us?” Burns demanded, distracting the man.

Edward pursed his lips, enjoying the uneasiness of the three. Billy waited impatiently for him to respond. The girl was frightened but also defiant at the same time. Only the mountain man seemed lost to the dire situation they were in. He gazed toward the hills, studying the distant skyline. He ignored everyone else.

“Money. That’s what we want,” Edward finally said. “We figured you and the fat man had gone after the old man’s girl. He must have paid you something in advance. We want it!”

“Take the money and be off with you then,” Charlotte snarled.

Jeb glanced over at the girl, surprised by her sudden outburst. Then he calmly said. “And if we refuse?”

“Talk sense,” Edward smiled, “If you refuse, we kill all three of you. And take the money anyway.”

Jeb's face strained with pent-up rage. His chest swelled up as his breathing became faster. "You bastards plan to kill us anyway," he shot back.

"Cut the gabbing, Edward," his partner demanded. "Let's take the money and get the hell outta here."

"And them?"

"Hell, kill them," Billy spat out, cocking the long rifle.

"Shoot that thing off again, boy, and we're all dead - including you and your partner."

Both men snapped their heads and rifles toward the mountain man who stood motionless in front of them. His face registered no emotion. The statement came out in a monotone and without guise. Billy started to laugh, then realized his partner wasn't.

"Whaddya talkin' about? We're packin', you're the ones that…"

Pony cut him off with a simple gesture. An upswung arm said everything. It shot up toward the east. No words were spoken. Eyes shifted east and everyone knew.

There, on the horizon, a ribbon of smoke curled its way up into the sky. Then Pony swung his arm over and pointed toward the west. Another narrow plume of smoke danced its way upwards. One ball of smoke meant 'an enemy is near' in Apache. They'd been spotted by the Apache telegraph and their location pinpointed.

"Smoke," Billy said.

"Apache smoke!" Jeb corrected him.

"That's 'paches sure 'nuf, Edward," Billy announced the obvious. "Let's kill these three and get outta here."

Jeb took a step forward, his hands still at his side. "You two against those murderous Apaches, don't be stupid. They'll have you both strung up before midday."

Here's our chance, the scout thought quickly. *A slim chance, but it's our only argument to stay alive.* He knew the two wranglers had been sodbusters not that long ago. They couldn't handle themselves in the wilderness and they knew it. Even now he could see the fear etched blatantly on their faces. They had heard what the Apaches did to their prisoners; white or Mexican.

Burns became aware of Charlotte siding up next to him. He would have one chance to make his play at convincing Billy and Edward to let them live. The mountain man's face was still stoic, as if he had already decided his fate and couldn't care less about the others.

"You've only got one chance," Burns explained, "Give us back our guns. We'll all try to make a run for it. They've heard the gunfire, but won't pin us down for a while. It gives us time."

"Let you go, hell," Billy said with clenched teeth. He cocked his rifle. The metallic trigger click sounded very loud in the still quiet of early morning.

"Fire that again, you fool, and they'll be down on us in minutes," Jeb growled back.

"He's right Billy," Edward said reluctantly.

"Listen to me, both of you," Jeb demanded, "Pony knows these hills like the back of his hand. If anyone can get us out of here, he can. Without him, you don't stand a chance of losing those Apache. They'll pick up your trail and corner you. It was your damn gunfire that brought them here, now let Pony get us out."

Nervously fingering his rifle, Edward finally said in a controlled tone of voice, "All right then, fat man gets us outta here and we let you go, but no guns."

"Damn it," Billy exploded, "you can't do that!"

"Shut up, Billy," his partner let out with fear and frustration "You two remember one thing. You try anything funny and the girl is the first one to get it."

"We don't move without our guns," Jeb countered.

"But..." Charlotte protested.

Billy broke in. "Then let's take the girl and leave these two for the Apaches to deal with." He looked away at growing dust clouds coming from both directions. "Let's do something!"

The scout braced himself for a rush. The two men had both Winchesters aimed in their general direction. A sudden movement might startle them to fire, perhaps hitting the girl in the first round.

He'd have to risk that. Every second they hesitated brought both war parties closer to them and certain death.

Edward swung his rifle straight at Jeb as he stooped to pick up the gun belts. Billy raised his rifle to fire.

"Alright then, it's a deal," Edward said reluctantly. "Now let's get the hell outta here."

Jeb briskly collected his gun belt from the ground. Pony sprang to his horse. He slapped heels against the mare's flank and it leapt away. Charlotte grabbed Jeb's crocked elbow and was hoisted up behind him. They followed Pony, bunched close together. The riders swung out across the bottoms. Two rolling clouds of dust were rapidly converging just over the hill. There was little time to reach the breaks. Their vexed mounts were lathering fast.

The two wranglers' horses were bad; spent and sorely handled. The frantic dash to the breaks was wearing them down all too quickly. Burns horse was also lagging under the added load. The sandy bottoms provided good running but sent up plumes of dust floating behind the five. The Apaches would know they'd been spotted and their prey was trying to escape. Black dots appeared suddenly, almost motionless, along the crests of several ridgelines.

"I can see them," Charlotte shouted in Burns' direction. He snapped back a look. The two war parties were merging. Pony started to draw away, heeling his lathered horse savagely. The others were left even farther behind.

The mountain man whipped his horse down through a depression and raced up the other side. All the horses were tiring now, with heaving flanks and faltering gaits. They couldn't take the pace much longer. In the rolling distance, sagebrush and cactus gathered near the end of the basin.

Edward and Billy hung low in the saddle, still gripping their new rifles as if they were gold. Fear was clearly evidenced on their pale faces and white-knuckled hands gripping the reins.

The breaks were not far now. If they could reach those intertwining corridors of canyons with their rock strewn razorbacks, they might be able to throw off their pursuers, at least for a little while. Up ahead, Pony dipped down again below the ground level. The others followed behind him over a slight hill and down on a long slope which bottomed out near the maze of breaks. The tiny horsemen were growing larger, getting closer. The dust cloud was closing its gap.

Pony should have spotted the yellow cactus wrens startled off the saguaro. He should have swung over a low lying hill bordering the depression. Instead he chose a trail which converged into a well-defined corridor leading straight through the congested sage and thickets. He should have caught the signs of an ambush but his concentration was riveted on a canyon looming just ahead, the one that would lead them into a crazy quilt of canyon razorbacks and draws to elude their pursuers.

Burns saw the sun flare reflecting metal. He shouted into the roaring wind and a dozen guns exploded in response. Pony and his horse went down in a heap, dropping into the sagebrush. The others reined back, sending pommels of dust shooting high into the air, laying a blanket of blinding dust between themselves and the ambushers. A battery of fire slashed the air in front of them.

Burns made no effort to find Pony. The mountain man had to be dead. He sought cover in an upheaved jumble of basalt and rock just behind them. He shouted to the wranglers and they followed, riding bent over their horses' necks.

They made the rock pile with bullets whistling right behind them. One sieved Billy's hat brim and sent it spinning. He cupped his bare head and fell-jumped out of the saddle. A chorus of whining ricochets screamed as they tumbled down behind the rocks and moved their horses farther back. Burns could hear the lead splash all about them. They didn't have to look to know the Apaches had repeating rifles like the wranglers.

"Stay down and pick your shots," Burns ordered, levering his Spencer. "Make every shot count. Make them come to us."

The situation perplexed and angered Burns. The Apaches must have been waiting in ambush for some time. Probably the same party Pony had detected the night before. No doubt the wranglers' gunfire had drawn their attention. The rest was all too evident around him, Pony gone, bullets screaming past, shrill war cries piercing the air. With the mountain man dead, their last chance of eluding the Indians was gone. Immediate survival became more urgent than thoughts of escaping.

Edward and Billy, nervous and openly afraid, snap-fired shots at any flash of brown skin or war cry. The Indians were baiting them and the men were wasting shots.

"Damn it, pick your shots, don't waste shells," Burns cursed the two of them. They nodded their understanding but continued to fire at any movement. Cursing didn't reach them. A sharp jab to the ribs settled Billy down for the moment but Edward's tense frame shook so Burns dared not risk touching him.

Charlotte was back with the skittish horses, trying to calm them.

"Lottie," Burns shouted back, "hold on to those horses. If they get away, we're done for." The girl shouted something back to him but the words were lost in the clamor of gunfire. The scout turned to his pale faced partners lying with him in the forward rocks.

Jeb spoke calmly this time, trying to steady their high-strung nervousness. "Just pick your shots, God damn it, don't fire at anything unless you've got a clear shot."

"Christ, I ain't gonna die," Billy babbled to himself, "Come on you red bellied sons-of-bitches, come and get me!"

"Damn you, shut up," Edward yelled, ducking a whining bullet overhead, "you're so almighty big for your britches, prove it for once. Use your god-damn gun instead of your big mouth."

Smart mouth Billy, the one with a ready gun and a quick answer for everything, burrowed deeper behind the rocks and knuckled his gunstock until his hand turned white.

Now this one is going under on me, thought Burns. *Christ, what more could go wrong?* The shelling died down a bit. Their return fire subsided.

The men held their fire, waiting for a target. The Indians, hidden among the sage and thickets, kept up a light curtain of slugs singing into the rock pile. Other Apaches continually moved forward to improve their positions and gather for the slaughter soon to come.

One glance back told Jeb why. The pursuing Apaches were drawing closer, their dust cloud even larger in the cloudless sky. They were 10 minutes away at the most, riding their wiry ponies hard to be in on the coup.

"Jeb!" Charlotte screamed.

Burns rolled over and caught the tag end of movement in the rocks behind him. Rushing over a rocky ledge mere yards to the right, a lithe Apache, naked but for a breechcloth, leapt behind a boulder.

A rifle cracked in the sage by their fort up, but it was a different kind of gunfire. Burns cocked an ear. It roared again. A buffalo roar. The report came from a Sharps, not a Spencer or Winchester the Apaches were using. It was Pony's Sharps! He had to be alive and fighting in the sage right among the attacking Apaches. The Sharps roared again and a man cried out. That sound held Burns' attention for a second and the Indian moved again.

The Apache sprang up again, topping a sheet of granite and sprinted toward the horses. Charlotte screamed and Burns steadied his rifle in the cradle of his arm. He fired. The slug glanced off a rock just behind the Apache's head. The scout levered another shell in the chamber. He sighted in. Then the warrior jumped in line with the girl. Burns' shot might hit her if he fired. The warrior was almost there. Charlotte stood petrified, gripping the reins, her arm jerking as the horses skidded and backed away from the rushing Indian. He waved his arms to spook the horses. The appaloosa started to rear up, lifting the girl to her toes. More bullets crashed into the rocks, sending Jeb back against the cover.

"Move!" Burns screamed. The girl didn't respond. His time was up. The Apache reached out for the reins. Charlotte kicked out at him with her leg. It hit her attacker in his stomach and threw him off stride. He crashed into the horse; throwing the girl back against the blue while he rolled by her feet. Then the Indian leapt up, shouting. Charlotte still clutched the reins, tottering off balance next to the pitching horses. Burns fired.

The .50 caliber slug caught the Apache below the waist and doubled him over. He started to fall then caught his balance. He whipped out a knife from his breechcloth and slashed out at the girl. Burns' Spencer roared again. The bullet tore into the Indian's face and spun him into a half circle before dumping him to the ground.

Another cry came from the thickets. The Sharps was taking its toll. An idea hit Jeb. It was a slim chance but likely their only chance. In his barricade behind the sage and overlooking the breaks, Jeb knew it was only a matter of minutes before both war parties converged on his spot and wiped them out. But with Pony attacking the core of ambushers, the Apaches had two adversaries to fight, with one right in their midst. It was a distraction but perhaps enough to provide the chance at escape they so desperately needed. The wranglers had kept up a shaky, but steady stream of bullets into the thickets, pinning down most of the Apaches. If they could break out and rush past the thickets, they might catch the Apaches off guard and make it through.

"Lottie," Burns waved, "get them up here." She came quickly. "Mount up, you two." The ashen-faced men got to saddle. "When I give the word, we're riding out of here. Head straight for the canyons, and hope to God we've still got time. Edward, if Pony's still alive, you take him."

He turned to the girl, gathering up her arms in his hands. She pressed close to him, looking up with fearful eyes. She said nothing but understanding all. "We'll get out of here Charlotte, but be strong. You've got to be strong." He put her on his nervous blue. "Let's ride!" he shouted.

They burst out of the enclosing rocks, firing into the surrounding thickets as they rode. Apaches surfaced, firing loosely, trying to get off as many rounds as possible. The Apaches shouted and yelped, leaping off rocks close to where the three men had laid. Pony burst through the sage, running at an angle to intercept the riders. He had a saddle bar and medicine bag on each shoulder. Bullets tore off pieces of sage around him, singing closely.

Burns dropped one archer, drawing a bead right behind the mountain man. Edward slowed his mount and Pony leapt up behind him, not missing a step in the rush. Billy was gaining back his confidence, riding with one hand on the reins, the other blasting away with his colt.

Behind the five, hostiles appeared beneath the dust cloud. The figures on horseback waved their arms and echoed shrill war cries. The little distance that had been gained at the offset was completely lost in the ambush. The horses were laboring badly. They could not last more than a couple of miles; certainly not enough to get them into the maze of canyons and possible escape. Pony took the party into a branching canyon and went up the side at a long angle.

There were at least eight Apaches from the ambush, screaming close behind them now. Their fresh mustangs were gaining ground quickly. Pony went up the ridge, topping it. Suddenly before him there was a long gray slide of shale. But there could be no stopping. The horses plunged into it, fought for footing, and went down.

Pony and Edward were thrown from the saddle. Billy clung to his mare's neck. Burns and the girl almost toppled over but their mount fell back, rump down, and then slid down the rough slope. The five were lost in a swirl of dust, the horses scrambled madly, fighting for a foothold.

Pony and Edward stumbled down the slope, hanging onto the saddle straps. Billy's horse slipped and slammed sideways into an outcropping before reaching bottom. Dust and dirt followed them all, rolling down around them in a great brown cloud.

Pony leapt to saddle, dragging Edward behind him. He kicked the mare's heaving flanks, but the horse was spent. It went only a few yards before it collapsed. Burns and the girl rode out of the cloud, Billy close behind.

Apaches appeared on top of the ridgeline. They stood dismount, rifles braced, and shot in careful aimed sequence. Billy's horse screamed, kicking up his legs and pitching over, tossing Billy off. Edward was limping ahead. Pony stood his ground, firing back at the marksmen along the ridgeline.

"Look!" Charlotte shouted, pointing behind Burns. He spun around, his mouth dropped in amazement.

Across the canyon bottom, fitted into a cliff wall, was an ancient ruin. Like a castle, it stood some fifty feet above the valley floor. It had been fitted so skillfully into its cliff pocket that it was little damaged by the elements. Below the main embodiment, reaching it from ground level, were a series of ledges and ladders. Upon the ledges were individual rooms, isolated apartments, and aeries literally honeycombed into the canyon wall. Standing tall among the ruins was an ancient tower. Only an arroyo lay between them and the ruins.

"There!" Jeb screamed, pointing toward the ruins. "It's our only chance!"

Billy rushed past and Jeb spun him around by the elbow. The boy's face was white with fear. "Strip your horse, damn you!" Jeb shouted.

Billy looked dumbly back at the dead animal then at the Apaches charging down the hill. He hesitated. Jeb pushed Charlotte toward the ruins, "Go on, I'll catch up," he said. Then he grabbed Billy by his arm and together they ran back to the horse. Bullets thudded into its still form. Burns quickly stripped off the canteen and saddlebags. He threw them in Billy's face. "Take these and go." The boy sprinted off.

Dropping behind the cactus, Jeb threw in a new tube of shells and steadied his aim on the lead rider who was plunging down the shale. A gun roared only feet away. Pony was behind Edward's dead horse. The Apache pitched forward off his horse, rolling down the slope. The other attackers stopped, back riders crashing into the hesitating front ones as the scout fired again. Another Apache tumbled off his horse and the others moved back up the slope. More Apaches appeared on the ridgeline.

"Go!" Burns waved to the mountain man, "I'll cover you." Pony gathered up the canteens and started back. Tiny puffs of dirt kicked up around his legs. Then Burns sprang to his feet and raced back, not even looking at the Apaches who again were coming down off the ridgeline.

CHAPTER TWELVE

The arroyo cut deep and wider than most. Like a jagged scar, it twisted along the sandy smooth valley bottom. It cut straight across the party's path to the pueblo ruins. The ground slash was too wide to jump and too long to skirt. There was no choice. Jeb and the others would have to enter it to get across and reach the ruins.

Charlotte and the two wranglers with their legs flying across the sand, eyes locked in front, plunged into the arroyo. Their bodies went down slip-sliding to the rock strewn bottom. They scrambled across the narrow bottom then propelled themselves up the other side. The swish of arrows pierced the air around them. As the trio rushed up the far side, their hands and knees clawed away at the loose shale and gravel. Sandy topsoil crumbled at their touch, making footholds tricky and the climb back agonizing.

Jeb and Pony caught up with the trio as the party sprinted across the elongated bowl. Their blood hammered against their brains and they took long drawn out gasps for air. They could hear yelping war cries close behind. No one dared look back.

The closest kivas and out buildings were only yards away. Cedar posts still remained as far as the settlement had once extended. Now time and the elements had reduced those apartments and ceremonial chambers to crumbling ruins that stood just three to four feet high. Drifting sand had filled in most of them, but the thick adobe walls afforded protection enough. These ruins could provide a first line of defense until the party got farther back into the main citadel.

Remarkably, Charlotte was first to reach the walls. She flipped her nimble body over the crumbling adobe and dropped to the ground. Her partners landed almost on top of her. Billy was the first up. He wedged himself in a corner and tapped out a notch with his rifle butt. As Burns and Pony dashed behind the wall, Billy's big Winchester discharged in their ears.

"Billy, hold your fire until you've got something to shoot at," Burns cautioned him. The boy mumbled a reply then fired again anyway. The others followed Jeb back into a kiva. It was filled with deep sand and plenty of dust kicked up by their trampling boots.

Frustration flared in Jeb's eyes but he blinked it away. Billy's empty head was reacting with pure emotion; anger and hatred. Common sense had been forgotten. Burns had to ignore him and think quickly. The horses were gone and with them their only chance of escape. Both wranglers were running low on loads and from the looks of their own cartridge belts neither Burns nor Pony had a large supply left either. Only two canteens remained and they were both nearly empty. The little food in their saddlebags wouldn't last the five of them for more than a couple of days.

The ancient pueblo was protection from immediate slaughter but not eventual starvation or torture by the Apaches. It was buying them time, for what Jeb wasn't sure. Edward and the girl watched him, waiting for a word. Pony watched the arroyo and the Apaches who were riding into it, dismounting, and lining its slopes.
For a few brief moments, the gunfire and fusillade of arrows had stopped. Their attackers were milling around the arroyo's bottom and filling the rock-strewn canyon's basin around it. Occasionally a head would pop up for a second, note the position of the whites and then disappear back into the arroyo.

Pony settled in, resting his Sharps on a notch in the brickwork. He said nothing as he focused on the edge of the arroyo. He took several deep breaths and waited. The next head that popped up looked around for a split second then exploded in a red ball of blood and brain matter.

"We've got to move out of here and push deeper into the ruins," Jeb shouted. He turned to Edward, "Get your partner back here," he said, "we're moving out."

Charlotte was sucking in gasps of air, still shaky from their mad dash to the pueblo's outskirts. She crawled up to her hands and knees, glancing at the ruins behind them then the arroyo.

"Lottie," Jeb said, "stick close to me." She swallowed hard and rose up off her knees behind Burns. Edward went back for his partner.

Burns and the girl crept through a back exit and into the next series of ruins. Pony had scrambled still farther back into one of the few standing rooms at ground level. He sat perched behind a small slit in the wall which served as a window. From it, he could draw a bead on the Indians hiding in the washout. Only his long black barrel poked its ugly nose out the hole and spoke. Yelping war cries rolled toward the ruins in response.

The Apaches were using the arroyo as a rifle pit, concentrating their fire on both Billy's and Pony's positions. Pony's sniping frustrated their bombardment and kept most of the marksmen ducking for cover.

Edward came around the corner of the wall, running. He was alone.

Jeb grabbed Edward's sleeve and stopped him, face to face.

"Where the hell is Billy? I told you to bring him here!" Burns shouted in anger. Edward glanced over his shoulder and answered, "He said he wasn't movin'. He's got a score to settle."

"Who the hell does he think he is, General Grant?" Jeb shouted in heightened frustration. "I need him back here, right now!"

Edward protested with a shrug of his shoulders. "You tell him, he won't listen to me. Once he's got a mind made up, there ain't nothin' in hell that's gonna change it. He's meaner than a bobcat when he's like that."

"Pony!" Burns called out, "Wait at the base of the main pueblo. We're moving up there as soon as I bring that damn fool kid back here."

The mountain man flung his bags over his shoulder and jokingly flipped Burns a quick sloppy salute. Pony was back in form. Since he had had his horse shot from under him, the mountain man was into the elements so familiar and satisfying to him. He was fighting and killing Apaches and loving every minute of it.

Edward and Charlotte followed Pony back into the ruins, winding out of sight among the jigsaw walls and mounds that were once rooms and homes.

With the absence of Pony's driving gunfire, rifle bursts from the arroyo had increased. Lead splashed into the mud walls above Jeb's hat as he scrambled, hunched over, back toward the kid. Billy was not keeping the Indians pinned down as Pony had. The boy was still nestled behind the first wall, squeezing off shots like a new recruit in practice. The hat he'd retrieved was cocked at a crooked angle on his head. He chuckled to himself with each blast fired from the yellow boy.

"Billy, come on. We're moving back. They'll be over this place in a minute."

"Shove your orders, mister; I'm not listening to you anymore. I got me a score to settle."

A bullet exploded just outside the notch, showering Billy's face with rock and mud chips. The boy spat out dirt and cursed, "Go on back," he shouted at Burns, snap-firing three quick rounds in retaliation. "I ain't movin'. Them red bastards is gonna pay hell if they want to take me."

Billy wasn't about to move. He'd die first in self-esteemed glory, rather than run any farther. Burns shook his head at the young man's arrogance and belligerency. He looked for another way to pry him loose. He leaned back against the wall, pondering the tough situation they were all in. If Billy's existence could help to keep the others alive, then his arrogance was worth tolerating. More bullets whined overhead, ricocheting off rocks and screaming past Burns' head. He'd have to pry Billy loose with force and risk the boy turning on him. If his temper snapped under the strain of combat, he was liable to act irrationally, but it was Burns' only choice.

The mud wall exploded against Jeb's ear. Rock chips stung his cheek. He flung himself down and rolled over, springing up with rifle aimed. An Apache was almost on top of him, axe raised, flash-burn close. Burns fired once, levered his rifle then fired again into his assailant's stomach. Momentum propelled the Indian three more steps before he pitched over. Another bullet plowed into the adobe inches from the scout's face. He realized some Apaches had flanked their frontal position.

He shouted at the boy above the commotion of rifle fire. "Billy, we're almost cut off, now hump yourself outta here, damn it. Let's go!"

The scout raced back, not bothering to see if Billy was following or not. The boy was on his own now. Something flashed brown behind a neighboring wall. A cane arrow snapped over Jeb's bunched up body. The scout didn't stop. He ran through a crumbling room and ducked behind its sidewall. The archer poked his painted face up and Burns' shot sent him diving for the ground. Then the scout crossed the sand filled room and rolled over a three foot wall in back. Up ahead he caught sight of the last string of apartments lining a rocky base below the main citadel's superstructure.

Footsteps pounded up behind him. He ducked into a partially collapsed building. Its roof lay at an angle across half the floor. The room was dark and dank. He spun around, his Spencer waist high, pressured to fire. It was Billy, framed in the doorway and gasping for breath. Something was bounding up behind him. The boy turned to fire.

"Watch out!" yelled Burns.

An arrow slammed into Billy, throwing him back into the dirt. An Apache, large and streaked with paint, leapt through the T-shaped doorway. Burns shot him just inside the room. He was dead before his body hit the ground.

Billy tried to get up. One hand propped up his quivering body, the other wrapped around a shaft protruding from his chest. The arrow was reed; a tri-feathered three foot frail piece of wood. A one inch quartz tip protruded from Billy's back. It had torn into his flesh with explosive force. Blood ran freely from the wound, bathing his chest in blood. The boy's face was ashen and pale. His hand jerked nervously, afraid to touch the wound. Droplets of blood dripped from the corner of his mouth. He tried to speak but couldn't form words. Blood bubbled on his lips.

"Don't talk," Jeb tried to reassure him. He slipped an arm under the boy's underarm and lifted him to his feet. Yelping war cries echoed off the ruins nearby. The Indians were in the first line of ruins already, following the others that had flanked their position.

Burns and the wounded boy moved clumsily out the rear entrance, and ran at a faltering pace into the encircling walls of another apartment. The loud crack of Pony's buffalo rifle rolled past Jeb's ears. Cover! Now they had a chance.

Billy grasped the Winchester tightly, knuckle-white fingers dripping blood on it. He'd lost his hat. Dark hair, matted down with dirt and grime, lay in tangles above his downcast eyes. His chest was a scarlet blob, which settled in around his waist. He was trailing blood with each step. Charlotte covered the two as they wobbled into the building and fell, arms intertwined, against the wall and slid to the dirt floor.

"Billy!" exclaimed Edward, rushing to the boy.

"Stay where you are!" Jeb snapped at Billy's partner.

"But….!"

"Stay put. I'll take care of him," Jeb spat out angrily. "If he'd listened to me, this wouldn't have happened." The scout was frustrated and upset. Their defenses were crumbling and there was little he could do about it.

A staccato of bullets peppered the wall driving Edward and Charlotte down into the dirt. Pony just burrowed a little deeper into his corner and waited for a target. He didn't have to wait very long.

Three warriors sprinted around a high wall and suddenly found themselves confronting the building where the five were forted up. The first Apache brought up his Springfield carbine to fire. Pony blasted him full in the face. The other two Indians grabbed at the falling leader and were cut down in a withering crossfire from Edward and Jeb. The rest of the attacking force slipped back into the maze of ruins, suddenly quiet and still.

"That was probably a chief," Pony spoke out loud, "should hold them up for a little while." True or not, the firing stopped and silence fell over the ruins. Movement and voices could be heard beyond that killing field but the Apaches were not in sight.

The brief respite gave Jeb a much needed moment of rest. He tore open Billy's shirt and probed bluish skin around the embedded shaft for damage done. It was obvious to even his untrained eye that more than one vital organ had been torn and ruptured. Blood had soaked down to Billy's pants and his head rolled to each side, as he lapsed in and out of consciousness.

"Let me help," Charlotte said. She had moved close by, leaning over Jeb's shoulder. Dirt streaked her flushed face and tangled hair. Discolored bruises on her chin marked her fall down the slope. Despite the hair, scratches, and tattered clothes, the girl radiated a breath of life that Burns hadn't seen for a long time. She seemed eager to help and unafraid of the gore of Billy's wound. She didn't wait for Burns to respond.

Gently moving Billy's hand to one side, she produced a cloth from her saddlebag and dabbed it around the wound, soaking up blood. She tried to run a little water down the boy's mouth but it only rolled off his lips. One eye weakly tilted up to her face, but then dropped back behind an eyelid.

The boy was moaning and turning his head. Pain and anguish wrapped his face in a distorted mask. The new shiny rifle lay across his lap, speckled with splotches of red.

Edward kept glancing over at the two and his partner. He bit his lip as the boy moaned and coughed up blood. "Let me help," he said finally, unable to take it quietly any longer.

"If you want to help, stay where you are!" Jeb commanded him. "Keep your eyes peeled. We're doing all we can. You'd only be in the way."

A tobacco aroma curled Jeb's nose. Pony was puffing on a short cigarrito, cupping the tiny cigar in his hand. His Sharps was lapped across his wide belly and he wore a look of complete calm, unattached to the violence and danger just beyond the adobe walls. He drew in deeply on the stub, and then flipped it to the ground, presenting his sneer again.

The girl wrapped a cloth tourniquet around Billy's chest. Blood immediately soaked through the first layer of cloth, dyeing it dark red.
"He won't last an hour," Jeb whispered softly to the girl. Charlotte continued wrapping the cloth while her head slowly nodded in agreement. She glanced up at the scout just once with deep penetrating eyes that bespoke not fear but concentrated determination. It was a message Jeb got loud and clear. Charlotte was a fighter, someone he badly needed at his side if they were to survive this Apache onslaught.

They bandaged Billy as best they could and leaned him up against the wall. Burns motioned Edward over and let him talk to the youngster. He positioned the girl in back of the doorway with Billy's new Winchester and gun belt.

"Know how to use one of these?" he asked her. She ran her hands over the stock and trigger mechanism, then looked at the scout with her steel green penetrating eyes. They were focused and full of earnest. She spoke slowly and with confidence.

"I have only shot a couple of old shotguns back East," then added, "but I'm a quick learner." She smiled and Jeb had his answer. Someone he could count on, and a tenderfoot at that - but unlike any he had ever known.

Jeb shimmied along the wall to Pony's corner above the others. From that vantage point he could examine the rocks and boulders that lay in jumbled heaps behind their room. There was little fringe cover to hide any passage back to the series of ledges which wound up into the pueblo. Crumbling roofs and walls had turned these ledges into a maze of twisting paths and dead end trails. There was too much open space to risk a rush up that way. The only certain way to reach the pueblo was through a series of intertwining rooms, eyras, lookouts and dwellings. To reach those corridors, the party had to either risk crossing the vacant space bordering their apartment or moving farther down closer to the first level of buildings.

As he scanned the ruins more closely, trying to spot a suitable fortification, Jeb's eyes crossed the tower. His eyes snapped back, focusing on the tall slab of layered stone. It was isolated, tucked away in the corner of the ruins, up against an overhanging cliff face. It seemed the only position which looked down on the rest of the stone ruins. Its entrance was an opening on the bottom, and from the looks of a shadow, the door appeared to be partially open.

If Burns and the others could reach that tower and block the door, they might be able to hold off their attackers - for a while at least.

"All right, we're moving out of here," Jeb announced. "We've got to go higher before they surround us entirely. There's a tower on top of that structure in back of us. We'll try for that."

He motioned Charlotte toward the exit. Edward came to help Billy. "Get him up and follow Pony," he ordered the cowboy. Levering his Spencer, he heard an empty chamber click. Dropping to one knee, Burns quickly pulled a tube of seven shells out of his saddlebag and shoved them up the stock, jacking a cartridge into the chamber.

The others were gone. He was alone in the room.
A slight scraping sound reached his ear. He moved quickly, his back to the wall. A face appeared around a wall, several dozen yards outside his room. He fired. The face disappeared. They had reorganized. The Apaches were closing in. Jeb dashed out the back exit and ran parallel to the crumbling walls.

Most of the pueblo's frontal structure on the lower level had been worn down over time. The log ceilings over the apartments had been eaten away with erosion. Heaps of logs and building materials lay scattered about where rooms had collapsed under accumulated weight. The upper levels were in better shape mostly because of the protection of the cliff face which hung over it.

Jeb could see a rough-cut walkway leading to the lookout tower's base. It ran by waist high mud walls. If they could reach that third level, the party had a chance to reach the tower itself.

The scout cornered a low wall and almost ran into the others.

"What's holding you up?" he asked impatiently.

Pony jerked his finger back over the wall they were pressing against. Burns peeked over. Although they had moved closer and a series of rooms lay only ten, perhaps fifteen yards away, the area before that building was wind swept clean. There were no ruins, cactus, or cedar posts to protect their passage. It was open ground.

Burns' total attention concentrated on the area in front of him. He didn't hear the war cries lifting up from the ruins behind him.

"They're coming closer!" Charlotte gasped.

"Steady!" Burns said, still concentrating on the open ground before him. He could see an apartment whose roof had pushed one wall out, exposing a gaping hole large enough for a man to fit through. It still required a mad sprint uphill but would afford the five much needed protection from the Apache snipers.

A rifle cracked. Lead splattered against the wall above their heads. Pony moved outside the wall, with Burns and Edward laying down a screen of protective fire as Charlotte supported Billy. Pony locked one paw onto his gear, the other onto his Sharps. He spat out a long stream of tobacco juice and winked at the girl. He sprinted out, dancing to the right, then left, dodging bullets which peppered the ground around him. In one sailing leap he was through the hole. In seconds, his rifle was trained in on the Apaches, driving them back behind cover.

Charlotte was next. Bunching up her skirt around the knees, she jumped out and ran, flat out, in a straight line to the hole. She dove in, legs flying and hands cradling the rifle tenderly.

"Billy's too badly hurt to run, I can't get him in there," Edward protested.

Burns' patience snapped. "Do as I say or I'll let you both stay out here and cool your heels. Now move!" He shoved the man by his elbow.
Edward snapped back, jacking his rifle up into the Jeb's face. "Damn you, I've had enough of your bossing us around. Billy's hurt bad and he's gonna die if we move him anymore."

"Come on!" shouted Pony from the room.

Edward inched the rifle closer. "He ain't gonna die, you hear me! He ain't gonna die. If he goes, you're gonna die with him, mister."

"If he stays here, he'll die for sure," Jeb shot back, his nose to the rifle barrel.

"He can't go no farther!"

"Then stay here, damn you," Burns exploded back. He pushed his way past the man, bunching up his body for the dash.

Edward looked on helplessly. His bluff had been called. He didn't know what to do. "No, wait!" he pleaded, "Don't leave him, please. I just don't want him to die."

Jeb spat his anger at the ground and helped Edward with Billy. The boy had lapsed into unconsciousness. His body was heavy and burdensome. His legs dragged on the ground. The scout waved his rifle at the others for a signal and shouted, "Now!"

The two ran bent over, dragging Billy between them. The boy's boots toed groves in the sand behind them. Bullets ricocheted off the stratified layers of adobe. Pony shouted something but it was lost in the bedlam. They had almost reached the hole when a bullet plowed into Billy's back with a dull thud. Edward slowed down from the shock of it all. He mouthed indistinguishable words to Jeb. Burns screamed at him to move. A bullet hit Jeb's hat and sent it cart wheeling. Burns staggered back. Edward and Billy fell in a heap. Another slug ripped Jeb's scalp open just above the temple, smashing him to his knees and blinding him with sudden blood.

Jeb lost consciousness for a second then grasped it again. As he stumbled to his feet, numbed and aching, his legs rubbery, he heard a familiar voice yelling at him to "Move! Hurry!" Then he saw, through streaming blood, Charlotte's blurred form. She was firing out the hole and shouting at him.

He stumbled toward her, his hand locked unconsciously onto his Spencer. Bullets whizzed past his head. His feet lacked all feeling. He saw the hole coming. He ducked down and propelled his body through the opening, smashing his knees in the process. Hands grabbed at him and dragged his limp body up against a wall. Gunfire battered his eardrums, rolling across his brain.

Charlotte's face loomed above his; those blue eyes, that mouth - frightened, concerned, wanting. He tried to say something but the words wouldn't come. His head pounded in pain and he felt himself falling back, off a large cliff into blackness below. He made a frantic grasp to cling to consciousness but failed and slipped away.

A minute passed, then two. The scout stirred, moaned guttural sounds, and pushed himself up into a sitting position. Something touched his arm and he jerked it away. The sudden movement shot stabs of pain through his head and he almost fell back.

"Steady," a comforting voice soothed him. It was the girl, kneeling right next to him. She still carried the rifle and had Billy's gun belt around her waist.

Jeb seemed to pay her no attention. His head was bent over to his knees, eyes clamped tight as he concentrated on clearing the dizziness away. When he finally cracked them open, the dim light brought only minor relief.

"You're lucky to be alive," the voice said softly. Hands dabbed something soft against his temple, rubbing the dried blood off his cheeks and eyelids. Fingers, soft yet toughened, pressed against his cheek and secured a strip of cloth around his forehead.

Burns cocked an eye open to a slit. He managed a weak smile and slowly rotated his head to clear his vision and the pounding in his brain. A rifle roared within the confine and it echoed in his head.

"What about the others?" he managed to ask.

Charlotte leaned close to him, her lips almost touching his cheek. "Edward's in here with us. He got shot up pretty badly. I think he's delirious. He isn't sure where he is or who he is."

"And Billy?"

"He's still out there. He's gone."

Something was wrong. Burns could sense it. He managed a slow turn and saw Edward in one corner. His chest and arm were bloodied. His head hung against his chest and he seemed to be talking in hushed tones to himself. Pony was in the same sniping position, peering through a thin shaft of light coming into the dark room. Then Jeb realized the something strange was an absence of gunfire - a silence which seemed to resonate almost louder than gunfire itself.

Charlotte handed him an open canteen. He gulped down a little of the tepid water and licked his lips. It helped clear his head some. He moved over toward Pony. As he moved, he surveyed the room they were in.

It was a tiny room compared to the other rooms which had been eaten away over time. It was cool in the dim light. The air was stale and musty and smelled of death. Dark walls rose 10 feet to a log ceiling, which seeped cracks of sunlight filtering through. In the rear, light framed a narrow exit. It led down a dark hallway, lit at odd intervals by faint shafts of sunlight filtering through the ceiling. That ceiling would be the floor of the rooms overhead.

To his right, Jeb could see an open area where other rooms, once laying parallel to theirs, had collapsed under the weight of rain-washed mud and erosion. The low-lying ruins provided a perfect cover for any Apaches closing in.

"Do you see anything out there?" he asked Pony. The mountain man looked over then returned his noncommittal gaze out the hole.

"Well?"

"Can't see them, but they're out there, inching closer all the time," Pony replied without bothering to look over. His Sharps had slipped down to his side and he leaned heavily against the wall. His smile returned, "Thought we'd lost you for a minute back there," he said. "Would have been a shame. No one to take the little woman back to her ranch. Figured I'd have to care for her myself."

"I've got your word," Jeb growled, "don't forget that!"

"Until we get outta here or one of us is dead!" replied the mountain man.

Stupid talk, thought Jeb. Pony was in his element, killing and fighting and living up to his own self-image. He could feel his body collapsing inside as the adrenaline wore off. He shot back at Pony. "Ay, shit, give me a cigarette!"

"Who the hell do you think you're giving orders to now?" demanded Pony.

"You! Now give!"

The Spanish cigarrito flew over reluctantly. Jeb lit it and thought out loud. "What are they waiting for?"

Pony laughed at the question.

"Nothing," he said, "they're waiting for nothing. Got all the time in the world now. We're near cornered in here and they're sure to have flankers out trying to cut us off entirely."

Then, feeling in his element and in charge, He added, "If you want to make that tower, we best get up there pronto. Before they flank us on both sides." Pony flipped his spent butt out the hole and asked, "We going?"

"Right now," Burns shot back. He stubbed the cigarrito into the ground.

"What about him?" Pony nodded toward Edward, who was still semi-conscious and being re-bandaged by the girl. "You plan to drag his sorry ass along too?"

"Damn right I do," Burns shot back, his teeth clenched tightly in firm control. "You think I'm gonna leave him here for the Apaches to find, you're crazy. I'm not leaving anyone behind, no matter what. That even goes for you!"

Pony sneered at him and brushed past. He entered the darkened hallway. His face, streaked with dried mud and chips of adobe planted in his beard, still reflected a complete calmness. But with it, something evil and sinister.

The old shrewdness had returned. The silent, watchful stare of a mind thinking again of the girl and those shiny black scalps he meant to have.

The scout checked the hole before leaving. Nothing stirred outside. No sign of Apaches. Only the burning sun reflecting off rocks and boulders. Hot air warmed his cheeks in the shaft of light.

Moving as quickly as they could with their wounded charge, the three passed through the corridor and into a narrow open space. A ladder to the second floor was there, leaning against the wall.

Steadying the crude ladder with tightened fists, Burns stood below while Pony reluctantly prodded the wounded man up each rung, one painful step at a time. Charlotte stood behind in the shadows, cradling her big Winchester and listening for any sounds behind them.

Edward moaned and Pony continued to push him up, even harder. When the wounded man reached the top rung, he fell over to the floor. Pony came up quickly, followed by Burns and the girl. They were in the first apartment on the second level.

Still nothing stirred in the rising heat outside. Peering down to ground level, neither Burns nor Pony could see any movement. Scanning the shadows and dark crevices among rocks and ruins, they probed for signs of Indians; a sun flare, a flash of brown skin, a colored turban, a moving bush, anything. But they saw nothing.

The room they now occupied was much larger than the first one. Its walls were still covered with ancient scratching. Broken pieces of crockery, plain and painted, lay scattered about the log-dirt floor. A small hole served as a window, looking over a courtyard. The front entrance looked out onto a veranda or roof over the first level.

Burns moved about the room, peering out both front entrance and side window, trying to gauge their position in relation to the tower. The edifice loomed like a cracked, crumbling arm extending from one corner, straight up. It raised above the third level of the stone fortress. Its curving sides were slit by narrow openings - perfect holes for defenders. The area around its base was sleeved by a series of crumbling low lying walls. They once housed ceremonial chambers before the limestone rock ceiling had dripped down enough elements to reduce the mud to mere formations of what they had once been.

"How do we get there?" Charlotte asked, as she examined the rifle in her hand. Pony gnawed off a piece of tobacco and waited for the answer. Jeb studied the tower.

"There is a main corridor through the apartments behind us. It should lead to the tower." The scout turned to Edward, "Can you make it alright?"

The man nodded weakly. Pony grunted.

"I'll help him," Charlotte volunteered.

Burns gave her a smile and a soft grasp by the elbow. She returned his smile.

They filed out, moving through the door and along the open air walkway. Pony went first, running close to the outside walls of the apartments. Packed tightly behind him came the girl and Edward, then Burns, always looking around.

The Apaches let them get completely out into the open, then they opened fire.

Shots exploded on both sides of the running targets. Whining ricochets screamed around the four like banshees wailing. Apaches came spilling out from their hiding places, ducking and weaving among the crumbling walls and buildings, firing as they closed in.

At the end of the run, the four found a ladder. It was weakened by time and lying against the wall. It led to the final level and hopefully the tower. Burns let Pony climb it first, his Sharps ready. He called the others up quickly. As he started climbing up, Jeb saw forms breaking the shaft of the dark corridor at the other end of the walkway. He fired down the hallway entrance. The movement stopped. He scrambled up the ladder. The gunfire continued but was more intermittent. The rock corridor protected the party. The Apaches waited for them to surface again.

The four were in a tiny room, five by five, which stood directly across from the tower and safety. Between the room and the tower lay the low lying crumbling adobe wall the scout had seen from below.

Pony stuck his head out the doorway but a bullet drove him back in. Apache marksmen had positioned themselves along the lip of the cliff face, directly opposite the room. From their concealed position, they could fire down on the entrance to the room.

"We'll have to go out that side entrance and follow the wall to the tower. No time to lose," Jeb said, "They're right behind us now."

"I can't. I can't!" Edward mumbled, pressing his fingers tightly against his chest. His face was pale and drawn, bloodless. The girl reached for his arm. She propped him straight up and nodded at Jeb.

Apache yelping rose from below them. It was chorused by other wolf yipping between the ruins and the corridor. The Apaches were moving toward the tower.

Pony wiggled through the small back exit to the room and ran along the wall. Shells fried the air over his head, chipping away at the adobe wall. The mountain man sprinted to the tower. It was a direct head-on rush. Bullets kicked up clods of dirt at his heels. He threw his weight against the door, slamming it back.

Moments later, his rifle barked out the tower's top floor slit.

"Now," shouted Burns to the pair behind him. He caught Charlotte by her elbow and pressed it gently. Then he pushed her ahead. When she hesitated, he assured her, "I'll take care of him."

Charlotte wiggled out of the hole and ran the gauntlet of fire, clipping her heels to both sides, and pushing through the entrance. She was followed by a shower of lead, which tore into the thick pine door.

Jeb could see Apaches filtering among the ruins right below and behind him. If they had been closer or Pony wasn't in the tower, he'd have been a dead man.

"This is it," shouted Burns to the gasping man beside him. His words fell on pain-deafened ears. The girl's rifle cracked along with Pony's. It was their only chance. Jeb rose up, pushing Edward quickly through the hole and along the wall. Bullets sang overhead, coming lower with each step they took. They would have to run the rest of the way. He dug his heels into the ground and began.

Edward's weight became crushing as his body went limp. The man had passed out, hung like a heavy chain around Jeb's neck. Jeb tried to grasp him tighter, but lost his balance instead. He felt himself dropping Edward. The ground came rushing up and slammed him in the face.

Edwards's body lay sprawled over Burns, shielding him from bullets, which tore up the ground on both sides. Two slugs tore into Edward's back almost simultaneously. Blood ran freely down Jeb's face, blinding one eye. His wound had reopened. He dragged himself free of the body and stumbled toward the door.

Jeb hit the door and glanced off it, rolling into a heap in the corner. Long feathered arrows hissed through the air, slamming into the door behind him. Charlotte shouldered the heavy pine affair. It slowly creaked closed.

By the time the girl had closed the door, Jeb was on his knees, steadying his vision and feeling the cold steel pressing against his belly. He had his rifle and canteen and that was all. The girl was safe and they were in the tower. At least three of them were still alive … for now.

CHAPTER THIRTEEN

The army encampment was surrounded with guards. In a makeshift corral, their hobbled horses encircled the cluster of bivouacked soldiers. Nightfall hadn't come too soon for the bedraggled troopers. It was the end of another futile day of chasing tracks that disappeared into the sand and cutting alluring signs that went nowhere. It was another day of tense, cautious traversing of the harsh desert landscape in search of an elusive foe. Seeking an enemy that never showed itself except in a quick deadly ambush that usually cost the troop casualties.

Tomorrow promised nothing but more of the same frustration and still no trace of the Apache war party or the girl they had taken hostage. Branan and Badger shared the frustration of the chase but for very different reasons.

The captain had said next to nothing during the day. He had few words for Badger. The hard scrabble rancher seemed to be in his own world of aches and pains and complaints. For his part, Branan was still troubled by nagging thoughts about the scout's exact identity. There was a connection between the captain and that cowboy but Branan couldn't yet pin it down. It was like a bad aftertaste that distracted the captain from his mission on hand. Old man Badger seemed his only link with that illusive person.

Instead of interrogating the rancher, Captain Branan let the old man babble on about fighting Apaches and trying to make a living off the harsh and unforgiving land. Badger babbled on all day but his words didn't add up to much of anything. There was nothing in the old man's rambling that could tell the captain any more about the scout and why he seemed such a menace.

Finally after a bad meal of hardtack and sour water, the captain made his move. He pulled out a small metal flask of whiskey and offered it to Badger. He would let the liquor loosen up the old rancher. Then he could begin his inquiry. Finally he began by setting the tone with an innocent question.

"That scout," the Captain said, "the one who brought in my supplies, did he ever tell you where he was from?"

Badger shook his head. "Not really. Just another galvanized Yankee who had a belly full of the war. He said losing the war was more than he could handle so he just disappeared into the mountains for a spell. Them Johnny Rebs could never stomach the thought of bluecoats telling them what to do." Badger let the thought and satisfaction of the defeated South stay there for a while. Then he continued, "Seen a lot of them in my time. Most were able to let go; go back to farmin' or driftin.' But some just couldn't. That scout wasn't letting go. He was still carrying a load of hatred in his gut for the other side."

"You sure about that?" the captain inquired in a monotone voice. *Maybe I'm finally on to something here,* he thought.

"Not sure, just guessing," Badger answered, "but I'd say it's an educated guess. He said that after his bunch was wiped out at Glorieta Pass, he just couldn't get the thought of killing union soldiers out of his head. That's why he lit out for the Rockies and then drifted down south into the Sierra Madres for a long time. Just to give the bad memories time to fade away. But I guess they never did…fade away."

"Glorieta Pass. Did he say he was there?" Branan asked, trying to hold back his excitement at making a connection. *Finally!* "You sure he said he was in that battle?"

"Well, I think that's what he said," Badger replied with a shrug of his shoulders. "Cursed those hard rock miners who cut down his men. He said they wiped 'em out to the last man. He was the only one to survive and get away." Badger paused for a moment, throwing a glance at the captain who was staring at him. "I don't know, it was late and he was dog-tired after that skirmish with the Apache. Maybe he was just passing time, you know, telling tales to boost his ego. Man can do a lot of talking when folks aren't listenin'." Badger paused, sucking in his cigar deeply before letting the smoke exhale out his whiskered mouth. "Maybe he was talking nonsense or just confusing one battle for another, but I think that's what he said about Glorieta Pass and all."

There it was! Captain Branan had his answer, and it wasn't good.

The scout must have been the last man of that Confederate squad Branan had tried to wipe out. The lone survivor who knocked him down and got away. The one hobbled gray soldier who saw his face full and then took out one of the captain's eyes. The scout knew what Branan had done. Battle or not. The scout knew that killing unarmed wounded men was not part of the code of battle - for either side.

Captain Brannan knew it too. No matter that too much time had passed for it to make any difference. There would never be a Court of Inquiry nor any judgment placed against the captain. Nevertheless the scout knew who he was, and if he still had killing on his heart, he meant to kill the captain if the opportunity presented itself - unless the captain could kill him first.

Now Branan had a legitimate reason to find the girl and therefore find that man. Badger was right, either way they had to find out what happened to the two men sent to rescue the girl, and if she had been saved.

No Chance of Escape

Death stalked the ancient stone tower. Lurking in the shadows, it waited for the three whites to make their next move; to show their faces or attempt another getaway. Flint and quartz tipped arrowheads were aimed at the narrow slots in the tower's enclosure. Apache rifle notches were lined up on their entrance. If their prey made attempt to escape, the Apache would put a quick end to it.

Time favored the Apache. The trio had a day or two, maybe three, but no more than that before hunger or thirst would drive them from their fortress. Certain death awaited by arrow, slug, or knife. There was no escape from the tower that protected the three for now.

Minutes before, the Apaches had tried storming the building but the gang's bullets had broken the back of their rush. Pony's sniping hit with pinpoint accuracy, driving all but the most eager young bucks behind cover. The attack had taken its toll on the Apaches.

Three brown bodies now lay scattered in the bright sunlight. Young warriors who hadn't estimated the mountain man's third floor overall view of the ruins. Caught in his killing range, they couldn't escape his shower of slugs.

In the dim light of the stone edifice, the survivors waited out their time, readying for another attack; another rush that would break down the door and bring death rushing with it. The Apaches could starve them out or charge again. The Apaches were patient. They'd bide their time and weigh their advantages first. All Jeb, Pony and Charlotte could do was wait and wonder what the Apache would do next.

Outside sounds were muffled by the tower's thick layers of stone and adobe brick. In most places, the wooden floors had completely dried out, creaking and straining under the pressure of new footsteps. In spots, it had also begun to rot and fall away, making for unsafe and treacherous for footing. Snakes and rodents scattered at the approach of strangers invading their nesting place. The air was pleasantly cool but stale with a smell of mustiness and decaying wood.

Once he had caught his breath and re-bandaged his bothersome scalp wound, Burns moved to secure the door permanently. Their attack had brought the Apaches up to the door but they hadn't thrown their weight against it. An ironwood branch, jammed into a brace, was its only lock. Grabbing a fallen timber, Jeb buried one end in the dirt and propped the other end up against the door, jamming it tightly against the door.

The old tower door was constructed of pine and had never been repaired. Its hinges were fashioned with a series of wooden plugs and crudely cut holes. In some ancient battle long before, those hinges had been attacked with axes and the battered pieces never replaced. Now only the timber acted as a brace, lodging the door tightly into its frame.

Jeb Burns scratched his beard and peered through cracks in the door's panels. The Apaches gave no signs of attacking again. A brown movement here and a sun flare there were the only hints of anyone prowling outside.

It doesn't really matter, Jeb thought. *We're not prepared for a long siege.* Two canteens and a meager ration of food wouldn't be enough to sustain the three of them for more than a couple of days. Shells were running low and all the horses gone. Charlotte was calm but Pony was acting crazy again, and the two wranglers were dead. If Jeb was honest with himself, it didn't matter when the Indians came again, he had nothing to stop them with anyway.

In his gut, a foreign feeling was starting to emerge - a need to protect this woman at all costs. He desired to save Charlotte's life if for no other reason than to see her off to California. She was a woman like no other he'd ever met before. This woman stirred up in him emotions he hadn't experienced in many years; primitive, and at its core, craving her close to him.

He wanted to touch her pale white skin. He wanted to inhale her womanly smell even in the dust and dirt and heat. He hadn't missed her surreptitious glances at him when she didn't think he would notice. It was very complicated and confusing for a man left alone in the mountains for far too long, too long drifting in the desert's scarifying heat, and too long ignoring the danger of death lurking behind every rock.

Edward's body was 20 feet from the tower. The cowboy was lying twisted in an odd shape where he had slipped out of Burns arms. His face was exposed to sunlight, mouth agape, eyes staring vacantly skyward. Already flies had begun to dot his hands and face like black spots. It would get worse as the heat increased. One of the Apaches, in the attack, had driven a lance into the body. It loomed above the still figure, its stub feather dangling in a slight breeze.

The scout thought of Charlotte and smiled to himself. There they were; two men and a girl; a woman really. The only survivors of a party of five left trapped in an ancient pueblo tower and cut off from any help. They were surrounded by Apaches intent on killing them, and that woman hadn't uttered a word of desperation or fear. Charlotte held her fear inward, unlike the other two who died whimpering in fear.

Despite the girl's confidence, their situation still looked hopeless. One more concentrated rush and the tower door would come down. The thought consumed Jeb and he tried to push it aside for anything more positive, but nothing surfaced. The utter fact that they would, in all probability, die in that stone tower without room to maneuver or fight back hung like a death wish over his head.

"Can I come back down?" a voice asked. It was the girl, peering down through a small circular hole in the second level floor. Her hands were already on the ladder, her agile body ready for the descent.

"I guess; one place is as unsafe as the next!"

Charlotte bounced down two rungs at a time, almost losing her balance at the bottom. She carried a piece of jerked beef in one hand. "Here, this is for you," she said, "I took a piece up to Pony but he doesn't want anything to eat".

Jeb took it without breaking his concentration out the door slits. Ripping off a piece with his teeth, he handed the rest back. "Save it," he said, "we'll have to ration whatever is left."

Charlotte leaned against the rough cut stone, her back to the coolness. She stood motionless for a while then said, "Pony's not the least bit worried. I think he actually enjoys all of this. I think he has a fascination with killing." Her eyes sought out Jeb's. He glanced over at her. Their eyes locked for a moment, no emotions exchanged. They just stared at one another, Charlotte trying to read him, Jeb trying to do the same back. Then the scout broke his concentration and returned to stare out the door.

"Maybe he does like killing," Jeb said to no one in particular. "Pony's a hard one to read."

"Impossible, I'd say," Charlotte replied.

They lapsed back into silence. Charlotte sorted through the saddlebags, rearranging food into one bag and cartridges and extra clothes into the other. "What do you think is going to happen to us?"

"You don't want to know. Let's not talk about it," Burns answered.

Charlotte's face bristled for a moment. Then she caught herself, regained a calm composure and continued, "Yes, I do want to know. That's why I asked." Her eyes pleaded innocence and curiosity, but also firmness and a determination to get an answer. She was not about to be turned away.

Subconsciously Jeb ran his tongue across his overhanging mustache, chewing on it. He removed more dirt from his forehead and tipped chin to chest, sighing deeply. Then he cocked an eye up at the girl. If she wanted to know, he'd have to tell her.

"I'd be lying if I told you we've got a chance in hell of getting out of here. They've got all the advantages and pride is on their side. They've lost too many warriors to let us go now. They'll stay until those deaths are avenged. That's why we will have to save our last cartridges for ourselves." He paused. "If they don't attack soon, they'll probably wait until just before dawn."

"Apaches don't fight at night, is that always the case?"

"Usually," Jeb answered, "nighttime spooks them. Comanches will attack at night. They're the only Indians that will, but not the Apache. It has to do with their belief that if they die at night their souls will wander this world forever." Jeb let his thoughts collect again. "They've got plenty of food with our dead horses, water nearby, and no reason to charge us tonight. They can just wait us out, then walk in and take our scalps." Jeb caught himself and felt stupid at his bluntness. "Sorry," he offered up.

Charlotte felt the seriousness of their predicament welling up inside. It was a hard and cruel land worlds away from the civility she'd known in Philadelphia. "I wish the cavalry had stopped them before they reached Badger's place." she commented. "None of this would have happened then." Her voice raised an octave. "I wish we could just rid the territory of those heathens."

"Those are mighty strong words for a refined lady," Jeb said.

"Well, that's how I feel. The Apache won't stay on the reservations. They won't stay at peace. This territory would be a better place to live if they weren't around."

"For whom?" Jeb asked suddenly.

Charlotte's forehead wrinkled as her eyes questioned the scout's statement. He was very serious. His intent gray eyes stared back at her, digging in. "What do you mean?" she asked.

Jeb let out a low sigh, "The army will never defeat the Apache. General Crook tried using Indian scouts and he had some success but the Apache kept turning up in pockets of a dozen or so, raiding and killing and hiding across the border. Now General Miles is doing the same. He'll probably meet with the same results."

"Why can't the army defeat them?" Charlotte asked.

Jeb smiled. "The average Apache can cover four miles an hour, maybe 15 to 20 miles before he takes a break. That's on foot. If he has a horse, he'll probably have several spare mounts along. When the mount gets tired, the Apache will cut him loose and grab the other mount. One Apache can easily cover 100 miles a day that way. Army can never keep up that kind of pace. Their horses are meant for strength, not speed or endurance."

Charlotte looked at the scout, studying his hardened face and tired eyes. Beneath his haggard countenance, she could sense a gentler side of the man seated next to her. Jeb gave her a quick glance then continued.

"Apaches know this land like the back of their hand. They've been here for centuries. They've fought and defeated the Conquistadors, Spanish Colonials, the Mexican Federales, and the U.S. Cavalry. They're as stealthy as a mountain lion and as cunning as a wolf. If need be, they can strip down to their breechcloth and moccasins and blend into the terrain and you'll never ever spot them, even if you're standing right over them."

Charlotte continued staring at Jeb, captivated by his calm demeanor and quiet analysis of their attackers. He was calm and collected almost as if he had come to grips with his fate and that of his companions. There did not seem to be any fear in the man.

"The problem with fighting the Apache is predicting what they'll do next - because you can't. You end up fighting them on their terms. They're cruel and ruthless to their enemies. You don't want to get taken alive. I once found a trapper the Apaches had ambushed. I had to pull him out of a cactus tree and then wait for him to die..."

"Please!" Charlotte shuttered at the thought of that wretched soul.

Jeb grew quiet. "I didn't mean to upset you," he said, "I just want you to know what we're up against."

"You know a lot about the Apache," Charlotte said, trying to ease the tension in the room. She moved closer to the scout.

"I do," Jeb agreed. "And I respect them. I'll kill them if need be, but I still respect them."

Jeb rested his chin on his hands wrapped around the gun barrel. "It's funny, you know; but they're probably thinking the same thing about us. Wondering why the white man came out here to kill their game, settle their land, mine their sacred mountains, and move them to good-for-nothing plots of dirt and rock called reservations."

"I don't understand," Charlotte offered. "Settlers never did the Apache any harm. All they wanted to do is build their ranches and raise their families. There's nothing wrong with that, is there?"

Jeb was hardly feeling in the mood for an argument. "Nothing wrong with it except they're doing it on Indian land. Settlers are taking land away from the Apache just like those Yankee blue-bellies are taking over plantations and farms right now in the South. Nothing wrong with it, if you subscribe to the theory that the victor gets all the spoils."

Charlotte was perplexed. "I don't understand you," she said, "the Apaches are trying to kill us and you tell me you think they have a right to do it?"

"A right to? No! But I understand why they're after us," he quipped.

"I don't understand," said the girl.

"Forget it; in a short time it won't make any difference what either one of us thinks about the Apache. They'll kill us and the whites will eventually kill all of them. That or herd them onto reservations. Same as killing them. In the end, what difference will any of this make?"

The silence grew heavy between them. "Look, I don't want to argue with you. Now is not the time to debate the plight of the Apache," Charlotte said.

"You're right about that. Wouldn't make any difference anyway," Jeb replied.

Charlotte surprised the scout with her next question.

"So you lived and trapped among the Indians for a long time," she said, still staring away from him. She saw him turn and look at her out of the corner of her eye and turn away again.

"I did."

"It must have been lonely for you. All that time spent in the mountains away from your family." She glanced over at Jeb but he was staring out at nothing.

"Did you have a family? I mean, was there a woman back then?" Charlotte asked hesitantly.

Jeb registered surprise at the question. He looked over at Charlotte. She kept looking away from him, pretending to be preoccupied. "Yes. She was back in Texas, waiting for me to come home."

"And?" Charlotte asked.

"She died before I made it back," Jeb answered.

"I'm sorry."

"So was I."

"Was?" Charlotte repeated, now turning to look at Jeb with a concentrated stare. Her eyes searched his face but it told her nothing. Jeb's face was vacant.

"Was," Jed repeated himself. He said it as a statement of fact. "That was a very long time ago. Far too long to hold on to. That memory has faded like a lot of other things that used to be my life back then."

"You've been alone ever since?" came the next question.

Jeb looked over at Charlotte. She was staring at him, blinking her eyes in the dim light. The question took him aback. He hadn't thought of all those years alone as anything but the norm. When he needed a woman, he knew where to find them. He seldom did … until now.

"Too bad," Charlotte blurted out, surprising even herself. She didn't dare look over at Jeb. She was afraid what his reaction might be. "What I meant was that you seem like a good man Jeb Burns, a kind man … unlike anyone I've ever met."

"You need to get back to civilization," Jeb laughed. Charlotte joined him with a soft chuckle. He cracked a fleeting smile, then it disappeared. "I'm not a good man. I've sent a lot of men to heaven or hell - whichever the good lord chose for them. Red legs in Missouri. Federals out West. Apaches. A couple of drifters that tried to rob me once. It didn't really matter. Nothing made sense back then."

Charlotte wanted to probe deeper into this mystifying man's difficult life and uncertain future, but before she could utter a word, Jeb was on his feet and moving toward the window slit. He stared out the window briefly, and then faced Charlotte.

"If the Apache don't get us, the thirst will. We can't go very long without water. Not in this heat. Not trapped in here." He went back to staring out the narrow slot of a window.

"What are you ruminating about?" Charlotte asked softly.

Jeb turned back to her again. "Talking to you has stirred up a whole parcel of memories," he answered.

"Good ones, I hope?"

Before Jeb could reply something caught his ear. He turned to look out the window. At the same instant he caught the flash of red movement among the ruins directly across from the tower, the snipers opened up.

A staccato of shots rattled against the towers window slits.

"Get down," Jeb shouted as he threw his body against the stone wall.

Flickers of flame lit up shadows back in the ruins. Apaches popped out of dark recesses, fired and dropped behind cover again. Others ran forward in a wide skirmish line, firing as they advanced. Some bullets ricocheted off the stone layers, singing through the air. Others went through the slits and thudded into wood. Splinters leapt off the door as slugs ripped into it. The centerboards cracked and broke open as concentrations of bullets literally ate their way through the wood.

Jeb grabbed Charlotte by her arm and shoved her into a corner as the first barrage smashed through the door. He pressed himself against the wall next to it, waiting for a chance to fire back. The air was alive with spent pieces of hot lead and wood fragments.

"I've got to go upstairs. My gun is there," Charlotte shouted.

"Stay down," Jeb threw back. "It's too dangerous to move."

"No, I need to help," the girl shot back, jumping up and dashing toward the ladder.

Jeb reached out to stop her but missed. He landed flat on his face. Charlotte jumped past his outstretched hand and scrambled up the rickety ladder.

On the third level, slugs ripped through the open slits, sending Pony diving to the wooden floor. The whining slugs ricocheted off walls, dropping like white-hot raindrops to sizzle on the floor. A look of glee lit up the mountain man's bearded face. He shouted and cursed the Indians, daring them to approach the tower. As bullets continued battering against the stone, he leapt up, shooting out the slit at an awkward angle.

There was no lull in the attack. Even as sniper bullets began to diminish, the skirmish line tightened and a body of warriors, a dozen in number, rushed the door. Carrying their Springfield's and Spencer's at hip level, the wild-eyed Apaches fired into the door, driving Jeb farther back into the corner. Jeb climbed the ladder quickly to the second level. He lay flat on the floor, aiming his rifle at the door below.

Sniper fire was effectively keeping Pony's shots wild and inaccurate. Try as he might, the mountain man could stay up only seconds before another slug struck the inside wall, bouncing around above him.

From a second floor slit, Charlotte tried to fire down on the attackers, but she too was sent to the floor as bullets sought out her position. The sounds of rifles beating against the wooden door sent a chill down both their spines.

"Get that ladder up," Jeb shouted as he emptied his Spencer down at the door.

The pounding continued. A rifle butt broke through the slug-eaten wood. Burns emptied his revolver through the door. The pounding stopped only for a moment. The scout scrambled up the ladder to the next floor.

Then a shoulder hit the door, loosening the timber brace behind it. Two more bodies hit the door in unison. It bulged in, creaking on its broken hinges. The centerboards cracked and broke through.

Gunfire riddled the air. The Apaches were on the other side pumping slugs into the first level. Burns slapped another tube into the Spencer's stock. He dropped cartridges into the revolver's chamber. *This is it,* he thought.

The ladder was pulled up and propped against the wall. If the Apaches broke through they would find an empty room. Gunpowder drifted up to sting Jeb and Charlotte's eyes. He and the girl readied themselves for the charge. Gunfire sailed up at them, thudding into the wooden floor under their stomachs. Any second now, bodies would come spilling through the doorway.

Burns remembered his cavalier statement about saving the last slugs for themselves. But now he wondered if he could really do it. Charlotte inexplicably and marvelously meant something to him. He wouldn't try to pin a logical explanation to the feeling. It was there and that was trouble enough.

The door gave way. The timber brace, loosened by constant pounding, was slack enough to slide up as three warriors burst through the doorway, jarring the door back. Jeb dropped his Spencer's barrel to fire down.

Then, it happened.

A blinding flash of yellow light and a deafening roar silhouetted the group of Apaches spilling through the doorway.

An explosion lifted the attackers off the floor and dropped them back down. Dust, smoke, and acid clouds filled the first and second levels. Where the Apaches had been standing a second before, nothing remained. Only rag tag remains of bodies were slumped in a pile in the doorway. The gas and smoke was blinding. The girl coughed feverishly. Jeb instinctively fired his carbine down past the bodies. There was no returning gunfire.

Heckling erupted above the pair. Pony was rolling on the floor in fits of laughter. He shouted and cursed and fired his Sharps rapidly out the window slit.

Gasping for fresh air, Jeb maneuvered Charlotte's face to one of the slits, then crawled himself to his window. The survivors of the attack were stumbling back, some bleeding badly, others limping, all in a daze and shock. Protective fire failed to stop Pony from cutting down several Indians before they reached cover.

Jeb dropped his Spencer and climbed the ladder to the third floor. "What the hell was that?" he coughed out.

"A little surprise of mine," came a reply followed by more laughter. Yellow teeth, framed by a tangle of beard, filled the mountain man's face. "Couple of sticks of dynamite. Some surprise, eh? I found them in my medicine bag."

"Do you have any more?"

"Nay, that was all I had," Pony said with a frown followed by a swift grin, "but they don't know that."

Jeb slumped against the ladder. Now the Apaches had no choice but to try to burn them out or starve them out. They wouldn't risk rushing the tower again. They'd probably try fire arrows on the door next time.

The door!

Jeb dropped down the ladder to the second level. The girl wasn't there. Before he could think, he saw her on the first level, trying to move the wreck of a door back in place. Jeb dropped down and stopped. The smell and sight made him nauseous.

Bodies lay piled up just outside the doorway. Bits and pieces still stuck to the inside walls. A hand in one corner, part of a brain smeared against the back wall. The force of the explosion had torn the door off its hinges, throwing it back against the wall.

Charlotte struggled with the heavy door.

"What are you doing down here?" Jeb demanded.

"What does it look like I'm doing?" she snapped back, "I'm trying to get this thing back in place. Are you going to help or just stand there and watch me work?" She capped her statement with a playful smile and Burns' face went from perplexed to irate and back to bewildered.

What the hell, he thought, *why try to figure her out? Living with her 24 hours a day is driving me crazy anyway. Why rush the process?*

Risking rifle fire, Jeb slipped behind the broken door and edging Charlotte to one side, he slowly moved the heavy door back into the shattered doorframe. He could feel his skin pressing against the holes peppered throughout the door itself. *An inviting target!* Nothing happened. There was neither gunfire nor arrows from the Apaches. *They must be licking their wounds after that last one,* Jeb thought.

After scrounging up more timber, Jeb was able to jam the door into its frame and lodge scattered wood pieces behind it again. It was a crude job at best. Not enough to hold back any concentrated attack or stop fire arrows but it was a blockade and it was in place.

CHAPTER FOURTEEN

Nightfall came slowly, wrapping itself over the pueblo like a gray shawl. Before the sun's fading orange light had dipped completely behind a neighboring hillside, Burns carefully inspected the terrain below. Up and down the valley, little escaped him and nothing relieved his concern. A brown hawk, out hunting, flew high over an outer valley beyond the neighboring shale hillside. Along the ridgeline a mule deer appeared only for a moment, sensed humans, and promptly disappeared. A hundred yards in the other direction, a covey of Mexican quail whistled cheerfully to a second hatch nearby. Darkness and the cool of evening would rouse a variety of nocturnal animals.

Since their disastrous attack hours before, the Apaches had kept well hidden back in the ruins. Sniper bullets kept the trio on edge and ever cautious of the window slits. Still the Indians gave no indication of an imminent attack. To amuse himself and unnerve the Indians, Pony kept up a constant chorus of hooting and long drawn out owl sounds. The Apaches remained unmoved, neither angered nor frightened by the sounds of the feared spirit - the owl God.

The little light that remained had cast the second level into an eerie shadow of dullness which was punctuated by two shafts of dying light coming from the window slits. Pony dropped down the ladder without warning. Burns and Charlotte had burrowed up against one wall. They could still see the area directly in front of the tower. The first level ladder had been hauled up and plunked against the rail. Both revolvers and rifles were on their laps, ready.

"What's to eat?" the mountain man demanded as his boots landed heavily on the groaning wood.

Charlotte reached into the saddlebag but Pony grabbed it out of her hand. "Hey!" she started to protest.

"There's enough for all of us," Burns said, his mouth curling at the corner.

Pony rummaged through the bag, drawing out a large piece of jerked beef and a handful of dried hard biscuits. He turned for the ladder. And as he did, a smirk came across his face, his shaggy beard jerking as lips chomped on the powdery biscuits.

"Did you leave any for us?" Jeb asked sarcastically. "We've got to eat too. We don't know how long this siege is going to last."

The mountain man turned. He looked at the food in his hand and then back at the pair. "Who are you trying to buffalo?" he said. "They'll be back tomorrow for sure. If we aren't outta here by morning, we're as good as dead." He paused for effect then continued, "We won't need this food then. If we do get out, we can always live off the land." He started up the ladder and threw back, "So either way, this ain't too much and I'm eatin' now!" and he was gone.

Jeb watched Pony climb the weak ladder and roll over the third level floor. The old mountain man was telling him something in his own bragging manner.

"You found anything up there we should know about?" Jeb called out after him.

Pony's hairy face appeared by the opening. "I ain't found nothin' yet, but I'm looking." He answered then he stuffed another whole biscuit in his mouth and rolled away.

"Was he serious?" Charlotte asked. "Do you think he's found a way out of here?" Her eyes suddenly alive with surprise and hope. "Easy, don't get your hopes up," Jeb cautioned her. "I've heard that some of these places have crypts or hidden rooms. That doesn't mean this particular one does or that the chambers lead anywhere." He needed to calm the girl down and squash any unrealistic hopes she might have. He continued, "I'll go up after a while and see if he's found anything." The last thing the scout needed was an excited girl, pinning her hopes on the bragging jest of the wrinkled mountain veteran. Charlotte settled back, deflated.

They ate uneasily, picking at the little food that remained. There was only enough water to wet their lips and wash some of the dust off their faces. Lottie turned from her food and ran one hand loosely against the wall behind her. She kept searching the walls with her eyes. Even in the dim light, growing steadily darker, she studied the layers of rock and adobe, one stratified layer at a time, desperate for signs of loose stone or blocks. Jeb sighed to himself as he watched her concentrate on her search, lost in a hope of release.

Burns finished his meal, washing down the powdery crust and dryness of beef with a short swig of water. He checked his belt loops, less than 20 cartridges left. Then he leathered his revolver and climbed the ladder to Pony's third level. Poking his head through the hole, he surprised the mountain man who was busily picking at a wall with his long cruel-looking hunting knife. Pony spun around on his knees, eyes flashing anger, his knife braced.

"Damn you!" he spat out. "Don't ever sneak up on me like that or I'll run you through."

"Take it easy, old man," Jeb said calmly. "You were so busy with that damn wall you didn't hear me. Have you found anything yet?"

The mountain man cocked an eye at the scout then shook his head. "Not yet, but if there's anything here, I'll find it."

Burns dropped back to the second level. By now it was dark inside the room. The girl was up against one wall, running her fingers deftly along the rock layers, probing with the tips for something. She turned as Jeb came off the ladder. She still wore the face of concern and steady determination.

"You're sure they won't attack us tonight?" She asked.

"It's true," Jeb replied. "Like I said, Apache religion says if they die in the darkness, their souls will wander in eternal darkness. But come first thing tomorrow morning…" he paused, examining Charlottes' face, "Well, it's true what Pony said about them coming back."

"What are we going to do?" Charlotte pleaded in an oddly controlled tone. Only her eyes betrayed the fear held back by her steady voice.

Jeb didn't know what to say. He could tell her the truth that in all likelihood they would be dead by early morning. Or he could try to convince the girl that help was somehow on its way. She didn't give him a chance to say anything.

"You don't have to answer me," she said. "It was a foolish question. I guess I know the outcome already." She quit her probe and leaned an elbow against the saddlebag, resting her head in the cup of her hand. She looked at the scout with a plain yet questioning look. Her hair hung in dirty tangles down her shoulders and her face was still streaked with dust from the explosion. She wanted to say something, Burns could sense it. She hesitated, seemingly debating the question in her own mind first.

"Something you want to say?" he asked.

"How'd you know?" she asked, turning toward him in amazement.

"I could read your face, like an open book," Jeb answered. "You didn't come over here just to pass the time. What's troubling your mind?"

"What you said about the Apache and our taking his land? Do you really believe that?"

Jeb pursed his lips in displeasure. He knew he shouldn't have brought it up. She wouldn't understand how he felt or why he compared the white settlement of the territory with that of the South overrun with carpetbaggers and military adjutants. Charlotte was an Easterner. Not his kind of people. Certainly not the kind to understand his Southeastern Texas way of thinking. But she would persist until he explained what he meant. Jeb knew Lottie wouldn't quit with her questions until satisfied.

"I'm sorry I brought it up," he said.

"No," she insisted. "I want to know."

"Yes," Jeb interjected. "I didn't mean to begin a debate. I don't expect you to understand." His eyes tried to tell her he was sincere. "I'm not sure I understand it myself. Killing Apaches doesn't bother me if they're killing whites. But I'm no scalp hunter or bounty man. I don't like fighting and killing for no reason. I can't blame the Apache for fighting for what they believe in or what they think is right. I'd do the same myself … I did the same myself."

"In the War Between the States?"

"In the war."

"Why did you say it doesn't make any difference in the end?" Lottie asked. "Why are you so fatalistic?"

Jeb pulled out the half burnt cigarrito butt he'd gotten from Pony. He lit the stub and drew in deeply on the noxious fumes. He slid his beaten hat farther back on his head and absentmindedly scratched his forehead. "Fatalistic! What about realistic?"

He settled back for a long discussion. "There's no way in hell the Apache can stop the white man from taking over his land. There are too many of us and too few of them. He's a scrapper all right and he won't quit. But the cards are stacked against him. A lot of whites are going to die before the Indians are wiped out. But neither side can stop now. It's too late. It's only a matter of time, but I won't be around so it won't affect me."

"Don't you care what's going to happen out here in the territories?" Charlotte questioned.

"I told you, I already know," Jeb answered. "And no, I don't rightly care." His eyes grew vacant. His thoughts were a million miles away. After a pause he said, "And besides, if I can get out of here, if we get out of here, I'm heading farther west. I've heard say that towns along the coast are growing and there's work to be had. The railroad is coming and will connect this country soon. Besides I'm through fighting and killing and not knowing where my next meal is coming from. There's work out on the coast. That's where I'll be heading."

Charlotte watched the scout with a mixture of envy and confusion, doubt and confidence. Her dark eyes searched his face for a reading of his thoughts. She read nothing. But still she couldn't let it go at that. "You're so certain of everything," she said. "About what you're going to do, if and when you get out of here. About going to California. About the Apache. What if you're wrong? Have you ever thought of that?"

Words, words. They had been bantered back and forth for so long; Jeb was no longer paying attention. His mind had drifted back to years ago. Back to a small Texas cabin and a girl in the doorway. Waiting for her young lover to return. Waiting and waiting … until the Comanches came instead.

Whatever had been alive in Jeb back then was no longer there. Jeb Burns was a different man with no resemblance to his past. Nothing remained except the memories that were fading fast.

"Jeb!"

The scout looked up, jarred back to reality.

Charlotte had raised herself up and was leaning against the wall. He could make out her face and form in the dim light. "You said there's work along the coast. What do you know about San Francisco? I'm a seamstress. Maybe there's work for me there. I mean, if we get out of here alive. I want to leave this part of the country too."

Jeb looked up, surprised. "You should go back East," he cautioned her. "A woman like you is too good for this part of the country. It will either kill you or leave you dried up and worn out like an old bear skin."

Her reply came quickly. "I told you I won't go back East. There's nothing back there for me anymore. Someday I want to settle down and have a family. Perhaps I might own my own business like my father. I want to be in control of my life, my destiny."

Crazy talk, thought Jeb, but he wisely decided to say nothing.

"And Badger's ranch? You won't go back there either?"

"No, I told you…"

The words sat heavy in the air. Jeb looked over at Charlotte and saw something in her eyes. *She has her reasons*, he thought. *I'm not about to push it. If she doesn't want to return to the ranch, I'll forgo my pay and let the girl have her way.*

Charlotte continued as if she hadn't heard the scout. "I think you and I understand one another. We care about the same things."

"Wait a minute!" Jeb protested, "We just met and not under the best of circumstances. You've been through a lot. That's quick judgment about an old saddle tramp long in the tooth."

"You're not being honest with yourself," Charlotte said softly. "I think I'm a good judge of character and you are a man of honor," she paused, hesitant to let out the rest, "…for a man with a troubled past."

Jeb couldn't help but smile at the girl's intuition as well as her perception of his character.

They looked at one another for a long time, letting their eyes do all the talking. If either had a slight curl on their lips, it wasn't perceptible to the average eye. But they both felt it. In their hearts.

"A man with a troubled past," Jeb repeated in a mocking tone, followed by a wide smile.

"Stop it!" Charlotte shot back, smiling at his self-deprecating humor. It broke the tension and they both laughed at the thought. "I was just making conversation."

"You shouldn't think so much. It's bad for the brain!" Jeb offered up.

"You talked about the thirst," Charlotte said.

"You don't want to know."

"Don't do that to me, Jeb Burns," Charlotte shot back. "I want to…"

"A man only lives for three or four hours after the thirst craze hits him. By then it's too late. Strange thing…" Jeb stopped.

"What?"

"A man dying of thirst always takes off his clothes. I don't know why but they always do. I found a miner once lost in the Sonora. His face was black as coal and his tongue had swollen up so that it stuck out of his mouth by a couple of inches."

"What did you do?" Charlotte asked.

"I only had enough water for myself and my horse. And a 100 miles still to go. That old man was too far gone to be saved."

"And?"

"I helped the man to heaven. It was the right thing to do."

"Would you shoot me, Jeb Burns?" Charlotte asked.

"And run the risk of your Irish wrath?" Jeb answered. "I don't think so!"

Charlotte laughed again, stronger this time, more sure of herself. She could talk to this man about horrible things and yet still feel comfort by his mere presence.

She felt good inside. He did feel something for her. No matter how much he tried to deny it, she knew in her heart that he wasn't as aloof or cold as he pretended to be. She was felt something for this peculiar man. She couldn't pin it down. She was afraid to explore the thought any deeper. Not now. Not under these circumstances.

"You know…"

"Go to sleep," Jeb interrupted her.

Charlotte smiled then laid back, her head still resting in the cup of her hand. Her shirt rose and fell in long gentle swells. Her mouth fell slightly open and she seemed at last content.

Jeb hadn't noticed the light until it lay across the girl's face. Two thin shafts of moonlight poured in through the second level slits. One glance outside told him what he feared. The tower had been situated so that even at night, it was still bathed in moonlight. Nowhere except the corners was there protective darkness. They were still in a fishbowl. It was quiet inside the room. *Even Pony is unusually quiet,* Jeb thought. *Perhaps too quiet?*

Jeb went up the ladder quickly. He stuck his head up to the third level, his chin even with the wooden beams on the floor. He blinked once, and then twice, there was little moonlight to illuminate the room. Even in the dimness, it was evident.

There was no one in sight. Pony had disappeared!

The mountain man's medicine bag was still in one corner alongside his Sharps buffalo rifle. Pony had to be close by. He would never leave his tools behind. Jeb climbed up and sat on the floor. There was no one on the third level. For a foolish second, Burns looked at the window slit then realized no human could possibly fit through there.

A sound caught his ear. A scraping sound, close by. It came from the left, in a far corner, hidden in pitch darkness. The scout moved towards the sound.

He spotted it. A hole, no more than a foot and a half high at the most and only two feet wide. Gripping his six-shooter, Burns crawled on hands and knees to the hole and cautiously stuck his head in. It was pitch black inside. He could see nothing. The coolness of the crypt struck him. It was a stale air, smelling of decay.

"If you're coming through, move in. Otherwise stick your face someplace else."

Pony was in the crypt.

The scout wiggled through still gripping his revolver tightly. He couldn't see a thing. Then the blackness was split with a tiny pinprick of light flickering in the corner, four or five feet away. It was a match lighting a candle.

"That from your medicine bag too?"

"Where else?" Pony chuckled in satisfaction with himself. "Them ancients did a damn fine job covering the crevices with rock dust. But I found this here crypt anyway."

"How do you know it's a crypt?"

"I found two wrinkled pieces of injun over here in the corner. That's how!"

Jeb could feel excitement rising inside. *Escape! Now there's a chance!*

"Does this vault lead anywhere? Can we get outta here?"

"It may, but it'll take a long time to find it." The mountain man shook his head. "It's blacker than pitch in here and this candle ain't gonna last long if I burn it all up now." He shifted his weight and resumed scratching away. "I'm gonna have to do my fingering in the dark." With that, the Pony snipped out the tiny flame with his pinched fingers.
"I'll help you. You take one side. I'll take the other," Burns suggested.

"Who you giving orders to?" Pony shot back, "You didn't find this tomb. I did. I'll do my own digging. You want to go snooping, go look up the little girl's skirt. But do it outta my hole."

Burns paused, trying to judge how close Pony had moved toward him. He felt his presence close, too close for comfort. If the mountain man found a tunnel which led out of the crypt and away from the ruins, he might knife the scout, take or kill the girl and be gone. But if Burns stayed in the tunnel, he'd have to depend on his ears and instinct and hope Pony didn't try to kill him. Either way, it was a dangerous proposition.

Then the scout remembered Pony's bag. He moved quickly, backing out the hole, his six-shooter still aimed in Pony's general direction. When he got out, he checked to make sure his eyes hadn't deceived him. No! The bag was there, and with it the mountain man's rifle.

"Pony," Jeb called back into the hole, "I've got your medicine bag and rifle out here. You find a tunnel and decide to leave alone; you'll go without your rifle or scalps." He could hear the mountain veteran growl and curse in the darkness. Then Jeb added, "If you want to work alone, go right ahead, but tell us when or if you find anything!"

"I want that bag!"

"Not on your life," Burns stated flatly. He moved to the opposite wall facing the hole, his Spencer on his lap and the medicine bag by his side. The odor of scalps rose off the leather skin and the scout had to push the bag away because of the repulsive smell.

The mountain man grumbled to himself and soon began scraping again against the stone, feeling the blackness for holes. Content to be by himself, Pony soon forgot about his medicine bag and concentrated on the black walls and the possibility of escape.

The air was still and cool. Pony's scraping worked as a rhythmic easing against the scout's brain, moving him toward sleep. His head bobbed and jerked as he fought sleep. Finally he let it trip him into a shallow dozing

Consciousness came so quickly Burns didn't know if he'd been asleep only seconds or a lot longer. His vision swam a bit, and then steadied. The Spencer was still lying across his lap. The Sharps and medicine bag lay by his side. He looked around. A dim light was growing stronger inside the room. *It must be nearing dawn*, he thought.

Dawn!

If the Apaches were to attack, it would be now!

Pony's scraping had stopped. No sound came from inside the crypt. The scout peered down to the second level. Charlotte was still asleep just as he had left her. Her chest was moving slowly up and down, her hair splayed across her face. Everything seemed the same.

But everything wasn't the same. Jeb could feel a difference. Perhaps a noise, a sound he had heard in his subconscious, something warning him to awaken.

Jeb rolled over and looked out the narrow window slit. He saw them. Apaches moving out into the open, still a safe distance from the tower. They filtered silently over the ruins, weaving through rooms and corridors. Archers arose with the riflemen. They were carrying fire arrows.

Before the scout could shout a warning, several arrows hit the door with a soft whooshing sound. Powder smoke bloomed among the ruins. Shells bracketed the window slits. The hint of smoke began to drift up inside the tower.

"Fire!" Burns shouted to the girl. Charlotte jerked her head up, startled, afraid. She looked around confused for a moment, forgetting where she was, then she saw Jeb on the level above her.

The sound of reed arrows cracking off in the flames reached Burns ears. The door was on fire. It would spread to the wooden interior of the tower in minutes. Charlotte huddled in a corner, afraid to rise for the bullets crashing above her head.

Jeb wriggled to the black hole. He shouted inside, "Pony, have you found anything? They've fired the door. We've got to get outta here!"

No answer.

The scout rolled to the hole in the floor. Bullets cracked over his head and below him. Charlotte still lay in the corner. The tinder-dry floor she lay on was showing smoke between its cracks. Jeb knew it could ignite at any second.

"Lottie," he called down, "you've got to get up here. That floor could go any second now. Come up the ladder, I'll help you." The girl still hesitated; looking up with alarmed eyes. "You can do it," Jeb encouraged her.

Gathering up her courage, Charlotte grabbed the canteens and saddlebag in one hand, her Winchester in the other. She rolled over and over until she reached the foot of the ladder. A slug burst through the wooden floor by her head, shattering splinters over her face. Lottie spit them out and leaping to her feet, she tossed the contents up and into Jeb's lap. Then she scrambled up the ladder after them. Jeb grabbed her arms and in one sweeping motion, had her up and over the lip and rolling on the floor next to him. He hugged her body tightly against his, her head against his lips. Then he slowly released her.

"It's happening," she confessed with a whisper.

"It'll be all right," Jeb lied. He pointed toward the black hole in the corner. "Let's go," he said.

"What is it?"

"It's a crypt Pony found last night," Jeb shouted above the racket. "I hope it's part of a tunnel. Come on!"

Together they wiggled toward the hole. The air above their heads was alive with spent bullets bouncing in all directions. Burns called out again for Pony. Still no answer. They could see nothing but blackness inside. The heat was growing with intensity beneath their bellies. Already the smoke was filling the second level room. As the smoke increased, the firing outside subsided, wolf yipping and yelps rose instead in the early morning air. Their eyes began to water from the choking gray smoke cloud filtering up.

"What are we going to do?" Charlotte pleaded as they reached the hole.

"Crawl inside," Jeb ordered the girl. He levered the Spencer and shouted into the hole. "Pony, we're coming through."

The scout nudged Charlotte as she reluctantly wiggled through the black hole. He shoved the rifles and saddlebags in but he held back the medicine bag. The heat was growing worse. Below he could hear the wood cracking and splitting as flames licked at the ceiling of the first level. The heavy smoke had grown so thick he could hardly breathe. His eyes stung and refused to open. He was blinded for the moment. Holding his breath, the scout flattened his face against the floor. Heat pressed against it.

"There's no one in here," Charlotte yelled back.

The scout could wait no longer. He shoved in the medicine bag, the Sharps, and his own saddlebag. Then he wiggled in himself.

As Jeb entered the near total darkness, a voice broke the silence. It was Pony, calling from a short distance away. His gruff voice was muted and distorted. Jeb could feel Charlotte's presence nearby. He moved until he brushed against her then gently but firmly moved her out of the way. He felt for his revolver still in its holster and asked the girl. "Where did that voice come from?"

A soft hand lay on his arm and she answered, "He's over to the right of us, I think. He sounded like he was in a tunnel or something. Maybe he's found a way out of here."

"Maybe," Jeb replied grimly, still not ready to believe it could be true.

Outside the crypt, only a few feet away, the sound of wood igniting and bursting into flames rose in volume. Smoke was seeping through the hole, growing thicker in the stale air. Charlotte coughed back the fumes. Burns did the same.

"What the hell's going on back there," a gruff voice called out. It was closer this time. As if it was just around a corner nearby.

Jeb palmed his revolver and answered, "They've fired the tower. We've got to get out of here." The scout felt desperation sweeping over him but he fought hard to keep his voice level and calm, hiding the desperate urge inside to run anywhere, just away from the flames.

"Lucky for you two I found us a way outta here," Pony grunted.

"Thank God," Charlotte exclaimed. "Let's go!"

"Not so fast!" the mountain man stopped them. "Where's my rifle and my bag. I ain't going nowhere without them."

Jeb thrust the Sharps and medicine bag in the mountain man's direction. "Here," Jeb said, "Take them. Now let's move!"

Since the tunnel carried little to no draft, most of the smoke stayed inside the crypt. Only the heavy smoke fumes followed the trio into the small, dank tunnel. Despite the lack of draft though, the air was still thick with stirred up dust. Jeb moved the girl in behind Pony and then followed their sounds down the narrow rock tube.

Jeb could see nothing. Only the soft hint of legs brushing along the dirt floor in front of him. Behind the trio, inside the tower, the fire's intensity had grown until it was a roaring conflagration. Wood crumbled and broke as timbers collapsed and fell apart. Jeb sucked in the cool air and realized a chill over his body. He was drenched with sweat. He blinked his eyes but it did no good. Total darkness enveloped his world. He could feel Charlotte's presence just inches away from his outstretched hands. Ahead of her, he could hear the mountain man dragging his medicine bag and rifle in the dirt.

The tunnel walls seemed to close in. Something scraped against his back. It was the ceiling. Inch by elbow inch, the ceiling was dropping down farther and farther until all three were on their stomachs, cheeks in the dirt, burrowing still farther into the side of the mountain.

Suddenly Charlotte stopped. Burns' hands hit her outstretched foot.

"What's wrong?" he asked hurriedly.

Pony's voice came through as if he were talking down a long pipe. "This damn thing splits off into two different directions. I can't tell which one will get us outta here."

Jeb became impatient. "Well, just pick one and let's go!"

"Go to hell, coon," Pony shouted back, his voice booming in the narrow confines. "I'll decide which way I'm going to take."

"Then decide," Jeb shot back, "Now!"

Suddenly behind them, the tower collapsed in an explosion of bursting rocks and white-hot flames. A roar rushed down the tunnel, echoing through their ears. They felt a wave of heat roll over them, followed by stifling smoke fumes. The girl coughed and choked and fought for her breath. Jeb pressed his cheek flat against the dirt and closed his eyes.

"My God," Charlotte coughed out, gasping for air.

"It's all right," Jeb tried to assure her. He laid his hand on her leg, trying to calm her down. "We're still alive. We'll make it out of here, I promise," he said.

Pony moved out again, choosing the wing which forked off to the right. It was larger than the one they had crawled through and the trio could rise up to their knees again. Their pace quickened, each moving as swiftly as their dancing fingers against the rock walls would allow.

Burns lost track of time. It seemed they had crawled for hours. Yet he was certain it was only minutes at the most. They still breathed in stale air. Stale but life-giving. The dirt floor was almost cold, a refreshing change from the heat of the pueblo.

Jeb's mind was still too confused to plan anything beyond getting out of the tunnel and assessing their position once they got to wherever the tunnel led them. No horses, little ammunition, little food, and a scant amount of water left their options very limited. Pony's actions, once he was a free man, would be impossible to predict. And there was still a long ways to go, on foot, back to Badgers spread.

"Found it!"

The words swept a feeling of relief into Jeb's brain. His whole body seemed to turn to liquid and he bowed his head in thanksgiving. He still couldn't see a thing in the pitch-darkness but the mountain man obviously had. Burns could hear him grunting satisfaction and moving faster. Charlotte followed Pony around a corner. Jeb hurried to follow their sounds.

Feeling his way around a sharp turn, Jeb saw it! A tiny patch of light centered in the black distance. The tunnel walls expanded and the trio could stand up, just barely. They moved quickly toward the light. The tunnel opened up into a tiny compartment just inside a hole, which opened to the outside. A dazzling brightness came through the opening, hurting the trio's eyes. Jeb could see sagebrush and bear grass had all but covered the exit. Shafts of light streamed into the tiny hole, warming it.

Pony stuck his head outside the hole, parting the bear grass with his beard. He grunted satisfaction and threw his bag into a corner. Without bothering to say a word to the others, he nestled in the corner and quickly fell asleep, snoring softly.

Charlotte blinked the dust out of her eyes and let out a loud, conscious sigh. Relief was written all over her dirt-streaked, weary face. She smiled at Jeb and then, following Pony, she slipped to the dirt floor and nestled in a corner. She seemed at last content, safe for the moment.

Jeb Burns looked cautiously out the tiny exit hole. The ruins were far below them, off to the right. Whiffs of smoke drifted lazily past their hole along with the sounds of men and horses.
Checking the entrance carefully, Burns could see a narrow, rock-strewn ledge just outside their hole. Peeking his head as far out as he dared, the scout could tell that access to the ledge was by way of a narrow camouflaged track which climbed up to it from a winding dried out stream bed. The track ran at least a quarter of a mile along the side of the mountain and finally dropped almost vertically into the dried bed. Yet the trail was so jammed with cottonwood, sycamore, and mesquite growth that only a determined, watchful eye could ever see it.

That would be their escape route, Burns thought to himself. If they weren't caught first. He had no idea how they would ever make it back to the ranch. Not with the hills alive with Apaches.

"What can you see?" Charlotte questioned him.

Jeb turned to her, a slight smile planted on his face. "I think I see a way out of here. We'll have to wait until nightfall before we can move out. It looks good from here."

The girl was too emotionally drained to respond. She nodded understanding.

Jeb squatted next to her. He said, "Try to get some more sleep. We'll stay here for now. The Apaches will search the tower once it's cooled off. We can't risk leaving in the daylight. Not now. Give them time to move out. When we leave tonight, there'll be no resting for a long time. We've got to put as much distance between this place and ourselves as we can."

"Do you really think we'll get away?" she asked in a tired voice.

"We'll get away. I'm sure of it," he lied.

In short order, Charlotte had fallen asleep and Jeb was lying next to her, staring up at the sky. His eyes were taking in the clouds but he couldn't shake the look that Charlotte had given him when he spoke of heading west, and why it perturbed him so much.

The woman befuddled and fascinated him. She scared him and stirred up emotions he had thought were gone forever. He had no idea where they were headed or what might happen once they reached the safety of a border town and freighters heading west; if Captain Branan wasn't on his trail - or Badger for that matter.

A slow meandering glance toward Pony brought Jeb up suddenly. Pony was gone, medicine bag and rifle with him. Only the sound of the wind remained in his place.

CHAPTER FIFTEEN

Branan's bad luck broke the next day. After a week of tracking ghost trails that went nowhere, his outriders finally crossed the tracks of three horses. Badger quickly identified the two mares from his ranch and a third mount brought along for the girl. The tracks were heading away from the suspected Indian encampment and back toward the ranch.

Later on that same morning, the column found two more sets of tracks; heavily shod horses. Two more white men tracking the trio. It was anyone's guess who the two new tracks might belong to, but Badger was certain he knew. Those tracks belonged to those cowboys who had lit out after Burns and Pony had left. The rancher was sure of it.

Captain Branan's first assumption was that the scout and mountain man had snatched Badger's niece away from the Apaches and were heading back toward the ranch. That is until their tracks converged with the two other riders who were following them. At that point, all five riders had left quickly, riding hard toward the deep recesses of the surrounding hills.

Apache ponies followed them into the hills, converging in from several different directions. There was a firefight not far away and signs of blood. Whether it was white or Apache blood didn't matter. There were no bodies, either white or Apache. Then the tracks had scattered, regrouped, and moved away quickly toward the enclosing hills.

With his outriders moving cautiously ahead of the troop, Captain Branan lead his column toward a pale gray swath of smoke that lingered up ahead, just over a small rise in the flat desert expanse.

A half hour later, the column drew up on the smoldering ruins. The

Apaches had long since cleared out. Amid the hollowed out shell of adobe and brick, the tower was still giving off traces of smoke and ash from the day before. Branan sent two squads out combing the grounds for signs of any kind. There were none. A few spent cartridge shells scattered about the grounds and several arrows still embedded in the burnt out hulk of the tower door. Other than that, the ruins gave no indication if anyone had survived the fire and collapse of the stone tower.

A shout from one of the troopers brought Branan and Badger over to a small gully cut in the embankment that bordered the pueblo ruins. There they found two pasty white naked bodies. They were cut up and mutilated beyond recognition. From one of their hats, Badger identified the body of the younger cowboy. The one with the big mouth. But no more; his nose and eyes had been cut away and stuffed down his throat.

"That's them," Badger announced. "Those two that lit out and stole my stock and killed one of my men. Bastards got what they deserved, I guess."

The captain turned to his sergeant. "Burial squad, Sergeant. Be quick about it. I want to move out before the hostiles' trail goes cold."

The sergeant left quickly with a squad.

The captain turned to Badger. "Mr. Badger, I can only assume that your niece and those two men are in the ruins of that tower. Burnt beyond recognition, I would have to say. I'm sorry."

Badger pursed his lips, chomping on an unlit cigar. "I gotta know for sure. Her parents and all, you know."

"I thought you said she had no living relatives?" Branan asked.

"Just in case there is, I mean," Badger backpedaled. "I gotta know if she died here or got away."

The captain grew irritated at the old rancher's insistence on continuing his search.

"There are no signs of horses leaving these grounds other than Apache ponies. The dead mounts we found came to three. Two others were led away by the Apaches. That would mean the survivors, if there were any, would have no horses and no way of escaping that inferno. If they did get away, the Apaches would have caught them before they got out of sight of this pueblo."

The captain paused to let his statement sink in. "Forget it, Mr. Badger, your niece is gone. So are those two you sent to get her."

"I gotta be sure."

"I have my orders, sir. You may do as you wish. I intend to pursue the Apache until I make contact with them or they cross the border into Mexico. You are welcome to continue on with the troop or go back to your ranch. Decide soon. We'll being leaving as soon as those two drifters are in the ground."

Erratic Behavior

Pony reappeared in the middle of the night without notice or explanation. Jeb watched him settle back into his nest, but said nothing. *No sense in asking,* he thought. The mountain man wasn't quick to say where he'd been. Unless he wanted to talk, Pony wouldn't be sharing anything with Burns or the girl.

But Jeb wasn't about to wait around for Pony's explanation. Just before dusk, a massive cloud formation had moved into the area, blocking out all but faint patches of moonlight. Now the night held little reflective moonlight. Black voids filled the land around the trio. It was time to move out of their cave and back toward civilization.

"Let's head out," Jeb said, "the cloud cover's too good to lose." Expecting an argument, Jeb steeled himself to head out with the girl if need be. Instead Pony arose without an argument and moved out ahead of Jeb and Charlotte.

Slipping down the narrow pathway, Pony was quickly enveloped in sagebrush and bear grass. Burns and the girl followed him, careful to conceal the entrance again with scrub brush. They moved down the wild twisting track quickly and silently, following Pony's bobbing backside to the creek bed.

From the dried up creek bed, the three could see the pile of rubble that was once the pueblo tower, silhouetted against the curving cliff face. All that remained of their tower were whiffs of smoke still curled up from the burnt timber and ruined adobe. They listened for voices, sounds of horses, or movements. They heard nothing. There were no signs of the Apaches.

However, Pony was not easily convinced. He rubbed his dirty matted beard with greasy fingers and scanned the ancient ruins with squinting eyes. The mountain man hadn't spent years trapping alone in the Sierra Madres or hunting in the Mexican deserts without tasting in blood the cleverness of Apache instinct. He knew firsthand the caution needed to remain alive in Apache country. He knew if the Apache had searched the ruins and spotted their escape hole into the crypt, the entire war party would be crawling the hills at that moment, searching for their exit hole. The trio couldn't assume the Indians were gone. They could only assume that danger was close by and would be until they reached safety - somewhere.

Charlotte didn't study the wilderness around them like the two men. Instead she was trying to fend off the flood of memories. She moved mindlessly, letting exhaustion slip her back into a fog. Her mind kept wandering back to the tower, to Billy lying in the sand, and Edward slipping off the scout's shoulders and that lance that had been driven into his body.

To distract herself, she crudely brushed back her thick hair with deft fingers, gathering it in a bunch at the nape of her neck. But as she tried to adjust it and throw a string around the mass, it slipped away, flowing across her back. Her hands were still shaky from the ordeal. They refused to cooperate.

"Here, let me help," Burns said, moving up behind her. He gathered up her matted hair with a gentle sweep of his hands. He held the hair securely while she tied the auburn mass tightly. Jeb rested his hands on her shoulders for a brief moment, and then resumed their journey.

Jeb's walk was more a limp, Charlotte observed, watching him move away. He looked tired and sore. Though not an old man, the ordeal had worn heavily on his face, caking his skin with dirt and fatigue. Only his dark eyes remained ever alert, constantly scanning the ridgeline, back and forth, searching for trouble.

I wonder what he's thinking about, she pondered. *Probably the fastest route west, good riddance to me, and hello California!* It was silly, she had to admit, this thing she felt for him but couldn't define. His story was probably no different from the many sad tales drifting around any spread when the whiskey flowed and men's minds returned to the good old days; the days of misspent youth and the women that got away.

Yet this man was a different. There was more than a faint trace of sensitivity in him. Charlotte could feel it more than see it. It was a gentle nature that was rare out in the wilds of the Southwestern territory. He was a man of character and vision and yet still troubled by something in his past.

At times Jeb did seem to be on the verge of revealing something to her. Saying something he hadn't said before, only hinted at. What that might be she could only try to guess. But from his touches, his glances, those quick smiles that were just as quickly covered up again - from all those signs she knew Jeb was trying to tell her something. The whole thought formed a lump in her stomach and confusion in her head. She tried to dislodge it from her brain. For now, he was the only obstacle between herself and Pony.

Pony seemed crazy and uncontrollable when he gave her those unsettling looks. *Ah, to be back East with my family,* Charlotte thought carelessly until the sharp realization came slamming home again. Back East was no longer her world, her kind of life. She had left it behind for good. Although the territory hadn't been the world she had imagined, it was not bad enough to make her want to return to the old world that had rejected her. She was caught between two worlds, rejecting both, and left searching for a third to choose from. It left her very tired and confused.

Jeb Burns soft-padded alongside Pony. He produced a cigarrito and stuck it in the corner of his mouth. Pony glanced at the cornhusk paper and curled his lips, growling softly to himself. Burns had taken the Mexican cigarettes out of Pony's medicine bag while the mountain man scraped out the tunnel.

"Want one?" the scout asked, barely concealing his joke. He reached for his shirt pocket where the others were jammed. Pony spat at his feet and turned away. "You think you can find a way out of here?" Jeb asked after drawing in deeply on the cigarrito.

"What if I do?"

Jeb blew out a long stream of blue smoke and removed the stub, spitting out flecks of tobacco. Pony's old arrogance was coming back again. His strength was building up in the open; out of confinement. He was in no mood for the scout's attempt at humor. "If you do know, then let's hear it," Jeb said.

Pony turned to face Jeb. The mountain man's face was stern and tight. Burns had seen that expression a dozen times before. His eyes were vacant and hollow. Pony's hand rested on the hilt of his Green River.

"You heard me," Burns interjected before Pony could get a word out. "We've got a lot of miles to cover. I'm not playing games with you. If you know the trail, let's move out. If you don't, say so! Then I say we take that canyon immediately behind us, flank the pueblo ruins, and move straight north." He let the mountain man know he meant business. "Well, what is it, your way or mine?"

"I'll show you the way outta here. You still got my word, but don't forget."

"Don't remind me," Burns interrupted him. "I've heard that threat before."

Charlotte walked up behind the pair, holding her arms tightly against her chest in the early morning chill. "How far to the closest town?" she asked, "Perhaps we could get horses there."

Pony spat out another wad of tobacco and leered at Charlotte, letting his eyes trail down her arms to her torn skirt. "San Miguel, but you won't find any horses there, just a bullet in your back, if you're lucky. You don't walk in there and expect to walk out alive, unless you're a greaser"

Burns threw in, "Our best chance is to skirt most of the towns around here and travel only at night. We can follow this mountain chain and hope we don't run into Apaches. They hang out around towns like San Miguel - the renegades do, for rifles and ammunition from the Comancheros. That's why they didn't level that town years ago."

The night stars poked their tiny pinpricks of light through the dissipating cloud cover and twinkled above the trio. They were fast fading in the growing light that was rising over the distant mountains. A gray shroud still lay over the land, concealing silhouettes on all but the sharpest ridgelines. By skirting the wide expansive areas and keeping to the darkness of deep gorges and twists in the hillsides, the trio was able to cover a couple of miles an hour and keep their presence well hidden.

By midday, they had wound their way deep into a maze of canyons, old wandering riverbeds, and rolling ground swells. Scrub and mesquite brush covered the ground, up to waist height. It provided the trio little protection from the sun during the late morning brightness, but at least it proved valuable for hiding if Apaches suddenly appeared on the horizon.

When the sun became too hot for traveling, they found a backwash near the canyon cliffs. Water from an ancient source had eaten deeply into the side of the limestone rock. The worn hole was deep enough to offer them ample protection from the sun's harsh rays and concealment from approaching riders. Scooping away loose dirt and gravel, they slid into the pocket feet first, and chewed on the little food that was left.

After Jeb and Charlotte had fallen asleep, Pony slipped out of the hole and silently walked away. He prowled the trail for a couple of miles, searching for horses or signs of riders. When he returned, Burns and the girl were watching him approach back into camp.

"What's wrong boy, think I left you?" Pony asked with a grin as he slipped back into the hole.

"Not really," Jeb assured him, "If need be, I can get us out of here too. With or without your sorry ass to lead us."

Pony stared at Jeb for a moment, trying to figure out in his head if he had been insulted again or not. Oh hell, it didn't matter. He'd have the girl, his money, and more scalps in a couple of days at the most. He wasn't in a hurry.

"Break time," Pony announced. Then he tipped his leather hat against his face and lay back in the sand, immediately falling asleep.

Jeb motioned to Charlotte and they both sat back down, collapsing against the sandy bottom. "Save your strength for the march tonight," he said to her. "Get as much rest as you can."

"What burr has gotten under his saddle?" Charlotte whispered to the scout. "His actions are quite bizarre."

Jeb whispered back. "It's almost as if he's liquored up but he's got no hooch. So I don't know what's swimming around in that head of his. Don't worry … I've got his word."

"Can you trust him?" Charlotte asked.

"No choice," Jeb answered. "Now get some rest."

Soon all three were fast asleep.

A hand came to rest on Burns' shoulder. The scout awoke with a cold start. Even before his eyes could focus, his hand had instinctively reached for his six-shooter.

"No!" came a startled response.

Jeb looked up with dazed eyes at Charlotte. She was up on her elbow, lying next to him. "Don't ever do that when a man is asleep." He cautioned her, "You could get shot that way." Looking up past the girl, Jeb could tell by the shadows on the ceiling of the ledge that it was late in the afternoon.

"Sorry, I was trying to awaken you carefully. Pony is gone again. I suppose he's checking something but I thought you'd like to know."

"He'll be back," Burns assured her. "Don't know why I know but I do."

Even as Jeb spoke those words Pony suddenly appeared from the brush directly in front of their concealment. He slipped quietly up the embankment, slipping back into the hole. After a light meal, the trio moved out again into the dying sunlight.

By the time the sun had burnt itself out, the party had made its way far from their resting spot. Soon they were out of the maze of rock distortions and corridors and into open country. From the crest of one of the rolling ridgelines, they could see the vastness of desert and mountain ranges; the remnants of the Sierra Madres chain they had been following.

The second night of marching proved no easier than the first. The three survivors, dirty, haggard, and tense from constant vigilance, kept up a steady but faltering pace across the endless patches of desert mixed with rolling hills. Charlotte trailed the men, stumbling in tight-lipped fortitude and pain. Burns and Pony, their carbines hiked waist high, watched each other as cautiously as they did the terrain. Burns kept up the pace out of sheer willpower born in the rigors of battle and again in the mountains afterwards. Pony's solid pace came from pleasure.

Despite their ordeal, the lack of food, and near brush with death, Pony felt more alive and free than ever before. It was just like in the old days when he was fighting Sioux and Pawnee up North. He was a man born of the hunt. When the tables were turned, he became an elusive, deadly prey; eager for battle and scalps. It was him against all the others: the scout, the Apaches, and even the Army. He was his own man and he wanted the girl for his own - like a brave takes a squaw. Before they reached the Badger spread, he meant to have her. He wasn't worried about the scout. He'd have his scalp before then. Time was on his side.

Even if Charlotte could have read the mountain man's mind, it probably couldn't have moved her to action. She was too exhausted. Her hair had worked itself loose again. Chestnut curls hung in lifeless tangles to her tired shoulders. Her skirt had been snagged and torn even farther through careless scraping against teddy bear chollas. Her alabaster arms were pricked bloody by the barbed spines, which seemed to leap off jointed stems and stick on her brushing arms.

A breeze lifted some dirt off the coarse ground. It cooled the air but filled three gasping mouths with fine dust. Pony spat out his tobacco. The others spat out their dirt. They all wanted a drink desperately, but only Pony carelessly upended his canteen and let the liquid run off his cheeks. Burns watched him and thought about the fight forthcoming if they didn't find water and soon.

Pony purposely led the party over rocky beds and rough outcroppings that paralleled many of the hillsides. His skillfully laid out, twisting path would cause hours of searching and backtracking before most Indians would light upon the right trail. He had been in the mountains so long that his instincts were honed to a fine edge. He could almost sense a suspicious change in the terrain, a wrong way bush that meant an ambush or just a sign of someone passing by. His body flowed fluid and loose, but his mind was rock steady - ready and able.

Near midnight, they stopped near a high rock encrusted waterhole. It was more a trickle than a puddle, but the water was still wet - a little brackish but good. It gave them relief for the moment and renewed energy. The meager food they could scrape out of the bottom of the saddlebag felt better going down with the water. Jeb noticed there were the foundations of buildings nearby; a ragtag collection of broken and abandoned structures scattered about the grounds around the waterhole.

"Reminds me of Tesorababi," said Pony, nodding toward the ruins, "used to be a large prosperous Mexican spread in the foothills of the Sierra Madres. Did some business with them way back. Nice folks for

Mexicans." Pony laughed, "til the Apache came and killed them all, every man jack of them - women and kids too. Told there was so much blood no Mexican ever came back there. Just let the whole place rot away."

Jeb looked over at the stone walls of rock and adobe; what was once the proud framework of a very large ranch house. Mesquite trees choked up the corral and he could see where outbuildings once stood. Now there was nothing, not even debris on the ground. The wind and the years had taken it all away.

"Apache must have been through here some time ago. Funny 'cuz they never go back to a place once they considered it a dead place. Never! These Mex never came back either," Pony stated, shaking his head. "Only the ghosts of all them dead greasers just staring down on us." Then he laughed and laughed.

Jeb and Charlotte watched the mountain man's fat belly rise and fall as he chuckled at his own joke. Then he began talking to himself in soft, barely audible tones. His mannerisms were getting more erratic, Jeb noticed. He was still rock solid on the outside, but Jeb wondered what he was like on the inside. If he were as strong as he seemed. Pony grabbed his medicine bag and walked up to a knoll nearby, squatting down, standing guard.

Charlotte had fallen asleep. Her breathing was very faint. Her head rested against the familiar saddlebags and she held her heavy rifle close to her breast. As Burns eased himself down next to her she moaned and jerked her body. Jeb laid a hand on her shoulder.

The negligible weight broke into the girl's dreams. She snapped up her head, eyes wide and unfocused. Recognition grabbed her mind and she sighed with relief.

"You were having a nightmare," Jeb said.

"It was nothing," Charlotte lied.

"Must have been something. You were pretty upset."

"I said it was nothing," Charlotte replied, then caught her breath, "I'm sorry. I'm just so tired, so exhausted I don't know what to do."

"I'm not prying. You were upset. I was worried." There. It was said. Whether Jeb really felt that way, he never gave himself time to think about.

But yes, he did feel that way. He was concerned. He continued looking at her, not sure what to say next.

Charlotte was touched. The nightmare had brought back the reality of her situation. She had to tell Jeb what happened back at Badger's place. But how? She wasn't sure how to begin. So she just did.

"I never told you about what happened back at the ranch. I think you need to understand why I won't…." she caught the words in her throat. "Why I can't go back there. Ever."

"I assume it has something to do with Badger. Perhaps the way he treated you."

"More than that … much more. The boy told me how Badger was defrauding the army on the stock he was selling. I don't know if the captain was privy or not. No matter if he was. Badger had been thieving for a long time and he was getting away with it. The boy knew of his double-dealings and wanted no part of it, but Badger threatened to kill him if he ever told. That wasn't all either."

"What else?"

The pause stuck in the air for a very long time. Neither Jeb nor the girl moved to interject a thought or word. Finally Charlotte let it all out.

"He tried to have me."

"Badger? One of his men?"

The girl didn't look up. She spoke softly yet firmly. "It was my uncle. I heard his voice even though he covered my head"

"My God," was all Jeb could say.

The girl continued in a soft voice. "He didn't manage to, but he hurt me. He meant to have me." Her eyes stitched anger on her face and Jeb finally understood the deep hatred she felt for that place. He understood completely why he could never take her back.

He started to explain, "We won't be heading back in that direction. Let's just say I don't want to meet up with the captain again myself."

Charlotte didn't pick up on his statement. *Just as good,* Jeb thought. He had no inclination to talk about his past or Glorieta Pass. *What's done is done and past – best to let it lie.*

"You still look pretty tired," he said, changing the subject, "better give yourself more time to rest."

As quickly as she had begun, the girl shut down again. Her exhaustion came back in waves and she lay back down. "How long do you think it will be until we reach the border?" she asked.

Jeb looked down; studying Charlotte's beaming eyes. They penetrated his skin like nothing had ever done before. She had a way of looking which bordered on staring, yet it grabbed on, holding tight. He liked the feeling and hated it at the same time.

"Well?" she asked.

"Oh, we should be there in a couple of days. As near as we can figure, we're still a ways out."

As he turned to lie back, Burns noticed Pony watching them from the knoll.

His teeth glinted as he smiled down on the two of them.

CHAPTER SIXTEEN

Dawn split the early morning sky in the vast and empty land. A veil of pearl gray sunlight drew long shadows off two riders descending out of the mountains. They were mere specks almost invisible among their sage and cactus surroundings.

Both riders spotted the rendezvous campsite as they crested the last of several ridgelines. They kicked their mounts into a gallop, eager for the food and whiskey awaiting them. Their horses were dirt brown sorrels, bred for climbing steep grades and winding mountain ridges. Behind them came two mules, tied in line and loaded down with canvas-wrapped boxes. All were securely tied down with gut string.

Old Ramon sat on his aging gray and watched the tiny figures winding their way down the steep, loose gravel slope. His large drooping sombrero shaded a face of tough leather, set with narrow eyes and a mouth of blackened teeth. His hairy paw caressed a Henry repeater, which lay across his tooled saddle. His boots of tailored Apache mule skin hung outside the stirrups, twisting slowly in circles to move the circulation back up his stiff legs. Thick and dirty hair hung in strands down to his stooped shoulders.

Ramon was a Comanchero; a trader, a raider, and a businessman who was always looking for new opportunities to extend his trade and business. Unlike his Mexican counterparts who mainly traded with the Comanches, old Ramon was a mixed breed; part Mexican, part Indian, and some white thrown in someplace back in history. He was an outcast to even his own kind.

His band of renegade Los Chaguanosos, along with their Indian allies, had worked the Old Spanish Trail for years, raiding commercial traffic from Santa Fe far into the California desert and stealing horses for the lucrative New Mexico and Missouri markets. Among his band were several runaway blacks; army deserters who had escaped from the cruel treatment they had endured at the hands of their white superiors.

The horse trade had served the old man well for many years. Now a new commodity was showing even greater promise. Guns, especially the Henry repeaters, were very lucrative trade goods for the bandit chieftain.

Now that the rifles had finally arrived, old Ramon could get on trading with the other renegade bands and then beat it deeper into Mexico. Two scraps with the United States Cavalry in less than four days had upset all of his plans. The troopers were persistently dogging his trail. Times were changing and he didn't like it. He needed a rest and these new rifles would pay for that.

When the riders got within shouting distance, Ramon took off his wide sombrero and yelled at them. He motioned toward the clearing where other riders were already gathered, then galloped to meet them there.

The Comancheros had made camp on the banks of a dried up river, cradled in the curve of a thickly wooded area. The horses, all eight of them, were hobbled and set to grazing. Men squatted around small campfires. Most of them wore tall Mexican sombreros which flopped around thick black hair. Their pants were buckskin, reinforced with leather chaps and riveted metal pieces for toughness. Several bandits wore bandoleers across their chests and carried new Winchester repeating rifles.

Exquisite Mexican craftsmanship had gone into their saddles and tooled boots, as well as their shiny new revolvers resting in cowhide leather holsters embroidered with silver conches. When they robbed, they only took the very best.

When the shouts of recognition and backslapping were over, Ramon led the two men to his tiny fire. He poured himself a steaming cup of java from an old tin pot and sprinkled it liberally with rye whiskey. He slugged it down and offered it to the two men. They quickly took him up on his offer. The hot liquid burnt its way down his throat, spreading a grin across his worn face.

The rifles were good, as much as he had hoped for. Once his younger brother and the others arrived, they could all migrate deeper into the country; selling the rifles as agreed upon and settling down to tequila and fat women for a change.

Old Ramon joked with the pair about their plans and the grand things awaiting them far from the border. No more Rurales or Federales, no more United States Cavalry, no more Arizona ranchers or Tombstone raiders, just good times. The others grunted their approvals.

They were, for the most part, silent companions. Their work was good; deadly when it had to be and professional when it was called for. They were killers and bandits but with a sense of propriety. If they could steal without killing, they would. Robbing without killing brought fewer posses on their trail. Not like years earlier when Ramon had driven cattle and horses across the Staked Plains from Texas to New Mexico, almost at will, and met Comanches and Kiowas on the Tongue River to barter.

The old bandit leader finished his drink and poured another steaming cupful. His boastful words fell again on disinterested ears, so he dropped the words and contented himself with his rifles. He ran his fingers over the shiny metal and smooth wooden stock. Casting glances out into the spreading sunlight, he felt an air of satisfaction.

"Are you sure they are still coming, Ramon," a voice asked from behind.

The old man turned and looked up at a young bandit with a long drooping mustache. Ramon opened his mouth with a grin, black teeth showing. "They'll come, don't worry," he assured the youngster. "My brother Pablo will be here shortly. Then we can go home and make good times."

The young bandit persisted. "I am not as certain as you," he said. "This is not a good place to wait for them. The Americanos might still be close, we are only a few miles from the border." He pointed outward. "They could easily cross the border, find us, and be back before any Rurales found out."

"Miguel, you worry too much," Ramon scolded him.

The young man stood up, looking down at the bandit chieftain with respect and yet uncertainty. He turned and walked toward his horse. Before he could reach his pony, a party of riders broke into sight.

"Ramon, you are right," he shouted, "here they come!"

The o1d man rose as fast as his stiff muscles would allow. He gulped down the rest of the spiked coffee and tossed the tin into the fire. Everyone was there. Now they could head home at last and enjoy a rest well deserved.

The riders were clearing brush and trees and coming into the open. Ramon shielded his eyes in the brightness. He counted them. Four horses, but there were five riders; only four had left that morning.

As they got closer, he inspected the rider that was not his own. The stranger riding saddle with one of his men had a long shaggy beard and carried a bag across his chest.

Apacheria

Jeb and Charlotte were ragged. They'd trekked mile upon mile in the desert heat with its stinging clouds of alkali dust and dirt. Ahead of them the mountain mass grew higher and the land began to buckle upwards. Their safety and sanctuary lay ahead, but first they had to traverse the coarse and cruel flatlands.

Despite their parched throats and sore legs, the pair was very much alive. Jeb's survival skills, finely honed over years in the mountains and deserts of the Southwest, had served them well after their escape from the pueblo ruins.

They walked slowly during the early morning hours and just before dusk. During the midday intense heat, the pair found whatever shade they could, settled in and barely moved. Jeb taught Charlotte to breathe through her nose so her throat wouldn't get so dry.

Nesting quail provided a tiny diet of meat and eggs and small water holes held just enough water to keep them alive. "As long as we sweat," Jeb reminded the girl, "we're doing all right. If we stop sweating, we're in trouble."

At night, Jeb dug a channel in the soft sand for their hipbones and curled up against the girl's back to provide body heat and comfort for her. Together they nestled under the dark star speckled sky and slept fitfully.

Over the last several days, Jeb continued to be surprised and amazed at the girl's resiliency and stubborn determination to survive in those harsh conditions. She was becoming one with the country; instinctively picking up on the signs and sounds and ebb and flow of desert life.

Her clothes were tattered from crawling through the confining tunnels of the tower. White flesh poking through holes contrasted with her sunburnt face and arms. Her auburn hair hung in matted clumps every which way.

Despite her desperate appearance, Jeb found Charlotte remarkably attractive and stimulating. She was arousing a feeling in him that he hadn't felt for a very long time. A feeling that made him uneasy; warm and uncomfortable all at the same time.

That afternoon, after finding a well hidden watering hole cut back into an arroyo, they rested and dozed off and on. The afternoon air was heavy with heat, but by not stirring they found it tolerable and almost soothing. As they sat, legs dangling in the warm water, they reflected in the afternoon stillness on their close brush with death.

"Do you think we've gotten away from the Apache?" Charlotte finally asked.

"You never get away from the Apache," Jeb replied without irony. "They call this territory 'Apacheria' because it is Apache country. Always has been. Until we started to push them off their lands. There's an area called the Camino Apache, translated the Apache Road. It goes from the Santo Tomas crossing of the Rio Grande to the Arizona territory, and south into the Sierra Madres in old Mexico. It even goes as far north as the Sierra Diablos. Like I said, this is their country. We're just passing through it."

Charlotte nodded her understanding, "I mean, do you think we've hidden our tracks well enough that they won't find us?"

Jeb cocked his eye at Charlotte. "Never say never," he said. "If the Apache are looking for someone or something, they will find them." He paused for a moment, reflecting on their predicament. "Only a question of how soon, but they will find our tracks."

"And there's no safety in Mexico?" She asked.

Jeb just smiled. The girl was getting an education and he was the teacher.

"If we go far enough south we'll run into the sub mountain rough lands; the rolling terrain before we enter the mountains there. If we went that route, we'd run into Mexican Apaches like the Bedonkohe or the Nednhi. If we head toward Sonora we'd run into the Yaqui Indians." He let the information sink in. "No, our best chance is to stay out of Mexico and just continue heading west."

"Have you ever been to Tucson?" Charlotte asked suddenly.

"I have," Jeb answered. "Stay clear of it. It's no place for a lady like you."

"Why?" She asked, "I thought I might go there instead of out West. I have read that it's purported to be a prosperous town and growing."

"Tucson is a growing all right. But it's still a rough and tumble town; full of traders, trappers, gamblers, horse thieves, and vagrants. The kind that goes where the gold coins roll. Not a lot of common folk or good people there."

"But…"

Jeb cut her short. "You asked why I have sympathy for the Apache. I'll tell you why. The Tucson Committee for Public Safety."

"What is that?" Charlotte asked.

"A group of vigilantes made up of American and Mexican residents who launched a surprise attack on a village of peaceful Apache families near Camp Grant a couple of years ago. They killed more than a hundred Apache women and children. No reason other than they wanted them all dead."

"That stirred up the Apache?" Charlotte asked.

"More than you can imagine," Jeb replied. "So yes, the Apache could find us if they wanted to. Our only hope is that they believed we all died in that pueblo fire."

There were other things weighing heavily on Charlotte's mind. "What about Badger? What if he's searching for us too?" She asked. "I don't know if he suspects that I know about his horse trading or that it was him who came into my room that night. Either way he might not want to see me again." She paused, letting the next thought linger on her mind for a moment. "…or he might not want to see me alive."

"Then why did he pay me and Pony to come after you?"

Charlotte pursed her lips, pondering the question. Then she answered. "My guess is that if you brought me back to the ranch, he would see to it that I never left there alive."

"Strong words," Jeb said.

"I told you what he tried to do to me!"

"You're probably right," Jeb responded. "Let's assume your uncle is out looking for us. With or without an Army escort, the man knows the lay of this land. He and his hired hands are masters at tracking all kinds of livestock, and humans."

"I won't let him take me, Jeb!" Charlotte announced, her eyes a cold steel again. Her body stiffened as she spoke. "If he comes after us. If he wants to take me back, I won't let him."

"I understand," Jeb answered. "I won't let him take you away either."

"I mean to kill him for what he did to me Jeb!"

"You said he only tried to..."

"I mean to kill him!" Charlotte spat back. "I won't go back!"

Jeb could feel the woman's rage, but he had no stomach for a fight - not against the Apaches or the U.S. Cavalry, if he could avoid it.

"If Badger's got himself an Army escort, we'll be dodging them instead of fighting them," Jeb responded. "Two of us against his hired guns and the Army; we wouldn't stand a chance of surviving a fight. Our only chance is not to be found. A trooper told me the captain lost his two Tonto scouts a week or so ago. Those were his eyes and ears. The captain's regulars aren't trained in cutting trails. They won't to be of much help. Branan's only got a couple of veterans, including his sergeant, that know the territory well. I can't say just how much help they'll be or what their chances are of finding us."

Silence fell between Jeb and the girl again. After a spell lost in their thoughts, Charlotte finally spoke as she looked towards the cloudless blue sky.

"So what are we going to do?" She asked.

"Keep moving. Be watchful. Trust our instincts."

"I guess that's all we can do."

Looking over at the girl, Jeb said, "We've been lucky so far!"

Charlotte returned his gaze and smiled, "Like meeting one another," she said out loud, before catching herself and registering embarrassment. She looked away, hoping he hadn't heard her comment, but he had.

"Yeah, like meeting one another," Jeb agreed. A smile crossed his face momentarily.

Charlotte smiled deeply and went back to staring up at the sky. The feelings were coming back again; emotions that didn't make sense and only clouded her perception of their predicament. Was Jeb trying to tell her something? Was he warming up to her? Was he feeling that same sense of attachment she had begun feeling toward this rough-hewn timber of a man?

The afternoon wore on slowly, peacefully. Neither one of them wanted to disturb the quiet. After quite some time Charlotte sat up and announced, "I feel putrid and downright indelicate."

"No surprise," Jeb answered.

"I'd love to take a bath or at least get in the water."

"Go ahead," he answered.

She looked at him in a funny way, "With you watching me?"

Jeb smiled, "After what we've been through, you're worried about someone watching you undress?"

Charlotte responded with a snap, "I'm still a lady. Don't you forget that?"

"I'm just saying…"

Charlotte could feel the smile crossing her lips. "Sort of silly isn't it," she admitted. "I mean if you wanted to…"

"Go ahead," Jeb interrupted her before she embarrassed them both any more. He turned away.

Reluctantly at first and then with confidence, Charlotte peeled off her skirt to reveal her skivvies beneath. Turning her back to the scout, she removed her shirt. Feeling secure with Jeb so close, she discarded the rest of her clothes and slipped into the water, settling on the muddy bottom,

"If you don't move a lot you won't stir up the mud on the bottom," Jeb warned her, after glancing in her direction.

"Really!" she said with a smile.

"Suit yourself, but it will be easier washing your hair without the silt in it," he added and went back to dozing.

Charlotte let herself float to the top, not caring if Jeb was looking at her or not. She was amused at the whiteness of her breasts and stomach as they contrasted with the deep brown and burnt red of her arms. She let herself sink back to the bottom and wiggled her toes slowly through the silt without disturbing it. She felt good with him there. She felt protected, safe, and scandalously aroused by his presence.

"Do you think Pony will come back?" She asked in a soft voice.

"Not likely!"

"So he's gone for good?"

"He's riding with the devil now. He means to do us no good.

Jeb looked over at Charlotte, not even noticing her only partially submerged nudity. "At this point if he does come back, it will be with malicious intent. He has his medicine kit and his rifle. That's all he needs to survive. If he comes back, it will be to kill me and harm you. We don't want him to find us."

"Is that why we've taken such a roundabout route?" Charlotte asked.

"Exactly!"

Jeb absent-mindedly rubbed his boot heel in the sand and shook his head. "We need to keep on moving and hope he doesn't cut our tracks someplace back there. If he does, it won't take him long to catch up with us."

"Then we fight him?" Charlotte asked.

"No," Jeb replied without emotion. "Then we kill him before he kills us."

Army Disease

Old Ramon counted again; yep, four horses, five riders. Even hidden behind his man, Ramon could tell the stranger was a huge man, dressed in leather and wearing a slouch hat hung low over his bearded face.

The man carried himself like a veteran even though he was camped behind a younger rider. As they got closer, the man slid off the back of the horse and quickly approached Ramon. Despite his bulk and unkempt clothes, he moved with the ease of a panther on the hunt. He carried a large Sharps buffalo rifle and a leather satchel under his arm. He had all the trappings of a trails man, a frontier trapper.

"Buenos Dias, Amigo," the man said, extending his hand out in a sign of peace. Immediately Ramon could tell the man was sure of himself and completely comfortable in his new surroundings. "Found your boys this morning. Thought I'd hitch a ride back to your camp and palaver a bit. Might have some tradin' for you."

Ramon said nothing. He just stood his ground, trying to size up this brash newcomer.

The tall man continued, "They said you was trading along the border and always looking for something more to trade."

Old Ramon smiled at the boldness of this stranger. "True," he agreed. "I'm always looking for something to trade. But between the Querechos, the Federales, and them soldier boys, I got me a lot of distractions. Whaddya got for me?"

Pony nodded, "I've got a proposition alright, but first I got me an empty belly that's been complaining for two days now. You got some grub for a hungry man?"

"Travelers are always welcome in our camp," Ramon smiled and waved over toward the first campfire. "Make yourself at home." Ramon walked with Pony to the campfire and seated himself across from the grizzly old man. The others walked away to give the boss time alone with the new stranger in camp.

Ramon poured Pony a tin of coffee. "Not half bad even if it's mostly mesquite bean," he said with a laugh. "Rabbit's just as poor, but it'll go down with the coffee."

The coffee was lukewarm and dull, but Pony nodded his satisfaction with the food and settled down alongside the smoldering campfire. He laid his Sharps and satchel on the ground beside him. His hat came off and landed on top of the bag.

"You from around these parts?" Ramon asked, as Pony bit deeply into the burnt rabbit from the spit. Pony nodded and continued ravaging the meat. Old Ramon was intrigued and suspicious at the same time. A mountain man this far south wouldn't be trapping this late in the season, nor would he be hunting the normal game. He was a man out of place and pretty haggard from the looks of him.

"Hard travelin'?" he asked.

Pony nodded again and continued ripping off the last shreds of meat. Ramon studied the man for any hint as to his motivation for being in his camp. He eyed the satchel the mountain man had laid on the ground beside him.

"What's in your bag?" the bandit chieftain asked. "Something you want to trade?"

Pony laughed and dug a hairy paw into the bag. He drew out several ears on a string and a fistful of pills. "Apache ears and some pills. The ears will spook any injuns I come across. The pills; they calls them the Army disease, if you get my drift."

Ramon laughed and extended his hand for several of the opium pills. Pony dropped several pills into the Comanchero's cupped hand. He threw them in his mouth and washed them down with a gulp of bad coffee.

"Give you shining times, they will!" Pony laughed as he popped several pills into his own mouth. He put the ears back in his satchel and continued with his burnt rabbit.

"So what have you got to trade?" Ramon asked. "I'm a business man and I'm looking to do some business. You look like a man who has something to trade. What might that be since you wouldn't have furs or pelts this time of year?"

Pony finished the rabbit and threw the bones in the fire. He side swabbed his beard with the back of his arm and sat back. He dug out an old twisted cheroot from his medicine bag and fired it up. Finally, after he was settled in, he spoke.

"I got me something you want alright. Something that will bring you plenty of money down South or with other traders you deal with."

"Now what might that be?" Ramon asked, fairly intrigued by Pony's bold statement.

"A woman. Nay," Pony corrected himself, "a young girl. Strong looker though. Unspoiled merchandise, I'm guessing. Catch the eye of every randy cowpuncher and overheated man this territory and beyond." Pony waited for a reaction. He got none but continued anyway. "I know where they are or where they're headed to."

"They! Who are they?"

"She's got an old scout travelin' with her. A Galvanized Yankee. Protecting her as if she needs it." Pony eyed the old Comanchero. "Scout's good. Knows the land about as well as I do. And the Apache. But I can still find them."

"But you're looking for some extra guns?"

"Exactly. I find them. I kill the scout. You get the girl. You do whatever you want with her after I get a piece. She'll be worth more than most of them rifles you just got. Fair enough?"

"If she's a looker like you say, I am interested."

"That she is!"

"How long to cut their trail?"

"They can't be more than a day or two west of here. They got no horses. No food or water. If we leave now, we can find them by tonight or tomorrow for sure."

"Then let's ride," Old Ramon smiled. "Get yourself a horse from the corral, we got extras. I can use something special for a trade. If she's that good looking, I just might share her with my boys, then trade her across the border - or give her to the Federales to get off my back."

Pony smiled. At last he could get the girl and get rid of that damn Jeb Burns at the same time. A piece for himself and he was back to the mountains and his old way of life. Good riddence to the rest of them all.

Poor Man's Fight

The afternoon wore on and neither Jeb nor the girl wanted it to end. Jeb stirred from his fleeting slumber and looked over at Charlotte still floating in the tepid water. Her pale breasts were bobbing on the surface by her island belly.

"Time we best be on our way," he announced softly.

"Do we have to?" she asked, dropping down into the water. She knew the answer already.

"If we want to make those mountains before dark, we do."

Charlotte sat up and smiled at Jeb. Without warning, she stood up and climbed out of the muddy seep. The nudity didn't seem to bother her as she stepped out and shook her hair. Jeb was way past being shocked; way past anything.

Jeb rolled over, got up, and began to gather their meager belongings. The girl dressed quickly and followed the scout out of camp. They walked for a long distance in silence.

"How much longer until we reach that butte?" Charlotte asked.

"Two or three more hours," Jeb said, glancing up once at the looming rock confluence in front of them. "Should be caves up there to give us some shelter, or at least there were on the backside if I remember correctly."

"Long time ago?"

"Yeah, a very long time ago."

Jeb's instincts were right. As they labored over the loose shale up the side of the butte, he could see shadows among the boulders and crags. There were some caves up there. He had no idea how shallow or deep they might be, but one of them would provide some shelter from the winds that were starting to pick up.

It took an hour to reach the far slopes of the butte and another hour until they found a suitable cave cut back far enough to escape detection from the surrounding desert flats. They settled in for the night, lying next to one another.

Charlotte turned to Jeb and asked, "Tell me about the war. Before I left Philadelphia, I heard rumors that Jefferson Davis just walked out of a courtroom a free man. They had him in prison for two years."

"I hadn't heard that," Jeb answered. "He was a good man, the President."

"You were in the cavalry?"

"Under Stonewall Jackson for a spell," Jeb answered. "He was a gloomy man most of the time but he stood tall against the union. Got his name because they say he stood like a stone wall at the first Battle of Bull Run."

"And Jeb Stuart?"

"Never served under him but they say he was a dandy. They say he wore a red love knot in his lapel and a peacock plume in his hat, but he was a fighter, no doubt about it. I wish we had had him at the Pass. Might have turned out differently if we had."

"Do you want to talk about it?"

"No," Jeb answered. "It was a rich man's war and a poor man's fight. Men like me were fighting for our country, our way of life, and our families. But in the end, we lost it all. That's why I never went back. Nothing to go back home to."

Silence fell between them again.

"I wasn't trying to pry…I just want to know more about you…what happened to you back then."

"You need to get your rest now," Jeb said.

Charlotte inched closer to the scout until her face was just inches away from his. "We need to talk…"

"About?"

"Us."

"You're tired…"

"If I had to be in a situation like this, I'm glad it's with you," Charlotte said softly. She reached up and placed her hand gently on his cheek. Jeb flinched, a momentary hesitation. Charlotte kept her hand resting softly on his skin. His body slowly relaxed. Then he brought his hand and rested it on her hip. Her eyes seemed to sparkle. They bore deep into his psyche. An understanding grew, unspoken and unexplained.

"Wish we weren't here," Jeb replied, responding to her soft touch. "Someplace safe. Away from this danger."

"Yes, but if I'm with you…"

"You need to get your rest…"

"Jeb, I…."

"I never thought I would ever feel this way again," Jeb whispered softly. "I never expected to meet someone like you. Kind of sets me off to feeling real unusual a lot of the time."

"Don't fight it," Charlotte said. She smiled and drew his face to hers. They kissed slowly, touching lips that hadn't felt another human being or such kindness for a very long time. Jeb drew Charlotte's body to his. He could feel the warmth of her body pressed hard against his. He could smell her hair and feel her soft breath against his neck. He tentatively cupped her firm breast. She let out a soft moan – a signal he heeded by pulling her body closer still. She drew up one leg and wrapped it against his thigh.

Slowly, methodically, Jeb drew up Charlotte's skirt and rolled on top of her.

She looked up into his eyes. She moved her body to accommodate his next gentle probing. For a brief moment he paused. She urged him onward, pressing her hands firmly against his back.

Their lovemaking grew in intensity. It was time. It was right. It was safe for both of them.

Afterwards they lay together, arms and legs woven together. As the nighttime chill descended, Jeb gathered their clothing on top of them, and they both fell into a deep sleep.

CHAPTER SEVENTEEN

Pony's hunch was right. After leaving the Comancheros camp, his party headed southwest, angling away from the site of the pueblo ruins and toward a distant spot on the horizon where Pony felt the scout and girl would be heading. His hunting and tracking instincts served him well. Even in the barren wilderness of the desert, he felt confident he would find their trail.

Cutting signs depended on the weather and the type of terrain Pony was traversing. There were few grasses or twigs to peruse. Instead, a ground cover of sand, shale, and gravel offered little in the way of telltale signs of the pair's passage. But even on bare rock, there might be the slightest scrape or mark of a boot.

Pony was a hunter back on the hunt and relishing every minute of it. He was in no rush to find his prey. If he found the scout, he'd cut him down in moments - or let the Comancheros do that for him as he tended to the girl. It would happen, sooner than later. His instincts told him he was close. Time was on his side. He relished the opportunity to study the land, watching for the minutest indication of their passing.

In the deadly heat of afternoon, the pair would either be camped out someplace shady or dead by now of heat stroke. He kept his eyes furrowed into scant slits, perusing the ground for any sign of them.

By the evening of the second day, Pony had cut two sets of footprints coming out of a sandy arroyo and heading straight for the confluence of buttes and outcroppings in the far distant skyline. Both tracks were moving slowly, pausing frequently by the shade of a scrub tree or tall cactus.

"Good. You got them," Old Ramon complimented Pony. "We'll settle in for the night and pick them off tomorrow."

"No, let's keep riding. I got me a score to settle"

"Not as long as you're riding with me," Old Ramon scolded Pony. "I'm not about to crest some ridgeline and have them pick me or my boys off in the setting sun. It can wait until tomorrow morning. You'll have your scout to deal with and I get the girl."

"After…" Pony started in.

"We stop now!" Old Ramon interrupted Pony, "Time to get drunk and play some Monte." The Comanchero ignored the grumbling from the mountain man and signaled his band of desperados to stop. He barked out several commands in Comanche-Mex and dropped out of his saddle. The old rheumatism was acting up again and he needed his drink to relax. The killing and woman taking could wait until tomorrow.

Comancheros and Apaches Together

The troop had halted by a collection of cactus which surrounded a shallow, rocky outcropping of boulders. The cactus gave off enough shade to provide some relief from the heat. The horses were hobbled in a group and the soldiers gathered around several campfires. Coffee and beans were the offering that afternoon.

Captain Branan and the sergeant sat across from Badger who was fidgeting with his revolver, cleaning the mechanism. The old man kept looking around, scanning the surroundings.

"Don't think we should be stopping so often, captain," the rancher offered. "Good way to get caught off guard by the Apache - or the Comancheros if their group is large enough."

"Troops need the rest, Mr. Badger. I'll handle this my way."

"No offense captain…"

"If the rumors are true about Comancheros trading nearby then we just might find them and the Apaches together. A surprise attack would be a real feather in our caps. And ridding the territory of those scoundrels would be welcomed by the Army and civilians alike. I mean to take every opportunity given to find and destroy them all."

"I'm not questioning your motives, captain, I'm just saying…"

"No offense taken, Mr. Badger. There are pickets stationed out there. We won't be ambushed under my command. I'm confident we will run into either the Apache or Comancheros very soon. Sanchez and Paco may not be Tontos but they're good. They say the hostiles are close. And if they are close, then the Comancheros are probably in the neighborhood too."

"And my niece?" asked Badger, faking his heightened interest.

"I wish I could be more certain about those three," the captain said. "but I can't. Their bodies weren't in the ruins back there, you saw that. But that doesn't mean they aren't someplace out there in the desert, sun dried and bleached white. Probably picked clean by buzzards by now."

"Or…" Badger was insistent.

The captain cut him off. "We have our priorities. We will concentrate on the exchange that is supposed to take place soon between the Apache and the Comancheros. After that, we may continue our search for the three."

Found

Jeb raked a match across his rifle barrel. It fizzled then burst into a pool of light, casting an eerie glow on his face. Cupping the flickering light against an early morning breeze, he swept it up to connect with a cigarrito, jutting out beneath his shaggy mustache. He settled back against a cradle of rocks.

Late the night before, he and Charlotte had climbed the butte and spent the night in a cave by the rim. Now from their nest near the cave's entrance, Jeb had a panoramic view of the flat, windswept desert patches and neighboring hills. Anyone approaching would be spotted long before they reached the bottom slopes of the butte.

Charlotte sat across from the scout, staring intently at the dancing reflections the flame drew on his face. She watched his eyes, unfocused, as he listened to the world around them. He made a slight turn of his head into the wind. From the distance came the very faint sound of a bird calling and another responding. The quiet was interrupted by a blowing wind, which stirred up sand at their feet and hair in their faces.

"Jeb," Charlotte said, breaking silence, "a penny for your thoughts. What are you thinking about?"

"You … us."

"What about us?" Charlotte questioned. She leaned forward and tilted her head, looking up at Jeb, smiling, "Tell me, please."

Jeb crushed the cigarrito out between two fingers and dabbed at his moist forehead. His eyes wandered across the plains, sweeping over cactus-studded areas interrupted by rolling hillsides. Nothing moved; nothing stirred in the early morning heat.

"I was thinking how different we both are. You were raised back East, in a fancy home with loving parents and a good upbringing. You've got refinement and manners. You're not rough like most of the women out here. You're like…"

"And you…?" she inquired.

Jeb looked at Charlotte with deep penetrating eyes. He wanted to say so much but he didn't know how. "And yet how much we still understand one another. We're comfortable with one another. Yet two completely different worlds … you and I. Right confusing for a simple man such as myself."

"We just need to take it slow," Charlotte replied. "Neither one of us knows what's going to happen. But if we're together, we…"

Burns suddenly turned away. He stared keenly at the landscape, focused on some spot she couldn't make out.

"What is it?" Charlotte finally asked.

"Shh!"

"What?"

"Listen!" Burns said, as he tilted his head. The girl froze in position, afraid to breathe too hard. She wanted to ask what he heard or saw but she was afraid. He wore that look again. The intensity was back and the controlled anger overtook his countenance. He sensed something or someone approaching and that meant danger.

Charlotte looked out across the wide expanse, searching desperately for a sign; some dust, a sun flare - anything. Then she saw them before she heard a sound. *Riders approaching!* They were tiny dots in the distance, almost indistinguishable from the land they were moving across.

"What is it?"

"Get the rifles and ammunition, the saddle bags." Jeb said. "Now!"

Charlotte scurried into the cave, her skirt flaring behind her.

Burns didn't need to see the riders up close to understand his fear. Although the figures weren't distinguishable, one of the men was leading his mount, and stooping over to study the ground for tracks. The others behind him rode loosely bunched up, their rifles reflecting sunlight across their saddles.

The party stopped, a second rider bent over in his saddle, examining a sign that the tracker was pointing out. They had found the pair's footprints! The tracker was pointing ahead. He mounted and the dozen or so riders broke into a gallop, lifting dust as they rode toward the butte.

Charlotte returned at a sprint, panting and puffing. "Here is the ammunition we have left." She handed Jeb two bores of tubes, keeping one box for herself. She caught her breath and asked, "Are they Comancheros?"

"Yes, Pony's tracking for them!"

"So he did find us," she stated in a factual manner.

"It's Pony alright! The old scoundrel found some Comancheros trading someplace and hooked up with them. Dollar to a dime, he told them about us and especially you."

Charlotte started to say something.

The scout raised his hand to silence her. "Listen carefully. We've only got a couple of minutes. Best guess is that they're certain we're up here but they don't know exactly where, or that we see them. If we can hit them on that narrow trail leading to the top, we've got a chance. If they reach the summit and spread out, they'll surround us eventually or trap us in the cave. They don't mean to take us alive. Do you understand?"

"I understand," Charlotte said. "What do you want me to do?"

Jeb pressed the girl tightly against his chest then just as quickly released her. "Go to the top of the trail," he said, "wait for me there. I want to see if I can hit them down below near the base of the trail. If not, maybe half way up. They'll try to get to the top and you can pick them off as they do."

Charlotte moved off quickly and Jeb turned back toward the approaching riders. They were closer and more distinguishable. Pony still carried his medicine bag across his saddle and his Sharps in one hand. He raised the rifle up toward Burns' position and spoke to the bandit next to him. They nodded agreement and continue riding toward the butte.

Burns concentrated on the topography of the bottoms surrounding the butte. His eyes probed every rise, every dip for an ambush position. There were none. He would have to wait until they began their ascent single file on the narrow trail before he could hit them.

As his eyes scanned the rough terrain, Jeb's mind kept racing back to Charlotte and her wanting to go to California with him. Her face, crystal clear and radiant, came back like a cloud superimposed over the vast panorama of desert and hills and riders. She was floating, hazy, just beyond his consciousness. He snapped his head, jerking her away, focusing his mind back on the approaching menace. Fingering his belt loops, he counted twelve cartridges left. That and his Spencer shells were all he had. Not much against a pack of Comancheros intent on killing him and getting the girl.

The trail leading up to the rim was a winding, cramped affair. Rough outcroppings of rock and shale lay bare along the side of the slope. On one side of the trail, the slope fell away, dropping to an alluvial fan below. On the opposite side, it edged in closely to the narrow shelf-like cut in the rock, making it accessible to only one rider at a time. The party would have to climb that trail single file if they were to top the butte. That was where Jeb intended to ambush them.

Charlotte was waiting by the trail's last switchback. Her hair was tied back and her Winchester lay neatly across her lap. She arose quickly, grabbing her box of ammunition, as she saw the scout approach at a run.

"Where are we going to hide?" she asked.

"We're going to separate. I want you to hide in that pocket of rocks near the rim. That'll give you good protection and still a view of the trail."

Charlotte nodded.

"I can't get a good shot of the trail base so I'll have to hit them half way up. If they get past me, they will have to get past you. Understood?"

"I understand," Charlotte said, grasping her rifle tightly.

"Let your hammer rest on an empty cylinder until they're close. That way you won't let loose until you're ready. Otherwise you could blow off a shot by accident."

Charlotte smiled at the lecture. "I think I know how to shoot a gun…." She started to respond but Jeb quickly turned around.

The riders were already approaching the bottom slope of the canyon, just before the butte. One of the Comancheros was separating from the main party, spurring his horse into a hard gallop, and starting up the winding trail. His rifle flashed in the sunlight. The others had spread out, in a rough line, watching him begin the climb.

"Damn!"

"What's wrong?"

"They've sent up a man to ride point. They'll try to get us to fire and reveal our position. But it makes no difference. Don't fire until I do." Jeb watched the rider separate from the group and begin his accent.

"I'm going to let him pass so the others think it is safe. You hit him at the top," he told the girl.

Without thinking, Jeb bent over and kissed Charlotte. Before he could lean back, she grabbed him tightly behind the neck and kissed him hard in return. He unwrapped her arms. "Don't worry," he said. "We'll make it outta here"

Then the scout quickly turned and was gone.

The lead rider was now letting his horse walk with the reins slack. The mount worked its way along the narrow winding trail. Its ears twitched constantly and head bobbed up and down. Then the ears went up-pricked and the horse nickered. The rider raised rifle higher against his chest. He scanned the terrain for any sign of the pair.

Charlotte slowly levered the Winchester, feeling a shell slide into its chamber. She leaned forward, resting her stomach across the warm smoothness of rock and hoped she could shoot when the time came.

Burns sprinted to his spot. He checked the Spencer mechanism to make sure there was a shell in the chamber. Crouched on one knee, he made a final survey of the trap he had laid. Then he stretched out and stared at the first switchback the party would have to negotiate. The heat, though still early in the day, was very hot on his back. His clothes were soaked through already.

Silence lay over the ambush. It was the same breathless, waiting silence the Apaches had laid over the trio when they were trapped in the tower. Only now, Jeb was on the other side of the trap. He was the hunter instead of the hunted. Everything was quiet except the wind which never died down.

On the trail, where it cut its last curve and entered the first switchback, the point horse stepped on a loose stone. The noise lasted only a split second before silence returned, but Jeb heard it. The point rider was nearing the top. Jeb gently raised the carbine to his shoulder. His cheek rested on the stock and he lined up on the trail below him. His eyes were narrow slits, cat-eyes, intent and determined. The skin beneath them was drawn up tightly. The front sight caught onto the first rider, following him slowly up the trail. He was young, with a shock of thick black unruly hair that flowed from under his wide sombrero. He kicked his roan up the last part of the trail and reached the rim.

The rest of the party was still at the bottom, their rifles covering the trail. Pony seemed disturbed, unsure of the trail and lack of cover. His voice drifted up over the rim, ever cautious, warning, but old Ramon would have none of it. He slapped heels against his mare's flank and it leapt away, moving up the trail. The others gave a shout and followed him. Pony remounted and trailed behind.

The point rider spurred his horse across flat sheets of rock, approaching the pocket of boulders where Burns was hiding. The point rider was humming a little tune. He scanned the rocks and foliage carelessly, barely glancing over Jeb's position. The scout let him pass. He was moving quickly to the top, closing in on Charlotte's position.

A second rider was now fast approaching the crest of the trail. Jeb also let him get closer, closing the distance to the first rider who by now was nearing the top of the ridgeline. When the second rider was only a few feet away, Jeb arose and shot him out of the saddle.

The shot reverberated out across the butte, shattering the silence. Another rifle barked in reply. Charlotte hadn't failed him. The rider toppled off his horse. The other riders spurred their mounts, moving quickly up the narrow trail. Jeb and Charlotte let them come, waiting for the right moment. It came very quickly.

Their crossfire caught the bandits halfway up the trail. Roaring out from behind and in front of them, bullets cut down three riders before the others could react. Men fought to steady their frightened mounts and fire back at the unseen ambushers. They failed in both.

Burns vaguely heard his own rifle exploding along with Charlotte's, but he was numb with concentration. He aimed and fired with mechanical precision, working the lever and pulling the trigger only when a bandit was centered in his front sight.

He jammed a new tube up the stock, jacked a shell into the chamber and searched for targets. Below him, the trail was littered with struggling men, firing back up at the rim, trying to turn their horses back down the trail. Two of the tail end riders retreated safely to the bottom with Pony and quickly began pouring a volume of fire in the girl's direction. Her rifle stopped. Then it opened up again. A cloud of dust rose from the ambush site on the trail. Two horses stumbled off the trail, tumbling over and over as they rolled down the slate slide.

Three riders sprinted on foot toward the rim and fired over their mount's head toward the top. The rest of the party struggled to make its way up the bloodied trail. Bodies littered the pathway; three on the slope, two halfway down the trail. Riderless horses broke through the trail hanging over the trail and ran back down the slope, terrified.

Burns leaned carelessly over the rim edges, trying to sight in on the approaching bandits. A bullet whistled past his ear and sent him flying back behind a rock. But not before he spotted three riders breaking through the dust which engulfed the trail, and galloping toward the rim.

Each rider laid over his horse, not bothering to fire, concentrating instead on reaching the top. Charlotte's rifle boomed, bringing down the last rider. His horse screamed and threw itself to one side, striking the hindquarter of the horse in front of it.

The second horse faltered, lost its balance, and tumbled over the crest line, but not before its rider threw himself off and sprinted behind the first rider to reach the top.

Now three bandits were over the rim, dispersed among the boulders and rocks. Gunfire from the bottom of the trail was growing heavier. The survivors had concentrated their firepower on the two ambush spots. Burns didn't need to lean over the edge to know that several if not all of the bandits were moving up the trail again, past the carnage of their first attempt, bent on reaching the others already on the rim.

Jeb could hear the gunfire lessen and hoof beats pounding up the rocky trail. Shots broke out among the rocks and boulders bordering the trails end. The three bandits were moving forward, closing in on the pair. One bandit suddenly appeared between two boulders, snap-fired three rounds in Charlotte's direction and just as quickly dropped behind cover. The girl's rifle went silent. Jeb jerked his head in that direction. Silence.

He rose up, gripping his last tube of shells, and sprinted toward Charlotte's concealed spot. Shells whistled past his head. He pitched forward, landing just short of a sandy spot. The hard rock surface tore at his elbow, burying grit deep into the exposed flesh.

One of the bandits broke into the open, running hard toward him. He fired his Winchester repeatedly as he charged. Burns snapped his Spencer up, centering in on the Mexican. But before he could press the trigger, the face centered in his sights disappeared in a spray of blood. Fingers clawed at the mass of pulp as the man tumbled to the ground, rolling over and over. Then he laid still, his face no longer there. The girl was still very much alive!

Jeb found Charlotte where he had stationed her. She was working the rifle with deadly precision, concentrating on the trail and the new riders fast approaching the rim. The girl's face was covered with a layer of rock dust and sweat-streaked dirt. She managed a weak smile and a nod. Burns needed no more.

"Come on," he said, "they're closing in. We've got to move farther back. Find some place to hold them off." He motioned toward an open expanse directly behind them then ran off, hunched over. Charlotte followed him without a word.

Shouts rose, followed by shells crashing against the rocks behind them. The pair ducked into a shallow depression in a rock, once a pool for rainwater that had long since dried out. The hollowed out rock, lodged above the other layers of stone, gave them a good fortification for anyone approaching from the direction of the trail.

Before they could fire, before the rest of the bandits on horseback even reached the top of the trail, new gunfire broke out. The riders crested the rim and just as quickly broke into a hard gallop across the butte ignoring the pair. The attacking bandits rose up from behind boulders and ran back, following the riders in a sprint across the rock-strewn butte.

Charlotte heard it the same moment Jeb did.

A bugle!

The cavalry had come - or Rurales. The sound of hoof beats pounding up the trail sounded heavenly in their ears. Charlotte moved next to Jeb; overjoyed, exhausted, and too happy to say a word. Soldiers appeared on the trail, charging toward the Comancheros.

The troopers engaged the Comancheros near the top of the trail. Jeb and Charlotte saw Captain Branan and Badger at the same time. Both were stunned.

"I can't believe it," Charlotte was first to shout above the din of gunfire.

"Stay down," Jeb shouted at her, "Let them fight it out themselves. They haven't spotted our position yet."

"No!" snapped Charlotte, watching intently the two figures leading the charge. "Let me be."

"What are you going to do?" Jeb asked. But already Charlotte was moving away from him, exposing her position, as she started to climb over the rock strewn ground toward the fighting. She began snaking between the boulders, edging closer to the firefight.

Jeb watched Charlotte go, fearing what she intended to do, yet unwilling to stop her. He understood the rage within her and what it meant to purge one's soul.

An officer crested the trail, his sword waving in the air. Sunlight flashed off of it. A column of troopers followed him and spread out. They fired their carbines and cut down the fleeing Comancheros.

Captain Branan was in full view, silhouetted against the clear blue sky. *A perfect shot,* thought the scout. *In the pandemonium of battle, no one would know where the shot came from.*

The carbine tightened in Jeb's hands. He started to bring it up into position then stopped in mid-swing. His face was frozen; skin stretched tight, his eyes focused only on the blue uniform of the officer he had vowed to kill.

Suddenly Badger was also in full view, riding hard between the captain and Jeb's shot. Jeb hesitated, waiting for Badger to move. Waiting for his shot.

The old man shouted something to the captain and then spurred his mount toward Jeb's position, but he wasn't riding hard toward Jeb. Jeb looked over and saw Charlotte standing by an outcropping, her Winchester resting across her chest.

Badger spurred his mount toward Charlotte, leaning forward in the saddle, drawing out his rifle as he fast approached her position. He was shouting something at the girl, but his words were lost in the uproar. He raised his rifle to shoot.

Jeb brought his rifle up, slammed it against his shoulder and squeezed the trigger to get off his shot before Badger could reach the girl.

He was too late. The old man's chest exploded in a burst of red, showering the mare with bone and tissue as Badger tumbled backwards off his mount. Jeb looked over at Charlotte. She was standing firm, her rifle still planted on her shoulder. Slowly she brought it down then turned away, never looking at the prone body no more than ten feet from her.

No one had seen Charlotte shoot her uncle. The captain and his troop were still chasing the remaining bandits down the far slopes of the butte, cutting them down as they tried to flee.
Jeb stood his position, stunned by Badger's sudden death.

Charlotte appeared moments later, scrambling among the rocks as she came back to the scout's position. She slumped against a boulder, exhausted yet calm. At first she said nothing then she turned slowly to the scout.

"It's done," was all she said.

"It's not right. It's not wrong," Jeb said. "It just is." He slumped against the rocks next to her. Sweat ran down his face and he loosened the grip on his rifle. He turned toward Charlotte. His face was wrought with pain, exhaustion, and yet a deep calmness. His face cracked open an ever so feeble curl of the lips - a smile.

"We have to go before the captain finds you," Charlotte said.

"No, I have to leave. You have to stay." Jeb replied. "You'll be safe with the troop. They'll have to get you back to the fort or the nearest safe town. They won't take a woman on patrol. I can't let the captain see me here. He'll kill me for certain. It's the only way…"

"But…"

"You'll be out of danger, Charlotte. We have no other choice."

Jeb rose and walked over to where one of the first bandits had fallen. He gathered up the reins of his mount and walked the horse back to Charlotte. She watched him and didn't say a word. She sat quietly and watched the scout prepare his gear. He secured his bags behind the saddle.

The horse was a strong looking roan. It would give him plenty of miles between himself and the cavalry. He shoved his Spencer in the boot and checked the cinches. Armed with ammunition and food in his saddlebags, he mounted up.

"Are you sure about this?" Charlotte asked. "Are you sure the captain knows who you are? He might not. He might just let us go."

"Charlotte, I can't take that chance," Jeb replied. "If he recognizes me he's just as likely to take me prisoner as he is to let me go. I can't take that chance. If he takes me back to the fort under any pretense, I'm just as good as dead. Maybe I should have shot him when I had the chance."

Jeb looked down on Charlotte staring back at him. "Doesn't matter now," he said. "I have to leave. You're in no danger. Badger's gone and the Army will escort you to the nearest settlement."

"I don't want you to go!" Charlotte suddenly blurted out.

"I know but…," Jeb began to protest.

"I know, I know," Charlotte threw back at the scout. "You're not sure about all this - but I am certain. We could still find a way out of here. We haven't been spotted yet. We could find a place for us in California."

"Lottie, you know I can't do that."

Charlotte's face was flush with anxiety and emotion. Tangled auburn hair hung in her face, framing her pleading eyes. She reached up to touch his hand. Flesh touched flesh for a moment then Jeb leaned away, out of her reach.

"I'm sorry," he said, 'I'm not ready to…."

"Then go!" she shouted. "Damn you, Jeb Burns, just go!"

Jeb kneed his mount back, looking down into the tear-filled eyes, not sure how to answer Charlotte. He wanted to explain but the words were hard in coming out. "If we meet again, it's because it was meant to be." He said, not sure where the words were coming from or if he really meant it. "I'm heading straight west. Tell the captain otherwise. Goodbye."

Jeb broke away, kneeing his mount to one side, and then quickly, almost lost in a hush, he said: "I'll miss you, Charlotte Barrington." Then he was gone, riding hard across the back end of the butte.

Charlotte fell apart; her emotions erupted into a cascade of tears. Her hands trembled and her body shook... She collapsed to the ground, drowning in her tears. She buried her face in her hands and sobbed uncontrollably.

CHAPTER EIGHTEEN

Old Ramon and his brother Pablo were nowhere to be seen. The other bandits had scattered among the boulders and crags with the cavalry in hot pursuit. The stronger, heavier Army horses ran them down in the rough terrain until only the few remaining stragglers had given up or died under a fusillade of repeating rifles. Old Ramon and Pablo were gone.

During the fight, Branan had been in his glory. He relished the mayhem and elimination of his prey. In the height of battle, he sent his mare crashing into another bandit and shot him on the rebound. One bandit stumbled to his feet and felt the cold blade of Branan's sword impale him through his throat. Another died running away from the captain. The slaughter was complete. Only two bandits remained after the conflict had ended.

Badger's body lay where he had fallen. The old rancher was crumpled down among the rocks and safe brush. Too bad, the captain thought as he rode up to the still figure. He so wanted to find his niece and rescue her. Siding up to the captain, the sergeant agreed it was unfortunate that Badger had been cut down before seeing her one last time. Captain Branan tossed a blanket over Badger's expressionless eyes.

"See that he's given a proper burial," he told the sergeant.

The captain looked on dispassionately as his men moved among the fallen bandits. His troopers gathered up the fallen weapons. There would be no guns for the Apaches. Without these guns, the hostiles would probably cross the border and hide in Mexico for a while. His orders had been completed. He would return his troop to the fort and wait for word of more hostile movement. Then he would be out again, hunting Apaches.

It wasn't until the sergeant motioned to his left that Branan saw a girl moving out from among the rocks and boulders on the far side of the butte. It had to be Badger's niece. Alone. There was no sign of the scout who had gone out to rescue her, nor the mountain man. As the girl approached, Branan saw her slow defeated gate and torn clothing.

"Glad to find you alive, ma'am," the captain said as Charlotte got within earshot.

She didn't respond, just kept on walking toward the captain and his gathering troop.

As she got closer, the captain moved his mount in front of her. She stopped and looked up at the officer. Branan tipped his hat and said. "I'm sorry to have to tell you that your uncle was killed in the fight. Right at the beginning. I'm sorry."

Charlotte acknowledged the captain and sat down exhausted.

Captain Branan dismounted and sat down beside her. He offered Charlotte water, which she waved away. "Anything else you might want?" he asked her. Again, she shook her head. After a short while, the captain began to address her again.

"Excuse me, miss, I have to ask you. What happened to that man who rescued you? The scout who left with the mountain man from your uncle's ranch?"

"We got separated after the Apaches burnt up the pueblo tower," was all Charlotte could say.

"So he's gone? Do you know where?"

"Just disappeared. Couple of days ago. He might have gone for help. Could have been caught by the Apaches. I just kept walking until I got here. Then you came along just as those bandits were hunting for me"

"No idea which direction he went?"

"No," Charlotte repeated. "I told you he just disappeared after the fight with the Apaches. So did the mountain man. Both just left."

"That seems mighty strange," the captain said. "I mean their leaving you alone in the desert like that. What with the Apaches and Comancheros around. You're sure about this? You were traveling through some mightily harsh country. Perhaps the sun got to you; made you forget what really happened."

Charlotte stared at him, saying nothing. Then she spoke. "I told you what happened, captain. Yes, we were all dying out there. Yes, we just escaped the Apaches in those ruins. And yes, the two of them just left me. Just like that." She paused to gather her thoughts. "I believe they were going for help and I would have slowed them down. That's what happened."

Captain Branan couldn't read the girl. He had no idea if she was telling the truth or not. Certainly she was exhausted and who knows what kind of trauma she might have experienced since leaving Badger's place - or what those two men might have done to her. Still, Captain Branan wasn't about to let the issue drop. Not if there was any chance that the scout might come back.

He continued his interrogation. "Did that scout mention anything about the war when you two were together?"

Charlotte turned to the captain. Her face was still flushed but the tears had been wiped away. Her determination to mask her true feelings painted a facade across her dirt-streaked face. She looked at the captain with the same steel in her eyes that had caught Jeb up short several times.

"The war? No, captain," she said. "He never mentioned a thing about the war. I don't even think he was in it. Why do you ask?"

"No reason really, ma'am," the captain lied, "but the scout… that man reminded me of someone I seem to remember from a long time ago. I thought it might have been someone I ran into during the war."

Charlotte shrugged her shoulders. "I need a horse and supplies. I'm not going back to my uncle's place. I'm heading west instead."

Burns rode the roan hard, trying to distance himself from Charlotte and the conflicting thoughts jumbled up in his brain. He was confused; angry at himself for leaving her, yet sure that he was doing the right thing for both of them. Deep down he felt it was right as it stood, but he still wasn't reconciled with his conscience.

After crossing a series of ridgelines and rolling foothills, the scout led his mount into a succession of high hills where the air was cooler. The chaparral was thicker there. The ground was broken into a series of ridges and volcanic boulders thrown into formidable shapes. He kept heading west.

His mind was in turmoil; battered by contradictory thoughts crashing into one another, making his decision to leave the girl a gut-wrenching choice. *Is this a mistake?* He didn't rightly know at that point.

Part of him wanted to turn around and find Charlotte. Part of him knew he wasn't ready for such a commitment. Part of him knew he'd given up the best thing that ever happened to his miserable life. The anguish of a past love lost and the fear of a new life kept him handicapped by hesitation.

Jeb Burns, like most other trappers and scouts, didn't know or care where the territory ended and Mexico began. If it existed on paper, Jeb had never seen such a thing. The bleak sand stretches and wandering mountain chains would tell him when he was near Mexico. Burns had traveled the old route into Sonora long enough to know the end of the United States territory was not far off. He would find the small village of Tejia's, have a long night in some saloon and be off to California.

On top of a ridge, like fringe on a buckskin coat, a cluster of palo verde trees stood strung out in a long rolling line. Dropping down from the cluster, smoke trees lay scattered about like soft, gray puffs in the distance.

There was something in the air that made the scout tense up, suddenly very aware of the tree line. He couldn't put a finger on it. It came from within. Instinct perhaps from uncounted trips through the desert highlands. He moved cautiously. He pulled out his rifle and laid it across his saddle. His hand lay across the trigger guard, a finger on the trigger. His eyes scanned the tree line. He saw nothing. He continued riding slowly toward the tree line.

The sound of hoof beats caught his attention. He swung around, jerking his carbine back toward the sound. A rider was fast approaching, along the same trail, now hidden by the side of outcroppings. She came around the bend, riding hard. It was Charlotte. Her hair was blowing freely in the wind. She waved at him. The girl wasn't going to let him go.

Jeb reined in. He twisted in the saddle and squinted his eyes for the most likely spot a man might be hiding. The mottled coloration of the trees, cactus, and flowers blended together, wiping away distinguishing forms and structures.

Charlotte was almost up to him. She shouted something he couldn't understand. His focus was still riveted on the hillside. It was a split-second flash of sunlight caught on metal that caught his attention. Someone was deep among the palo verde trees, waiting. It was an ambush!

"Get down," Jeb shouted at the girl as he leapt off his startled mount.

Charlotte reined back. A crack of gunfire scattered all pretense of quiet. She screamed, clutched her reins and rolled backwards off the horse. A shower of blood sprayed the air, enveloping both girl and horse. Even as Burns scrambled toward Charlotte's rolling figure, another heavy slug whined overhead, inches past his face. He grabbed the girl and rolled her over.

A gasp caught in his throat as he looked down on the face covered with blood and skin gone ashen-gray. Another shot exploded among the trees. A third slug whistled past his ear. It brought him to his senses. Charlotte was dead.

He laid her broken body back down and grabbed his Spencer. He rolled over toward a clump of underbrush to his left. As he rolled over once, then back up, another slug hit his hat, sending it spinning into the air. A shock wave slammed his head into the ground and he lay flattened out, gasping for air. He stumbled to his feet then collapsed into the underbrush.

Jeb had no idea how long he had been unconscious if at all. The tiny puddle of blood in front of his eyes was still moist in the hot sand. His fingers traced it back up his check to an open shell burn bordering his temple. Somewhere in the back of his brain, a hammer kept up an incessant pounding. It ran through his suddenly tired body, reducing his limbs to rubber. The air was alive with buzzing insects. They crawled on his hands, along the edge of the blood. He wanted to smash the repulsive scavengers, but he let them be to focus on the task ahead.

Risking a bullet, the scout edged up and peered through the flat beaver tail cactus. Nothing had changed along the tree-lined ridge. He studied the terrain carefully, working back to the ridgeline and then forward among the thickets to him. Jeb felt alone, like the last man for hundreds of miles around. Yet only feet away, he could see the girl he had lost. Her body was turned over to one side. He must have moved her without realizing it. Jeb couldn't remember. Everything was a vague, hazy memory. Only one thing was certain in Burns' tortured mind - that Pony meant to kill him. Now he was the hunted. Pony the hunter.

Jeb's motions, slowed by his aching head, were coming back into form. Long ago he had learned the art of patience. It served him well in trapping and keeping clear of Indian parties. Now it might mean the difference between life and death. The first to move would probably be the first to die; that was the unwritten law. Both he and Pony knew it.

His attention jumped back to the ridgeline and the trees there. Something moved by one of the trees, just for a second, and then disappeared. A black-green coloration among the trees and thickets hid whatever it was. But in that second, Burns had spotted something. A hump, barely visible like a man's back, had appeared, moved to the right of a single palo verde tree, then dropped down below the surrounding thickets. There had been no sound, no disturbance. Birds still flickered from one tall saguaro to another, undisturbed. If Pony had seen the scout wasn't dead, Jeb was still in danger.

Jeb wormed his way past Charlotte's still form, at a perpendicular angle to the thicket. If Pony had been that hump Burns had seen or thought he had seen, then he would be working his way down toward the scout's location. Jeb could catch him on the way down if he made it to the rough outcropping of rock up ahead. It would give him an ideal spot to catch any movement down off the ridgeline toward the horses.

The crawl seemed to take ages. Flies buzzed his face, and insects lighted on his back.

Reaching the pile of rocks, Jeb nestled into a worn notch among the formations and waited. He propped his back up against a stone and laid his rifle on the lip. Now the wait began. If Pony were true Apache, he'd wait until dusk, many hours away, to make contact. But Jeb was gambling that he wouldn't; that the mountain man's instinct would win over and greed would send him in for the kill right then and there.

Jeb's hand slipped down on the trigger of the rifle. He carefully eased back on the hammer. The metallic click seemed to echo off the rocks, a hundred times louder than it actually was. His senses rode the fine edge of trickery, keened up to hear or see anything that might spell danger. The man squinted his eyes until they watered but he still couldn't detect any movement past his spot.

A bird lighted on a mesquite branch and quickly darted away, scolding. Pony was there! Jeb was certain of it. But that location was much farther down from where Jeb had estimated the mountain veteran would have been by then. The bird returned moments later and landed, staying this time. Pony was past already. At that pace, the mountain man would be down to Burns' spot in only minutes, and then back up toward the outcroppings. It was happening much quicker than Burns had anticipated.

Out of the corner of one eye, ignored by his intense concentration on Pony's movements, Burns thought he saw something move far from Pony's spot - where the girl had fallen.

It was a blur of something dark, reddish, and with it came a sound. A moan, hardly audible, as if someone or something were in pain. He tossed his attention between the two spots, where Pony must be crawling and this new disturbance where Charlotte had been.

Then it came again; a blur, but more distinguishable, like someone's head. Disheveled hair flashing among the growing darkness of the thickets.

The thought struck him like a fist across his face. No! It couldn't be! He had held Charlotte's still, lifeless form in his arms. He'd seen the blood-covered face and felt her cold hands. She couldn't be alive! Charlotte was dead.

Yet his eyes weren't deceiving him. He saw it again, longer this time as if someone, yes, Charlotte, was attempting to sit up. It moved, a chestnut smudge among the brush between them. It had to be her. *Charlotte must still be alive!*

Jeb felt energy surging through his body. A renewal, a regeneration; it was the realization that he hadn't lost her after all - but Pony had seen her too.

Again, out of the corner of his eye, Burns caught movement. A form arose from the thickets off to Charlotte's right. A long barrel, black and shiny, pointed at Charlotte's swaying head.

Instinctively Burns fired, ripping off three snap-fire shots. Bullets exploded the thick chaparral, sending branches filling the air. Pony dove down. Now he knew the scout was alive, where he was, and that the girl was not far away. Pony was directly between them.

The scout's first reaction was to tell Charlotte to get down. But knowing the impact of the bullet which must have creased her head, Jeb knew she would probably not be able to hear his words clearly, and his yelling might prompt her to try standing.

Although the gunfire had driven the mountain man back down, it hadn't stopped him. As Jeb scanned the foliage between Charlotte and Pony's old spot, he saw birds suddenly fly away, several yards from where he had fired. The mountain man was moving again, much quicker this time. He was moving directly toward Charlotte. If Burns moved himself, he'd risk getting caught halfway to the girl. If he stayed put, Pony might reach the girl before Jeb could stop him.

Sheer desperation brought the Spencer to Burns' shoulder and cold, calculating fury pressed the trigger. It bucked against his torn shirt as he patiently laid down a blanket of fire where Pony should have been crawling.

Seven shots, then a lightning fast jam of new cartridges up the stock. Three more shots fired. Then silence with only the echo of gunfire roiling off the slope into the valley below.

Charlotte was getting up, struggling to hold onto a loose limb. She was calling out his name. She was in pain. He had to go to her. He had to help her. He couldn't let Pony kill her again.

It has to be now! Burns had to make his move. He broke out of the rock formation at a run, violating every rule of survival. He sprang through the thick brush, kicking his legs at the entrapping limbs. Gun at hip level and eyes straining for a sign in the bushes where Pony should have been, Jeb smashed ahead.

Halfway to Charlotte a shot exploded in front of Jeb, burning the air past his face. Jeb braked, digging his heels into the dirt. He pumped two fast rounds at the spot. A muffled cry arose. He pumped his last two shots into the brush and tossed the piece aside. His revolver was cocked, pressured to fire when Pony staggered to his feet out of the bushes. The mountain man stumbled up slowly. His left arm dangled lifelessly to one side. His face was covered with dirt and a smear of blood where a bullet had clipped off one ear. A spreading dark patch oozed blood on his chest. He coughed blood when he spoke.

"Damn, you're good, pilgrim," he muttered. Blood spittle formed on his lips.

Jeb eased back, letting some of the tension in his body go. His pistol hand started to relax. Then Pony suddenly drew out a revolver from his breeches and fired off one shot.

It tore through Jeb's rib cage, knocking him off his feet. Instinctively, he fired as he fell; once, twice, three times. Two of the shells hit Pony chest high. He staggered back, flailing his arms.

'Coon,' he muttered, "them was shining times, they was." He swayed back and forth, more blood trickling out the corner of his bearded mouth. He tried to focus on Jeb with glazed, pain-filled eyes. He fell, crashing forward into the thick brush like a giant slab of rock.

Jeb sat motionless for a moment, drained to the bone. A girl's voice broke through. It was Charlotte. She needed him; but more importantly, he needed her. *Now more than ever!* Jeb dropped his revolver and rolled over to get up. He started to rise but then the ground came rushing up to slap him in the face.

A tiny candle flickered and swayed in a faint nighttime breeze. In the distance, a whiff of charcoal smoke tickled Jeb's senses and then gradually disappeared. All was quiet except for the distant sound of animals baying and small children laughing. It was near dusk. A rough-cut window in the adobe wall showed only faint glowing traces of a dying day.

The scout was someplace unfamiliar. It was a location full of confusing sounds that left no identity other than of a small village by the faint noises outside his dark adobe walls.

When he finally regained enough of his senses to sit up, Jeb found himself in a dark room, dank and smelling of old furs and cooking grease. He lay on a crude bed made of tree branches and covered with a torn cloth. His head had rested on a grass filled satchel. The room was empty but for his crude bed and a small wooden cross on the wall next to the woolen blanket that covered the doorway.

The sounds and smells of a meal being prepared came from the other room. Jeb could hear voices talking, one more pronounced than the others. Someone speaking in broken Spanish intermingled with English. It sounded like Charlotte's voice. Yes, it was her. He was sure of it. She was talking to someone on the other side of the blanket. Jeb fell back and lay still, trying to listen to what she was saying. But other voices kept interrupting her and breaking his concentration.

Jeb lay there for a long time, moving his arms and legs occasionally and trying to lift himself back up, but the pain was too great and he just fell back, exhausted. He drifted in and out of consciousness most of that evening. Later when he awoke he could hear Charlotte's voice again, clearer this time. It lasted for a while until he drifted off to sleep again. Later that evening, Jeb finally awoke fully and began listening intently to the sounds around him.

The outside sounds had gone away and now only the sound of kitchen utensils could be heard on the other side of the blanket.

Charlotte appeared from behind the blanket with a smile on her face. She was carrying a plate of meat and potatoes. Her clothes were cleaned and pressed. She smelled of bathwater. Freshly washed hair tumbled down her shoulders. Even in the dimness of the room, her beauty radiated.

"Oh good, you're awake," Charlotte said, "have some of this." She sat down on the edge of Jeb's cot. "Eat slowly. It will give you your strength back." She held out a ladle of chopped mutton and vegetables.

Jeb tried to lift himself up but again fell back. Sharp pain gripped his chest. He took a deep breath and slowly rose up a second time.

"Don't get up," Charlotte scolded him. "The bullet passed through your side. You're still pretty well torn up. Just lay back and I'll feed you."

He started to protest but Charlotte cut him short. "Enough already! No more arguing. Either eat or go hungry. These people have been gracious enough to host us until you get well. Don't complain."

Jeb looked at the girl and smiled. Charlotte was still a feisty, head-strong woman after all that had happened to her. *More woman than any one man could handle,* he thought. He said nothing and just ate.

Charlotte fed him small portions in silence. When he was finished eating Jeb collapsed back in the bed. "Where are we?"

"South of the border someplace," Charlotte answered. "I don't really know exactly where. It's a small village far enough away from the overland freighters that they get few outside visitors. Maybe its Tejia's. Anyway, it's a safe place to heal."

"No sign of the captain?" Jeb asked.

Charlotte shook her head. "No," she replied, "but the villagers are talking about Comancheros. They're raiding villages south of here, killing the people and taking their stock. These poor peasants fear it's just a matter of time before those bandits come in this direction. But I think we're safe for now." Charlotte stepped toward the doorway.

"How long have I been here? Like this!" Jeb asked.

"Almost a week now." Charlotte answered. "You were lucky. Your wound will heal in time and I was only grazed." Charlotte paused then said "Pony is dead. I left him where he fell." The girl's voice was matter-of-fact and to the point. She didn't look at Jeb as she continued. "So I got you over your saddle somehow and kept going until I found this small village on the other side of the Rio Grande. I had enough gold and silver coins from Pony's saddlebags to buy their help and then some."

"Your grubstake."

Charlotte ignored Jeb's comment. "There is also enough to get us to anywhere we might want to go ... if you're interested. These are wonderful people. They won't tell the Rurales or Federales if they come snooping. I've paid them enough that you can stay until you're well enough to travel."

"You came back," Jeb said, surprised at himself for saying it.

Charlotte said nothing. Her face registered reaction to his statement. "Of course, I couldn't let you leave like that … there was too much left unsaid… You are in no condition to travel now. We must stay here until you are convalesced."

She gathered up the dinner plate and started to leave.

"Charlotte, it won't work," Jeb suddenly blurted out.

Charlotte stopped, her back to Jeb. He could see her shoulders visibly sink down as if weariness had descended over her. She stood in place for the longest time and finally started to turn around.

"It can if you let it" Charlotte replied as she slowly turned to face Jeb. She stared at him without saying another word.

Jeb fell back on his cot; chest fallen. His voice was sad and soft. "Charlotte, I know what you want from me, but I don't think I can give it to you. I'm not ready for this. Maybe I'll never be ready. I'm too old of a cuss to change now…and you're too young to be with a relic like me."

"You're not that long in the tooth, Jeb Burns. You just think you are," Charlotte said as she moved closer to the cot.

"Charlotte, I just…"

"I'm not begging you." Charlotte said.

"I'm just saying…"

"I have to ask you," Charlotte interrupted.

"What?"

"About that night…" she paused, afraid to continue. "Did it mean anything to you? I mean besides…"

"Of course it did," Jeb answered quickly. "It was real. It meant something."

"Good," Charlotte answered. "You'd be one neutered mare if it hadn't."

They both smiled at one another and let the silence return.

"What are you going to do?" Jeb asked, not wanting to hear the answer.

"What am I going to do?" She repeated his question. "Stay here with you or head due west. Perhaps north to San Francisco. What am I going to do, Jeb Burns? You tell me."

Jeb lay still, staring up at the rough-hewn log ceiling. He said nothing. Silence filled the room and lay heavy between them.

"I … don't know," Jeb answered slowly, "I don't know."

Jeb was lost for words. He was a fool to think that such a fine woman would want to stay with an old codger like himself. A war veteran who still hadn't let go of the wounds, physical and mental, that had plagued him for so long. He didn't deserve such an exquisite woman.

Charlotte came in the next morning. She was dressed for traveling with a leather jacket and riding chaps. She stood by Jeb's cot as he leaned up on one arm.

"Villagers say you can stay here for as long as you want. At the very least until you're able to travel," she said then added slowly. "You're right. We were probably never meant for one another. We're too different, you and I. You're too set in your ways and I in mine. I realize now that a man has to learn to live with himself before he can live with another person. I love you, Jeb Burns…but I can't live with that uncertainty for the rest of my life."

There, it was said, Charlotte thought to herself as she slowly turned around and left the room. *The hard part is over. I am going and he is staying. No protest, no teary goodbyes - just a simple parting of ways.*

Jeb wanted to protest. To talk about his jumbled up feelings - his fear of commitment and the confusion and elation at seeing Charlotte after he had left the butte. He stared up at the dark ceiling, his eyes lost in a fog. He wanted to better explain but his words were mixed up, just vapid thoughts in his brain not coming out. He said nothing and let the silence be between them.

"Things change," he began to say, but when he looked up she was gone. All he could see was the blanket slowly swaying back and forth from her passing through the doorway. Jeb lie back on the cot and fell into a deep troublesome sleep.

Charlotte was long gone when Jeb awoke. The villagers, knowing only cursory English, weren't much help. He could decipher from their motions that she had left early that morning; but they didn't know exactly when, nor which direction she was heading. An old man simply told him, "Siga el sol." *Follow the sun.* Another pointed toward the west and nodded.

Charlotte was gone like the cool morning breeze that was now dissipating under an ever-growing, stifling heat. His chance at redemption had left and with it any reason to care about living.

It took two more weeks for Jeb's chest to heal well enough for him to venture out of bed and around his small stifling room. It was another week until he could leave the house entirely and shuffle down the dusty dirt footpath that was the main thoroughfare for the tiny village.

The villagers stared at him but said nothing. His roan had been fed and cared for by the village blacksmith. Everything had been taken care of. His debt to the villagers had been paid off. Charlotte had done everything she could to see that Jeb was going to pull through. The womenfolk still tended to his needs and he grew stronger by the day.

Charlotte had done everything but explain why she wouldn't stay. Why she had to go off to California. There had been no protracted arguments between them. The Irish woman had made up her mind and without an encouraging word from the scout to hold her back; she had gone her own way. Jeb couldn't blame her. He had closed that door when he wasn't able to commit to her way back before the Comancheros had caught up with them on that mountaintop.

In a way Jeb had made Charlotte the strong, forceful, self-reliant person she always wanted to become. He had created the auburn wanderer who now had left him back in a Mexican border town while she followed her dreams to the West Coast. A big town like San Francisco or Sacramento or the smaller village of Los Angeles would be to her liking. She was ambitious. She would make do and be successful no matter what she did.

Jeb had let her go and he had no one to blame but himself. He was too old and too tired to take another chance at love. And if the truth were to be told, he was too afraid of losing another woman to take another chance at love. He was a fool and he knew it. He had let the most important thing in his life get away and he couldn't do a damn thing about it.

Jeb was packing his saddle bags a few days later when one of the villagers noticed him packing to leave. It was a middle-aged man who walked with a limp and wore a wide sombrero laced with eagle feathers. He said nothing at first. He just stood his ground and watched Jeb tighten the saddle cinch and slip his rifle into the scabbard.

Finally the man broke the silence. He motioned with his hands, asking if Jeb was riding back toward the border. Jeb nodded in the affirmative. The peasant quickly turned around and ran away in a painful gate. He disappeared into a ramshackle structure across the plaza.

Within moments, the peasant quickly reappeared out of the building with another man. Jeb recognized the other man as the village elder, a wrinkled gray haired man who began walking in slow deliberate steps toward Jeb.

Jeb was still standing by his horse when the village elder removed his sombrero and nodded slighted toward him. He began to speak slowly in rough Spanglish. "You leave now, my friend?" He asked.

"My thanks for your hospitality," Jeb answered as he swung up onto his mount. "I think it's time for me to head back up North. I trust you got paid enough by the woman. If not, I've got more coins."

"De nada," the old man answered, "de nada." He seemed nervous and hesitant to speak. Jeb sat in the saddle, watching the elder struggle to find his words.

"I know you must leave," the elder began, "but we have work for you…if you will have it. There is no other one who can help. Your woman says you are a man of the gun. But you are a good man and can be trusted."

Jeb shifted his weight in the saddle and leaned forward. "I'm listening," he said.

The peasant stepped forward, nodded at the old man, and began explaining. "There are two brothers, ruthless killers, who have raided our villages many times in the past. They were in a battle with the Americans several weeks ago and their gang was wiped out except for the two brothers. They escaped and now they are in hiding south of here, trying to put another gang together. If they come back here, many of our people will die. Someone must stop the brothers."

Jeb stared at the village elder but said nothing. The first peasant looked at the elder and then stepped back.

The elder began speaking again, "They hide from Rurales now. But there are others, much south, in canyons trading. If brothers come with them, many will die."

"You want me to find them before they form up another gang and…?"

The old man smiled through his tobacco-stained teeth and quickly answered. "Para llevarlos al diablo."

"Take them to the devil," Jeb answered and a weak smile escaped his lips.

The other peasant tentatively looked up at Jeb, over to the elder, then back to the scout. He nodded in the affirmative.

"We pay you much," the old man said, "in gold and silver."

The scout absentmindedly let his hand pass over his holster belt and his revolver. This was probably the same gang that Pony had led when he tracked down the scout and Charlotte. Jeb knew of the Comancheros and how they liked to raid small villages like this one. They would show no mercy to these people, men, women or children for that matter. Jeb was probably the village's only hope for stopping what might be total carnage if the raiders came.

"I will do it," Jeb answered slowly, "but not for pay. You gave me back my life. I will do what I can to save your village. Ojo por ojo." *Eye for an eye.*

"Es un hombre valiente," the old man replied.

Jeb shook his head. "No, I'm not brave," Jeb replied. "Man has a debt to repay. I will take care of those brothers."

"They drink every night and take women from the saloon," said the first peasant. "It would be best if you fight them at night when they are drunk on whiskey and rum."

Jeb swung around in saddle and leaned over toward the two men. "It'll get done. I'll kill them anyway I can. You have my word on it."

"Will you follow the woman?" The village elder asked.

"Don't know," Jeb answered. "Man's gotta do what his head tells him to do." He sat back up and swung his mount around. With a tilt of his hat, he kneed the roan and rode out of the village.

It took eight hours of hard riding before Jeb reached the canyon draw which split his trail in two directions. One gravel pathway cut south toward the village. It would still be another hard day's travel before he got there. The other trail moved up into the high country toward the mountain passes which allowed entry north toward the coast.

Jeb reined in his mount and sat for a long time. The air was hot and still. Overhead the black streaks of vultures slowly circled high against the blank sky. On the other side of those mountains were a dozen trails heading north toward the California territory where Charlotte might have gone.

To the south was a sure gunfight and better than even odds of his own demise. Jeb had a saddle bag full of gold and silver coins and a full load in his rifle. Even if he killed the brothers, he had no assurances that other Comancheros wouldn't track him down. He would become a hunted man, a man on the run, without a woman beside him and sure death coming from a dozen different directions.

Jeb had already made one big mistake by letting Charlotte go. He could try to rectify that mistake if he was willing to take the chance. Jeb smiled to himself. A gambler he wasn't. At least not when it came to love. And besides, he had given his word to the villagers.

Jeb swung his reins against the horse's neck and turned. The sound of gravel under hoof was the only sound heard as he headed south.

ABOUT THE AUTHOR

Denis LaComb is a storyteller.

Dissatisfied with a single title such as novelist, screenwriter, or playwright; Denis decided that the most apt description of his work would simply be: Storytelling.

Regardless of genre, the essence of Denis' work is storytelling in its purest form. While the characters may change and the story may vary, at the core of all of Denis' work is a story to be told. A story that might involve mystery, passion, conflict or the intricacies of relationships.

The catalyst for Denis to begin writing full time was a decision to wind down his video production business. With the threat of retirement looming in his future, Denis went back to work on a Western novel he'd written forty years earlier. The original Western project has become Apache Death Wind.

Denis has completed three more novels and four screenplays. He has also decided to take some of the made-up tales he'd created for his grandchildren and turn them into picture books. Denis is also writing scripts for television movies and has completed several plays, which he is shopping around for the proper venue.

Denis and his wife Sharon divide their time between Minnesota and Southern California; with long layovers in Colorado, where three of their grandchildren live.

Connect with Denis online at:

www.DenisJLaComb.com
www.ApacheDeathWind.com

Facebook
www.facebook.com/denisjlacombofficial

Blog
denisjlacomb.blogspot.com

Twitter
@AuthorDLaComb

CPSIA information can be obtained at www.ICGtesting.com
Printed in the USA
LVOW05s1935180214

374219LV00029B/1257/P

9 780988 420335